Acclaim for *Si*

'Lovely bubbly' *The Times*

'Wickedly witty' *Esquire*

'Wonderfully high-spirited . . . a writer poised to become formidable in her field' *Sunday Telegraph*

'A comedy of modern manners . . . frothy, frivolous, and fun' *Harpers & Queen*

'Fast paced, funny romp' *The Big Issue*

'Bitingly witty' *OK Magazine*

'Well observed and witty' *The Mirror*

'I'm Absolutely Furious, but secretly very flattered' Tara Palmer-Tomkinson

And the critics loved *Bad Heir Day* too:

'A romp of a novel . . . Holden writes with delicious verve and energy . . . she is superb at sending up style fanatics . . . lie back and enjoy it, girls!' *Mail on Sunday*

'Fiendishly witty' *Marie Claire*

'Wendy Holden should survive and prosper . . . the perfect antidote to the blues' *The Times*

'Restores the pun to literary respectability – an amazing feat' *Esquire*

'Savagely amusing . . . the satire is deadly, the plot addictive and the pace exhilarating' *Metro* (London)

'Fulfils the old definition of comedy' *The Sunday Times*

'Poshness, puns [illegible] it's combination of society froth and personal embarrassment is a genuine and enjoyable form of escapism' *London Evening Standard*

'So delicious, funny and heart-warming that I turned straight back to page one after I'd finished it in order to guzzle it all over again' Fiona Walker

'Devilishly witty' *Elle*

SIMPLY DIVINE is the first novel by journalist Wendy Holden, former deputy editor of society glossy *Tatler*. She has worked on *Harpers & Queen*, *The Sunday Times*, the *Sunday Telegraph* and the *Mail on Sunday*. Her second novel, *Bad Heir Day*, was published in January and was a *Sunday Times* bestseller for eight weeks. She lives in London and is currently writing her third novel *Pastures Nouveaux*.

WENDY HOLDEN

HEADLINE

First published in hardback in 1999 by
HEADLINE BOOK PUBLISHING

First published in paperback in 1999 by
HEADLINE BOOK PUBLISHING

10 9 8 7 6 5 4 3 2 1

ISBN 0 7472 6129 6

Typeset by Avon Dataset Ltd, Bidford-on-Avon, Warks

Printed and bound in Great Britain by
Mackays of Chatham plc, Chatham, Kent

HEADLINE BOOK PUBLISHING
A division of Hodder Headline
338 Euston Road
London NW1 3BH

www.headline.co.uk
www.hodderheadline.com

To my husband

Chapter 1

The organ swelled as Jane approached the altar, light-headed with happiness and not eating. It had been worth it – the tiny waist of the wedding dress now fitted her with ease, and she was blissfully aware of her slender form moving gracefully beneath the thick satin. The air was heavy with the scent of white roses as, smiling shyly beneath her cathedral-length veil, Jane drew up alongside Nick. Looking at her with a gratifying mixture of awe and wonder, Nick's face lit up in a tender smile . . .

The organ swelled and made Jane, fast asleep and revelling in her favourite dream, wake up suddenly. A dead, heavy weight was dragging itself across her chest. Realising it was Nick, Jane groaned more with discomfort than relief as her boyfriend groped clumsily to get his bearings before starting to saw away at her like a lumberjack. She barely had time to let out more than a couple of dutiful moans before, having galloped past the finishing post even faster than normal, Nick dismounted and rolled, grunting, back to his side of the bed.

As usual, Jane was left to lie in the wet patch.

She sighed as she stared out into the darkness, feeling vaguely violated. Quite literally, a rude awakening. She'd never get back to sleep now. Still, perhaps she ought to be grateful. She and Nick rarely had sex at all these days, and when they did, Nick preferred entering from behind, lying on his side, usually semi-conscious. It was, apparently, too much effort for him to get on top any more. A clear case, Jane thought ruefully, of Missionary Impossible.

It had not always been thus. They had met as students at Cambridge, a city which had afforded ample opportunities for thrillingly spontaneous lovemaking. The shelf stacks of the university library had quite literally been pressed into service, as had the backs of bike sheds, the Backs at midnight; punts, pubs, teashop loos and even the Master of Magdalene's garden. Most memorably of all, Nick had once pulled out all the stops in the organ loft of King's College Chapel. The Festival of Nine Lessons and Carols had never seemed quite the same after that.

Trying to anchor her head more comfortably in the pillow, sleep still as remote as the stars, Jane recalled the moment she and Nick had met in the campus cafe. His brusque Northernness had struck her as rather thrilling, as did his rugged handsome face and the fact that he seemed Terribly Politically Committed. Besides, as an English student specialising in Hardy, Jane quite fancied the idea of a horny-handed son of toil.

The horny part, unhappily, had recently made its excuses and left. As she lay dozing in the dark, Jane tried to pin down the exact moment when she realised Nick didn't fancy her any more. If she was honest, it was about six months ago. Around the time she had moved into his flat in Clapham.

The bedside table exploded into frantic sound as Nick's irritating Mickey Mouse alarm clock announced six thirty. Oblivious of Jane deeply asleep beside him, Nick swore loudly, swung his legs out of bed and yanked back the curtains. A weak sun struggled through the dingy window-panes and illuminated the pile of dirty washing over which he leant to switch on the radio.

Jane groaned inwardly as the quarrelsome tones of John Humphrys flooded into the room. Not *more* current affairs. It only seemed five minutes since Jeremy Paxman had been switched off the night before. But, just as Nick could not sleep without having seen both the nine and eleven o'clock news and *Newsnight*, he seemingly could not rise without having the *Today* programme reverberating through the flat from dawn onwards.

Jane's conspicuous failure to be as obsessed with current affairs as he was drove Nick to distraction. 'Your idea of political awareness,' he once accused her, 'is the length of Cherie Blair's skirt.' Jane had bridled at the unfairness of it. Had she not, over the years, helped Nick canvass his way on to every committee from the college JCR to a seat on the local council, all landmarks along the course of political achievement Nick had set for himself? She knew more about politics than most. But she *was* interested in the length of Cherie Blair's skirt. Very much so. And what was wrong with that?

Nick's small blue eyes were screwed up with concentration as he listened to John Humphrys mauling a minister.

'How can they get so cross about things so early?' moaned Jane, sticking her fingers in her ears.

'Shush,' said Nick, flapping his hands like an irritable dowager and glaring at her as the minister's voice came on again. 'He's interviewing James Morrison, the transport minister. My boss, in case you've forgotten.'

Jane rolled her eyes. Forgotten? If only. In the two months since Nick had started working as a special adviser in his office, she had learnt more about the transport minister than he probably knew about himself. None of it remotely interesting.

'I put it to you, Minister,' shouted Humphrys, 'that if caravans were only allowed to travel between the hours of two and five in the morning, the world would be a happier place.'

'Quite right,' muttered Jane, who had been stuck behind more swaying beige mobile homes hogging the middle lane than she cared to remember.

'Look,' growled Nick, 'it may be a joke to you, but the caravan debate's a political bloody hot bloody potato of the first bloody order. Caravan owners have rights too, you know. James Morrison's been under a lot – a hell of a lot – of pressure to champion them recently.'

'Should start calling himself Van Morrison, then,' said Jane flippantly, diving back under the duvet as the interview ended.

'Hilarious,' said Nick, crushingly, stomping out of the room as best he could in his bare feet. His sense of humour, Jane reflected, had been another casualty of their cohabitation.

Minutes later, she heard the shower crank reluctantly into action and hoped he wouldn't take all the hot water. It was a vain hope; he usually did. Her standard of living had never been lower. Moving in with Nick may not have been a good idea.

'Are you sure it's a good idea?' Tally had cautiously asked at the time.

'Of course!' Offended, Jane had rebuffed her best friend's obvious conviction that it wasn't with all the brio she could muster. 'Nick needs me,' she had explained. Tally looked unconvinced.

'Are you sure he doesn't just need you to pay half the mortgage?' she asked gently.

Jane winced. Nick was not exactly famous for his generosity. Tighter than a gnat's arse, if she was to be frank. Last Christmas she had bought him a Ralph Lauren bathrobe and a Versace shirt. Nick had reciprocated with a twig pencil and a teddy bear which had been a free gift from the petrol station.

'Honestly, Jane,' Tally went on, exasperated, her big grey eyes wide with sincerity, 'you've got so much going for you. You're so pretty, and funny, and clever. I just don't understand why you're throwing yourself away on him. He's so *rude*.'

Tally was right. Nick *was* rude, especially after a few drinks, and especially to Tally. The fact that she was grand and had grown up in a stately home brought Nick out in a positive rash of social inferiority.

But it was all very well for Tally to be censorious, she thought defensively as she burrowed yet further beneath the duvet. It was just fine for Tally to declare she was holding out for Mr Right. Or Lord Right probably, in her case. She didn't understand that relationships simply weren't that straightforward. They didn't just *happen*. You had to work with what you had, particularly if you were twenty-four and didn't want to be a spinster at thirty.

'You'll be saying you want to marry him next,' Tally had almost wailed. Jane judged it injudicious to confess that this was the whole point of her moving in. Not that it had worked. On the contrary, judging by present form, Nick's plighting his troth looked more unlikely than ever. Plighting his sloth, however, had been the work of seconds.

Once Jane was on site, Nick had seen no further point in squandering both time and money on trendy restaurants when there was a perfectly good TV at home to eat Pot Noodles in front of. Similarly, all trips to cinemas, bars, concerts and parties had come to an abrupt end now that they no longer needed to leave the flat to meet each other.

Jane's evenings consequently divided themselves between working out how to fit her clothes into the minute amount of wardrobe space Nick had allocated her and scenting and oiling herself in the grubby little bath that no amount of Mr Muscle made the faintest impression on. She, at least, was determined to keep up her standards.

Nick, on the other hand, now picked his nose with impunity, refused to shave at weekends and after she'd been living with him a month, no longer bothered to hold the farts in. From French kisses to Bronx cheers, Jane thought miserably, as Nick's sex drive wound down to a sputter. Her own, by contrast, had revved up alarmingly. Practically sex-starved except for the occasional middle-of-the-night grope, Jane had lately begun to fantasise about everyone and anyone who so much as smiled at her.

Especially that gorgeous man who had just moved in upstairs.

With a guilty thrill, Jane thought about last night's encounter. The man upstairs had been sticking his key in the lock of the outside door of the building just as she had been opening it from the inside. Talk about Freudian. She frowned, trying to wrench her thoughts away from the hulking figure with the tumble of fair hair that had greeted her when the door opened. She could still recall the enormous size of his . . . grin.

Jane sighed and yawned, knowing the water would certainly be cold by now. She peered over the top of the duvet into the chilly, dusty air. The scant warmth from

Nick's storage heaters – turned permanently down to low – went straight out of the ill-fitting windows. Even in summer you could practically see your breath.

Not that Nick was around much to notice the Arctic atmosphere of his flat. Now he had finally realised his dream of working at Westminster, he came home later and later. Night after night, he stayed in his office, doing Jane knew not what. Taking phone calls from furious caravan owners, apparently. She sighed. Perhaps she should invest in one herself. It would be a way of attracting his attention.

Nick may have been bitten by the Westminster bug, Jane reflected, but it could have been any one of the insects in his flat. The place was crawling, and it was the discovery of a new itchy lump on her leg that finally drove Jane from under the duvet into the chilly embrace of the morning. They simply had to move out of here. Finding a new flat, Jane felt sure, would cement their relationship, as well as heat it, roof it and supply it with windowboxes. So far she had not had much luck.

'We found a lovely first-floor flat in Kentish Town,' she told Tally, 'but Nick was worried about the carpet glue. He was afraid it might bring out his asthma.' She did not voice her suspicions that he was afraid it might bring out his wallet. Nor, to her credit, did Tally.

Shuddering, Jane stood before the wardrobe mirror and stared at her naked body. Her legs, at least, were reasonable, even if her waist was too thick, her breasts too small and that stubborn spare tyre spread like a swag across the front of her tummy. The plump tops of her arms also gave her cause for concern. Still, Nick had never said he wished she was thinner. Then again, he'd never said he wished she was anything.

She wrapped Nick's Ralph Lauren bathrobe round her

and went into the freezing kitchen. Something about Nick's appearance caught her eye. She stared at him covertly over the top of the paper he was reading. He had obviously been spending at least some of his time in the bathroom squeezing a stubborn spot above one of his eyebrows, and his efforts had left an angry circular red weal that made him look as if he had been shot through the forehead. Jane could imagine how this had wounded his vanity.

'I'd put some toothpaste on that,' she said helpfully. 'Dry it up a bit. It's what all the supermodels do.'

Nick tutted and continued his perusal of the *Telegraph* leader column. 'Trust you to know that,' he said scornfully.

Jane shrugged and started to examine the *Sun*. Most of the inside page was taken up with a picture of some ragged-looking, wild-haired environmental protesters at a planned bypass site. They were surrounding, and apparently arguing with, a tall, rather debonair figure whom Jane recognised as the transport minister, James Morrison.

There was something oddly familar about the protester pictured closest to Morrison. With his high cheekbones and funny little snub nose, he looked astonishingly like Tally's brother, Piers. He even had her small, thin lips and the same large, sloping eyes which, in that patrician fashion peculiar to inbred aristocratic types, looked as if they were about to slide away down the side of his face. The resemblance was extraordinary. It just showed, Jane thought, dwelling on one of her favourite theories, that there really were only so many facial types in the world. There must be, if some wild crusty could look so like someone who, at this moment, would be sitting in the chapel at Eton with his hair plastered down and looking as if Matron wouldn't melt in his mouth.

'Bloody crusties,' Nick exclaimed, his attention drawn by the amount of time she had spent staring at the page. 'Drug-crazed hippies. All sponging off the state. Too busy making trouble for everybody else to do any work.' It was not, Jane saw, the time to start arguing the case for conservation. Clearly, the official view from the transport minister's office was that his press coverage that morning was not all it might be. Jane swiftly turned over the page.

A huge colour photograph of an extremely glamorous blonde girl sprang out at her. So pneumatic were her lips, so vast and plunging her cleavage, so huge and confident her smile and so contrastingly tiny her dress that one almost didn't notice the handsome but ineffectual-looking young man with her, who was gazing into the camera with vacant eyes. 'Bubbling Champagne!' proclaimed the headline. 'Society girl Champagne D'Vyne, snapped last night at the Met Bar with billionheir escort the Hon. Stretch von und zu Dosch,' said the caption.

'Oh, Christ, it's that stupid Sloaney tart again,' exclaimed Nick, looking over and seizing on another target for his ire. He took a swig of tepid tea from his Houses of Parliament mug. 'She's absolutely bloody everywhere,' he snorted in disgust. 'And why's she got such a bloody stupid name?'

'Apparently she was conceived after her parents drank a bottle of champagne,' said Jane. She'd read it somewhere or other, and, having offered the information, felt acutely embarrassed as Nick razed her with a withering glare.

'The things you know,' he remarked in mock astonishment.

Jane flushed. It was true. Her ability to retain unfeasible amounts of trivia was ridiculous. Against her better judgement, she could remember all the words to 'Bohemian

Rhapsody', and recall every contestant in *The Wacky Races* but had forgotten her own telephone number on more than one occasion.

'It's a good thing her parents weren't into Newcastle Brown, then,' snorted Nick in his grating voice. 'Or Horlicks. Anyway, why's she so sodding famous?'

Jane looked at Champagne D'Vyne's lithe, athletic form, a riot of curves gloriously set off by her practically nonexistent clothing. She wore no bra. Her gravity-defying breasts seemed to be of that elastic variety that needed no support other than their own exuberance. 'I can't imagine,' she said, her light tone laced with sarcasm.

'Well, there must be some reason,' Nick insisted, Jane's irony utterly lost on him.

Jane stared. Could he really not see? Or perhaps it was because Champagne D'Vyne had a cleavage like the Grand Canyon that she, acutely conscious of her own rather more Cotswoldesque *embonpoint*, had no difficulty pinpointing the root of Champagne's attractions. 'She's famous for having huge tits,' she said finally. 'And for being fantastically posh. A lethal combination, wouldn't you say?'

'Well, you should know,' Nick sneered. 'That's your department, all that frothy, titsy, celebrity stuff. Great campaigning journalism, I must say.'

Jane flinched. Her career wasn't all it might be but did Nick *have* to be so nasty about it? Working on an upmarket glossy magazine might not be the socialist ideal but it was undoubtedly something a lot of people would kill for. The problem was, after six months at *Gorgeous*, Jane rather wanted to kill herself. Commissioning endless in-depth investigations into the contents of celebrity fridges and the dinner party games of the rich and famous was a soul-destroying business.

The sound of footsteps in the kitchen overhead derailed her train of thought. She wondered what the man upstairs was doing.

As she had passed him in the doorway last night, her all-quivering senses had caught a whiff of his aftershave – a delicious, clean, sharp scent the other end of the smell spectrum from the aspirational, peppery Jermyn Street potions Nick seemed so fond of.

By now, Nick had disappeared into the bedroom to get dressed. Jane could hear him rattling through the rail of expensive Egyptian cotton shirts that he had recently wheedled out of her for a birthday present, any one of which cost almost as much as her best office jacket. He emerged eventually, his bullet-hole smeared over with what looked suspiciously like her expensive new MAC spot cover.

'Good luck with celebrity underwear drawers,' Nick sniped as she went to kiss him goodbye at the front door. 'I wouldn't ring up Champagne D'Vyne about those,' he added. 'I can't imagine she has much use for knickers. She's obviously dropping them for every chinless wonder in town.'

Lucky old her, thought Jane as the door slammed in Nick's wake. She heard the click of his Church's shoes receding down the path as she headed towards the bathroom. Time to get ready for work. Make herself *Gorgeous*. There must be some hot water now.

Jane went into the bathroom and shot out again instantly. The air was filled with an ear-splitting shriek which she realised, after a few seconds, was her own. To accompany it, a series of crashing thuds from upstairs shook the flat above. But Jane hardly noticed. The last thing to register with any of her senses was the huge spider crouched in the bottom of the bath. Vast, malevolent and murderous looking, with terrifying markings on its back, it had evidently marched in from the garden while they were reading the papers.

Still screaming, Jane bolted through the hall and out into the entrance passageway, leaving the door of the flat wide open. As she paused for breath, she heard it click shut behind her.

'Need any help?'

Head spinning with fear of the hideous beast in the tub and the dawning, dreadful awareness that she was locked out of the flat, Jane stared wildly up the stairwell to the next floor. *The man from upstairs was leaning over the banister. Grinning at her.* Grinning, it had to be said, more widely than the circumstances merited.

Jane gasped as she remembered she was wearing nothing but Nick's bathrobe. As she looked down at it, lolling off her shoulders and gaping open, she realised she wasn't even really wearing that. Mortified, she clutched the edges of towelling tightly to her and felt a warm tide of embarrassed crimson flood her face. How much had those knowing racing-green eyes managed to see of her? Had he spotted her spare tyre? The way her unsupported breasts scraped the floor? He must think her a loose woman in every sense of the word. Talk about the woman who put the common in Clapham.

'Well, aren't you going to tell me what's happened?' asked the man upstairs on the stairs, by now slowly descending the stairs. His faded burgundy bathrobe, stopping at his knees, revealed long, finely-muscled golden calves. 'I think it's the least you can do, personally,' he added, flashing her a smile so brilliant it could have been spotted from the moon. 'I was just in the shower myself, and you gave me such a scare screeching like that that I lost my balance and fell over. Face down on the taps, as it happens,' he said, arriving on the ground floor and raking her with a rueful glance from beneath his thatch of damp, butter-coloured hair.

Despite herself, Jane sniggered. Falling face down on the taps was *too* ridiculous.

'Glad you find it funny,' remarked the man from upstairs, raising an eyebrow. 'I'll have a couple of shiners by the morning. Guaranteed.'

Contrite, Jane realised she wasn't giving him the best of incentives to assist her. 'I'm terribly sorry,' she stammered. 'Perhaps if you rub some steak on them?' She had a vague idea from somewhere that this helped.

'I'd rather eat it, frankly,' he replied. 'Anyway, what *were* you yowling about? What's the problem?'

'Well,' Jane muttered, suddenly feeling silly. 'There's, um, there's a rather large spider in my, um, bath.'

'Spiders won't hurt you,' said her neighbour breezily. 'It won't even move unless you make it. The whole point of a spider is being a spider. They don't go in for sightseeing or aerobics.'

'Well, this one's got a leotard on, actually,' flashed back Jane, remembering the nasty markings and determined to claw back some dignity out of the situation. She turned on her heel to re-enter the flat, only to encounter the closed door. 'Oh, and I'm locked out as well.' She banged her fist on the door in frustration.

'Hang on a minute.'

As if she had much choice, Jane thought, slumping against the door and watching the long legs lope back upstairs. She was hardly going to rush out and catch a bus dressed like this, was she? Not that it stopped some people.

Two minutes later, he had bounded down again, opened the latch with a credit card, entered the flat and flipped the spider out of the bathroom window. 'Thank you so much,' said Jane, stiff with embarrassment as well as cold. She had noticed by now that her legs were not only blue with the chill, but needed a shave. Her standards were beginning to slip after all.

'It's a pleasure. I'm Tom, by the way.' He flashed her another knee-trembler of a grin.

'I'm Jane.'

'Yes,' he said. 'I know.'

'You *know*?' Her heart swooped in a somersault. He knew her name. Jane surrendered herself to the thrilling thought that he must have more than a passing interest in her to bother finding out what she was called.

'Yes. There's a pile of bills with your name and address on them by the door.'

Chapter 2

'I want *ideas*. Big ideas. *Huge* ideas. Circulation-rocketing, magazine-of-the-year-award-winning ideas.'

The editor of *Gorgeous* put the tips of his manicured fingers together, pursed his lips and glared at his staff. Jane shifted uncomfortably on the sofa between the art director and the fashion assistant, both of whom were gazing vacantly into space.

Josh flicked an invisible bit of dust off the lapel of his Prince of Wales check suit and stared through his monocle at his features department. In other words, Jane. There had been talk, when Jane started, of recruiting a crack ideas team to help her, but it had so far failed to materialise. Nor, Jane knew, was it now likely to. *Gorgeous* operated on the principle common to most publications, that keeping staff costs down was as important as keeping the circulation up. The standard belief that the overworked staff would feel elated by the enormous responsibility and positively revel in the lack of support also applied.

'What I particularly want,' Josh continued, 'is some really *brilliant*, original, ingenious, attention-grabbing *gimmick*. I'm *sick* of seeing *The Sunday Times* stealing a march on us with Tara Palmer-Tomkinson. She should be writing for *Gorgeous*. She's done wonders for their figures.'

No mean feat considering she had a chest flatter than an airport runway herself, thought Jane, who was no fan of the celebrated sybarite.

'And *Fabulous* is snapping at our heels,' continued the editor testily. It was true that *Gorgeous*'s great rival, the society magazine *Fabulous*, was putting on readers at an alarming rate. 'We *can't* let them overtake us in circulation.' He banged his fist dramatically on his desk. A collection of silver-framed photographs of Josh with Princess Diana, Josh with Karl Lagerfeld, Josh with John Galliano and Josh with Kate Moss fell over with a crash. 'What's *new*?' he demanded, wiping Kate lovingly with his sleeve as he propped her up again.

His staff quaked. Everyone was terrified of Josh. Impeccably dressed and sharply good-looking, he had the reputation of being one of the most gifted and competitive editors in London. He was devoted to *Gorgeous* and expected everyone who worked there to be as obsessed with it as he was. He had, after all, taken it from a mumsy rag to a glittering social glossy in the four years he had been editor. No one could doubt his talents or his commitment. But his management skills were from the Darth Vader school.

'I see Champagne D'Vyne's all over the tabloids again,' ventured the chief sub. Her voice trailed off as she waited for Josh's reaction.

'Yes, doesn't she look wonderful, bless her,' said Josh, exposing his exquisitely-capped teeth in a dazzling white smile. He shook back a lock of hair that had had the impertinence to detach itself from its smoothed-back auburn fellows and stared thoughtfully at the chief sub. She blinked at him through eyelashes so thick with make-up they looked more black leaded than mascara'd.

'Ye-e-es,' said Josh, slowly, a gleam appearing in his eye. The chief sub blushed and put up a self-conscious hand to further tousle her moussed-up hair. She'd had a crush on Josh for ages. Had her moment finally come?

A stream of breathless excuses announced the sudden arrival of Valentine, *Gorgeous*'s deputy editor who, despite his lofty title, received almost as much flak from Josh as Jane did. 'Oh, you won't believe what happened to me on the way here,' he gasped.

'You're right, I won't,' Josh cut in rudely. 'So don't bother.' Valentine visibly slumped. But Josh hadn't finished with his unfortunate number two. He picked up a page proof from his desk and waved it at Valentine. 'Have you had these interior pages legalled?' he asked.

'Legalled?' echoed Valentine. One of his responsibilities was to make sure every page in the magazine had been through the in-house lawyers before publication. 'Why ever would the lawyers want to read "That Sinking Feeling: How To Choose an Amazin' Basin", or "Pale and Interesting: Picking the Right White For Your Home"?' he demanded. His chest swelled defensively, straining the hard-pressed buttons on his suit still further. His eyes bulged.

'Well, you never know, someone may have slagged off a scatter cushion,' said Josh. 'Better talk it through with the lawyers, there's a dear.'

Valentine snatched the proof from him and rushed out in the direction of the legal department.

The meeting was dismissed and Jane settled herself behind her desk which, as usual, was a sea of last week's newspapers and possibly last century's page proofs. Her heart sank at the mess of it all. The entire office was piled up with old papers, envelopes, post nobody bothered to open, unwanted faxes from unwanted contributors and, worst of all, boxes of everything from Tandoori burgers to savoury ice creams sent in for review to the food editor, whose rare appearances meant they rotted and stank in the office's overheated atmosphere until someone (usually Jane) had the sense to throw them away.

The last of all the staff to arrive was Lulu the fashion editor, who had never seen a morning meeting yet. As always, despite being over an hour late, she gave an impression of great speed and industry, bustling in as quickly as her combination of tight black leather skirt, impenetrable dark glasses and vertiginous heels would allow.

As Lulu sashayed past her desk, Jane noticed she was dragging something odd behind her. And this time it wasn't one of her exotic collection of photographer's assistants. 'What's that?' asked Jane, staring at something long, black and rubbery trailing in Lulu's wake.

'It's a symbol of Life,' declared Lulu theatrically. 'It represents woman's struggle on earth.'

'It's an inner tube, isn't it?' asked Jane.

'No,' said Lulu emphatically. 'Only if you *insist* on perceiving it that way. The circle is also a representation of the cyclical nature of Womanhood and the fact it is made of rubber refers to the eternal need to be flexible. Woman's inheritance, in short.' She sighed and rolled her eyes. 'All that juggling of priorities.'

Jane snorted quietly. The only juggling of priorities Lulu did was forcing her breasts into an Alexander McQueen leather bustier.

'Women should think themselves lucky then,' drawled Josh's voice from his office where he was, as usual, listening. 'All I'm going to inherit is Parkinson's.'

Jane grimaced. It wasn't as if Josh needed to inherit

anything. His salary, she suspected, ran well into six figures, he received more designer suits than he could wear and was courted by so many PRs he probably hadn't paid for his own lunch for years.

'Fancy a cup of tea, Lulu?' Josh's light, sarcastic tones floated across the room.

'Josh, darling, I'd just *die* for one,' breathed Lulu with her usual understatement.

'Off you go and get one then,' said Josh. 'And get me one while you're at it.'

Lulu grinned. 'Oh, you really are *ghastly*, Josh.' She always took his jibes in good part. Jane was unsure whether Lulu simply didn't get half of them or tolerated them because she realised she had an ally in Josh. Did Lulu, after all, know what side her sushi was wasabi'd on?

'She's a few gilt chairs short of a Dior front row, that one,' muttered Jane to Valentine, who had by now returned from the lawyers, as Lulu wobbled out of the office.

Josh overheard. 'It's so wonderful to have *someone* round here who knows about clothes,' he purred, shooting a loaded look at Jane. 'They're a very important part of Features.'

'Look,' said Jane, exasperated, 'I admit fashion's not my area but I pull my weight, you know.'

'Considerable weight it is too,' said Josh, who prided himself on his lack of political correctness.

'You could have him for sexual harassment, you know,' murmured Valentine in an undertone.

Josh's sharp ears twitched once more. 'I assure you,' he said silkily, taking his monocle out and polishing it, 'there's nothing sexual in it.'

Christ, and it's only Monday, Jane thought. Four and a half whole days to go before the weekend. And not an enormous amount to look forward to then. Nick was going to Brussels for a ten-day Euro transport summit, which put the kibosh on flat-hunting. On the other hand, there was always the delicious possibility of another on-the-stairs encounter with Tom . . .

Jane frowned. Just forget it, she told herself. There was no point, having worked away at Nick for the last few years and finally succeeded in moving in with him, to risk the bird-in-the-hand reality of a permanent relationship by having a crush on the upstairs neighbour. The thought of two in the bush with Tom remained a delicious fantasy nonetheless. But fantasy, thought Jane, was as far as it was going to get. Tom probably had millions of girlfriends anyway. And *she* had a boyfriend.

Around lunchtime, the telephone on her desk shrilled.

'Hello, *Gorgeous*,' said Jane, gritting her teeth, as she did the fifty times a day she had to give this absurd salutation.

'Jane, it's Tally,' came a distant, muffled voice from what sounded like the bottom of a mine shaft. The phone system at Mullions, the rambling manor in Gloucestershire where Tally's family had lived for four centuries, had not been rewired for the last two reigns at least. 'Please say you'll be around this weekend.' Even through the ancient and twisted phone lines a certain desperation could be detected. 'I'm coming to London. I need to see you. We have to talk.' Then, like a crumbling and decrepit actor who yet retained a fine sense of dramatic timing, the Mullions line abruptly cut itself off.

Talk about what? Was Tally in trouble? Surely not pregnant? Jane ran through a mental line-up of the workers on the Mullions estate and quickly dismissed the suggestion. There were two, and only one was a man – Peters the gardener who also, and often without washing his hands too thoroughly, doubled as butler.

Still, all would be revealed at the weekend, if Tally ever managed to reconnect to suggest a rendezvous. Feeling more cheerful, Jane went to the fax to send a second proof of his page through to Freddie Fry the restaurant reviewer. She prayed that this time it had no mistakes in it. Her ears were still burning from their recent conversation.

'It's preposterous,' Fry had blustered. 'Look at the second paragraph. Where it says "my newt's livers"?'

'Mmm?' said Jane mildly, looking at the offending line. It seemed perfectly properly spelt to her.

'My newt's livers?' boomed the notoriously brusque Fry. 'What the fuck are newt's livers? It should say "minute slivers", you bunch of morons.'

As the missive beeped and screeched its way through to Fry, Jane idly scanned the pile of faxes in the tray beside the machine. Near the top was a letter from Josh. She picked it up with interest but had not read five words before panic gripped her heart. 'No!' she gasped.

The fax was a letter commissioning a column and promising the writer not only all the editorial help they could possibly want, but £1,000 a shot into the bargain. It was addressed to Miss C.O.W. D'Vyne.

So this was the brilliant new gimmick. The circulation-soaring, award-collecting Great Idea.

'You're not serious!' protested Jane, shooting into Josh's office with the fax trembling in her hand. 'Champagne D'Vyne!' she exclaimed. 'But she's just a dumb Sloane. Tara Palmer-Tomkinson can at least write. Rather well, too,' said Jane, much as it pained her to admit it.

'Quite,' said Josh. 'And Champagne will write even better. With a little help from *us*, of course.' He grinned at her. 'But I don't just want a measly old Tara-sized column.

No point just repeating what she does. I want something much bigger and bouncier.'

'Well, you've certainly got that,' said Jane.

'I want a whole double-page spread of sparkling social froth.' Josh's eyes glowed. 'A good fourteen hundred words of witty, polished copy every month, Maybe two thousand words. Make it four pages, even. You'll easily manage that.'

Jane blinked. 'Me? But how can I? I'm not the one with the glamorous social life.'

'Well, you said it, dear,' said Josh, yawning and stretching his long perfectly-tailored arms to the ceiling. 'No, but seriously, as we comedians say. Champagne and I have discussed it. It's just a simple matter of you talking to her every now and then. Keep on to her. Ask her where she's been, who she's seen, what she's bought and, best of all, who she's slept with. Then just jot it all down. Keep her diary, in other words.' He paused. 'Brilliant, isn't it?'

'Fantastic,' said Jane sourly.

'I thought you'd jump at the opportunity.'

'Yes. Out of the window,' snapped Jane. She could tell she had no choice in the matter. She groaned inwardly. Nick was going to have a field day when he heard about this.

'I've already thought of a name for it,' Josh continued, triumphantly. 'Champagne Moments!'

'We'll be the laughing stock of Fleet Street,' Jane mumbled miserably.

'Nonsense! It's just what *Gorgeous* needs. It'll knock *Fabulous* into a cocked tiara. How can it go wrong?' Josh clapped his manicured hands, with their faint hint of clear nail polish, together in delight. 'Champagne's fantastically posh and has huge tits. A lethal combination, wouldn't you say?'

The very words she had said to Nick that morning. Jane's heart sank.

Much as Nick might – and did – sneer at the triviality of Jane's latest project, tracking down Champagne D'Vyne turned out to be investigative journalism of the highest order. Jane was initially encouraged by the fact that Champagne was signed up with a vast international public relations outfit called Tuff PR. But this turned out to be a false dawn, as brokering Champagne's deal with *Gorgeous* and banking the cheques seemed to be the limit of Tuff's interest. Even less concerned was a snappy and extremely camp-sounding creature called Simon whose responsibility Champagne apparently was.

The two telephone numbers Simon gave Jane for Champagne both turned out to be useless. One was an incomprehensible answerphone message which cut off halfway through and the other the full mailbox of a mobile phone.

'So how do you suggest I get hold of her?' an exasperated Jane finally demanded of Simon. 'Telepathy?'

'Look, I'll do you a favour, OK?' was Simon's miraculous response. Blistering rage, apparently, was the only thing that made an impact. When the going got tough, Tuff, it seemed, got going. 'Champagne's doing a fashion shoot this afternoon for a magazine. You'll have to go along to that. It's a bore, because I don't want any strangers making her nervous on her first big job.'

Jane was surprised. She had not had Champagne down as the shy type. In her tabloid appearances, at least, Champagne seemed to have the front of a hundred Moulin Rouge dancers.

The photographic studio where the fashion shoot was

to be held was in a converted warehouse in Docklands. As an entry into the glamorous world of Champagne D'Vyne, the building seemed unlikely. A poky, strip-lit, hospital-like corridor issued into a tiny office where someone with their back to Jane and almost completely hidden by a vast, battered leather chair was talking very loudly into the telephone. From the voice, and the pair of white-jeaned legs visible on the desk in front, Jane assumed it to be the studio secretary. She sat down on a shabby black plastic sofa to wait for her to finish her conversation, and wondered where in the building Champagne was. She felt faintly apprehensive at meeting a real life bombshell in the flesh. Particularly when she felt such a bombsite herself.

'What do you mean, hang on a sec?' the girl suddenly screeched. The back of her chair wobbled violently. 'No one tells me to wait for secs.'

Jane blinked. She'd dealt with some uppity secretaries at *Gorgeous* in her time, but this was a whole new ballgame. Models and photographers were, she knew, a notoriously imperious breed. She hadn't realised their secretaries were as well.

'Yes, I should bloody well think I'm connected.' As she got angrier, the girl's voice sounded increasingly like the honk of an extremely patrician goose. But not for long. Having reached the person she wanted to speak to, her voice suddenly dissolved into a syrupy, lisping, Sugar Kane wheedle.

'Is that you, Rollsy?' she gushed. 'Darling, I've been thinking about our trip to Paris tonight. It's just *too* wonderful of you to take me in your private plane but *could* we *possibly* take that glorious red Gulfstream instead of the blue one? I know I'm a silly, darling, but it's just that my nail varnish is the wrong colour for the blue . . .'

Jane swallowed. Clearly, studio secretaries moved in more elevated circles than she thought. Literally.

'The *red* one, darling, yes.' A hint of the imperious honk was creeping into the girl's breathy tones. Rollsy was obviously having trouble recalling which of his hundreds of Gulfstreams she meant. 'You know, the one with that divine little inglenook fireplace . . . Yes? Fabulous, darling. Big kiss. Bye-ee.' She slammed down the phone. 'Fucking idiot.' With a push of her long leg, the chair swung round.

Jane found herself staring at an arrogant-looking blonde with indignant grass-green eyes and a petulant, full mouth big enough to seat a family of six. She had cheekbones like knuckledusters, cascades of shining hair and a tight white jersey top through which her nipples could clearly be seen. Jane realised it wasn't the studio secretary at all. She was looking at Champagne D'Vyne.

'What the fuck's going on?' a voice behind them demanded suddenly.

A small, profoundly tanned man with intensely blue eyes, tight jeans and stack-heeled boots was standing in the doorway of the office. Three cameras, all with enormous lenses, were slung round his wrinkled brown neck, as were a number of thick gold chains. Jane recognised him instantly as Dave Baker, a well-known fashion photographer who had launched more models than NASA had space probes. He waved furiously at Champagne, tapped his huge, expensive-looking watch and frowned. 'For fuck's sake, we haven't got all day,' he shouted at her. '*Scusi* my language, darling,' he said to Jane, his Italian sitting oddly with his Cockney. 'We've been here three hours already and Her Blondeness has only just turned up. Only just got out of bed, apparently – though *whose* I wouldn't like to speculate.' He turned on his stack heel in disgust and minced back in the direction of what Jane imagined was the studio.

Champagne took absolutely zero notice. Her entire attention was focused on the telephone, which had just rung again. She listened intently, then let out an indignant yell into the receiver. 'I don't *believe* it, Rollsy,' she shouted furiously, completely abandoning her sugary tones. 'You've lent it to Prince *who*? Well, can't you get it back? No, the blue's simply *not on*, darling. *Nada*. I'd have to have a whole new manicure and you *know* how busy I am, angel.'

Jane's fingers crept towards her pad and pen. May as well make a few notes. You never knew.

'Oh, I *suppose* I could bear BA first class, if you simply *can't* get it back,' Champagne lisped petulantly. 'But *must* we go to boring old Paris *yet* again? Another weekend at the Crillon and I'll *kill* myself.'

After a few more minutes in this vein, Jane was stopped mid-scribble by a touch on her arm. It was Dave Baker again.

'Look, I'm sorry to bother you, *carissima*,' he said, the muscles in his wrinkled cheeks working like galley slaves as he cast a furious look at the still-chatting Champagne. 'But would you do me the most *enormoso* favour? I need to find out *urgimento* whether the light is OK for these pictures. Would you be a complete *cara* and sit for some Polaroids so I can check everything before we start shooting on film? Sorry, we haven't been introduced. Dave Baker, *fotografico*.'

'I know,' said Jane, touched by the modesty and friendliness of one at the top of a profession not noted for its humility. 'Of course. I'd be delighted. If you're sure I won't break the camera.'

Dave laughed. 'You're a very pretty girl, dear.'

Jane packed up her notebook and followed him into a large, light room where snake-like black cables writhed over the floor like the inhabitants of a reptile house. A beautiful make-up artist, arms folded, awaited Champagne's pleasure beside an array of pots and brushes while a wide-eyed young man wearing very tight white trousers busily altered the angles of the photographic lamps and measured their strength with a light meter.

'*Molto bene*,' said Dave, sitting Jane in front of a huge backlit white screen and encouraging her to suck her cheeks in. '*Bella, bella*. Amber, *carissima*, a spot of make-up if you please, and *una piccola* tweak with the hair perhaps?'

Amber breathed mintily and absorbedly while she dabbed Jane's face with a bit of powder and lipstick and pinned her hair loosely up behind her head.

'Gosh,' said Jane, gazing at herself in the mirror Amber held up when she had finished. The soft, shadowy light made her face look fragile, her blue eyes huge and her hair a soft haze of piled-up gold. Amber had also done all sorts of clever things with a lip pencil so Jane's thin mouth, while not quite rivalling Champagne's six-seater, at least now provided respectable room for two.

'You've got lovely bones, you know,' Amber said matter-of-factly, snatching away a stray eyebrow hair with a pair of tweezers. 'You should wear your hair up more often. Or get it cut short to show off your face a bit.'

'Do you really think so?' asked Jane, settling back into the chair happily. She was beginning to enjoy being a supermodel. She hoped Dave would give her a Polaroid shot to take back to Nick. He could keep it in his wallet. On the other hand, as he so rarely opened it, that might not be the best place.

'What the fuck's going on?' It was Champagne's turn to sound indignant. Her demanding tones echoed round the studio.

'I didn't realise this was a shoot for Evans the Outsize,' Champagne snarled, striding up to Jane. Her heels clattered furiously on the wooden floor. 'Who the fuck are *you*?' Her brilliant green eyes homed pitilessly in on the greasy roots of Jane's hair. Nick had taken all the hot water again that morning.

'I'm Jane from *Gorgeous*,' Jane stammered, terrified despite herself. Being sneered at by someone so beautiful was an intimidating experience. 'I've come to write your . . . I mean, I've come to discuss your, er, column.'

'Well, what the hell are you doing in front of the camera then?' Champagne's drill-like gaze moved from Jane's scuffed shoes to the sagging bra beneath her not-very-well-ironed white blouse. Jane's cheeks burned with shame.

'Jane very kindly stepped in to help us with the light reading since you were so *busy*,' said Dave.

Champagne seethed. Pausing only to throw a glance as green as a glassful of Chartreuse at Dave, she flounced out of the studio, muttering a stream of invective of which only 'fucking old poofter' could clearly be heard.

There was a short silence.

Dave sighed. 'Go and sort her out, Fabergé,' he murmured to his snub-nosed assistant. Fabergé started eagerly forward. But his services, it seemed, were not required.

'I'm ready.' Husky tones had replaced the honk. Turning round, Jane saw Champagne standing in the doorway wearing nothing more than a challenging gaze.

There really was, Jane saw, nothing holding those breasts up. Full and glorious, they soared onwards and upwards like helium balloons, each topped with its rosy nub of nipple. Champagne grinned at her astonished and silent audience. She strode forward, long muscles sliding up and down her slender thighs as she moved. She walked up to Dave and, thanks to the disparity in their heights, thrust her nipples practically in his face. 'Dress me,' she said in her huskiest tones, running both hands down the sides of her body. 'If you want to, that is.' She shot a searing glance from beneath her thick lashes and pouted at the room.

Jane sighed. Champagne had turned a tantrum into a triumph simply by taking her clothes off. Satisfied at the sensation she had caused, Champagne swung on her heel and began to sashay up and down the room like a supermodel. Watching her prance around, utterly uninhibited, it struck Jane that nakedness was a concept that only really applied to those with less than perfect figures. People with bodies as stunning as Champagne's were always dressed, in the sense that there was never anything embarrassing to conceal.

Delighted to be the centre of attention, Champagne now dazzled the assembled company with a radiant smile.

'She can certainly turn on the charm when she wants to,' Dave muttered grudgingly.

'She can turn on more than that,' Jane whispered. 'Look at Fabergé!'

Dave turned round to see his assistant bending over some boxes. He was clearly trying desperately to conceal an enormous erection in his tight white trousers.

'*Well*,' said Dave delightedly, raising both eyebrows and grinning widely. 'I had no idea he was such a talented boy.'

Dave's good humour restored, the shoot proceeded. Champagne was in her element, posing, pouting and slinking about in a succession of tiny, tight evening dresses that Jane could barely imagine getting her own right leg into. As Champagne's grudge against her seemed to have completely dissolved under the hot studio lights and the attention, Jane bit the bullet and suggested, after the shoot was over, that it was time to talk through the first instalment of Champagne Moments.

'Well, it had better not take long,' Champagne snapped, looking at her diamond-studded Cartier watch. 'I've got a colonic at three,' she announced. 'Then a leg wax. Then Rollo's picking me up.'

'Fine,' said Jane briskly, fishing out her notebook and flicking the ballpoint release mechanism of her pen. 'Let's be quick then. Talk me through your week. What have you been doing?'

Champagne, slumped on an orange box in the studio with her elegant legs wound round each other, fished a cigarette out of her snakeskin Kelly bag. She lit it and frowned. 'Ah,' she said, addressing the far wall. 'Um,' she added. 'Er,' she finished.

Jane felt panic rising slowly up her throat. Of the many difficult situations she had imagined Champagne Moments might involve, the one in which Champagne was unable to remember anything she had done had never occurred to her.

'Um, I saw in the *Sun* that you had been out with Robert Redford when he came to London earlier this week,' Jane prompted.

A slight pucker appeared between Champagne's perfectly-plucked eyebrows. Robert Redford, Robert Redford, her bee-stung lips mouthed silently. Robert Redford. After a few minutes of profound frowning, a faint glow of remembrance irradiated her face. *'American!'* she pronounced triumphantly.

Jane nodded eagerly, encouragingly.

'*Actor!*' Champagne added a few seconds later.

Jane nodded again.

'Oh, *yah*,' pronounced Champagne eventually, her face glowing with the promise of full recollection.

The promise remained unfulfilled. Champagne could remember nothing more.

'I suppose I had a lot of QNIs last week,' Champagne concluded. 'Quiet Nights In.'

Heart sinking, Jane realised this was not going to make four sentences, let alone four pages. And if she returned to the office without the fourteen hundred words of sparkling copy Josh wanted, it wasn't going to be Champagne D'Vyne who got the blame. Why, if he'd wanted an It Girl, hadn't Josh simply signed up Tara Palmer-Tomkinson, Jane seethed to herself. She, at least, had the two vital skills Champagne lacked – the ability to string a sentence together and some idea of what she'd been doing all week.

Sighing, and sending up a silent prayer to the god of ghostwriters, Jane took her mental pickaxe and determinedly and repeatedly attempted to break the surface of the substance which lay like impenetrable rock between Champagne and her ability to recall anything whatsoever that had happened to her in the past few days. Thank goodness she had taken those notes when Champagne was on the phone.

It took several increasingly frantic phone calls a day for the rest of the week before Jane managed to extract enough information to make up the first column. The latest *Gorgeous* had been about to hit the printing presses, but Josh insisted the issue was held until Champagne Moments was written and slipped in at the last minute. At the end of the week, Jane staggered, utterly drained, into Josh's office and handed over four pages of print-out to her boss. Heart hammering, she sank on to the sofa and folded her arms to await the verdict. It was always nerve-racking showing Josh a piece. Few things ever seemed to come up to the standard he demanded. She crossed her fingers so hard that it hurt.

Josh read. He clapped his hands and rocked with mirth. He laughed so much at the Gulfstream stories that his monocle fell out. 'It's hilarious,' he gasped, dabbing his streaming eyes with the handkerchief from his top pocket. 'It's fantastic. A star, my dear, is born.'

Damn, thought Jane, uncrossing her fingers.

Chapter 3

Whatever it was Tally desperately wanted to discuss, she wasn't going to break the habit of a lifetime and arrive on time to do so. Sitting waiting in the corner of the local wine bar on Saturday night, Jane had got through one glass of house white and half a bowl of peanuts already. Not that she was too annoyed. No one could hold a candle to Champagne in the irritation stakes. And anyway, it was impossible to be angry with Tally. She was much too sweet and awkward. With her funny nose, large eyes, long legs and towering height, Tally had reminded Jane irresistibly of a startled ostrich the first time they clapped eyes on each other at Cambridge.

'Do you remember,' Jane often said long after she and Tally had become friends, 'that first English tutorial on Memory when we were asked what our earliest recollections were and you said yours was of the line of servants' bells ringing in the breakfast room at home. I thought you were the most ghastly snob!'

'I suppose I should have said they were ringing because the window sash had broken again and there was a howling gale blowing through the room.' Tally sighed. 'And that I was in there because my bedroom ceiling had collapsed and I was sleeping on the breakfast room floor.'

Tally, Jane soon realised, was not your typical upper-class girl, despite having had almost a textbook grand upbringing. From what Jane could gather, her mother had wanted her to ride but Tally was almost as scared of horses as she had been of the terrifyingly capable blondes strapping on tack at the Pony Club. Lady Julia had managed to force her daughter to be a debutante, with the result that Tally was now on intimate terms with the inside of the best lavatories in London. 'I was a hopeless deb,' she admitted. 'The only coming out I did was from the loo after everyone else had gone. I once hid in the ones at Claridge's for so long I heard the attendant tell the manager she was going to send for the plumber.'

Tally did, however, live in a stately home, Mullions, and was the descendant of at least a hundred earls. The earls, however, had done her no favours as far as the house was concerned. 'Trust' was the Venery family motto. 'I *so* wish it had been Trust Fund,' Tally sighed on more than one occasion. For the heads of successive generations had, it seemed, trusted a little too much in a series of bad investments and their own skill at the card table. A sequence of earls had squandered the family resources until there was nothing left for the upkeep of a hen coop, let alone a mansion.

'It's embarrassing really, having such hopeless ancestors,' Tally would say. 'These wasn't a Venery in sight at Waterloo or Trafalgar, for instance. But once you look at the great financial disasters, we're there with bells on. The South Sea Bubble, the Wall Street Crash, even Lloyds; you name it, we're there right in the middle of it, losing spectacularly, hand over fist.'

Tally's own father, who had died in a car crash when she was small, had tried to reverse the situation as best he could while saddled with a wife as extravagant as Lady Julia. But without much success. The result was that Mullions had been more or less a hard hat area for as long as Jane had known it. Nonetheless, Tally had, after Cambridge, decided to dedicate herself to restoring her family home to its former glory, continuing the work of her father.

Highly romantic though all this sounded, in practice it seemed to consist of Tally rushing round the ancient heap doing running repairs to stop it falling down altogether, and using any time left over to apply for grants that never seemed to materialise. As time had gone on, Tally seemed to have gently abandoned hope of getting the place back on its feet. She had confessed to Jane frequently that getting it on its knees would be a miracle. 'Although I suppose it possesses,' she sighed, 'what *House and Garden* would call a unique untouched quality.'

Jane scooped up another handful of nuts and looked forward to what was always a plentiful supply of stories about Tally's insufferably grand mother. Lady Julia was as determined as her daughter that Mullions should go on – as long as someone else did all the work. She was markedly less willing than Tally to struggle into waders to drag weeds out of the oxbow lake or crawl along the Jacobean lead gutters pulling leaves out to stop blockages. Even more useless was Tally's brother, Piers. He seemed to prefer spending all his time – including holidays – at Eton. She must remember, Jane thought, to tell Tally about the crusty in the paper who had looked so like her brother. Tally would be amused.

Tally did not look amused, Jane thought, as the tall, grave-faced figure of her friend finally appeared in the wine bar. But she certainly looked amusing. What on earth was she wearing? Tally had never exactly been a snappy dresser but even by her standards this was eccentric. As Tally threaded her way between the tables, Jane saw she had on what looked like an ancient, enormous and patched tweed jacket worn over an extremely short and glittery A-line dress.

'You look amazing,' Jane said, truthfully, leaping up to kiss Tally's cold, soft, highly-coloured cheek. 'Is that vintage?' she asked, nodding at the dress which, at close range, looked extraordinarily well-cut and expensive, if a little old-fashioned.

'Mummy's cast-offs, if that's what you mean,' Tally answered, slotting herself in under the table and stuffing what was left of the nuts into her mouth. 'All my clothes have fallen to bits now, so I've started on hers. I must say they're very well made. The stitches don't give an inch. When I was scraping the moss out of the drains yesterday—'

'You surely didn't scrape them out wearing *that*?' gasped Jane. 'It looks like Saint Laurent.'

'Yes, it is, actually,' said Tally vaguely. 'But no, I wear her old Chanel for outdoor work. Much warmer. This glittery stuff's a bit scratchy.'

'How is Mullions?' asked Jane. This usually was the cue for Tally to explode into rhapsodic enthusiasm about duck decoys and uncovering eighteenth-century graffiti during the restoration of the follies. This time, however, Tally's face fell, her lips trembled and, to Jane's dismay, her big, clear eyes filled up with tears. The end of her nose, always a slight Gainsborough pink against the translucent whiteness of the rest of her face, deepened to Schiaparelli. This, clearly, was what Tally wanted to talk about.

'Whatever's happened?' Jane placed her warm hand over

Tally's bony cold one. Tally swallowed, pulled it away and tucked her thin light-brown hair behind her ears before lifting her reddened eyes to Jane.

'Mummy,' Tally whispered. 'She's gone mad.'

Jane frowned slightly. Was that all? But surely Julia had always had a screw loose? She had more than once, Jane remembered, sent Tally back to the new term at Cambridge with instructions to 'drive carefully back to Oxford, dear'. After her father had died, the horses in the carriage block had been the nearest Tally seemed to have to a stable family background.

'How do you mean, mad, exactly?' asked Jane carefully.

'Don't ask how it happened. I've no idea. But she says she spent a night sitting naked on top of a mountain in the Arizona desert and it changed her life,' choked Tally. Julia had, she explained to an amazed Jane, recently flown off on holiday in all her usual first-class, chignonned splendour and had returned a barefoot New Age hippy with her hair around her knees. 'And now she wants to go round the world and enlarge her horizons with Big Horn,' Tally finished.

'What's that?' said Jane. 'A New Age travel company?'

'Her new boyfriend.' Tally closed her eyes as if to block out the horror of it all. 'He's a Red Indian she met in Arizona. Only now he's living at Mullions. And he never says anything. Ever.'

'*What?*' said Jane. It couldn't be true. Lady Julia Venery, a New Age hippy? A woman whose idea of crystal therapy was looking at the window display of Tiffany's. And a Red Indian boyfriend? Julia, whose only previous experience of reservations was the kind one made at The Ritz. 'I can't believe it,' she said. 'What does Mrs Ormondroyd make of it?' The powerfully-built, raisin-faced housekeeper at

Mullions was in a permanent state of outrage as it was.

'Big Horn's causing havoc,' sniffed Tally. 'Mrs Ormondroyd put his prayer flag in to wash with a red jumper and it came out streaked like a sunset. He was furious, in a silent sort of way. And now he's trying to build something called a sweat lodge in the rose garden. Mr Peters is not amused.'

The sour old butler/gardener had never been amused the entire time Jane had known him. Neither, come to that, had Mrs Ormondroyd. Unsure what to say or do in the face of such disaster, Jane ordered two more glasses of wine, and another bowl of peanuts.

'Can't Piers do anything?' she asked.

Tally sighed so heavily the top layer of peanuts rolled on to the table. 'Gone AWOL,' she groaned. 'No one at Eton has seen him for ages. Apparently he's—'

'Joined a gang of environmental protesters?' Jane leapt in as the photograph of the crusty clicked into place in her head. However unbelievable it seemed, it was only half as unbelievable as the Julia story.

'How on earth do you know that?' gasped Tally, shocked out of her misery to look quite her old self.

Jane explained about spotting his picture in the paper. 'Nick was furious,' she added.

A wintry smile crossed Tally's strained features. 'That makes me feel better at least,' she said ruefully. 'Piers was last heard of a hundred feet beneath a runway at Stansted, glorying in the name of Muddy Fox. He seems to be rather notorious. Been arrested at least twice, apparently,' she sighed. 'Still, he's not the first of the family to do that. My great-great-great-grandfather was thrown into jail three times for running up gambling debts. By my great-great-great-grandmother, apparently.'

They lapsed into silence. It struck Jane that the conversation was getting surreal. Two glasses of wine on an empty stomach plus Tally's mad family history was a potent brew – even without the week she'd had.

'Never mind,' she said eventually. 'Look on the bright side. If Piers goes on making headlines like this he'll get his own chat show. Then you'll really be able to put Mullions back to rights.'

But instead of cheering up, Tally's face fell even further. She took a deep swig from her glass and coughed violently.

'Now I have to tell you the worst thing of all,' she stuttered, after Jane had banged her on the back and her eyes had stopped streaming. Jane looked at her apprehensively. Short of Mrs Ormondroyd and Mr Peters opening a Tantric sex workshop, it was difficult to imagine what that might be. 'Mummy wants to sell Mullions.' Tally's voice was as tight and dry as her face.

'*No!*' Jane gasped. This really was a disaster. Nick at his most scathing and Champagne D'Vyne at her worst paled by comparison. '*Why?*'

'To pay for her travels. It's her right, she inherited the house in Daddy's will. And she can do what she likes with it – there's no title to hand down anymore since the Ninth Earl, my grandfather, lost it on a hen race in 1920.' Tally paused and swallowed. 'Mummy says the place is an old wreck and we'd be best advised to get shot of it while it is still worth something. She s-s-s-says,' Tally gasped, her self-control deserting her, 'that she suddenly realised she'd spent her entire life [gulp] perpetuating [sniff] an outmoded feudal system.' Tally clapped her bony hand to her mouth as the tears spilled down her long, thin cheeks.

'Well, she took a long time to work that out,' said Jane. 'Did she never get any clues from the fact she lived in a stately home with servants' bells and a stable block?'

Tally said nothing. Both red hands were covering her face now. With a twinge, Jane saw the signet ring with the Venery family crest shining dull and gold on Tally's little finger.

'But you've had that place for four hundred years, for God's sake,' Jane raged, feeling suddenly furious. 'You can't let go of it now. Can't you stop her?'

Tally shook her head. 'Not unless I can come up with some brilliant plan for it to make money. But as I can't even get grants to repair the place, I very much doubt I'll get them to start building restaurants and things. And quite frankly, Mrs Ormondroyd's cooking is hardly a draw.'

'You could always marry someone rich,' Jane suggested. 'Then they could buy the place off Julia.'

'Fat chance,' said Tally miserably. 'Who's going to want to marry *me*?' She raised her thin face hopelessly to Jane. 'It's not as if I'm pretty. Or rich. I'm going to die a spinster in a council house at this rate.'

'Hang on, hang on,' said Jane, seeing Tally wobbling at the top of the Cresta Run of self-pity. 'What about all that stuff about Lord Right? What about finding the perfect man?'

'Forget it,' said Tally, flashing her a hurt, how-could-you-mention-that-now glance. 'At the moment, I'm trying to hang on to the perfect home. Not that anyone thinks it's perfect except m-m-m-me.' She started to snivel again.

'Now look,' said Jane briskly. She was, she knew, at her best when she was trying to help other people out of trouble. Unable to solve any of her own work or Nick problems, she nonetheless felt completely confident she could sort Tally out somehow. The most appalling messes always had ingeniously simple solutions. Didn't they?

'There's got to be a way out of this,' she said decisively, sitting up straight and giving her slumped friend a challenging look. 'We need to get you a knight in shining armour. Sir Lancelot. Or Sir Earnalot, more like.' She grinned. Tally remained hunched and hopeless.

'He doesn't even have to have shining armour,' Jane added. 'You've got plenty of that standing around the Great Hall.'

'Well, it's not very shiny,' sniffed Tally, 'but Mrs Ormondroyd does her best. You know what she's like.'

'Half cleaner, half demolition squad,' grinned Jane. 'Well, a knight on a white charger then. Or, even better, a gold chargecard. A multi-Mullionaire.'

'But where am I going to meet someone like that?' asked Tally dismally.

Jane had to admit it was a good question. 'Let's have another glass and think about it,' she said.

After an hour more of lamenting the situation at Mullions, Tally suddenly decided she couldn't bear to be away from it another second. 'After all,' she said mournfully as Jane poured her into the train at Paddington, 'I might not be living there much longer.'

'We'll think of something,' said Jane, clunking the train door shut like a capable nanny. Tally was the only person who could make her feel in control. The only person more hopeless than she was.

Jane returned to the flat. As she opened the front door, she saw Tom and a fair-haired girl going slowly upstairs. His hand was spread tenderly across her back and he was talking to her. They seemed to be much too absorbed in each other to notice Jane crossing the hall beneath them. Anaesthetised by alcohol, Jane blinked, pursed her lips and nodded slowly and exaggeratedly to herself. Of *course* she was not disappointed. She had only had one conversation with Tom, and that had been in far from ideal circumstances. And of *course* Tom had girlfriends. When someone looked like that, it was only to be expected. Good luck to him, in fact, she thought, stabbing furiously at the Chubb with the key and a trembling hand.

Inside, Jane collapsed on the sofa with a cup of camomile tea which Nick always said looked like pee but which she hoped might do some overnight super-cleansing of her system and save her from the hangover she undoubtedly deserved. With an effort, she forced herself to think about Nick and what he was doing in Brussels. He had left this morning so early she had not even said goodbye to him.

She gazed vaguely at the bookshelves opposite the sofa and smiled fondly at the fat spines of Nick's vast collection of political biographies. The sudden need to find a man for Tally had helped put Nick into perspective, albeit the perspective given by several large glasses of dubious house white. There was no doubt that, at his worst, Nick was rude, unsupportive, mean and selfish. But she wouldn't be without him, Jane assured herself. She loved him. She lived with him. Occasionally they even had sex.

Poor old Tally, was Jane's last waking thought before passing out on the sofa. The only man who made the earth move as far as she was concerned was Mr Peters with his shovel.

'It's fantastic,' trilled Josh as Jane entered the *Gorgeous* offices one morning a week later. 'Blanket coverage,' he yelped, gesturing at the newspapers which lay scattered about the desktops. The new issue of *Gorgeous* had obviously hit the publicity jackpot.

'They've all picked up on her column.'

Jane grabbed a pile of papers. It was true. Only the *Morning Star*, it appeared, had resisted the temptation to carry a picture of Champagne D'Vyne on its front page.

'Eat your heart out, Tara,' crowed Josh. 'The party's over.'

Jane gazed in fascination at a vast picture of the multiple-Gulfstream owning Hon. Rollo Harbottle in the *Sun*. To say he was far from handsome was an understatement. Rollo looked as if his features had been thrown on from a distance by a group of near-sighted darts players. Teeth like tombstones and a receding hairline hardly improved matters; it was a face, in short, that only a bank manager could love. Most gruesome of all, it was gazing with lascivious appreciation at Champagne's barely-there knickers, clearly almost not visible beneath the near-transparent material of her dress. Talk about heir and a G-string, thought Jane. According to the caption, the Hon. Rollo Harbottle was poised to inherit a vitreous enamel fortune.

'He looks horribly pleased with himself,' observed Valentine. 'Flushed with success, in fact. But he *has* done quite well, I suppose. Considering he looks like something you'd find on a fishmonger's slab.' He gazed at the photograph in awe. 'I've never seen an overbite like it,' he said, shaking his head. 'They should preserve it for dental science after he's dead.'

'Well, she's obviously not with him because of his looks,' said Jane.

'Yes, the vitreous enamel fortune probably has something to do with it,' Valentine agreed. 'What you might call a chain reaction. He probably bowled her over.'

'And we mustn't forget his title,' grinned Jane.

'Champagne's obviously a sucker for the class cistern. I wonder whether he's taken her to the family seat yet.'

Josh, ignoring them, was flicking busily through the centre sections of the newspapers. 'Look at all these inside spreads,' he crowed.

It was true. The *Daily Mail* had run a line-up of every man Champagne had ever been out with and had calculated their net worth in a facetious paragraph beneath. The Hon. Rollo Harbottle, Jane noted, was the richest. Second was Giles Trumpington-Kwyck-Save, an equally ill-favoured supermarket heir Champagne had apparently dumped a couple of weeks before.

'That's market forces for you,' observed Valentine. 'Wonder how long it'll be before Harbottle's been passed on to the next gold-digging party girl. I'd give him a week.'

'Oh, I don't know. After all, do you love anyone enough to give them your last Rollo?' snorted Jane.

Even some of the quality broadsheets had made features of the story. The *Daily Telegraph* had lined up a collection of the most eligible bachelors in Britain for Champagne's consideration and headlined the piece 'Sparkling Possibilities'. The *Guardian*, meanwhile, had run a pious piece by some former millionaire's wife headlined 'Why I Prefer Poor Men'. Josh fell about laughing when he saw it.

All morning the phones rang with requests about *Gorgeous*'s new star columnist. 'Richard and Judy want her,' reported Valentine, putting the phone down after one conversation.

'So does Chris Evans,' smirked Josh. 'But I've told him TFI's got a long way to go to beat the Big Breakfast offer.'

'I can't quite believe what I've just heard, but I think that was the *Today* programme,' said Jane, putting down her receiver in horror. Surely people weren't taking Champagne seriously? 'It's a nightmare,' she moaned to Valentine. 'That column's going to run and run now. What have I got myself into? All these papers calling her the It Girl. Which makes me the Shit Girl, I suppose. The nearest I get to a trust fund is Sainsbury's loyalty points.'

'Keep your chins up,' said Josh, overhearing as usual and giving Jane the broadest of grins. 'You'll grow to love her in the end. You'll be twin souls soon. Sisters under the skin.'

But why, thought Jane miserably, do I have so much more skin than she does?

Tracking Champagne down for the second Champagne Moments column proved even more exasperating than the first. Her mobile was switched off and her home answer-phone was full. Simon at Tuff PR was just full of himself

'Look, Champagne's very busy,' he barked. 'She worked very hard promoting a new club last night. She's at home. I don't think she's even up yet.'

Jane saw red. 'I'm going round there,' she announced. Phoning was obviously useless. It might be good to talk, but only if the other person picked up the receiver. 'What's the address?'

Trust Champagne to live in one of the most exclusive squares in London, Jane grumbled to herself as, half an hour later, she piloted her battered red 2CV into a row of porticoed palaces, their white stucco gleaming in the afternoon sun. The vehicles parked outside resembled an al fresco luxury car showroom. A futuristic, white open-top sports model lounged decadently alongside a vermilion Corniche more brilliantly scarlet than Vivien Leigh with a double first. My love is like a red, red Rolls, thought Jane enviously, conscious of the dent in the side of her own door and the flotsam and jetsam of rubbish on the floor.

Appropriately enough for one of her probable bra size, Champagne lived at number 38. Standing like a shrunken Alice in Wonderland before the colossally oversized black-painted door, Jane dithered between bell pushes marked 'Visitors' and 'Tradesmen'. Which, she wondered, was she? Trade, certainly. Or perhaps both. She pushed first one and then the other, but there was no reply from either. Eventually, she pushed the huge door itself with her fingertips. Unexpectedly, it swung open.

Jane entered a vast, white-painted hall where a curving wrought-iron staircase mamboed its way up to a huge Edwardian skylight. A white door stood slightly ajar to the right. All was silent. Even the traffic outside was stilled, lost in the high-ceilinged space, the all-absorbing quiet of wealth. It was, Jane thought jealously, a far cry from Clapham, where Nick's windows practically cracked if Tom dropped a peanut upstairs. She did not, however, want to think about Tom just now. Especially, she did not want to dwell on the niggling feeling of betrayal after seeing him with the blonde girl.

Without warning, the quiet erupted into ear-splitting noise. It reverberated off the floors, resounded off the pillars, flashed back sharply from the huge chandelier that hung in the centre of the ceiling. It turned out to be a small, grey poodle with spiteful little black eyes, which had shot out of the door on the right and was now engaged in skidding round Jane in circles on the marble. It was a ghastly creature. Its high-pitched, hysterical bark was, Jane thought, the most irritating sound she had ever heard.

'Gucci, what the fuck's the matter?' Jane instantly

revised her opinion. The second most irritating sound she had ever heard.

'Champagne?' called Jane.

'Who's that?' bawled Champagne.

'It's Jane. From *Gorgeous*. I'm here about the column.' Silence followed. Jane pushed the glossy white door further open.

'Hang on,' yelled Champagne. 'I'm coming.' From the giggles that followed, Jane deduced Champagne was not alone. Nor was her last remark necessarily addressed to Jane. Did she have a man in there?

Jane picked her way between the piles of clothes, shoes and shopping bags that formed islands in the sea of cream carpet on the sitting room floor. The room was so enormous that even the huge, black Steinway grand filled little more than a corner. From the piles of dresses slung over the piano stool, Jane deduced its ivories had seen little tinkling of late and that its main function was to support the collection of silver-framed photographs which, in the best Belgravia tradition, crowded its gleaming surface.

Champagne had still not appeared. Jane crossed the room towards the photographs, waves of pale carpet ebbing about her feet as she moved. Although most of the pictures featured Champagne holding gum-baring contests with a string of celebrities, there were a few more personal ones as well. Jane peered closely at a large picture of two children: a blonde girl and a boy in front of a well-kept country house. There was no doubt that the girl was Champagne – the knowing smirk and the self-conscious pose were all there even then. As was the rest of it, Jane saw jealously. At the time she herself had been a pudgy-kneed child with a pot belly, Champagne already had a neatly-cropped mane of white-blonde hair (it must be natural after all) and the long, slender limbs of a thoroughbred. But, Jane comforted herself, if Champagne had the legs of a racehorse, she had the brain of one too. And her boyfriend, Rollo Harbottle, had the teeth of one.

Jane felt rather sorry for the pleasant-looking boy she imagined must be Champagne's brother. It was bad enough having to talk to Champagne for a few hours a week. Growing up with her was something she couldn't begin to imagine.

She picked up another photograph of a white-haired baby being pushed in a pram by a fierce-looking woman in a dark blue uniform. There was no time to put it back as the mistress of the house suddenly bounced into the room and strode quickly up behind her.

'Oh, that's me and Nanny Flange,' Champagne declared in her ear-splitting rattle. 'Sweet old thing really. Left after I bit her leg.'

'Did what?' asked Jane.

'I bit her leg,' said Champagne matter-of-factly. 'Mummy was furious.'

'Well, I suppose it was a bit naughty.'

'Yah, Mummy went ballistic. "Oh, darling," she said. "How *could* you have bitten Nanny's *filthy* leg?" ' Champagne put back her head and roared with laughter.

Her bare, brown flesh was scarcely covered by the tiniest pair of knickers Jane had ever seen. A tight, cropped, pink T-shirt evidently made for a two-year-old struggled to cover her exuberant bust. Her hair was a bird's nest, a cigarette dangled from the corner of her lipstick-smudged mouth and her mascara had run, but this, Jane was irritated to observe, only made her look more beautiful than ever.

As Gucci exploded into more high-pitched yapping,

Jane realised they were not alone in the room. Slinking his way along the back wall was the snub-nosed photographer's assistant whose trousers had been so excitable at the Dave Baker shoot. Matters had evidently developed since then. He stood, twisting his hands, by the door into the hall.

'Weel I see you again?' he mumbled to Champagne in a heavy French accent.

'Yah, course you will,' said Champagne, drawing on her cigarette as she bundled him out of the door. 'Buy *Gorgeous*, there's a good boy,' she added, closing the door firmly and padding back into the sitting room. 'Phew,' she said. 'Just in time. Rollo'll be here in a minute. He'd go ballistic if he bumped into Fabergé.'

Quite, thought Jane. Rollo probably had a vitreous temper. Nonetheless, disappointment flooded through her at the news that he and Champagne were still together. On the evidence of what she had just witnessed, she was beginning to wonder if she might bag Rollo for Tally. Whatever his shortcomings, he was at least rich.

The poodle's yapping continued unabated. Jane's head started to spin with the volume. 'Gucci, darling,' cooed Champagne, falling gracefully to her knees to pet him. 'You're hungry, aren't you?' Scooping the shrill scrap of noise into her arms, she left the room.

Jane followed her into a brilliant white kitchen where Champagne was rummaging in a vast metal techno-fridge much taller than she was. Like her, it had evidently not seen any food for several days. The only evidence of nourishment anywhere were the empty bottles of Krug thrust neck down in a Fortnum's box in the corner.

'Bingo!' Champagne, who had been throwing open a succession of empty cupboards, finally produced a tin. As she placed the scraped-out contents before the dog, Jane realised it wasn't Pedigree Chum. 'But that's foie gras,' she said.

'Yah, absolutely,' said Champagne, not batting an eyelid. 'Gucci adores it. Can't stand the stuff myself. *Bloody* fattening. And so cruel to the geese as well, forcing all that food down their throats. Worse than an anorexic rehab centre.'

Jane's antennae began to twitch. She fished out her pencil and started to scribble. 'Better mention my really cool new car,' Champagne honked, noticing.

'What car?' asked Jane.

'Parked outside. White sports car?'

Jane recalled the menacing machine lurking alongside the kerb. 'Hey, big spender,' she said, mock-chiding but envious.

'Oh, it wasn't that much,' Champagne said silkily. 'Rather a bargain in fact. Amazing after-sales service as well,' she added coyly, looking at Jane from under her eyelashes. 'So I'd love to give them a mentionette in the column, if possible.'

'Fine,' said Jane, wondering what sort of after-sales service Champagne had required. After all, the car was brand new. Perhaps someone had had to come and show her where the ignition key went. Or . . . It suddenly dawned on Jane that Champagne had probably been given the car for free. Bargain indeed, she thought furiously, breaking the stub of her pencil on her notebook.

There was an abrupt ring at the front door. 'Oh fuck, it's Rollsy,' groaned Champagne, leaping up. 'Sorry, have to run. Got to dash off to New York. But we've done the next column now, haven't we?'

Jane found herself being shown to the door just as the Hon. Rollo Harbottle manoeuvred his teeth into the hall.

Up close, he was even more repellent than he appeared in the newspapers. How on earth could Champagne bear to touch him? Nick may be grumpy, but at least he didn't have a face like a basket of fruit. And he was, Jane thought happily, finally back from Brussels tonight. Hopefully with a vast box of Belgian chocolates.

Chapter 4

Jane put the phone down, feeling numb with disappointment and fury. She'd spent all lunchtime buying, and all evening preparing, dinner for Nick's return. And now he'd called to say he would be late. Not by a few hours, though. *By another whole day.* 'There's a Caravanning League of Belgium Fringe Pressure Group fondue I can't afford to miss,' he informed her via a crackling mobile phone.

Depressed, Jane returned to the kitchen. The pasta had taken advantage of Nick's phone call to weld itself to the bottom of the pan, while the putanesca sauce, which she had hoped might set a spicy and whorish tone to their reunion, was starting to burn. Cooking, Jane knew, had never really been her forte. But then, what was?

At least, she thought, poking the flaccid, off-white mass of pasta, she could always beat Tally into a cocked cacciatore. No one this side of Macbeth's three witches was as bad a cook as her. Jane would never forget the evening at Cambridge when Tally had invited her round for supper.

'What's this?' Jane had asked, staring at a burnt-looking lump of bread running with sticky sweet goo. 'Sixth Form Special,' Tally had replied proudly. 'Toasted Mars Bar sandwich. You stick a couple of slices in the Breville and put a Mars Bar in the middle. Close and cook for two minutes. Delicious. We lived off them at Cheltenham.'

Jane felt a stab of guilt at the thought of Tally, Mullions and the missing multimillionaire. Locating one had sounded so simple after a bottle of wine on an empty stomach. In the cold light of day, it had presented certain logistical difficulties. Thumbing through her address book, Jane realised she didn't know a thousandaire, let alone a millionaire. The nearest she could manage was Amanda, an old friend from Cambridge who had married a merchant banker and swapped bedsit life for six-bedroomed, domestically-aided splendour in Hampstead. Jane wondered if she should get in touch.

The telephone rang again. Jane dashed to answer it. Had Nick changed his mind?

'Hi there,' said Tally mournfully.

'I've just been thinking about you,' said Jane, hoping she didn't sound too disappointed.

'Probably because Mullions has become one huge psychic energy transmitter since Mummy's come back,' said Tally grumpily. 'As I speak, my mother's making ritual fire towards the waxing moon and Big Horn is ceremonially constructing a mercurial harp in the paddock.'

'A what?'

'You don't want to know. Suffice to say, it is based on the ground plan of Stonehenge and the geometry of the magic square of Mercury. And, to top it all, quite literally, is a stone from the ancient Cheesewring site in Cornwall.'

'*No!*' said Jane.

'Oh yes. Apparently it is meant to bring harmony and peace to the house, but I can assure you that from where

I, Mr Peters and Mrs Ormondroyd are standing, it's war. *Damn!*'

'What was that?' asked Jane.

'I'd better go. Billiard room door's just fallen off.' Moral support wasn't the only kind Tally needed at the moment.

She could do with a boost herself, come to that. Nick's no show had hardly got the evening off to a flying start.

Wandering into the tiny sitting room, Jane stared at the candles on the table guttering in the breeze which swept under the door. The carefully wrapped little welcome home present (a pair of cuff-links) lying on Nick's plate suddenly looked pathetic. The polished wine glasses, shining in the candlelight, stood ready for the bottle of champagne and the bottle of Pouilly-Something she'd dithered over for ages at Safeway's, unable to decide between Fumé or Fuissé.

Pouring herself a stiff gin and tonic, Jane decided to spend the evening lying on the couch with an old bonk-buster. After all, snuggling up with Jilly Cooper was probably the nearest she was going to get to a sex life for the moment.

Ten minutes later, lost in the adventures of a raunchy TV executive and her well-heeled brute of a lover, Jane was suddenly brought down to earth. By something on her ceiling. She sat up and listened. A series of loud clatters from the flat above made her wince. All hell seemed to be breaking loose. It sounded as if Tom was playing Twister with a herd of elephants in platform shoes.

Jane tried to concentrate on her book. The TV executive and the brute were now indulging in some steamy bedroom scenes. She followed the bumping and grinding avidly, vicariously. The banging on the ceiling kept pace, a faint thump of music accompanying it.

Jane gripped Jilly hard by the spine and glared at the words. Five seconds later, she flung Mrs Cooper to the floor in despair, flew out of the door and up the stairs and banged her fists on Tom's door.

The door opened to reveal Tom naked from the waist up and rather red in the face.

'Hi, there,' he grinned, shoving back a clump of hair from his glowing forehead. Something around Jane's lower pelvis ignited like a gas stove at the flash of armpit revealed as he did so.

'Hi,' said Jane, shifting from foot to foot. 'Er, you're making quite a lot of noise, actually, and . . .'

'Am I? God, sorry. I'm just packing up a few things. I'm moving out, you see.'

'Moving out?' Jane looked up at him as he filled the doorway. His smooth, tanned torso suddenly struck her as eminently *lickable*.

'Yes. I'm going to New York. Tomorrow, in fact. So you won't have any more noise problems. I've just finished in any case.'

'Oh. Right.' Jane was suddenly filled with the wild desire to drop to her knees and beg him to make as much noise as was humanly possible. 'Well, good luck,' she said, starting to back away from the door. 'Goodbye.' This was beginning to sound like *Brief Encounter*. If only it was. An encounter with his briefs was just what she needed.

'Bye then,' said Tom, and closed his door.

Jane re-entered the flat. It was now frustratingly silent. Absolutely no reason to go upstairs again at all. She walked over to the window and, sighing, started to clear the table. She looked out. The sky was still light outside, the usual grey, featureless fading evening oddly characteristic of Clapham.

She gazed up beseechingly at the patchy ceiling, stained by generations of overflowing baths, broken-down shower units and rising damp. She willed Tom to break out into a foundation-shaking series of crashes, but there was silence. Except – Jane's ears pricked up – a slight, insistent tapping at the window behind her, which could have been a branch.

Only there were no branches near her window. Nothing grew in the scrubby, slimy apology for a back garden that Nick had neglected for as long as he had lived here. A rapist, then. A Jehovah's Witness? Jane whipped round, and drew her breath in sharply, her hand shooting automatically to her throat. Something huge, dark and misshapen was visible at the window, tapping gently against the pane.

She approached cautiously. The object seemed to be hanging from some sort of string. As Jane got closer, she realised it was a trainer. Poking out from inside it was a white slip of paper. Jane scrabbled frantically to open the peeling, scabby, moss-streaked window frame. She grabbed the piece of paper with a shaking hand and smoothed it out on the half-dismantled table, upon which one of the candles still flickered.

'Apologies for noise,' a decisive hand had written in blue-black ink. 'Can I take you out to dinner to say sorry?'

Jane's stomach plunged through the floor. Her knees shook. Should she ignore Tom out of loyalty to Nick? But Nick had let her down with his wretched caravanners' fondue. And what was the point of going out for dinner, piped up a Sensible Voice in her head, when there was a dinner all ready down here? She knew from experience that the putanesca sauce would respond well to treatment; if she added a little more tomato puree, only an interesting hint of smokiness would suggest how near it had come to disaster. The pasta was, well, just pasta. And there had never been anything wrong with the tomato ciabatta, the rocket salad and the Pouilly-Something.

Jane rushed upstairs before she could change her mind, knocked on the door and issued the invitation. 'It'll be ready in half an hour,' she said.

'Half an hour, then,' drawled Tom. 'Want me to bring anything?'

'Just yourself,' grinned Jane, instantly feeling mortified for sounding so cheesy. She was filled with a sudden terror that once he was across the threshold she'd be overcome with a form of socially maladroit Tourette's syndrome, telling him to 'sit ye down' and 'take a pew'.

Back in the flat, Jane threw herself against the door in an ecstasy of knotted-stomach guilt. Honestly, said the Sensible Voice. Anyone would think that you'd swung naked from the chandeliers, licked cream off his entire body and committed triple-chocolate adultery, the way you're reacting. You've only invited him to dinner. Jane pulled herself together. Half an hour, she thought, panicking. Five minutes for the food and twenty-five to make herself look more stunning than a 2,000 volt charge.

Twenty minutes later, Jane was standing despairing in the bedroom, having tried on and abandoned every outfit she possessed. He might think it odd she had changed, anyway, she thought, prising herself back into her jeans and white linen shirt. Ten minutes. She brushed her hair furiously, cleaned her teeth manically, re-applied her worn-off lipstick and gave herself another coat of mascara. As usual, it took longer to unclog her handiwork with a lash comb than it did to put it on in the first place. Five minutes. 'Aagh,' squealed Jane, giving herself a last slick of perfumeless Mum and a powerful blast of Chanel No 19. Three minutes. She rushed into the kitchen and uncorked the half-bottle of champagne for Dutch courage. Shame I never got round to the food, she thought, eyeing the reproachful mass of pasta as she knocked back an entire flute in one.

Right on cue, there was a knock at the door. Heart thumping, Jane opened it to find Tom waving a bottle of Moët. 'By way of apology, as you wouldn't let me take you out,' he grinned. 'And it's cold, so we can drink it now.'

As Jane sloshed it unsteadily into two glasses. Tom went straight to the bookshelves. 'What's this like?' he asked, selecting *Callaghan: The Man and The Myth* and *The John Major I Knew*.

'Not what you'd call a racy read,' said Jane. Even Nick had struggled with the Major book.

'But then,' she added, 'I'm not the one to ask. Politics isn't really my thing. Nick gets cross with me because he says all I care about are Cherie Blair's skirt lengths.'

'Cherie Blair's skirts are a crucial issue,' said Tom gravely. She had no idea if he was teasing her. 'Nick's away, I take it?' Was that a gleam in his eye?

'How did you know?'

'Elementary, my dear Jane. After you'd been up – and rightly, too – to complain about me, I simply put my ear to the floor and listened.' He grinned at her and emptied his champagne glass down his muscular throat.

'Yes. He's in Brussels.' She explained about the caravanners' fondue party. Tom raised an eyebrow.

He moved on from Nick's books to her own. Jane sent up a rare, silent prayer of thanks to her absent boyfriend for not allowing her room for her collection of bonkbusters. Those had been relegated to piles on the floor beneath the shelves while Nick had conceded a few inches of the shelves themselves to the battered old volumes of Keats, Yeats, Eliot and Shakespeare Jane had studied at university. Books that she still opened now and then to remind herself that she had once had a brain.

'It's when I read Yeats that I realise how hopeless it is to try and be a writer,' Tom sighed.

'Are you a writer, then?' Jane gasped. 'How *romantic*. What are you working on?'

Tom looked amused. 'I'm not sure it's all that romantic.'

Jane mentally kicked herself. How could she have sounded so jejune?

'It's about this serial killer driving around the Aberdeen ring road,' Tom elaborated. 'He's had a few lines of coke, his necrophiliac Alsatian's asleep in the back, and the man's bored, so he suddenly decides to follow this car and see where it's going. When the car stops at a service station, the killer gets out and does the business, as does the dog. This seems quite fun to them, so they start following another car at random, then strike again when it stops, then start following a van to see where that's going. And so on and so on until the man and the dog eventually drive off the Humber Bridge.' He stopped, and looked triumphantly at Jane. 'It's a sort of metaphor for our violent, haphazard society and the random nature of the choices we make in life. And death.'

Jane's heart sank. It sounded horrible.

'It's sort of *On the Road* meets *In Cold Blood*, so I thought I'd call it *Cold Road*,' said Tom, beaming. 'What do you think?'

Jane screwed up her courage. 'To be honest, not much,' she said. 'Ghastly, actually. I can't bear books like that.' She regretted it the moment the words left her.

Tom turned back to the bookshelves. Jane noticed his shoulders moving up and down. He was evidently struggling with his feelings.

'I'm so sorry,' she gasped, touching him on the arm. 'I didn't mean . . .'

Tom whipped round. His eyes blazed and his mouth quivered. Jane realised he was laughing.

'That plot,' he grinned, 'was suggested by my agent the other day. He told me that that's the sort of thing I would have to start knocking out if I ever wanted to make any money.'

'Ugh,' said Jane, relaxing a little. 'Well, I certainly wouldn't buy it.'

'Shock value equals publicity value apparently,' Tom said. 'Frankly, I'd rather write a bonkbuster. I see you've got quite a collection.'

So he'd noticed the Jilly Coopers after all. Tom grinned as Jane poured him another glass of Moët foam with a wobbling hand.

'Yes, of course. I can see the plot now.' Tom stared theatrically at the ceiling. 'Impecunious writer takes flat for a few weeks above beautiful blonde who lives in basement with boyfriend who doesn't realise how lucky he is.' He paused. 'Writer meets girl over romantic dinner, falls in love but has to leave for New York the next morning.'

Jane buried her reddening face in the champagne.

She'd read about sexual tension before, although all it had meant with Nick was that she wanted it and he didn't. But here it was now, the real thing. The air between Tom and herself felt thick with energy. Jane imagined a white flash of electricity if she touched him, like the opening credits of the South Bank Show. By now, Nick had receded to the far outback of her mind. Not waving, not even drowning. Not, for the time being, at all.

She stole a glance at Tom from under her triple-mascara'd lashes. He had all the careless glamour of one of those singlet-clad models in the Calvin Klein ads, except that Tom's seemed genuinely effortless. His hair had obviously not seen a comb for at least a day and his jeans were ripped at the knee. The most convincing testament of all to his lack of vanity was the T-shirt proclaiming 'Some Idiot Went To London And All I Got Was This Lousy T-shirt'.

'I always wondered who actually bought those,' Jane said, breaking the crackling silence.

Tom looked down at his chest, surprised. 'Got it from a jumble sale,' he said. 'Quite like it, actually. I find the implication that people come back from London laden with exotic gifts unobtainable elsewhere rather romantic really.' He grinned.

'Er, would you like to eat?' Jane asked. After all, it was the whole point of the evening. Wasn't it?

Tom nodded politely. 'Love to. But can we talk a bit more first? I find it practically impossible to have a conversation over food. I'm always shoving my fork in my mouth at the exact time someone is asking me a question.'

It was amazing. He wanted to talk to her. Jane racked her brains to recall the last time she had had a proper conversation with Nick. Or, come to that, the first time.

'We were talking about my bonkbuster, I believe,' Tom said lightly, igniting a Marlboro and gazing at her from between the slits in his narrowed eyelids. 'Now, where had we got to?' He stared at the ceiling again. 'Ah yes.' He blew a sequence of perfect smoke rings. 'Writer comes down for dinner with beautiful blonde, falls in love, but realises that as he is going away next morning and she has a boyfriend, it can never be.' He stopped, pulled a face and looked at Jane. 'Pity.' It was impossible to tell if he was serious. Nevertheless, disappointment flooded her.

'So.' Tom slipped from the armchair on to the floor and crawled across the rug to where Jane perched on the edge of the sofa. He looked into her eyes, took her face in his hands and touched her lips with his. 'So he steals a kiss anyway.' Jane's back locked rigid with excitement.

With a light finger, Tom traced the outline of her cheekbones and lips before slowly, deliberately, lowering his mouth again to hers.

Jane's brain flew round her cranium like a flock of disturbed sparrows. He couldn't do this to her. But, as his tongue gently slid between her acquiescent lips, she felt very glad that he had.

'Do you do this to everyone you've only just met?' she stammered as he came up for air.

'No, of course not. Anyway, we've met before.'

'What about your girlfriend?'

'Don't have one.' He was lying, Jane knew. So the girl on the stairs had been his agent, had she? 'More to the point, what about your boyfriend?' asked Tom wickedly. By now his hands had slipped inside her shirt. They were cool and dry, unlike Nick's, whose were always the temperature and moistness, if not the cleanliness, of the hot towels served in Indian restaurants. Tom's tongue, too, was miraculously free of the rivers of saliva that accompanied Nick's rare attempts at tonsil hockey.

'He's not here,' said Jane. Having decided that she would sleep with Tom, she felt quite calm now. What possible harm would one empty, brittle, mad, impetuous and utterly meaningless fling do? It was, anyway, Nick's fault for throwing her in temptation's way. Wasn't it?

Jane looked boldly into the clear eyes a few inches from her own. 'Let's just get something straight, shall we?' she said, as Tom's hand gently pushed down her jeans zip and started investigating her knickers.

'What?' mumbled Tom. 'I've got some condoms.'

'There's something else.'

Jane made no attempt to resist as he pushed her gently down on the rug. Thank goodness she'd hoovered it reasonably recently. And thank double goodness she'd shaved her armpits. As Tom's mouth moved down to her stiffening nipple she breathed in the heady scent of him – top notes of basil with a dash of salt.

'What?' muttered Tom. His tongue flicked thrillingly about her nipple. Jane gasped as every nerve in her body started singing the Hallelujah Chorus and her insides dissolved into molten metal.

'This is a one-night stand, isn't it?'

'Of course.' Tom looked up at her and grinned through his tangle of hair. 'This is far too much fun to last.'

'So you won't respect me in the morning?'

'I sincerely hope not.'

'That's all right then.'

Chapter 5

'Wore that yesterday, didn't you?' Josh asked as Jane came into the office the next morning.

Jane ignored him. Who cared if she'd rushed out of bed at the last minute and thrown on the clothes still lying on the floor from the night before? Josh was lucky she'd got them on the right way round. She sighed as her eye caught the clock. Tom would soon be leaving to catch his flight to New York. She would never see him again. Parts of her – very particular parts of her – regretted this intensely. But it was just as well, obviously. Last night had been a meaningless, mad and utterly shallow fling. But as meaningless, mad and utterly shallow flings went, it had been a good one.

Tom had made her feel more beautiful and desired than Kate Moss, a World Cup win and the National Lottery jackpot all rolled into one. He had been the gentlest as well as the most skilful of lovers, although admittedly her field of comparisons was limited. He had made her laugh. He had astonished her by his gentleness and sensitivity. And she had never seen such an enormous penis. It had looked big enough to pick up Channel Five. The World Service, come to that.

Nick would finally be on his way back from Brussels

now. He'd probably pass Tom in the air. Jane swallowed to combat a rising and recurring nausea, unsure whether it was an excess of champagne or guilt.

Two Nurofens later, Jane stood on the strand of the morning's news, preparing to wade through the tide of tabloids. 'Wondered when you were going to get on to those,' came Josh's voice out of his office. 'Then again, you should know everything about the big story already.'

Please don't let it be another transport minister disaster, prayed Jane. She couldn't cope with the thought of Nick sulking all week like he had after the run in with Piers and the crusties. Trembling, she scrabbled for the *Sun*.

'END OF A LAV AFFAIR', read the headline, breaking to an astonished world the shattering news that Champagne had swapped the vitreous enamel heir Rollo Harbottle, whom the tabloid unkindly dubbed 'Loo Rollo', for a more glamorous model. The paper revealed Champagne's latest consort to be 'brooding bad boy of rock Conal O'Shaughnessy, lead singer of moody Mancunians the Action Liposomes, whose "Make Mine A Large One" single, taken from their *Seven Deadly Cynics* album, was last summer's chartbusting sensation.' O'Shaughnessy's unsmiling face glowered from Champagne's side in the *Sun* photograph. His hairy eye-brows lay along the top of his brows like a draught excluder.

'She'll take to being a groupie like a rock chick to water,' observed Valentine. 'Although I imagine the only kind of rock that gets her going is the sort Burton gave Taylor.'

This new, although not completely unexpected, turn of events made the phone call Jane received later that day all the odder. There seemed to be no voice on the other end, just a series of agonising gasps and sobs.

'Who is this?' asked Jane anxiously. Had Nick somehow found out about her infidelity and collapsed into tears, realising how much he loved her? Her heart raced with guilt-fuelled panic.

'It's Sha-Sha-Sha-Champagne,' the voice on the other end managed to wail before dissolving into another round of sniffles.

'What on earth's the matter? What's happened?' Jane was alarmed. Her interlocutor seemed distorted by agony of the most unimaginable nature.

'I've just got [gasp] a crisis on my hands at the moment [gulp],' stuttered Champagne. Then followed some words Jane could not quite catch. Something about slashing. About cuts. Jane froze as the line went dead, visions of Champagne bleeding to death in the bath crowding in on her.

She immediately telephoned Simon at Tuff. 'Has someone died?' she demanded. 'Has,' she asked, crossing her fingers behind her back, 'Gucci been run over?'

'Leave it with me,' rapped out Simon, sounding concerned for once. If Champagne was hurt, Jane realised, the Tuff PR bank balance would hardly escape unscathed either. 'I'll call you back. Relax, I'm sure it's fine.'

But Jane could not relax. Listening to what had sounded like Champagne's last few minutes on earth had not been a pleasant experience. The surprising realisation that she didn't wish Champagne any real harm dawned on her. It was not, after all, Champagne's fault that they had been thrown together in this bizarre fashion. Christ, thought Jane, giving herself a thorough mental shake. I'm almost starting to feel sorry for her.

When the phone rang again, Jane dashed to answer it.

'Hello,' said Nick.

'Hello,' stammered Jane, wondering if he could tell by the timbre of her voice what she'd been up to. 'You're back.'

'Yes and no. I'm actually calling to say I'm not *coming* back. To the flat, I mean.'

His voice sounded distant. But then again, it was, thought Jane. Being in Brussels.

'Oh dear, what a pity,' she said. Damn, and she'd been shopping for dinner again, too. 'Have you missed your plane? Do you have to go to more meetings?'

'No,' said Nick abruptly. 'I'm leaving you.' The silence that followed his words reared up and buzzed in Jane's ear.

'*What* did you say?' She clutched the receiver, stunned. Had he, could he have, found out about Tom?

'You heard me,' Nick said calmly. 'There's no nice way of saying this, so I won't. It's over. I just don't think it's working any more.' Hang on, this wasn't in the script, thought Jane, her mind racing. He's dumping me and he doesn't even seem to realise I've been unfaithful. It was almost insulting.

'I feel we've grown apart,' Nick said. He could have grown all sorts of parts, Jane thought bitterly. It had been so long since she had seen him naked he could have developed an extra leg for all she knew.

'How long have you been feeling this?' Or rather, who, Jane added silently. It was obvious now what he was trying to say.

'Well, I've actually been seeing Melissa for a while,' Nick said, understanding her perfectly. 'She's in the same office. It's being going on for about five months.' Roughly the time she had been living with Nick, Jane calculated swiftly. So that's why he had been staying so late at Westminster. He hadn't been lying when he told her he was working on briefs. Jane scowled. Had whips been involved as well? No doubt there had been plenty of pairing. No wonder it was called the Mother of Parliaments.

'Was she with you in Brussels?'

'I, um, haven't been to Brussels,' Nick said, at last having the grace to sound slightly shamefaced. 'I've been in London, trying to decide what to do. About us. And now I have. I'm moving out.'

'Moving out? But it's *your* flat.'

'Ye-e-es. I'm moving in with Melissa. But there's no need for *you* to leave. Stay as long as you like. As long as you keep up with the, um, mortgage payments, of course.'

'Of course.' How magnanimous of him. With one bound he was free and had gained a tenant with a doubled rent cheque. 'Right, then,' Jane said, feeling thoroughly out-manoeuvred. 'Um, OK,' she added slowly, uncertainly. Suddenly, quite unexpectedly, a mist veiled her eyes and a warm flush spread across her face. A sob caught in her throat.

'Look, I'm sorry—'

'Don't.' It wasn't the loss of Nick that tore at her heart. It was his criminally appalling timing. Why hadn't he done this to her yesterday, before Tom had, well, done what Tom did? Their fling needn't have been quite so meaningless and shallow after all.

'I'll be round to pick up some things,' Nick said uncomfortably. 'I'll understand if you're not there.'

Jane put the phone down as hard as she dared without drawing Josh's attention.

It rang again immediately. 'I can explain everything.'

'What do you mean?' asked Jane.

'Nothing's wrong at all. I don't think you quite understood.'

'What?' asked Jane, too confused to place who was speaking.

'Champagne. When she called you. She's upset because the manicurist cut her nails the wrong shape, that's all. Got a bit emotional about it.' With an effort, Jane recognised Simon's voice. He had evidently recovered his sangfroid. 'She's fine now, though. Emergency over. Thought you'd like to know.'

Bugger Champagne and her manicures, thought Jane. Crisis on her hands indeed. 'Fantastic,' she said heavily.

Wishing the accelerator pedal was Nick's head, Jane shot over Waterloo Bridge like a 2CV out of hell. He had discarded her like yesterday's newspapers. Only even yesterday's newspapers had a longer lifespan with Nick. Some had hung around the flat for years.

The scales had fallen from her eyes to such an extent that she could no longer see straight, and completely missed her exit off the Elephant and Castle roundabout. The things she had done for Nick, she raged, shooting down the Embankment in the opposite direction to the one she had intended. The support she had given his career, particularly. When he was trying to get elected to the local council, en route to his goal of working in Westminster, was it not she who had stuffed endless envelopes for him? Wandered devotedly around in the pouring rain canvassing for him? Even stood in for him at his Town Hall surgery when he had been unavoidably delayed. Unavoidably delayed doing what? Jane now fumed, curling her lip with fury. It was not a surgery she wanted to see Nick in at the moment. It was Accident and Emergency.

She had stuck with him through thick and thin. Not that she had ever been all that thin. But she had certainly been thick. Stupid beyond belief, in fact. She ground her teeth as she remembered the answerphone choked with messages from Nick's constituents, all of which she had diligently noted down for him. People complaining to the councillor about stains on their bathroom ceiling. People whispering suspicions that their neighbours were beaming death rays through the wall at them. People railing about hospital waiting lists, including the never-to-be-forgotten Cypriot matron whose swollen legs had bulged and snaked hideously with fat varicose veins. She had arrived in person in the end, choosing a morning when Nick was particularly badly hungover to come and show him exactly how much she needed an operation on her calves. It had worked. Once he had forced down his nausea, Nick had been on to the hospital like a flash.

Then there had been Nick's many meannesses. The way he always forgot his credit card in restaurants; the way he always had his ear clamped to his mobile when the taxi needed to be paid for; the day he had claimed to have no money to pay the window-cleaner and Jane had subsequently found his wallet stuffed with notes. But far worse than any of this was the fact that he had not dumped her earlier.

If she got home in time, might Tom still be there? It was a vain hope, but Jane pressed the accelerator further down anyway. As she parked outside Nick's flat, now her own, she looked up. On the first floor, Tom's crumbling bay windows were in darkness. He had emphatically, definitely, undoubtedly gone.

So that was that then. No point in thinking about him any more. It was time to pick herself up, dust herself down and start a lover again. And her newly single state held certain compensations, Jane tried to tell herself as she let herself into the flat. For a start, she could run herself a bath since Nick was no longer around to take all the hot water. His dirty underpants would no longer litter the floor. The tide of foamy scurf encirling the basin each morning would be a ring of the past. John Humphrys would no longer shatter the early morning silence. But it *was* silent. Absolutely, ominously silent. When, later, she turned the squeaking bathroom taps on, the thunder of water sounded like Niagara Falls.

Lowering herself into the hot embrace of the tub, Jane was shocked to see the bathwater rise further up the sides than usual. She'd got fatter lately, there was no doubt about it. She stared down the length – or was it the width – of her body, plump, white and slick with moisture under the electric bathroom light. Little, shining, blancmange-like islands of tummy, breast and thigh rose above the foaming water line. I look like the Loch Ness monster, Jane thought in panic.

Her breasts lay along her torso, white and pointed like a couple of squid heads. Her waistline, never a strong point, lay conclusively buried under layers of spare tyre and water. All waste, no line. Jane stretched a leg out of the water and scrutinised her cellulite as calmly as possible, before despairingly concluding there was more orange peel there than an orchard in Seville. Somewhere inside me, determined Jane, there is a thin woman waiting to get out. She dared not contemplate the possibility that somewhere outside her was an even fatter woman trying to muscle in.

She stared at her face in the mirror in the bath rack. The overhead lighting minimised the blue of her eyes and emphasised the bags beneath them. They looked bigger and blacker than a Prada tote. Her lips were dry and looked thinner than ever and the spots on her forehead seemed of Himalayan proportions. Her crow's feet were at least size ten.

No wonder Nick had left her. Tom was probably glad to see the back of her as well. Which is more than I am, thought Jane, catching sight of her reflected rear in the mirrored cabinet as she heaved herself, pink and steaming as a fresh-cooked prawn, out of the bath.

Wrapped in a towel, she felt like a sausage roll, a stuffing of soft pink meat. She felt disgusted with herself. She was too fat to live. She could just stick her head in the oven and it would all be over. Easy. Except for the disgusting thought of all that gluey takeaway pizza cheese which had stuck to the oven bottom. She pulled a face, imagining the stench from the ancient slop of the pineapple and peperonis Nick had been so fond of. No, she wouldn't put her head in the oven.

She'd put it in the fridge instead.

It's at times like this that a girl needs her sense of hummus, Jane decided, shovelling in the remains of a Marks and Spencer's Greek dip selection that wasn't too far past its sell-by date.

She wandered through into the gloomy living room and switched the lamps on. One bulb pinged defiantly back at her and conked out. Jane slumped on the sofa and stared at the very rug where, barely twenty-four hours before, Tom had done all those unimaginably wonderful things to her. She clenched her fists and screwed up her eyes. She wanted Tom, desperately. But she had no number, no idea where he was. They'd been ships that passed in the night. That had been the point of the encounter. Then.

If she couldn't have Tom, she'd have to make do with Gordon, Jane decided, reaching for the bottle. This called for extreme measures in every sense of the word. Anaesthetising. Comforting. The deep, deep peace of the double gin.

Chapter 6

One of the bitterest pills to swallow, Jane considered, was not just that her love-life and work life were on the kind of downward trend not seen since the Wall Street Crash. Much worse was the fact that Champagne seemed set on an endless upward trajectory. For, if the first Champagne Moments column had been a sensation, the second almost caused riots. Within hours of *Gorgeous* appearing on the news-stands, it had sold out. People, it seemed, simply couldn't get enough of her. Champagne's combination of stunning beauty and astounding vacuousness seemed to have struck some kind of chord with public and media alike. The Lost Chord, a despairing Jane supposed.

Champagne, naturally, was well aware of her popularity. 'If there's no beginning to her talents,' Jane sighed to Valentine, 'there's certainly no end to her demands.' Only yesterday Champagne had called insisting *Gorgeous* hire a Learjet to fly her to a polo match, a request that followed hard on the Blahnik heels of a recent demand for a helicopter to take her to a shooting weekend.

'Doesn't she ever use roads?' Jane had marvelled aloud.

'Well, you always said she was an airhead,' Valentine reminded her. Josh then amazed them both by revealing he had promised Champagne a company car as a compromise, which left Jane wondering who was compromised, exactly. Josh had then played his trump card by saying he'd thrown in a chauffeur too.

'She's worth it,' Josh said shortly. 'Our circulation is on the up.' But it wasn't just her own magazine that Champagne dominated. International heavy-hitters from American *Vogue* to Russian *Tatler* were rushing to profile her. Her increasingly frequent appearances on TV translated straight into column inches in the tabloids. When she appeared on *Have I Got News For You*, Ian Hislop, after asking Champagne how she kept her figure, had been rendered unprecedentedly speechless when Champagne had said she worked out 370 days a year. The press had gone wild.

'What would you say to those who call you an egomaniac?' Bob Mortimer had asked her on *Shooting Stars*. 'Oh, they're completely wrong,' Champagne had replied. 'I absolutely *loathe* eggs.' This became Quote of the Week in every paper from the *Daily Mail* to the *Motherwell Advertiser*.

Most notorious of all was Champagne's appearance on *Newsnight* when Jeremy Paxman asked her whether it was true she spent each and every night out partying. 'Absolutely not,' Champagne had replied, apparently deeply affronted. 'As a matter of fact, I spent last night finishing a jigsaw puzzle.'

'A jigsaw puzzle?' Paxman had asked sardonically, raising one of his famously quizzical eyebrows.

'Yah, and I'm bloody proud of myself,' Champagne had declared. 'It's only taken me ninety-four days.'

'Ninety-four days? Surely that's rather a long time for a jigsaw,' Paxman bemusedly replied.

'Well, it said three to four years on the box,' said Champagne triumphantly.

On the strength of this performance, negotiations to give Champagne her own chat show were well advanced.

It was odd, Jane thought, that a public, not to mention a press, that had already endured years of Caprice, Tamara, Tara, Normandie and Beverley could possibly have the stomach for yet another pouting party girl, but stomach it most certainly had. Perhaps it was, Jane mused, because Champagne seemed somehow to combine all of them. She had Caprice's looks, Tara's class, Tamara's chutzpah, Beverley's shopping obsession, and probably now close to Normandie's money as well.

Oddly enough, Champagne never seemed to encounter any of her rivals. Jane had two theories as to why. Either they all avoided her or, as was far more likely, Champagne spent night after night with them in Brown's, Tramp and the Met Bar but could recall absolutely nothing of it afterwards. Champagne's memory, Jane considered, made a goldfish look like Stephen Hawking.

Not that this in any way held her back. No breakfast TV programme was complete without at least a reference to her; there was talk of her kicking off at Wembley, and rumours were beginning to circulate of a planned tribute in Madame Tussaud's. 'I hope that's true,' Jane said to Valentine. 'I might get more information for the column out of a waxwork.'

'What we need,' said Josh, 'is the new sex.' The Monday features meeting had begun.

'You're telling me,' simpered Valentine, examining his cuffs and pursing his lips in his best John Inman fashion.

'You know what I mean,' Josh snapped. 'I'm talking about what's the latest hip thing. The new rock and roll, the new black, the new brown, the new whatever. What's really, really hot just now?'

'Well, this office for a start,' said Valentine huffily. 'The air conditioning is a joke.' He flapped a plump hand about in front of his perspiring face.

Josh took no notice. 'Is being common the new smart?' he wondered aloud. 'Are men the new women? Is staying in the new going out?' He looked round the table. 'Where's Lulu? There must be something fashiony we could do. Are low heels the new stilettos? Is short the new long? Is underwear the new outerwear?'

'Lulu's still in bed,' said Jane, who had received a telephone call from the absent fashion editor to this effect a few minutes before. 'Her alarm didn't go off.' She paused. 'So,' she asked tartly, 'is absence the new presence? Is staying in bed the new getting up?'

'Poor Lulu needs her rest,' said Josh, leaping, as usual, to the fashion editor's defence. 'She needs to rest. She gets ill very easily, poor dear.'

'You're telling me,' said Valentine. 'She's certainly the only person I've ever known claim they had bunions in their ears.'

'Oh, shut up,' said Josh. 'Let's concentrate on the matter in hand. What's hot, what's hip. Is death the new life? Is being fat the new thin? Is,' his eyes widened as if knocked sideways by the brilliance of his own train of thought, 'rock and roll the new rock and roll?'

As she entered the sandwich shop at lunchtime, trying to psych herself up to a mayonnaise-free, butter-free and most of all fun-free lettuce leaf roll, Jane spotted Valentine. He was muttering darkly in a corner with Ann, the deputy editor of *Blissful Country Homes*. A monthly celebration of Agas, appliqué screens and City bankers downshifting to barn conversions in Bicester, *Blissful*, as it was known, was a stablemate in the same magazine company as *Gorgeous*.

Meeting her gaze, Valentine rolled his eyes and beckoned Jane over. 'I've just been telling Ann about Josh. How he can be so rude to me, considering the strain I have been under, I can't imagine.'

'Strain?' asked Jane, relieved that she wasn't the only one suffering at the moment. There was nothing like someone else's woes to take one's mind off one's own. She looked at Valentine's shining, agitated face. 'Why, what's the matter?'

'It's Algy, my cairn terrier,' wailed Valentine. 'I went away last weekend and put him in a kennel where he got in with all the wrong dogs. He now refuses to come to heel and poos all over the house. It's very upsetting.'

'I know just how Valentine feels,' Ann said sternly to a nonplussed Jane. 'One of my tabbies isn't well at the moment. It's dreadful. I have to inject my poor pussy twice a day.'

Never had a day been so designed to test Jane's patience to the full. She returned from the sandwich shop to find a letter from the BBC asking Champagne to go on *Desert Island Discs* and recommending she choose a mixture of contemporary and classical music. Jane snorted. Probably as far as Champagne was aware, Ravel was a shoe shop, Telemann someone who came to fix the video and Handel something that her bulging designer shopping bags were suspended from. None of this improved the fact that top of her list of jobs this afternoon was getting more column inches out of Champagne.

Jane delayed the evil moment as long as possible, rummaging about her desk and returning telephone calls, sometimes to people who hadn't even called in the first place. Eventually, however, she bowed to the inevitable.

'What the *fuck* are you doing calling this early?' barked the sleepy, furious voice at the other end. Jane looked at the clock. 'It's ten past three, Champagne,' she said with exaggerated patience. 'In the afternoon, that is.'

'Is it? Oh. Had no idea. Bloody late night last night,' honked Champagne.

Jane hardly dared breathe, let alone say anything that might knock Champagne off this particular train of thought. Like a truffling pig, she had caught the first tantalising whiffs of that rare and precious commodity Anecdote. 'Really?' she asked gently. 'What were you doing?'

'Went to the races with Conal. Bloody good fun, actually.'

'Which ones? Sandown? Kempton Park?'

'No, the East End somewhere.'

Jane frowned. Which of the racecourses was actually in London? None, as far as she knew.

'Bloody funny horses,' Champagne continued. 'Really weird and small-looking. Went bloody fast, though.'

The penny dropped. 'Do you mean you've been to Walthamstow?' Jane gasped. 'The dog track?' Conal O'Shaughnessy had clearly been attempting to inculcate Champagne into working-class culture. Jane was not sure how successful he'd been.

'Yah, and then we went for supper,' Champagne recalled after a few minutes' hard thought. 'Conal tried to make me have a green Thai curry but I told him no way was I going to eat anything made out of ties. Particularly green ones. Hermès ones I might have considered.'

'Have you seen this?' asked Valentine as Jane stopped scribbling and put the phone down. He flopped an open copy of *Vogue* on her desk. Jane coughed as the powerful smell of ten different scent inserts filled her nostrils. Below her on the glossy page Champagne sprawled across an advertisement spread for an aftershave called Leather, her ice-blonde hair spilling over a clinging leather catsuit and her nose hovering above an improbably large and clumsy frosted glass bottle. 'My favourite scent is Leather,' ran the slogan.

'Well, it would be,' said Jane. 'Essence of wallet.'

'On the other hand, it's great to see her getting a good hiding,' said Valentine.

'It's absurd,' grumbled Jane. 'Champagne's endorsing practically every product there is. Talk about a legend in her own launch time. Even that ridiculous poodle of hers is doing a dog food ad, for which I expect it gets paid more than I earn in five years.'

'Never mind,' said Valentine, putting a hot, damp palm on her shoulder. 'Just remember this. She may have the looks, the wealth, the boyfriend, the ad endorsements, the national newspaper columns, the TV appearances, the talk of film deals, the world at her feet . . .' His voice trailed off.

'Yes?' prompted Jane, fixing him with a beady eye.

'But she can't possibly be happy,' Valentine finished valiantly.

'Can't she?' asked Jane tightly.

Valentine was saved from answering by Jane's phone ringing. He scuttled across the room and disappeared behind the pile of newly-arrived gold lamé oven gloves heaped on his desk for review.

'I was just calling to say,' Champagne boomed, 'when you call me to read my column back to me, call me at the Lancaster.'

'The Lancaster?' echoed Jane. The Lancaster was the most expensive luxury hotel in London. A former office block off Piccadilly, the new, all-suite hotel had swiftly upstaged the Metropolitan's chic. Each suite famously boasted extensive views over its own butlers, hot and cold running individual fax lines and an outside temperature gauge in the wardrobe so you could choose exactly the right clothes to combat any hostile elements encountered between leaving the hotel lobby and stepping into the limo. 'But why?' asked Jane. Was Champagne's huge flat in Eaton Square no longer good enough?

'My cleaner's resigned and the flat's an utter tip,' drawled Champagne. 'So I called the Lancaster and they're giving me a suite for free. Told them I'd mention them in the column, so stick them in somewhere, will you? Oh, and mention the beauty treatments. Gucci and I are having the time of our lives. He's having a sauna and a seaweed wrap at the moment, in fact.'

'Is Conal with you?' Jane asked, quietly grinding her teeth. If he felt moved to trash the suite in rock-star fashion, please let him throw the TV at Champagne, she prayed silently. Followed by the minibar and the breakfast trolley.

'No idea where he is,' Champagne barked. 'Haven't seen him for ages. Not since he asked me if I wanted to go to Latvia with him the other day.'

'Latvia?'

'Yah. But I told him not bloody likely, he could go on his own. I mean, I haven't read a review of it anywhere. Might be awful.'

'Oh, I didn't realise it was a restaurant,' said Jane, embarrassed. Another trendy eaterie that had passed her by.

'Why, what else is it?' bawled Champagne, sounding surprised. 'A country? Oh. Well, I suppose that explains why Conal's been away all week. I thought there must have been some trouble over the bill or something.'

Weeks passed. Returning to the empty flat and seeing Tom's darkened first-floor windows got every evening off to a bad start for Jane. She had no doubt that Tom was now holed up in a TriBeCa loft with a long-limbed blonde, tapping out a bestseller between trips to Dean & Deluca. Even though she knew he was thousands of miles away, she still saw him everywhere. The world suddenly seemed to be full of tall men with tousled blond hair and deep-set eyes. It was rather like living in Stockholm.

Nick, meanwhile, had faded from her life almost as if he had never been there. He had shuffled round a couple of times to pick up such essentials as his peppery after-shaves, his Queen albums and the set of wooden coat-hangers that had fitted Nick's upmarket self-image better than they had ever fitted into the wardrobe. They had muttered to each other from behind the barrier of a cup of tea. But that was the limit of their contact. It was incredible to think they had ever lived together. And it was terrifying to think she had ever wanted to marry him. Tally, she knew, would sympathise with that.

It was while pondering this that Jane realised she had not heard from Tally for ages. Guilt swamped her. To think she had been spending all this time moping over the loss of a man, when her best friend might have lost her house. She had, Jane realised, agonised, done precisely nothing about finding Tally her Mullionaire.

'Nick's left me,' she told Tally when, at last, the telephone was answered at Mullions. She felt relieved. At least the family, or what was left of it, was still in residence. Jane waited for Tally to whoop with joy. But whoop came there none.

'So we're both young, free and single,' Jane pressed, eagerly. 'Both in the same boat.'

'Yes, except that your mother doesn't keep writing "Go For It" in lipstick all over the Venetian glass mirrors,' sighed Tally. 'Nor does she run up and down the Long Gallery with a net saying she's catching dreams.'

'Oh dear.' Jane's stomach knotted with guilt. 'Listen, why don't I come up? This weekend?'

Tally seemed to perk up at this. 'That would be wonderful,' she said with feeling. 'Then you can see what I'm up against. Can you remember the way?'

'Of course,' said Jane, reeling off a few directions. 'Just round the first bend past Lower Bulge, isn't it? Sharp right or you'll miss it?'

'You can't miss it now,' Tally said dolefully. 'There's a huge, glaring, red For Sale sign plastered all over the front of the gatehouse.'

Having put the phone down, Jane switched on the news and dug a fork into her pasta. She almost choked as Champagne immediately sashayed across the screen, on her way to some premiere with Conal O'Shaughnessy. Foaming at the mouth as best she could with a mouthful of pesto sauce, Jane hurriedly switched over, only to find herself staring into the face of James Morrison the transport minister, taking on the bypass protesters once again.

Jane squinted over her pasta at the screen, hoping to spot Piers. It certainly looked lively. Nick would be furious, she thought gleefully. Hordes of muddy, wild-haired creatures were rushing about the site shouting abuse at the hapless politician. Some were even throwing things at him. It was really rather exciting. Jane could almost hear the thuds and bangs.

She *could* hear the thuds and bangs. She turned down the TV and listened carefully. Above her head, a series of abrupt thumps followed by a crash confirmed that someone was in the first-floor flat. Her insides plunged suddenly downwards like a hi-tech lift, leaving her stomach with a curiously empty and airy feeling. Had he, was it possible, could she entertain the wild hope that Tom had come back?

Swaying on her weakening knees, Jane let herself out of the flat and walked slowly upstairs. Her palms were sweating, her back felt hot and her intestines were surging like a geyser. Her heart thumped with excitement as she tapped at Tom's door.

It was opened by a tall, spotty youth with an unfeasibly large Adam's apple and huge, smeared spectacles. He blinked shortsightedly at Jane. She felt almost sick with disappointment.

'Um, hello,' she mumbled, after a few seconds' shocked silence. 'I'm, er, your downstairs neighbour. Just come to say, er, hello.'

'Hi,' mumbled the youth, avoiding her gaze and tangling black-nailed fingers in strands of greasy hair. He looked a bit like Jarvis Cocker, but ugly. A sweet, fusty and greasy smell hung about him.

'I was wondering,' Jane gabbled, glancing fitfully into the flat behind him where several vast cardboard boxes filled up the sitting room, 'whether you knew anything about the person who used to live here. I'm trying to get hold of him. He, er, left a few bills behind, you see.'

'Dunno,' mumbled Jarvis vaguely. 'Landlord might, but I think he lives in Spain. Want his number? It's somewhere in there.' He waved a white and emaciated arm in the direction of the boxes, piles of clothes and upended furniture heaped in the room behind.

'No,' said Jane, clearing her throat aggressively as she retreated back down the stairs. 'No, it's all right.'

But it wasn't.

Chapter 7

Heading west for the weekend at Mullions, Jane derived a brutal satisfaction from making the poor old 2CV go far faster than it could really manage. It soon beat her at her own game, however, by obstinately refusing to stump up the horsepower required to overtake a man who was a Caravan Club Member, had a Baby On Board, believed Campanologists Did It with Bells On and as a consequence could see nothing at all out of the rear window. Which, thought Jane, furious but impotent, explained his snail-like pace but not the reason why he steadfastly and unstintingly stuck to the middle lane.

As a result, Jane arrived at Mullions not mid-morning, as she had planned, but at lunchtime. Tally was right about the For Sale sign. Subtle it was not. As she swung in under the crumbling gatehouse that announced the beginning of the park, Jane profoundly hoped lunch might be over. Mrs Ormondroyd was the kind of cook who believed all vegetables should be boiled to a gluey mass and regarded pastry that rose with profound suspicion. It was no surprise that Tally had considered toasted Mars Bar sandwiches a culinary breakthrough.

It had always seemed odd to Jane that no one in the Venery family seemed to expect their cook to be able to cook. The thinking appeared to be that generations of Venerys had got by on watery Brown Windsor soup and bony cutlets and hadn't come to any harm beyond delicate digestions and a generally fleshless appearance. And what was bad enough for them was certainly bad enough for their descendants. Given what she was expected to eat, it was no wonder Tally was so tall and thin. Looking like a beanpole was certainly the nearest she was likely to come to fresh greens.

And what went for Mrs Ormondroyd certainly went for Mr Peters the gardener, Jane was reminded, as the car bounced over the potholes in the drive. Like his colleague in the kitchen, Mr Peters was a retainer whose prime function, as far as Jane could work out, was to be retained irrespective of what his skills were. Or weren't. A generous critic might assume that Mr Peters' criterion of excellence was what would look good in the park in five hundred years' time as there was no evidence that he was interested in the contemporary landscape at all. His idea of a formal garden was distinctly lax.

Tally's hair-raising descriptions of the state of Mullions had prepared Jane for the worst. So, as the first view of the house slid along her windscreen, she was surprised and relieved to see it still seemed to be standing, more or less in its entirety. Across the shimmering oxbow lake, the pile of mellow stone glowed yellow as butter in the soft sunshine. The leaded glass in the eponymous mullioned windows glittered like slices of diamond, and over the crumbling stable block, the weathercock that pointed the same way no matter what direction the wind came from shone in what was almost a spirited fashion.

As she drove past the rose garden, heavy with over-blown, un-deadheaded blooms, Jane looked hard for the sweat lodge Tally had mentioned, and the mysterious mercurial harp. But there was no sign of either. She turned into the stableyard, which backed on to the kitchen wing. This, for the last hundred years at least, had been the main entrance to Mullions, ever since the massive front door had come off its hinges while being opened to admit Queen Victoria – who, on that occasion, had apparently been amused.

Mrs Ormondroyd came out to greet her, dressed, as always, in a checked nylon overall of violent turquoise blue, her massive calves covered with tights the colour of strong tea. Her large-nosed face with its uneven eyes and spreading ears was, as usual, the deep-creased pictur[illegible] disapproval and suspicion.

'You're just in time for lunch,' she grumbled.

'Great,' said Jane bravely. 'I was hoping I would[illegible]

'Well, you might change your mind when you see wh[illegible] it is.' Mrs Ormondroyd scowled, leading the way back into the kitchen. Jane followed, bewildered at this unexpected flash of self-knowledge on Mrs Ormondroyd's part. Had she finally accepted there were limits to her cooking skills?

Inside, the welcome was warmer.

'Jane!' shrieked Tally, clattering over the stone flags like an excited five-year-old. Jane found herself enveloped in a dusty, mothball-scented hug. 'It's so nice to see you,' Tally gasped. 'You look wonderful. Much thinner.'

'Do I?' Tally always said the right thing, but this really was the rightest thing of all. Hoping she meant it, Jane stole a swift look down at herself. Her stomach was a bit flatter, largely thanks to the steep drop in her wine consumption. Opening a bottle just for herself, alone in the flat, made Jane feel like an alcoholic. However, she permitted herself the occasional gin and tonic because she needed the lime slices to counteract the risk of scurvy from her unvaried diet of pasta and pesto.

'You look so smart,' Tally said, holding her at arm's length.

'It's only my jeans,' said Jane. Her white shirt wasn't even new. Yet it was newer by a generation than anything Tally had on. Her sharp, bony elbows protruded from a tiny, shrunken pullover. A pair of half-mast trousers ended halfway up her skinny calves. 'Amazing trousers,' Jane said with perfect truth, unable to tear her eyes away from the dark, wide-pinstriped creation that, like the dress Tally [illegible]d worn to the Ritz, had a faintly antiquated look about [illegible] 'More of your mother's Mainbocher?'

[illegible]h, these.' Tally looked down. 'No, Daddy's. They're [illegible]d school trousers. I found them when I was looking [illegible]r something to wear in bed the other day. They're very warm. A bit worn out on the bottom, but I expect it was all that caning.' She flashed Jane a strained grin. Her fine, mouse hair was scraped haphazardly back in a rubber band, and there was a more anxious expression than usual in her clear, almost lashless grey eyes. Tally's pale cheeks with their dusting of patrician high colour seemed thinner, which made her snub nose with its red-tinged tip look odder than ever.

Mrs Ormondroyd had stomped off a while ago, but Jane suddenly realised they were not alone in the kitchen. A large, silent figure was standing at the back, making almost imperceptible sounds and movements at the large stone sink. Jane started in shock. It wasn't any old large, silent figure standing there. It was a Red Indian in the finest spaghetti Western tradition.

'Jane, this is Big Horn,' said Tally, following the

direction of her astonished gaze. 'He's cooking lunch,' she added hastily, as if this somehow explained his appearance. Big Horn turned from his labours and walked slowly towards them, his large, bare feet moving soundlessly over the worn flagstones.

About seven feet tall, and naked from the waist up, he was impressively muscular, with a tan the same strong terracotta colour as Mrs Ormondroyd's tights. Above his deep-set, brilliant dark eyes, his centre-parted hair was thick, black and long, tightly plaited and wound with brightly-coloured thread. Across his torso he sported an impressive array of complex tattoos as well as several necklaces of shells and beads. From the waist down, what looked like a fringed apron of embroidered chamois leather seemed to be all that protected his modesty. Yet he was silently impressive, ready to take on General Custer at a moment's notice, despite being armed with nothing more than a slotted spoon.

'How do you do,' Jane said, smiling.

Big Horn inclined his large-featured head slightly. A faint smile thawed his thick, beautifully-cut lips and he raised one eyebrow a fraction of a centimetre.

'Big Horn and Mummy are on the Ayurvedic diet,' Tally explained, shepherding Jane out of the kitchen. 'They eat to suit their personality. By that reckoning,' she whispered, once they had reached the kitchen passage, 'Mummy's is all mung beans and Chinese worm tea. At least that's what Big Horn's been making all week.'

'How very unflattering,' said Jane. 'If someone was cooking to suit my personality I'd expect lobster and foie gras at the very least.'

'Well, Mrs Ormondroyd tried to cook a chicken,' said Tally, 'but as soon as Mummy saw it, she picked it up and started waving it about over everyone's heads. According to her, raw poultry absorbs negative energy.'

Jane giggled. 'And what about negative smells? All those beans must have had an effect.'

'Yes,' confessed Tally. 'I suppose there have been some rather ripe odours about.' She screwed up her snub nose.

'I suppose you could call it,' chortled Jane, 'the Blast of the Mohicans.'

Tally giggled, just as the housekeeper came back down the passage and swept past them, her face as stony as the floor. The sound of her thighs swishing together in their tea-coloured tights faded into the kitchen. 'And Mrs Ormondroyd's been driven to distraction,' whispered Tally.

'I imagine she finds that mini-apron thing of his very distracting,' grinned Jane. 'I bet Big Horn's the most exciting thing to hit the Mullions kitchens since the days they had naked boys turning the spits.'

'I think you're probably right.' Tally pushed back the tattered green baize door at the end of the kitchen passage and stepped out into the Marble Hall, the freezing, lofty space at the heart of the house. The black and white chequer board Carrara which gave the hall its name stretched away beneath their feet. A number of dusty statues on plinths stood desultorily about, while a massive, carved Jacobean oak staircase climbed wearily up to the house's upper floors, sagging slightly as if the effort was too much for it. Which, in some places, it evidently was. Jane spotted, beneath the treads nearest the hall floor, several piles of books that were evidently supporting the whole structure. She had no doubt that some of them were first editions, grabbed haphazardly from the Mullions library.

Adding to the atmosphere of weight and weariness were the Ancestors – Tally's name for the collection of heavily-framed oil portraits whose subjects' red-tinged nostrils identified them as Venery forebears. Two loomed from each of three walls, and another four accompanied climbers of the staircase up to yet more portraits in the Long Gallery on the next floor. There was, in fact, scarcely anywhere one could go in Mullions without contemplating the snub-nosed, thin-lipped visage of a long-dead member of the family. The Venerys as a dynasty had cornered the market in bold, unsmiling poses centuries before the likes of Conal O'Shaughnessy had smouldered on to the scene.

Suddenly, a terrifyingly loud and utterly anguished scream from upstairs shattered the brooding silence of the hall. Bits of plaster started to drift down like snowflakes. Jane's hand leapt to her throat as she stumbled towards Tally in terror. It sounded as if someone was being disembowelled, dying in childbirth and being burnt at the stake simultaneously.

Tally, however, looked oddly calm. Bored, even. 'Mummy, doing her primal screaming,' she explained, rolling her eyes in exasperation. 'She does it every lunch-time. It helps expel the tensions of the morning, apparently. But it doesn't do much for the roof.'

As the frantic beating of her heart subsided, Jane raised her trembling vision to the painted ceiling far up in the gloom above. Painted in the Italian Renaissance style by a pupil of Verrio, the ceiling's once-writhing congregation of plump gods and goddesses was indeed looking distinctly patchy.

'Only this week, Triton lost his trident and both wheels of Phoebus's chariot peeled off,' sighed Tally. 'Nymphs and shepherds are coming away all the time. It's falling apart up there. You can barely walk across the floor without causing some disaster among the deities.'

Jane shot a speculative glance at a wobbly-looking piece of the egg-and-dart moulding which seemed about to detach itself from the frieze which ran round the walls below the painting. One more shriek of Julia's might easily result in its leaping for freedom.

'Primal screaming?' Jane struggled with the concept of the former steely lady of the manor bawling her head off. Almost as amazing was the fact that it was before lunch. The Julia of old rarely stirred from bed before two.

'Yes, it's ghastly,' Tally said. 'The Ancestors are horrified,' she added, waving a long white hand in the direction of the portraits.

'They look it,' said Jane. And there did seem to be a certain, barely perceptible, alteration in their faces. Each painted eyeball, previously passive, now bulged slightly with what might have been horror, and each formerly straight, tight mouth had acquired a definite downward turn.

'Yes, the Ancestors are very shocked,' Tally said sadly. 'The ones in here are appalled enough, but the ones in the Long Gallery practically need counselling. They're nearer to the noise, you see. And it's not just the screaming that's upsetting them. Mummy's been round the whole of Mullions feng shui-ing it, and decided the chandelier in the drawing room was covered in bad chi.'

Jane stared. 'Still, I suppose Mrs Ormondroyd doesn't handle a duster like she used to,' she said.

Tally looked at her sternly. 'Really, Jane, this isn't all some huge joke, you know,' she said. 'Believe me, there's nothing funny about it.'

Jane determinedly turned down her irrepressibly curving lips.

'What is bad chi?' she asked, trying to keep her

shoulders from shaking; a challenge as they were shuddering from the cold anyway. However mild the climate was outside, inside Mullions the atmosphere was so icy you could skate on it.

'Sort of bad luck, I think,' said Tally. 'Anyway, she's taken the chandelier down and replaced it with a piece of nasty old dried buffalo skin that smells cheesy and looks very odd with the Grinling Gibbons. But the worst is what she's doing in the bedrooms. She's moved the eighteenth-century bed that Queen Victoria slept in and replaced it with a piece of carved bark to counteract what she calls the negative energy of colour chaos emanating from the Gobelins tapestries.'

Jane blinked. Tally was right. It wasn't funny. It was hilarious. Her lips started to quiver again at the corners.

'But at least they haven't built a sweat lodge in the rose garden yet,' she said comfortingly.

'No, but only because they're going to build a yurt on the parterre,' sighed Tally. 'And Big Horn's practically worn out the lawn with his ritual dancing at dawn. All the telephones in the house stink of Mummy's essential oils, which Mrs Ormondroyd hates. And when Mummy destroyed the vacuum cleaner the other day, Mrs Ormondroyd almost handed her notice in. It was only Big Horn's coming past at the crucial moment with his apron flapping that changed her mind.'

'Why, what was Julia doing with it?' asked Jane, genuinely curious. 'I didn't know your mother knew what a vacuum cleaner was, let alone how to use one.'

'She was trying to hoover her aura,' Tally confessed. 'According to Mummy, hoovering your aura – which is apparently a sort of spirit force surrounding you – draws out all the impurities in your soul.'

'Like a sort of spiritual spot wash?' Jane was worried she would laugh if she didn't say anything. It was, she could see, truly awful for Tally. Julia had obviously gone completely mad this time. More barking than a pack of hounds, in fact.

'Yes, but in Mummy's case the dustbag burst and she ended up with far more impurities than she started with,' said Tally. 'Including a contact lens she'd lost in the seventies, apparently.'

There was a rustle above them, accompanied by a faint tinkling of bells. Jane looked up, and gasped. 'Julia?' she exclaimed in amazement.

Nothing could have been further removed from the perfectly turned out Lady Julia of old than the pair of brilliant eyes Jane found staring down at her from a tanned, lined and completely unmade-up face. Julia's wild hair looked as if she had been dragged through a hedge backwards, and then dragged through it forwards again. What looked like bits of foliage were stuck in it for good measure.

Only Julia's voice was still the same – more cut glass than a factory of Waterford. It took more than a few months' New Ageism, it seemed, to make an impact on a lifetime's Old Money. 'Jane, darling!' declared Julia, as she descended the stairs amid acres of flowing white robe. 'So it *was* you!'

'What do you mean?' asked Jane, almost overwhelmed by the clouds of essential oil scent that floated in Julia's wake. She was aware of Tally squirming in embarrassment at her side. Julia took no notice. Her full attention was trained ecstatically on Jane. The intensity of it was unsettling.

'When I looked at the chart at midnight last night, I

noticed that Mercury was sextile with Venus,' breathed Julia, dramatically. 'Emotional change was in the air. It was *you*!' As Julia patted her cheek, Jane felt her toes curl.

'I see,' she said awkwardly. How exactly did one reply to this kind of greeting? 'Well, it's very nice to see you, Julia. You look very well.'

'*I feel* well,' said Julia, clasping her hands in apparent ecstasy. 'I have never felt *quite* so well before. My life was empty and unsustainable and now it's full of truth and spontaneity. Would you like some lunch?' she added.

'Er . . .' Jane prevaricated, remembering the mung beans.

'We're going out,' said Tally hurriedly.

'That's nice,' said Julia absently. 'Well, if you'll excuse me, I have a lot to do this afternoon. Mr Peters is very worried about it not having rained for a while on his roses, so Big Horn and I are going to appeal to the Great Earth Goddess on his behalf and perform a rain ceremony.' She wafted off through the door into the kitchen passage.

'Now do you see what I mean?' asked Tally.

Jane put an arm about her shoulders. 'Let's go for some lunch at the Gloom,' she suggested, leading Tally back down the kitchen passage to the door. The local pub, the Loom and Bobbin, or the Gloom and Sobbing as Piers had once dubbed it, owing to its mausoleum-like Victorian atmosphere, provided unmatchable therapy for depression. However miserable one was, one couldn't possibly be as dejected as the hatchet-faced regulars draped over the bar.

They drove along in a silence punctuated only by the 2CV's bouncing and jolting over the potholes in the drive. As they passed the lake, Jane glanced over at Mullions. Seen from across the water in the mellow afternoon light, it seemed to be floating serenely atop a great expanse of pearl. The rose window in the dining room, rescued from the ruins of a nearby abbey, flashed cheerfully as the sun passed across its ancient panes, and the oriel window by the entrance door bulged happily. The balustrade of Jacobean stonework, which formed the edge of the terrace in front of the house, undulated merrily along the wall and the turrets stood clear-cut and golden against a blue sky. Seen from this distance, it looked the epitome of the power and style of the landed gentry. No one could possibly have imagined that it was collapsing and that the cash-strapped family was having to sell it after four hundred years of ownership. No one, thought Jane, could possibly have imagined there was a Red Indian in there, either, not to mention a New Age lady of the manor. The depressed silence continued as she and Tally passed under the For Sale sign.

'Why will no one ever give you grants?' Jane asked, realising she had never raised the subject before. It did seem odd, though. From this angle, Mullions looked such a jewel. More idyllic even than those posters of sun-soaked castles amid undulating emerald downs that the English Tourist Board put inside Tube trains to upset commuters. 'Surely the National Trust or someone can help out?'

Tally sighed, and made an odd, scraping noise that sounded suspiciously like the grinding of teeth. 'Do you really think I haven't *tried*?' she asked testily. 'But Mullions is too run down for someone like the National Trust to take on. And even if they were interested, they would want enormous endowments to help with the upkeep. But they're not interested. Apparently it's not important enough a building.'

'Isn't it?' asked Jane in surprise. 'Why ever not?'

'Oh, something not quite right about the groin vaulting

in the antechapel,' said Tally wearily. 'And apparently our spandrels are below par. The Jacobean strapwork's been found wanting, and the neo-classical columns in the hall were, it turns out, made by one of Adam's less gifted pupils.'

'Alas, poor Doric,' said Jane, drawing up outside the Gloom and Sobbing.

Tally frowned.

Tally slammed the car door shut and following Jane into the pub.

Inside, the usual funereal atmosphere prevailed. A sullen fire spat in the cavernous hearth and a collection of locals who might have been there since Jane's last visit sat slumped over their pints of Old Knickersplitter, the Gloom's sour, home-brewed ale. Apart from gin and tonic, the pub sold practically nothing else.

'So Julia's still really set on selling it?' Jane broached the subject as she pulled open a bag of cheese and onion crisps so ancient they could well have been the prototype for the brand.

Tally nodded miserably. 'Yes. And the estate agents are egging her on. Even though the place is hardly in a state to sell. The electricity supply is totally erratic – the state of our connections would horrify Mr Darcy. The heating is a joke. You can hear the pipes banging and creaking for miles, but nothing ever makes it to the radiators. And the entire water supply is plumbed with lead.' She shifted uncomfortably on the hard bench they were sitting on.

'Doesn't that drive you mad?' asked Jane.

'No, I suppose it's what everyone in similar houses did at the time . . . oh, I see what you mean,' said Tally. 'Yes, lead piping was supposed to be one of the reasons behind the fall of the Roman Empire. You do go insane in the end, apparently.'

'Maybe that's what's happened to Julia,' suggested Jane.

Tally shook her head. 'She doesn't even use water any more. She washes her face in pee.'

'No!' exclaimed Jane. She had raised her glass halfway towards her lips. Now she put it down again.

''Fraid so,' said Tally. 'She says that, apart from doing whatever wonders it's supposed to do, it's quick, cheap and warm. Unlike anything that comes out of the Mullions bath taps, she says.' She gazed despairingly into her smeared glass. Old Knickersplitter was an even less cheerful prospect than her mother. 'The fact remains,' Tally finished, 'a damp-proof course and a new roof would do more good than all the feng shui in China.'

Jane frowned. 'We've got to find you this rich man fast,' she said firmly. 'Someone loaded and sexy.'

But the eyes Tally turned to Jane were utterly devoid of sparkle. 'Sexy? It's so long since I slept with someone I've practically sealed up'. Tally sighed. 'And it's too late for the house, in any case. The first person is coming to look round next week.'

'Who?' Jane asked. 'You never know,' she added, determined to see light at the end of the tunnel, even if it was another tunnel altogether, 'it might be someone gorgeous who'll fall for you.' If Tally had a radical makeover in the next few days, got her hair cut and stopped wearing her father's school trousers, there might well be a chance.

'Doubt it,' said Tally. 'He's a pop star, apparently. I can't imagine I'm his type.'

Jane was forced to admit this was not untrue. Tally's idea of contemporary music was probably 'Greensleeves'.

'Still, let's be thankful for small mercies,' Tally sighed. 'At least Mummy and Big Horn won't be there when he comes. They're off for a few weeks, to some ashram in

California. Apparently Big Horn's going to lock himself in a dark shed for a month and contemplate his inner child while Mummy looks for the wise woman in herself.'

'Well, that'll be a fruitless search,' said Jane.

Chapter 8

'What's bitten you?' Jane asked. She had just arrived in the office to find Josh with a face like thunder.

'Only that Luke Skywalker's had an accident ski-ing,' Josh grumbled. Luke Skywalker was the *Gorgeous* astrologer. Or, rather, the astrologer for *Gorgeous*. Even the most flattering of byline pictures had not succeeded in making Luke's unkempt, stringy hair, large nose and doleful eyes appealing. And he probably looked much worse now.

'Oh, poor Luke,' said Jane. 'Is he OK?'

'Not really,' said Josh irritably. 'The clumsy bastard smashed into a rock and now he's got amnesia. Can't even remember the past, let alone predict the future. You'd have thought he'd have seen it coming.'

Jane raised her eyebrows as she sat down and started to poke about her desk. In an attempt to impose some order on the chaos of her life, she had recently taken to noting down the next day's most important tasks on a Post It before she left the office the evening before. This morning, she gazed at the little primrose sticker and sighed. Top of the list was ringing Champagne.

She tried the mobile last. It ground away, unanswered. Jane had just decided to put it down when someone at the other end picked it up.

'Yah?' barked Champagne, over what sounded like loud banging and sloshing sounds in the background.

'It's Jane. How are you?' asked Jane, trying to sound enthusiastic.

'Fine. Just got back from shooting, in fact,' honked Champagne. 'With the Sisse-Pooles in Scotland. Bloody awful.'

'Oh, I hate blood sports too,' agreed Jane, starting to scribble down the conversation for the column. 'So dreadfully cruel.'

'Hideously cruel,' Champagne agreed, much to Jane's surprise. 'Making people stagger over the moors in the peeing rain wearing clothes the colour of snot is absolutely the worst, the most inhuman thing you can do to anyone. Let's face it,' Champagne added, in the face of Jane's stunned silence, 'I'm just not an outdoor type of girl. The only hills I care about are Beverly.'

And the only kind of shoots you care about are movie ones, the only Moores you're interested are Demi and Roger and the only bags that grab you are by Prada, thought Jane, working up the theme for the new column and scribbling furiously. And we all know whose butts you're most interested in at the moment. Unless, that is, you've been poached by a loaded gun.

That, at least, was a thought worth probing. 'Who were you shooting with?' Jane asked. It didn't sound like a very O'Shaughnessy activity. Perhaps Champagne had dumped him for some vague, weatherbeaten blond lord with a faceful of broken veins, a labrador and vast tracts of Yorkshire. Tim Nice Butt Dim.

'Well, Conal, of course, who the hell do you think?' came the booming honk. Slosh, slosh went the mystery background noise. 'The Sisse-Pooles asked him along as well. He had a blast, actually. Haw haw haw. God, I'm funny.'

Jane gritted her teeth. 'How did he do?' she asked, trying to imagine the determinedly working-class O'Shaughnessy stumbling around a moor with a collection of portly patricians in plus fours.

'Only thing he shot was one of the beaters,' boomed Champagne. 'But that didn't matter. Bloke was as old as the hills anyway. Oh yes,' hollered Champagne over the noise, 'Conal had a great time. He likes a good bang as much as the next man. Haw haw haw.'

'So you're still together?' The relationship with O'Shaughnessy had now lurched past the fortnight mark. In Champagne's book, that was practically the equivalent of a diamond wedding.

'Bloody right we are,' bawled Champagne. 'More than that, we're getting married!'

Jane's pen dropped with a clatter to the floor. 'Married?' Despite being separated from the conversation by the glass wall of his office, Josh's head shot up like Apollo 9.

'Yah, Conal asked me last night,' screeched Champagne excitedly. 'At least, I *think* that's what he said. Might have said "Will you carry me" as he was a bit out of it at the time. But by the time he came round, I'd dragged him into Tiffany's. Couldn't go back on his word then!' She roared with laughter.

The banging and swishing seemed to reach a climax. Champagne's voice was now barely audible over the terrific sloshing noise, as if she was caught in a terrible storm. Jane finally decided to voice the suspicion that had been building for some time. 'Champagne,' she asked, 'are you filing your column from the shower?'

'Not exactly,' bellowed Champagne. 'I'm just test-driving my new whirlpool bath. It's amazing. Some of the jets do frankly thrilling things.'

Jane put down the phone feeling sick. Champagne's wedding was a nauseating prospect. Day after day, Jane realised, she would be forcibly reminded of her own single status as Champagne banged on relentlessly about what would most certainly be the Media Wedding of The Year. The only bright side to it was the fact that if her wedding was splashed all over *Hello!*, even Champagne might be able to remember something about it for the column.

Still, when life failed, there was always food to fall back on. At lunchtime, Jane headed for the supermarket, deciding to buy herself something glamorous and comforting for supper. She headed automatically for the dairy counter, with its wealth of sinful lactocentricity. But here lurked disappointment. Disillusionment, even. Scanning the shelves, Jane couldn't help noticing the number of products that seemed to exist to mock the solitary, manless diner. Single cream, drippy and runny and the antithesis of comforting, luxurious double. Those depressing, rubbery slices of processed cheese called Singles.

Feeling self-conscious, Jane shuffled over to the more cheerful-looking Italian section, where she plumped for a big, squashy, colourful boxed pizza. Something about its improbable topping – four cheeses, pineapple, onion, olives, chicken tikka, prawns, peperoni, tomato, capers and tuna – struck her as amusing, and its mattress-like proportions looked intensely comforting. And Italians liked large ladies anyway.

Once the pizza box was in her basket, however, Jane felt racked with embarrassment. She was, she told herself, at least a stone too heavy to wander around in public carrying such a blatant statement of Intent To Consume

Calories. Hurriedly retracing her steps, Jane slipped the pizza box back on the cooler shelf and replaced it with a nutritionally unimpeachable packet of fresh pasta. No one needed to know she intended to eat it with eggy, creamy, homemade carbonara sauce.

Having secured the bacon, Jane went into a dream by the eggs, confused by the vast variety on offer. Was barn-fresh grain-fed more or less cruel than four-grain yard-gathered? Spending so much of her time in her own dreary office building, Jane was intensely sympathetic to the plight of battery hens. She picked up a cardboard box of eggs and shoved them vaguely in the direction of her basket. Only it wasn't hers.

'Oh, I'm so sorry,' Jane gasped to the tall, dark-haired, leather-jacketed man standing right next to her. 'I seem to have put all my eggs in your basket!' She retrieved them and giggled. 'I'm sorry. I was miles away.' But the man did not smile back. His handsome face didn't even crease. After staring at her hard for a second or two, he walked swiftly away. Jane gazed after him. Really, people acted very oddly in supermarkets. They were the strangest places. Some, she knew, were cruising zones. Some even held singles evenings.

Rounding the corner, hoping to happen upon some garlic bread, Jane bumped into Mr Leather Jacket again. 'Sorry,' she muttered again. He stared at her even harder. Annoyance flooded her. What was his problem?

Then a thought struck her. Jane flushed deeper and redder than a beetroot. Oh Christ, she thought. He thinks I fancy him. He thought I put my eggs in his basket on purpose. It's probably accepted supermarket flirting code. Eggs probably mean something very intimate and reproductive. Christ. How embarrassing. She looked round in panic at the contents of the baskets around her, suspecting the existence of an entire alternative universe of shopping semiotics. What, for example, did carrots mean? Or sausages? She hardly dared think about cucumbers. And meat? Were there such things as pick-up joints?

Even more embarrassing was the fact that her advances had been rejected, even though they had been unconscious. Or had they? Had there been some subliminal attempt to attract the man in the egg section? Had she been screaming out 'Fertilise Me' as she plonked her Size Twos into his basket? They had, she remembered been free range as well.

Jane returned, shamefaced, to the office. Mercifully, the day passed without any more interruptions from Champagne. Jane's relaying of the wedding news to Josh resulted in a six-foot-plus bunch of flowers and a six-pack of Krug being whizzed round to the Lancaster double quick. Josh was evidently putting in an early bid for a place on the invitation list.

At home, Jane put the pasta on to boil and opened the low-cal tomato sauce which she had eventually bought and which promptly spattered all over her. She gazed miserably at the sauce spots staining her new white blouse. Damaged goods. Shop-soiled. She may as well face it, she was, Jane decided, starting to snivel, on the shelf, and the one marked Reduced For Quick Sale at that.

She poured herself a stiff gin and tonic and felt pleasantly weak as the spirit flowed through her veins. So what if she didn't have a boyfriend. Plenty more fish in the sea, she thought encouragingly, raising the glass to the light. Even if they were probably sharks. Or, worse, tiddlers. Even worse, plankton. She'd clearly boarded the wrong train of thought here, Jane decided, finishing the glass. And now she'd upset herself. If depression was a black dog, she was currently presiding over a whole kennel full.

The telephone rang. Torn between the always lurking hope that it might be Tom, and the always lurking dread that it might be Nick, Jane decided to screen the call and hovered as the answering mechanism clicked loudly on. 'Oh, Jane, it's Amanda,' floated out the serene, clear and confident tones of a woman evidently at the other end of the coping-with-life universe from Jane. Amanda? Amanda who? Surely not Amanda-from-Cambridge. Amanda-with-the-vast-house-in-Hampstead. Rich-Amanda-she-had-meant-to-get-in-touch-with-about-Tally.

Since Cambridge, Jane and Amanda had seen each other only sporadically. The last time, Jane remembered, blushing, was when she and Nick had gone round there for dinner and Nick had attacked Amanda's merchant banker husband Peter for being a running dog capitalist. His opinions, Jane toe-curlingly recalled, had gathered force if not coherence from the gallons of Veuve Cliquot that Peter had provided, and Nick had soaked up like it was going out of fashion.

'Amanda!' Jane snatched up the receiver, hoping her words didn't sound too drink-sodden. 'Just got in through the door,' she lied. 'How *are* you? Haven't heard from you for ages.' She decided not to refer to the circumstances of their last meeting.

'Nor I you,' said Amanda smoothly; she had evidently reached the same conclusion. 'Which was why I was getting in touch. I thought you and Nick might like to come round to dinner Saturday week. Should be quite fun. If you can bear another tableful of City types, that is.' She gave a glassy giggle.

Jane blinked. Amid the clutter of her gin-fogged brain,

three clear possibilities gradually emerged: Amanda was very forgiving, Amanda had lost her memory, or Amanda had a *placement* problem. The latter seemed the most likely. Two guests had obviously dropped out of her dinner party and Amanda needed bodies quickly. She must, Jane thought, be *desperate* to consider having Nick back. She obviously hadn't heard they were no longer an item.

'I'd love to, but . . .' Jane started to explain about Nick. Then she stopped. A thought had struck her. What about Tally? A big dinner party at Amanda's would be full of City bankers. Men with money. The kind of men Tally desperately needed to meet. Jane's brain fizzed. Amanda didn't need to know about Nick. Hopefully she wouldn't find out, either. Jane would simply turn up with Tally, and break the change of partner to Amanda at the last minute. Fantastic. At last she was able to do something to help her friend.

'Actually, I think that might be OK,' Jane said slowly, shoving the receiver under her chin and making jabbing-frantically-at-the-Psion movements into thin air. 'Mmm, yes. It's fine. We'd love to. About eight thirty?'

Breaking the scheme to Tally would be simple, Jane decided. She would just tell her the two of them had been invited together. She hoped she could rely on Amanda not to make it awkward.

That decided, Jane went to bed, and dreamed of Tom. As she did at least twice a week, she recalled in vivid detail as much as she could remember of their night together. Frequent reminiscence would, she hoped, like water on a garden, keep the memory green. But she was already beginning to forget exactly what he had said to her. Admittedly, there had not been much. The sex, however, she could remember perfectly. Jane was reliving a particularly delicious moment, right down to the moans and sighs, when she realised that she was actually not asleep, but awake, and the moaning and sighing was happening directly above her head.

Jane opened her eyes wide and sat bolt upright. The moaning and sighing was more regular now, and was accompanied by rhythmic thuds. As the noises climbed the decibel scale to ecstasy, Jane realised that, in the flat above, Jarvis was apparently grinding some willing female into the shagpile.

The irony of it. Jane threw herself face down into the pillow and bit hard to prevent herself from screaming. Should she go up there and ask them to stop? Should she go up there and ask to join in? Jarvis and his partner were making so much noise now, moaning and sighing, panting and gasping, that Jane wondered what more they could actually do to mark the crucial moment. Blow a horn, perhaps? On the other hand, that was probably exactly what was happening now.

'Cheer up,' said Josh. 'Why not do some work to take your mind off things?' He flung a handful of A4 sheets across the room. 'There's a piece here to edit. Needs a bit of restructuring, I think.'

Shocked out of a delicious daydream in which Tom appeared in the office with a pair of first-class Eurostar tickets to Paris, Jane came abruptly down to earth. Or, even more depressingly, to sticky, stained carpet as she scrabbled to detach the pages from the floor. She scanned the opening paragraph. The appalling grammar, dreadful spelling and sentences looser than seventies Monsoon smocks made any kind of argument impossible to decipher. 'Restructuring?' snarled Jane. 'It needs scaffolding. It needs a whole team of builders with their bums sticking out.'

Oh sod it, she thought, half an hour later, looking at her watch. I'm going to lunch. Even the prospect of a lettuce roll in the local sandwich bar wasn't as depressing as staying in the office under Josh's baleful eye and the increasingly powerful aroma of rotting Thai prawn ready meal samples wafting over from the food editor's desk.

As it was early, Jane managed to grab a table. She bit into her roll, which tasted, as usual, of cotton wool, and allowed herself to daydream about Tom again. They were aboard the Eurostar now, stretching out in First, and she was just taking a crisp, chilled sip of a particularly rich and golden vintage champagne.

'Hi, there,' chirped a cheery, familiar voice. 'All alone, are you?' Jane did not look up. She didn't want to be disturbed. At least, she didn't want to be disturbed by fat Ann from *Blissful*, now bearing down on her with a plate full of pasta, a full-fat Coke and a bright chatty smile. Oh no, thought Jane in alarm, clutching her roll in panic. I don't want to spend all lunchtime hearing about her sick pussy.

'Actually, I'm glad you're on your own,' said Ann, plonking a pile of tomato goo that smelt strongly of sick on the table. That makes one of us, then, thought Jane. 'I've been meaning to have a chat with you for *ages*,' Ann continued. 'You see,' she stretched out an arm and placed it on Jane's, the thick hairs on her upper lip quivering, 'Valentine told me you split up with your boyfriend. And I wanted to say I was sorry.'

Thanks, Valentine, thought Jane. Then, as Ann did not immediately remove her clammy hand from her arm, the panicked thought that Ann might actually be trying her luck seized her. 'Thanks, Ann,' she said uncertainly.

'Welcome to the club!' said Ann, raising her Coke to the level of her thick, shiny nose.

Jane felt a rush of panic. 'What club?' she asked quaveringly. Could Ann see something she, Jane, had never been aware of? Maybe this was why she had never managed to make relationships with men work. 'The singles club,' beamed Ann, loading a forkful of goo into her mouth.

'Oh, I'm okay,' Jane said unsteadily. 'I'll put a Lonely Hearts ad in *Time Out* or something.'

'I'd be careful where you put your ads,' Ann said, with her mouth full. 'Personally, I've had very little luck with *Time Out*.'

'Really?' whispered Jane, wishing she hadn't bolted her sandwich so quickly. She could feel it lying like a slug at the bottom of her stomach. Her digestive system was in far too much of a tiz to let it progress any further. It lurked there, unmoving and uncomfortable.

'Yes, first there was the man who had inherited land.' Ann cocked her head to one side and frowned at the ceiling. 'But it turned out to be his grandfather's allotment in East Ham, which wasn't quite what I had in mind . . .

'Then there was the man obsessed with his mother. Then the man obsessed with his ex-girlfriend who picked his spots all the time.' Ann ran a ruminative buttery finger over her own far from flawless complexion as she spoke. 'Then I decided I'd have more luck going for the older man market, you know, the more mature, sophisticated sort.'

Jane nodded, fascinated, unable to speak.

'Which was when,' Ann finished, shoving the rest of her tomato mush in her mouth, 'I found myself having a night out with a retired brigadier from Basingstoke. Who didn't show the slightest interest in my pussy.'

* * *

Say what you like about Champagne, Jane thought a few days later. You couldn't deny she had the gift of the grab.

'It's *too* marvellous,' Champagne yelled excitedly with the eardrum-shattering tones she seemed to reserve exclusively for Jane. 'Everyone's being just *too* generous. Alexander McQueen's already offered to do my wedding dress and darling Sam McKnight's doing my hair as a favour. Plus the sweet Sandy Lane and the angel Hotel du Cap are fighting over giving me a free honeymoon!'

Hope it's the Sandy Lane, thought Jane bitterly. But only if Michael Winner's there.

'And,' Champagne added with what was meant to be a happy sigh but which sounded like Arnold Schwarzenegger giving artificial respiration, 'Mario Testino's agreed to do the wedding photographs! Such a darling. Just beyond *heaven*, don't you think?'

Champagne's neck wasn't merely brass, thought Jane. It was solid platinum. 'So where are you actually getting married?' she asked.

'Can't believe you're asking me that. It's so *obvious*,' Champagne bawled. 'Where on earth do you think?'

Jane's mind raced. Westminster Abbey? St Paul's? A beach in Bermuda? Underwater? The moon? San Lorenzo? Prada on Sloane Street? 'Er, no idea,' she admitted.

'St Bride's, Fleet Street, the journalists' church, of course,' barked Champagne. 'After all, it's my trade!'

Jane leant back on her chair and gritted her teeth. 'What will the dress be like?' she forced herself to ask.

'Oh,' trilled Champagne with what was meant to be a light tinkle of laughter but sounded like someone smashing up several industrial-sized conservatories. 'I can't remember anything apart from something about an eighteenth-century fantasia, inspired by Madame de Pompadour. Darling Alexander is stretching his ingenuity to the limit.' Not to mention his stitches, thought Jane. There was only one definite thing about what Champagne would be wearing. It would be tight.

'What about music?' asked Jane.

'A musical friend of Conal's is going to arrange some Action Liposomes hits, including "Hot To Trot", so everyone can sing them as hymns. And I've also asked the choir of St Bride's to sing "Wake Me Up Before You Go Go" by Wham, which is one of my favourite songs ever.'

'And where will you live?' Jane asked, wondering what Madame de Pompadour would have made of it all. Not much, was her guess.

'Well, a socking great mansion in the country, of course,' honked Champagne. 'Where the hell else does any self-respecting rock star live? I'm going to be lady of the manor. Opening fêtes, local hunt, that sort of stuff.'

'I thought you said you weren't the hunting type,' said Jane.

'Yah. Loathe it,' bawled Champagne. 'All that effort to look like a place mat. But they look rather sweet milling about the lawn. We're going to see a place tomorrow, s'matter of fact.'

'Where?' asked Jane, scribbling away. This was perfect column fodder. 'I mean, what county is it in?'

'Dunno. England, I think. Place has a very odd name. Called Millions. Very appropriate for Conal, I must say. Haw haw haw.'

Jane put down the telephone, feeling numb. So Conal O'Shaughnessy was the rock star Tally had been talking about. Poor old thing. She had no idea what was about to hit her.

Chapter 9

Tally sloshed the whisky into her mug. She felt in dire need of a stiff drink. 'I know it's not six o'clock yet,' she said to herself. 'But it must be six o'clock somewhere in the world.'

It was, in fact, just before twelve. Conal O'Shaughnessy and Champagne D'Vyne were coming to view the house at noon. Pacing backwards and forwards over the black and white squares of the Marble Hall, Tally's mind dwelled on every ghastly detail Jane had told her about Champagne. She could hardly believe such a person existed. Yet, sighed Tally, if her mother was forcing her to sell her home there was no use crying over spilt ilk. Money talked, although she wasn't entirely sure she liked what it said. Breeding, these days, was something Japanese people did when they cut themselves.

Tally took another sip. The whisky helped calm her jangling nerves. She gazed at the mug as she raised it to her lips. It depicted a strange-looking creature with what looked like an upside-down coathanger protruding from its head and bore the legend Tinky Winky. The mug had been a present from Piers and Tally had never understood what it represented.

There was a lot Tally had never understood about her

brother. Least of all why he seemed to think some rotten old scrubland outside an airport was more worth preserving than four centuries of family history. But to be fair, Tally thought, gasping as the iodine taste of the whisky blazed a trail down her throat, it was entirely possible that Piers, uncontactable and out of reach, didn't have the faintest idea what was happening at Mullions. She sniffed at the remaining alcohol in the bottom of the mug. Was it peaty island malt or TCP? It wasn't the first time she had suspected Mrs Ormondroyd of adulterating the bottles.

Tally gazed despairingly out through the vast and dusty floor-length windows of the Marble Hall. It was raining, as it had been ever since Julia and Big Horn had performed their rain dance for the benefit of Mr Peters' roses. That had been over a week ago. Big Horn and Julia had now jetted off in search of their inner selves, leaving behind them a swamp that was once a rose garden and a soggy hole where the ceiling of the Chinese Bedroom used to be. Tally had spent the morning trying to clear up the mess.

She sighed. Never had getting Mullions back on its feet seemed such an utterly hopeless prospect. She was getting tired of the struggle, not to mention cold and wet of it. Jane, on the other hand, had been firing on all cylinders when she called her about Amanda's dinner party, which she seemed convinced would provide the answer to all Mullions' problems. Jane had even urged her to get a facial. 'Oh, and go and buy something new to wear,' she had instructed. 'Something sexy.' Tally sighed again. Jane had to be joking. Shopping, in Lower Bulge, was Shangri-la if your idea of sartorial heaven was American Tan tights. And she couldn't even afford those. Still, there seemed no reason not to go to the dinner. It meant an evening away from Mrs Ormondroyd's cooking at least.

Spring had yet to make an impact on the naked trees in Mullions' park, which looked miserably bronchial, their bunched, vein-like branches black and lumpy against the sky. The mangy grass looked even patchier when wet and Tally could see that the bulrushes in the oxbow lake were getting out of hand again. Why didn't Mr Peters do something about it? she fretted. Well, he never had before, so he was unlikely to start now, especially after Julia's parting request was to ask him to make her a didgeridoo out of one of the Elizabethan bedposts. Unlike Tally, who had been beside herself at the casual vandalism of the idea, Mr Peters' objections sprang from his misapprehension that a didgeridoo was a sex aid. He had stormed off in high dudgeon and had not been seen since.

Suddenly, a long, white limo with blacked out windows glided into view and proceeded swiftly up the drive towards her. Tally knocked back the rest of whatever brew was in her mug and realised, panicking, that it was now too late to change clothes. The combination of her father's hunting pink, one of her mother's old tweed skirts and a pair of wellingtons would just have to do. She ran a hand hastily through her hair, hoping it was still reasonably presentable. She had brushed it yesterday, after all.

Giving herself a hurried spit wash, Tally rounded the corner of the house from the kitchen door, rubbing her forehead furiously. She was just in time to see a spoilt-looking blonde struggling out of the back of the car, her progress impeded by a tiny green miniskirt and perilously high heels. Tally gasped. Jane had warned her that Champagne was a beast but not that she was a beauty. The girl now swaying slightly on stilettos on the gravel had the rippling blonde mane, large eyes and full lips of a

Botticelli angel. Tally blushed for her own red-tipped nose and scraped-back hair.

Champagne's tiny skirt stopped at a point obviously designed to make her beautiful, tanned, finely-muscled legs look longest. Her minuscule blouse was made from a matt material Tally had never seen before, with a rippling, liquid, milky texture that clung to Champagne's bronzed and rounded breasts, exposing a wealth of golden if goosepimpled flesh. She certainly wasn't dressed for looking round a cold and draughty country house. Tally, who was, shifted uncomfortably in her ancient and mud-stained wellingtons. She felt like a cross between the town crier and the village idiot. And, from the way Champagne was staring rudely at her, she obviously looked that way too.

'Christ, what an old *dump*,' Champagne honked, lighting a cigarette. Her brilliant grass-green gaze swept pitilessly over the crumbling, wet bricks and soaked window frames which looked at their most irredeemably rotten in the rain. 'Could you tell whoever is in charge here,' she ordered in loud and patronising tones, 'that Miss Champagne D'Vyne has come to look round the house.'

'Actually, that's me,' muttered Tally, embarrassed. 'I live here. I'm Natalia Venery. How do you do.' It was only after she had stuck her hand out that she realised her palms still carried a fair proportion of the Chinese Bedroom with them. Champagne recoiled.

'I didn't realise you were coming alone,' Tally said, feeling rather disappointed. She realised she had been secretly looking forward to meeting the famously sexy rock star Jane had told her about. There hadn't been such a high-profile musician at Mullions since Thomas Tallis had dropped by in 1580.

'Yes, well, can't be helped,' snapped Champagne. 'Conal

can't come this morning, and as I'm in charge of spending his money anyway, I thought I might as well give the place the once-over myself.'

'I suppose he must be very busy,' Tally said brightly.

Champagne frowned. 'I'm pretty bloody busy *myself*, actually,' she said indignantly. 'I've got ten parties, three premieres, a dress fitting and a skin peel to cram in before the end of the week. Conal's only got the Brit Awards and a court appearance.'

'A court appearance?' asked Tally, before she could stop herself. 'Oh dear.'

'Yah,' drawled Champagne, her heels scraping on the mossy stones as she tottered in Tally's wake round the side of the house. 'It's very boring. Some ghastly drummer the Action Liposomes had long before they became famous has crawled out of the woodwork. He's saying that *he* wrote "Hot To Trot" and has the rights to all the profits from it. So he's suing Conal. Can you bloody *believe* it?'

'How dreadful,' said Tally, grateful to Jane for her crash course in popular culture, thanks to which she knew 'Hot To Trot' was the Action Liposomes' mega-selling hit and not a racehorse, as she would otherwise have assumed.

'Oh, it's all a fuss about nothing, of course,' Champagne said dismissively, pausing theatrically by the back door. 'Conal says the guy's just trying it on. Jealousy, you see. People can't cope with other people's success. It's just one of those ghastly things that happens to you when you're famous. Believe me, I *know*. People have no *idea* how hard you have to work to be successful. The *sacrifices* you have to make. Oh no, they just try and put you down. People want to put *me* down all the time.'

'Really?' said Tally mildly.

'Yah,' howled Champagne, whipping herself into a

frenzy of self-pity. 'I mean, people think I have the most *amazingly* glamorous life. But I don't. I get parking tickets on the Bentley just like everybody else. *I've* had to wait for delayed Concordes as well.'

There was a silence. Tally shifted from wellington to wellington, not quite knowing what to say. 'Would you like to see round?' she ventured nervously.

Champagne nodded and took another drag of her cigarette. 'Bit remote out here, isn't it?' she barked, suddenly, as if the thought had only just occurred to her. Under her thick eyeliner, her eyes snapped suspiciously around. She cocked her head in the direction of the few desultorily twittering birds that could be heard. 'Very quiet,' she boomed. 'Where's the nearest Joseph?'

Tally looked blank. 'Um, in the village church, I should imagine,' she said, puzzled. Champagne had not struck her as the pious type.

'What?' honked Champagne, her face contorted with contemptuous amazement. 'I mean Prada, Gucci, Joseph. Where do you go for retail therapy?' she shouted, as if to a moron. 'Shopping!'

'Oh, um, there's the village for milk and stamps and things,' Tally stuttered, panicked. 'Lower Bulge, it's called.'

Champagne threw her head back and laughed. 'Lower Bulge! Definitely my kind of town. Is there an Upper Bulge as well?'

Tally nodded, trying not to look too offended. 'Yes, there is, as a matter of fact.'

Champagne laughed so much she almost lost her balance on the mossy, cracked path. To hide her blushes and confusion, Tally started to force open the door of the kitchen entrance, which had swelled and stuck again with the damp. It took a few minutes.

'What time do you have to get up to milk the pheasants round here?' Champagne demanded as she strode ahead of Tally into the kitchen only to collide with Mrs Ormondroyd carrying a big bowl of evil-looking slop towards the back door.

'Ugghh!' shrieked Champagne.

The housekeeper looked thunderous.

'This is Mrs Ormondroyd,' stammered Tally. 'She's the housekeeper here. Mrs Ormondroyd, this is Miss D'Vyne. She's come to look at the house.'

'Charmed, I'm sure,' muttered Mrs Ormondroyd, sounding anything but. She took in Champagne's scanty clothing with a single, withering stare. Like a threatened peacock, Champagne immediately pushed her cleavage out still further and looked contemptuously at the housekeeper's nylon overall. The standoff ended only when Mrs Ormondroyd, who was still holding the slop bowl, moved off with massive dignity through the back door, where she could be heard emptying it down the drain. Tally let out a silent sigh of relief. The slop wasn't supper then, after all.

'Christ,' said Champagne. 'What a dragon.'

'Her heart's in the right place,' said Tally loyally.

'Shame nothing else is,' remarked Champagne. 'She looks like someone's driven over her face.'

Tally prayed Mrs Ormondroyd hadn't overheard. She would, she knew, be lucky if tonight's Brown Windsor was even tepid. Or brown, come to that. She led Champagne down the kitchen passage into the Marble Hall.

'It's *freezing*,' bawled Champagne. 'Haven't you got any central heating?'

'Just one old and rather unreliable boiler, I'm afraid,' faltered Tally.

'We just met. Back there. Haw haw haw,' honked

Champagne. There was a distant crash from the direction of the kitchen. Bang go the chops as well, thought Tally. She realised, guiltily, that the prospect wasn't too disappointing. 'We have some wonderful statues,' Tally said quickly, gesturing at the marble figures surrounding them. 'They're considered very fine.'

Much to her amazement, Champagne gazed at them. 'Talk about a six-pack,' she exclaimed, running her hand over the muscular stomach of Mars.

'It's a copy from Praxiteles, actually,' corrected Tally.

'You trying to be funny?' Champagne snapped.

Tally swallowed. She decided to try and interest Champagne in the portraits. 'These are all Venerys,' she said, waving an arm in the direction of the Ancestors.

Champagne looked at them with interest. 'Filthy bastards,' she pronounced delightedly, after peering at them for a few seconds. 'On the other hand, it's pretty obvious from their weird red noses.'

'I'm sorry?' said Tally, taken aback. The Ancestors' eyes were visibly bulging. More blue veins than the painters had ever intended stood out from the canvases.

'You just said they were all venereal,' honked Champagne. There was a visible frisson of fury from the pictures on the wall.

'No, no, not at all,' said Tally, horrified. 'Venery is the family name.'

Champagne raked the portraits over again with her brutally frank gaze. 'Oh,' she said. 'Still, who on earth would want to have sex with that lot anyway?'

'Would you like to see some other paintings?' Tally said brightly, aware of the Ancestors' painted pupils boring furiously into her back. 'We have a very important Dutch School in the Green Drawing Room.'

'How *boring,*' Champagne boomed. 'Who on earth wants to look at a painting of a *Dutch school*?'

To say that Champagne held the treasures of Mullions in low esteem was an understatement. Fifteen minutes later, Tally was close to despair. When shown Queen Victoria's corset, which lay in a display case in the Green Drawing Room, Champagne had expressed disgust that the Queen-Empress wore such filthy old underwear. She had been interested in the Library until she realised it contained no videos. Tally's offer to show her the Grinling Gibbons elicited enthusiasm until she proudly brought Champagne before the carved Blue Room fireplace and was asked where the monkeys were. Tally's explanation that the tapestries were by Gobelins met with blank disbelief. 'But how could they reach?' Champagne stormed.

Nor had she been impressed by Tally's self-deprecating explanation that the nearest Mullions got to an indoor pool was the parts that the fire buckets dotted about to catch the rainwater could not reach. What Champagne really wanted, Tally realised, was not a country house but a country house *hotel.* And, probably, the more overheated, overstuffed, overdecorated and overpriced the better.

There seemed scarcely any point in showing Champagne the bedrooms, but she insisted. She also insisted on grinding out her fifth cigarette in the ancient oak of the staircase. And it was as a near-desperate Tally led the way up to the first floor that disaster struck. As Champagne staggered by, her high heels sinking into the soft old oak, one of the biggest portraits of the Ancestors suddenly broke free of the wall, swung drunkenly on one nail and fell. The heavy frame containing the Third Earl crashed just inches from Champagne's feet. Another nanosecond and her skull would have been smashed. Oh, for another nanosecond, Tally thought. After all, Champagne's skull wouldn't have made much of a mess. It wasn't as if there were brains in it.

It took almost a full minute for Champagne to realise she was still alive. Her green eyes widened and her vast red mouth opened in a roar that brought down an avalanche of plaster and almost the rest of the portraits as well. 'Get me out of this hideous dump,' she screamed at Tally. 'Now! It's *disgusting*. I *hate* it. I don't want to live in some old *shithole* with walls covered in venereal disease and *goblins*! We're going to St John's Wood like everybody else. If it's good enough for Liam and Patsy, it's good enough for Conal and me.'

When the white limo finally disappeared from sight, a hugely relieved Tally examined the fallen picture. Miraculously, the heavy Jacobean frame had hardly a scratch, and the stairs had not sustained too much damage either. Tally sank to her knees on the damp marble floor and gazed around her. The Ancestors, their equilibrium apparently restored, gazed at her with approval. She could have sworn that there were twinkles in some of their painted eyes.

She pulled a face at them and sighed. Selling Mullions was going to be even more difficult than she had first thought. Particularly now the house seemed to have taken matters into its own hands.

Chapter 10

'Oh dear,' said Josh, devouring the front page of the *Sun*. 'He's been knocked off the number one spot and is plunging down the charts.'

It was a week later. Jane looked up from the papers in which she, too, was reading the sorry tale of how Conal O'Shaughnessy had lost his case against his former drummer. 'Hot To Trot' had after all been ruled to be the creation of one Darren Diggle from Wigan, to whom the humiliated heart-throb had been forced to pay a multimillion-pound compensation package.

'And you know what that means,' crowed Josh. 'Goodbye, Champagne. Farewell, my bubbly.' He was clearly thrilled. All stories about Champagne were good news for *Gorgeous*, as, Champagne being their columnist, the magazine always got a mention.

'That's nice,' said Valentine. 'Dumping him just before they were about to get married. What about for richer, for poorer? The poor sod needs her support.'

'Champagne would certainly have had the "for poorer" bit written out of the marriage service,' said Jane. 'And I don't think support is her strong point. You can tell that from looking at her underwear.'

When Champagne rang, Josh was proved right.

She had had absolutely no scruples in dropping O'Shaughnessy like a shot. 'Rather a pity, really,' she honked to Jane. 'I never liked his music all that much, and quite frankly he was a bit common. But he really had the most *enormous* willy.'

Jane's thoughts instantly flew to the other person she knew who was similarly equipped. She swallowed, but looked determinedly on the bright side. At least Champagne wasn't getting married now. She would be spared the details of bridesmaids, luxury Portaloos, honeymoons and the rest of it. And all for a marriage that probably wouldn't have lasted five minutes anyway. Jane had little doubt Champagne would have dumped O'Shaughnessy without a qualm the moment a better prospect presented himself. Champagne's idea of emotional baggage, after all, was being fond of her Louis Vuitton.

It was more than enough to make even Elizabeth Taylor feel cynical about marriage, Jane decided. And to think she had so fervently wanted a wedding herself. To Nick, of all people, who still rolled up at the flat with almost weekly regularity, ostensibly to unearth another armful of embarrassing albums and a mouldering jumper or two. Jane, however, suspected the real reason was to check she had not moved somewhere else. If only she had the energy to, she thought sadly. But at the moment the last thing Jane felt like doing on a Saturday was trailing miserably around the type of peeling, smelly South London prison-cell bedsits her single salary could afford.

Spending Saturday househunting would, however, have one distinct advantage. It would keep her away from the shops. Jane had always known life as a single woman was a social minefield. But it was not until the eggs-in-wrong-basket incident at the supermarket that she had realised it was a shopping one as well.

Saturday shopping, Jane had come to realise, actively conspired against the single. A recent visit to Heal's had almost resulted in a nervous breakdown as she found herself alone amid a sigh of blissed-out couples testing out vast, comfy sofas with names like Figaro and Turandot and bouncing up and down on enormous beds called Renoir and Picasso. As she fled from the mass of the young, beautiful and sexually fulfilled, Jane wondered vaguely what Thackeray would have made of the CD rack his name had been so freely given to, and also which of the Brontës the elegant silver wine rack was honouring. The alcoholic Branwell, perhaps?

There was no escape in John Lewis, where Jane found herself at close quarters with yet more cheerful couples weighing up the rival claims of seagrass and seisal. At Harvey Nicks, beautiful thin girls with perfect bottoms and unstructured-linen-clad boyfriends compared brands of aubergine crisps in the food hall, while at Selfridges dreamy twosomes dithered over duvets. Sainsbury's check-out queues were nothing less than a conspiracy of besotted lovers with trolleys full of rocket salad, parmesan, vine-grown tomatoes and champagne. Usually, Jane made her way home from these excursions with nothing but M&S knickers and a huge single-woman-sized chip on her shoulder.

Still, hope was in sight. There was Amanda's dinner party to look forward to. At least that should sort out Tally. Jane was beginning to realise she was rather counting on a result from it herself.

Champagne, by way of profound contrast, lasted barely twenty-four hours without a new man on her arm. Jane opened the papers two days later to find the centre spreads of the tabloids devoted to a shot of Champagne, skirt riding up to her waist and apparently innocent of underwear, snogging someone in the back of a limousine. The snoggee, according to the practically identical accompanying reports, was 'one of London's most eligible bachelors, dashing millionaire property developer Saul Dewsbury'.

'She's certainly met her match this time,' Valentine remarked. 'So to speak. Because from what I hear, Saul Dewsbury's responsible for more burnt fingers than the Spanish Inquisition.'

According to Valentine, Dewsbury had a reputation for being as ruthless in the bedroom as he was in the boardroom. Valentine accordingly suspected his liaison with Champagne was as much about business as it was about pleasure. 'It usually is,' he said. 'My father's in property, so I've heard a few stories about Dewsbury. His last girlfriend's father was leader of a council where he was apparently trying to get planning permission for some Princess Diana-themed wine bars. Dewsbury dumped her as soon as it was granted. And I think he got about five hundred acres of prime Sussex countryside out of someone else, which apparently he's made into a Space Experience.'

Jane sighed. 'That column's going to have more plugs than the John Lewis homes department. Not that it doesn't already.'

Her fears were justified. Suddenly Champagne, followed by the ever-eager paparazzi, seemed to be spending her entire life in one or other of the businesses in which Dewsbury had an interest. These ranged from a West End theatre which Dewsbury was converting into luxury flats with individual lifts and plunge pools, to a disused medieval City church he was transforming into a nightclub. A

Georgian townhouse had just been demolished in all but façade to accommodate a gym for the twenty-second century, whose colour-sensitive walls would reflect the collective mood of the gym-goers.

'Talk about making hay while the *Sun* shines,' remarked Valentine one day, scrutinising a picture of Champagne in a sparkling leotard bicycling for all she was worth while the wall behind her loomed an ominous black. 'It's ridiculous. The column's practically a prospectus for Dewsbury at the moment.'

In the end, Jane lost her patience. 'I've told her we're not running another word about him,' she told Valentine a day or so later. 'I absolutely refuse ever to plug him again. Champagne's furious. She says she couldn't think of anything else to say. Claims to have writer's block.'

'Well, I'd agree with the block bit,' said Valentine.

Champagne, however, seemed to be utterly in Dewsbury's thrall. And looking at the pictures of them that appeared almost daily in the papers, Jane didn't find it too hard to see why. Extremely handsome, and with cheekbones so sharp you could cut cigars on them, Dewsbury looked as cool and dangerous as a Smith & Wesson on ice. Thrillingly ruthless, thought Jane, feeling herself going emerald with envy. Damn Champagne. It wasn't fair how men came buzzing round her like bees to a honeypot. Or, in Dewsbury's case, a moneypot.

On the day of Amanda's dinner party, Jane finally screwed her courage to the *placement* and called her to say Tally would be replacing Nick as her partner that evening. Amanda's voice had been acquiescent, but tight. 'So up herself she could practically tickle her tonsils,' Jane giggled to Tally over a pre-dinner party departure gin and tonic in the flat.

'And her husband's so boring,' whinged Tally, who seemed to be going off the whole idea.

'He definitely puts the Square in Square Mile,' said Jane. 'But just imagine his incentive package. More to the point, think of those of his friends.'

Amanda cast a satisfied glance around the bathroom. She was particularly proud of the fleur-de-lis lavatory paper. To most people, the Balkan war had meant mass graves and Radovan Karadzic. To Amanda, watching the highlights on breakfast TV as she lunged backwards and forwards on her rowing machine, it meant that attractive Bosnian fleur-de-lis shield.

The hall was faintly scented from the light bulbs dabbed with essential oils. Not for the first time, Amanda congratulated herself on selecting precisely the right shade of paint for the walls. Biscotti, with the dado and picture rails picked out in Etruscan. She looked round brightly as she descended the stairs, the half-smile on her face fading as she noticed the morning's copy of *La Repubblica* loitering unread on the doormat. She hated being reminded that, having decided to take the paper to practise Italian for their Tuscan holidays, neither she nor Peter ever bothered to look at it.

She bent over the banister to look down into the basement kitchen. Yes, there was Peter, by the Aga, chopping chillis as requested. He looked distracted, as usual. The dinner party would, if nothing else, be a chance for her to catch up with whatever was going on in his head at the moment. Peter was always too tired when he came home to tell her anything. But at table, he would have to regale their guests with something of what had happened in his life for the past month or so. Really, dinners were quite useful in that way if you thought about it.

She trotted into the sitting room (or was it drawing room, she never could decide) to plump up the Kettle Chips. 'Peter,' she called. 'Peter, darling. Have you remembered to slice the lemons for the gin and tonic?'

There was no reply from the kitchen. Amanda returned to peer down over the banister. Her husband was nowhere to be seen. Panic shot up Amanda's gorge. It was almost eight sixteen. People would be arriving any minute. She hated it when everyone came en masse, requiring one to perform the feat of taking coats, pouring drinks and making small talk simultaneously.

Dashing inelegantly up the elegant, sweeping staircase to the first floor, Amanda banged on the bathroom door. A faint gasping could be heard from inside. Amanda shoved it open. She screamed.

Towering over the washbasin, her husband had his trousers down and his penis flopped into a sinkful of cold water. 'Peter,' she stammered, realising that, subconsciously, this was the moment she had always been expecting. The reason for his distraction. The moment when Peter confessed that his suppressed passion for Fish Minor back in the fourth form was why he could never love her as a woman needed to be loved. Amanda gazed at him in wide-eyed, speechless anguish.

'Sorry,' Peter said matter-of-factly, straining a watery-eyed smile in her direction. 'Just had a pee and forgot I'd been chopping chillis. Dick feels like it's on fire. Talk about a red-hot poker.'

Amanda descended in disgust. As if she hadn't enough to put up with. First there had been that wretched Jane Bentley ruining her *placement* by saying she was turning up with Natalia Venery instead of her boyfriend. Please God they weren't going *out* with each other, thought Amanda, sending up silent prayers in the direction of the decorative baskets suspended from the oak-effect kitchen beams. Merchant banks were hardly bastions of liberalism. A couple of lesbians at table could scupper Peter's chances of promotion until well into the next century. Then there had been that arrogant bastard Saul Dewsbury who had called at the eleventh hour – quite literally, at eleven o'clock that morning – to say not only would his girlfriend and Amanda's star guest, Champagne D'Vyne, not be coming, but he doubted he could make it himself.

Amanda stole a look through the glass oven door. There sat the boeuf en daube and the luxury coquilles St Jacques warming beneath. Thank goodness there were some things, Harrods Food Hall for instance, that never let you down.

She shuddered. It had been a close-run thing with Dewsbury; for a few minutes, her numbers had hung precariously in the balance. He had agreed to come in the end, though only after Amanda had gone through the rest of the guest list with him. He'd made an abrupt volte-face after that – there was obviously someone he wanted to meet.

But who? Amanda racked her brains as she circled the dining table, making sure the forks were tines down in the French style. Probably it was the deeply dishy Mark Stackable, the unfeasibly young head of investment with Peter's firm Goldman's. Through the medium of Peter, Dewsbury had often tried, without success, to get Stackable to underwrite his projects in the past. He was probably trying again. At the thought of Stackable, Amanda felt a frisson in her gusset. It wasn't just out of politeness she'd placed him next to her at table.

She scattered the cushions a little more, and gave a final ruffle to her artful-casual arrangement of glossy magazines. Then again, Dewsbury might well be wanting to catch up with Nicola Pitbull, Goldman's head of development. It was unlikely he had any interest in meeting her useless and deeply embarrassing artist husband Ivo who everyone thought must have got something on Nicola, otherwise she would never be seen dead with him. Not for the first time, Amanda wondered what that something was.

Apart from herself and Peter, that only left Sholto Binge, a financial journalist who was an old school friend of Peter's, and of course Jane and Tally. None of whom Dewsbury would give two hoots about.

'Everyone here now, darling?' Peter hissed half an hour later, as, firebucket style, he relayed the gins and tonic from the kitchen to Amanda in the hall.

'Apart from Saul,' said Amanda through clenched teeth. 'Honestly, the *cheek* of the man. I practically had to *beg* him to come, and now he's late. *Christ*,' she added, glancing through the sitting-room door at her guests. 'Ivo's eating the potpourri. He must think it's vegetable crisps. I'd better go.' She snatched up a bowl of Japanese crackers and dashed to the rescue.

'Ivo, my darling,' said Amanda, gliding up to him with the bowl. 'Do try some of these. They're delicious.'

Ivo stretched out a hand and stuffed one into his mouth. 'Hmm,' he said, after chewing for a few seconds. 'Not mad about peanuts, actually. Think I prefer the other things.'

'Have you met Natalia Venery?' Amanda interjected hastily, before Ivo could resume his consumption of Elizabethan Rose.

Tally, draped on a piano stool next to Ivo, nodded. 'Yes. We're having a lovely chat,' she said, gazing at Amanda with large and pleading eyes. Amanda, either unable or reluctant to realise that this was SOS code for Tally's having failed utterly to light the conversational blue touchpaper and wanting help, moved complacently on to the large navy-blue damask sofa where Jane was trying to put as much space as possible between herself and an edgy, skinny blonde wearing a bright red suit. The blonde was smoking furiously, a deep frown creasing the space between eyebrows so plucked they were practically nonexistent.

'Oh, I see you've met Nicola, Jane,' smiled Amanda. 'Works with Peter. Married to Ivo, who's sitting down over there next to Tally.'

'Yes,' said Jane. She was furnished with all the information already. Nicola had rapped it out before lapsing into a sullen silence. She had pointedly not asked Jane any questions at all. Jane cursed herself for having let Amanda plonk her down here. Her hostess had seemed determined she should stop talking to the dark-haired American still standing with Peter over by the piano. They'd arrived at the same time and he'd introduced himself as Mark Stackable, a banker from the same firm as Peter.

He was so handsome she hadn't even sniggered at his name. She stared over the room at him now. He was gorgeous. *And* smart. His expensive-looking suit gave way to a crisp white shirt which set off a tan just the right side of improbable. He looked, Jane thought, as if he could show a girl a good time. Though which girl, if it came to a choice between herself and Tally, remained to be seen.

She looked across at Tally, still valiantly trying to kickstart a conversation with Ivo. As instructed, she had made an effort, and as a result her usual eccentric appearance was so toned down it could even pass for classic-with-a-twist. The classic was the perfectly-cut black dress which looked like one of Tally's more successful raids on her mother's wardrobe. It showed off her long legs to perfection, and played down the broadness of her shoulders so that her bare arms looked elegant and endless. The twist was the battered fuchsia feather boa that Tally clutched and tore at nervously with her long thin fingers, but this, Jane noted approvingly, actually reinforced the bohemian-aristo air of Bloomsbury that hung about her milk-white skin, piled-up hair and huge grey eyes. Tally looked, in short, unprecedentedly presentable.

Jane shifted uncomfortably in the black silk shirt and narrow cigarette pants she had hoped trumpeted to the world her recent weight loss. She had looked positively svelte in the full-length mirror (a first), and had felt sufficiently emboldened to slick on a mouthful of Mon Rouge. Now, compared to a Tally bordering on the beautiful, she wondered if she'd made enough of an effort. After all, it was a two-horse race now.

'Nicola's the top woman at Goldman's.' Amanda yanked her back from dreamland and deposited her next to the blonde again. 'She's *terrifyingly* successful!'

Why not just give me her CV and have done with it? thought Jane, expecting to hear Nicola's bra size next. Not that she looked like she needed one. Nicola was so flat-chested, Jane thought waspishly, her only possible use for bras would be for the identification of sex in the event of an accident.

'What do you do?' asked Nicola languidly, obviously already uninterested in the reply. Jane stared regretfully at her empty gin and tonic glass and prepared to address the heart-sinking question. In her book, 'And what do you do?' came second only to 'Have you discovered the love of Jesus?' as a conversational show-stopper.

'Jane's a journalist,' said Amanda brightly. 'Be careful what you say to her,' she added gaily as she strutted off across the carpet towards Sholto. 'You know what these wicked journalists are like.'

Sholto, catching the end of the sentence, beamed at her. 'You *are* a tease,' he said admiringly.

'I work on *Gorgeous*,' Jane admitted, blushing. She could imagine the contempt with which Nicola, who had probably smashed more glass ceilings than the Crystal Palace demolition gang, would regard a society glossy.

Nicola stared at her. Jane shrank from her gaze.

'The one with the Champagne D'Vyne column, isn't it?'

Jane blushed again and nodded, embarrassed. She was surprised Nicola had even seen Champagne's column. Surely she was too busy being a Mistress of the Universe to read anything other than the share prices.

To her amazement, Nicola melted. 'Oh, but I *love* that column,' she gushed. 'It's wonderful.'

'So do I,' piped up Amanda, making a return circuit with a bowl of pistachios in one hand and the rescued bowl of Elizabethan Rose in the other. She proffered the pistachios. 'I *adore* it. And *so* interesting you should be talking about that, because tonight someone who knows—'

'It's true that she doesn't *write* it, isn't it?' Nicola interrupted.

Jane jolted with shock. Did people actually know then? Was recognition round the corner at last?

'I heard she doesn't write a word,' Nicola persisted.

Jane nodded, feeling months of pent-up frustration

prepare to pour itself out to a sympathetic audience. 'Absolutely,' she began.

'Not as much as a full stop,' added Nicola, inhaling half her cigarette in her excitement.

'Not even a comma,' Jane agreed. 'I—'

'No, her agent does everything,' said Nicola gleefully.

'What?' Jane felt the ebullience drain out of her, slide over the sofa cushions and disappear under one of Amanda's original-feature Georgian doors.

'Yes, I go to the same gym as her agent,' panted Nicola. 'Guy called Simon. Says he writes every word. Gets absolutely no thanks from Champagne either. Bloody ungrateful, I call it.'

'*Bloody* ungrateful,' added a voice from the doorway. 'But I think you'll find the agent is prone to exaggeration.'

Everyone stared at the newcomer. Black-haired and handsome, he lounged confidently against the doorframe wearing a suit as sharp as a razor. His glittering, black eyes were fixed on Nicola, whose furious expression said louder than words that she wasn't accustomed to being argued with. His sensual lips were pursed in an amused, dangerous, Tybalt-like smile.

'This is Saul Dewsbury, everyone,' said Amanda, proudly. Dewsbury moved across the carpet like a panther, his eyes sweeping the guests. Did Jane imagine it, or did his glance, impenetrable as a tinted limousine window, linger on her a second or two longer than it did on the others?

'I'm *terribly* sorry about Champagne,' Dewsbury said, turning his back to the fireplace and addressing Amanda across the room. 'She was *desperate* to come but she just had to stay in and write her column, I'm afraid.' He shot a look at Nicola. 'Deadlines, you know.'

Amanda nodded eagerly. 'Oh, I'd hate my little dinner party to deprive the rest of the nation of their monthly treat,' she twittered. An explosion of choking filled the room. 'Are you all right, Jane?' asked Amanda, concerned.

'Oh, f-f-fine,' gasped Jane, conscious of Dewsbury's glitter-eyed interest. 'Just went down the wrong way. I'm fine, really.'

'*À table*,' announced Amanda in her best French accent, motioning everyone to head next door into the canteloupe-coloured dining room. Jane looked apprehensively at the thin, grey iron chairs, complete with finials and fragile-looking strips of purple crushed velvet running over the seat and up the back to serve as both backrest and cushion.

Sitting down, she found they were every bit as uncomfortable as they looked. Particularly the prime slot Amanda had waved her to, next to the barking Ivo. There was an empty place between herself and Amanda. Would she hit the jackpot and get Mark Stackable? Or the booby prize, the scary Saul? A flock of butterflies rose in Jane's stomach as she saw Stackable come towards her, and settled down again as he was steered firmly to a seat the other side of Amanda. 'And you're here beside me, Saul,' Amanda called coquettishly, patting the ribbon of velvet between herself and Jane.

Mercifully, Saul was assigned to Amanda for the coquilles St Jacques. Jane, meanwhile, prepared to dig for victory with Ivo. Fortunately, her long apprenticeship getting conversational blood out of a stone with Champagne had its uses.

'What do you do?' She hated herself for asking the dreaded question, but this was an emergency. She was even prepared to ask him about discovering the love of Jesus if it didn't work. Across the table, Tally flashed her a grin. Jane half scowled back. It was all very well for Tally to look so jolly. She'd landed the coveted seat on the other side of Mark Stackable, and they were already chatting away like old friends. Even more annoyingly, Tally now looked positively gorgeous. The alchemy of the candlelight wiped the redness from her nose, gave her eyes a velvety depth and threw a halo of soft gold about her hair. As she moved her elegant fingers about the stem of her glass, the Venery gold signet ring caught the light.

'I'm an artist,' Ivo said, or sputtered, simultaneously revealing a cavalier attitude to oral hygiene and more plums in his mouth than an orchard of Victorias.

'What sort of an artist?' asked Jane.

'I work with kens, mostly.'

'Kens?' Visions of Barbie's boyfriend and Mr Barlow from *Coronation Street* segued rather confusingly before her.

'That's right,' said Ivo. 'Coca-Cola kens, baked bean kens, tomato kens, you name it. I collect them, crush them and make pictures out of them.'

'Do you wash them first?' asked Jane.

'Not always, etcherly,' said Ivo. Really, his voice was ridiculous, thought Jane. He was so grand he could barely speak. 'You can git some very interesting iffects when the kens are still full. For instance, I orften put a bean ken in the road, wait for a car to run over it and spletter it, then scrape it up and stick it on the kenvess.'

Amanda placed the daube on the table, along with a bowl of what looked like grey mashed potato. Jane's heart sank. Oh no. Of all things in the world she could never digest.

'Artichoke, Jane?' asked Amanda, digging into, and lifting, a huge chunk of the mixture and dolloping it in a heap in front of her. Fartichoke, thought Jane. They never had agreed with her. She looked warily at the grey pile on her plate. It had all-night stomach problems written all over it.

'So you're the famous Jane,' came a silky drawl at her side. 'I'm very glad to meet you at last. I've heard a lot about you, from Champagne.'

Jane looked into Saul's sharp, handsome face. His hooded eyes stared steadily back at her. He raised a single, elegant eyebrow and twisted his full, sensual mouth into the widest and most charming of smiles.

'Yes, well, I suppose I could say the same about you,' Jane said guardedly. She noticed he wore a watch chain. A sharply-folded handkerchief protruded like a knife blade from his waistcoat pocket. Jane took an enormous sip of nerve-steadying wine. 'You're very busy, from what I hear,' she blurted. She found the stillness with which Saul held himself intimidating, like a snake about to strike. 'What do you do to relax?' she added, trying to sound casual. It seemed wise on the whole to get him off the subject of his businesses, given that she had recently tried to ban Champagne from ever mentioning them.

'Oh, this and that,' said Saul, watching amusedly as Jane gulped back more of Peter's best Domaine de Vieux Télégraphe much too quickly. 'I'm quite keen on racing. I have an interest in a couple of racehorses, as a matter of fact.'

'Really?'

'Yes. One's called Dogfood so it knows what's in store for it if it loses. The other's called Knacker's Yard for the same reason.' Saul grinned wolfishly at her. Jane tried to suppress a shiver. He was so cold. She felt like the *Titanic* to his iceberg, but without the warmth and humour the word iceberg normally implies.

'I'm also quite keen on fishing,' said Saul.

He was not the type Jane could easily imagine standing for hours on a riverbank. 'You are?'

'Yes, I'm very fond of getting my rod out,' Saul enlarged. 'At the moment, as it happens, I'm trying to develop the ultimate fly.'

Despite herself, Jane's gaze flashed involuntarily to his crotch.

'Fishing fly,' said Saul, sounding amused. His eyes were curiously expressionless beneath their hoods. 'I'm developing a type of fly which always catches a fish.'

Jane was still not sure if he was teasing her or not.

'The secret,' said Saul, locking her gaze with his own, 'is to attach a female pubic hair to each one.' Embarrassment coursed through her. Ivo, on her other side, was riveted.

'Fish can't resist the female pheromone,' Saul continued. 'And oddly enough, different colours of pubic hair attract different types of fish.' He paused, and raked Jane's fair crown with a meaningful look. 'Salmon, like gentlemen, apparently prefer blondes.'

Ivo sniggered.

Jane became aware that, the other side of Tally, Sholto's interest had now been engaged.

'I say, is that really true?' Sholto asked, his rather Hanoverian, bulging blue eyes protruding even further. His spongy scalp flushed pinker with excitement.

'How very interesting,' Jane muttered, thrusting her fork savagely into the pile of abandoned and cooling artichoke mash.

'Yes, isn't it?' Saul purred. 'I was trying to persuade Champagne that she should mention it in the column, as it must be of interest to a great many readers.'

Something interesting in Champagne's column, thought Jane, would be a first in itself.

'But I understand from Champagne that, how shall I put it, that her column is subject to a certain amount of, er, *censorship*.' Saul gave Jane a dangerous smile.

'You edit Champagne's column rather, er, *enthusiastically*, from what she tells me,' Saul continued glassily.

Jane took an indignant swig. 'What do you mean?'

'I mean,' said Saul softly, his relentless gaze holding her own without blinking, 'that you sometimes even *remove* things she wants to put in.'

'You mean I don't let her plug your flats and gyms the whole time?' Jane snapped, conscious of a churning in her stomach that had nothing to do with the artichokes. 'Well, I'm sorry, but we have a readership to consider. I think they deserve slightly more than just an extended commercial for *your* business interests.'

'Since when did anyone give a toss about the *readers*?' drawled Saul, a sardonic smile playing about his lips. 'There are more important interests to consider. Champagne's, for instance. Not to mention yours.'

'I don't follow,' said Jane.

Saul raised his eyes to heaven and gave her a patronising smile. 'Put it this way,' he said, as if talking to the profoundest idiot. 'I happen to know quite a few things about Champagne.' He pressed his face conspiratorially closer to Jane's. Her nostrils filled with the scent of discreet but expensive aftershave. 'You wouldn't believe what she gets up to in the bedroom, for example,' he whispered. She gazed, fascinated, into his hypnotic eyes. 'Not the sort of things nice girls do at all. I've got photographs, naturally. Think what a shame it would be if they found their way into the, ahem, gutter press.' He paused, and calmly took another sip of wine.

'You *wouldn't*,' stammered Jane. It never occurred to her to doubt that he had the photographs he spoke of. He probably had the soundtrack as well.

'Of *course* not,' Saul smiled. 'Depending, of course, on the sort of, um, *editing* that Champagne's column receives from now on.'

'You mean if I don't plug your businesses you'll give the pictures to the tabloids?'

'I see we understand each other perfectly.' Saul pressed a cool, slim hand on her own hot one.

'What on *earth* are you two whispering about?' boomed Amanda, trying to sound jolly but feeling rather strained. For the past ten minutes she had been struggling with the realisation that Saul Dewsbury had apparently been persuaded to come to dinner to see, of all people, Jane Bentley. '*Do* tell the rest of us,' she shrilled. 'We're dying to know.'

'Oh, nothing,' stammered Jane.

'Change places for pudding, everyone,' ordered Amanda, piling the plates together and cursing under her breath as she remembered too late her recently-acquired new rule that plates should be taken out individually to the kitchen, as stacking them makes it look as if one is not used to having servants.

Saul was now sandwiched between Nicola, who lost no time in berating him about the colour of the towels in his new health club, and Tally, who began to tell Amanda the latest dramas from Mullions. Jane was hugely relieved to escape the Siege Perilous next to Saul and sit herself next to Mark Stackable who, anticipating the Inevitable Question, immediately started explaining in great detail exactly what it was he did at Goldman's. As she listened,

Jane noticed that Saul had stopped listening to Nicola. Much to the latter's annoyance, he was now blatantly eavesdropping on Tally's conversation with Amanda.

'How old did you say your house was, Natalia?' he suddenly asked her. He then launched into so many questions about periods, ageing and background that the place began to sound positively menopausal.

'Is Mullions listed?' he asked Tally lightly.

She shook her head. 'Too run-down and patched up,' she said, 'and we can't get grants to restore anything unless we can raise half the capital ourselves. So selling's the only option, really.' Tally sighed. 'Some more people are coming to look around tomorrow, in fact. Jane's coming up to lend moral support.'

'It's not listed as much as listing,' supplied Jane, who by now had drunk four large glasses of Télégraphe and was feeling wittier than Oscar Wilde. 'I always told Tally it would be the ruin of her.'

Beside her, Mark Stackable sniggered. Jane looked at him in delight. He was young, handsome and no doubt extremely rich. It seemed unbelievable that he had a sense of humour too. Amanda, meanwhile, seemed to have lost hers. She was passing round the petits fours with a face like a cat's bottom. Jane leant towards Stackable trying to expose as much of her cleavage as possible.

'Tell me more about yield curves,' she breathed.

Chapter 11

'So what happened?' asked Tally. 'What did you do after I left?' They were standing in the kitchen at Mullions, which, thanks to the absence of Mrs Ormondroyd and the presence of a number of dusty sunbeams, was looking uncharacteristically cheerful. The light, albeit muted, flooded like headlights on full beam into Jane's leaden eyeballs. It wasn't merely the mother of all hangovers she had. It was the mother-in-law.

'You don't want to know,' said Jane, slumping at the sink. 'Have you any Nurofen?' She wondered miserably if Mullions' plumbing was up to the demands she might be about to make on it.

'But I *do* want to know,' said Tally, gently but insistently. 'You looked near to death when we left this morning and you haven't said a word apart from the occasional "Stop the car, I need to be sick." Now fess up, do.' She placed her mug lightly down on the kitchen table. The noise reverberated round Jane's hypersensitive brain like a thousand slamming doors. She groaned.

'Did anything happen with Mark Stackable?' pursued Tally. 'You were getting on like a house on fire after I left.' She looked hurriedly around at the beamed ceilings and acres of oak kitchen table and quickly touched wood. 'Or perhaps I shouldn't say that. Anyway, you were both shouting your heads off during the Hat Game.'

'What about you and Saul Dewsbury then?' Jane retaliated weakly. 'He gave you a lift back, didn't he?' She must be feeling vaguely better. Until now it had not even occurred to her to wonder what had happened after Tally had taken her flat keys and disappeared with Champagne's saturnine lover.

'Yes, well, I couldn't wait all night for you to leave,' said Tally. 'And Saul drove me to the door. That's all,' she added firmly. There was no question that she wasn't telling the truth. Tally never lied.

'Well, nothing happened with Mark Stackable either,' Jane muttered, pressing her hot hands to her throbbing head. 'At least, not what you think.'

'But you didn't come back to the flat,' Tally murmured. 'I left the window open for you, like you said.'

Jane felt her salivary glands working overtime. Was she about to be sick? And was there a dignified way of telling gentle, strait-laced Tally the ghastly truth? That Mark Stackable had not as much driven but lurched her back to his flat, taken her up into his bedroom and . . .

'Ugh, no, no.' Jane pressed both hands to her temples in an attempt to literally squeeze out what had happened next. Remorselessly, the pictures reeled fuzzily past on the blood-red screen at the back of her eyes. They had even edited themselves down to the most gory bits. The bits where Mark flopped her on to his bed and peeled her clothes off one by one. The bit where he had slowly pushed her legs apart. Then, the crucial moment, the bit where what wasn't supposed to happen had happened. It could not be held back. It had spurted everywhere.

Jane shuddered at the memory. She had practically

exploded. First she had vomited all over *him*. Then all over his extremely smart Liberty waffle-cotton duvet. Then all over his sisal matting, which Jane knew from experience wasn't easy to get normal dust out of, let alone undigested artichoke mash. '*Nothing* happened,' she wailed to Tally. 'I threw up *everywhere*, fell asleep in a stupor and then snuck out and came home before Mark woke up. It was chaster than a night with the Pope.' It was true. A plateful of Amanda's artichoke mash had turned out to be the ultimate in safe sex. I should, Jane thought bitterly, recommend it to Marie Stopes.

'Oh dear,' said Tally sympathetically. Her eyes drifted faintly towards the back of the kitchen. Had she heard a faint thud? She prayed it wasn't Mrs Ormondroyd smashing yet more of the Sèvres. Then she remembered it couldn't be. Mrs Ormondroyd was away for a few days visiting her ailing sister. Briefly Tally's thoughts seized on the idea of Mrs Ormondroyd coming to one's sickbed. 'How ghastly,' she added.

Jane nodded. Still slumped against the sink, she was beginning to grasp the enormity of what she had almost loved and certainly lost. She'd got within a Y-front of a night of wild passion with a glamorous and sexy man and it had all gone more pear-shaped than a skipful of Conferences. She hadn't been in a fit state for a one-night sit, let alone a one-night stand. And there wouldn't be a second chance, as she could never face Mark Stackable ever again. Jane hung her head in self-disgust. The run of bad luck with men that had started with Nick and hit its lowest ever point with Tom showed no sign of ending. She was, and looked set to remain, officially the most hopeless single girl on the planet.

The faint banging sound continued. 'Oh,' said Tally,

light suddenly dawning. 'That must be the managing director of that gourmet sandwich company coming to look at the house. I'd better let him in.'

Jane greeted the news with an unpleasant swirling at the back of her throat and a nauseous lurch in her stomach. She hoped the visitor hadn't brought any of his wares with him.

Several hours later, after poking in every room and cupboard in the house, the captain of the sandwich industry told Tally that Mullions was a tad too small for the global staff incentivisation centre he had in mind. 'On the other hand, "The Mullions" could be a marvellous name for one of our products,' he remarked. 'It could be the flagship sandwich of our new Heritage range. I can see it now, roast pork with apple stuffing in sun-dried aubergine ciabatta with parmeggiano shavings and the merest hint of rocket and pecorino pesto. A real taste of Old England.'

'I'm not sure he was quite the right person,' Tally said after the sandwich Czar had left.

'On the other hand, he certainly wasn't short of bread,' observed Jane.

'Whatever is pecorino?' asked Tally. 'It sounds like a minor Italian painter.'

'Who did you say the next lot were?' Jane asked as a vehicle rounded the last bend and approached the house. Tally peered at the sheet of estate agents' notes on a marble-topped side table in the hall. 'Um, Mr and Mrs Hilton Krankenhaus,' she said. 'Americans,' she added.

'You don't say,' said Jane, as they left the back door and dashed round to the front.

At the foot of the terrace steps, a plush and gleaming hi-tech people carrier was just disgorging its contents. The vast, sports-jacketed man had a head as shiny, pink and moist as boiled ham, whilst at least a third of the height of the fur-swathed, thin-faced woman with him was a mass of sculpted and teased hair. Not so much big hair, thought Jane, as skyscraper. Of a determined auburn, it looked as delicate and brittle as spun sugar.

As they approached, it became obvious that Mrs Krankenhaus's face had more lifts than the Empire State Building. 'She's had so many tucks she probably farts out of the back of her neck,' whispered Jane. Mrs Krankenhaus's skin was stretched as tight as a drum across the bones of her face; it looked as if it would split if she laughed, although judging from her surgically fixed expression, there didn't seem much danger of that. Vast, knotty gold earrings the size of quails' eggs dragged down her wrinked lobes, and her eyes stared out like glass marbles beneath eyebrows that were a perfect, surprised semicircle of bright orange pencil.

The Krankenhauses evidently expected their arrival to be marked at the very least by the appearance of Anthony Hopkins and Emma Thompson in best *Remains of the Day* fashion. They looked at Jane and Tally with undisguised disappointment. Perhaps we should have put on Elizabethan costume, thought Jane. Then I could have looked as ruff as I feel.

'Hello,' said Tally, stepping forward towards the visitors and holding out her hand. 'Natalia Venery. How do you do?'

'Hilton P. Krankenhaus the Third,' bellowed the man, thrusting forward his unpleasantly clammy palm and almost yanking Tally's arm off. 'Well, let's not hang around, let's git going. Ah didn't git where Ah am today hanging around.' Neither Tally nor Jane had the faintest idea where

Hilton P. Krankenhaus had got today. But they guessed they were about to find out.

'Y'heard of Krankenhaus's Catflaps?' Hilton drawled as Tally began to lead him up the Ancestors' staircase. 'Biggest catflap providers in the Yewnited Stites.'

Tally was saved from replying by a commotion at the foot of the stairs.

'Hey! There no elevator here?' shouted Mrs Krankenhaus, wobbling perilously on her high heels as she clung to the newel post.

'Sorry, no,' said Tally.

If Mrs Krankenhaus could have frowned, she would have done so, but the relevant muscles had long since been removed. She hauled herself up the steps one by one, clinging to the banister as she went, with Jane hovering behind in case of disaster. 'These goddam stairs,' cursed Mrs Krankenhaus furiously, an expression of amused surprise fixed permanently on her face. As they passed the Ancestors, Jane felt their painted pupils contract in horror.

'I'm afraid I haven't heard of your catflaps, actually,' said Tally. 'I'm not much of a cat fan, you see,' she added apologetically.

'Doesn't like cats!' Hilton boomed over his shoulder to his wife who, having hauled herself to the top of the stairs, stood there open-mouthed. Not with surprise, however. She was busy checking her lipstick in a clouded, mould-spotted eighteenth-century mirror.

'Can't see a goddam thing in this,' she was muttering to herself, utterly ignoring her husband.

'Well, that's a darn' shame,' Hilton declared to Tally and Jane. 'Cawse the old place would sure liven up with a few moggies around.' Terrifying visions of Ann from *Blissful* and her poorly pussy sprang to Jane's mind.

'This is the Long Gallery,' Tally said, leading the way.

'Uh-huh,' said Krankenhaus noncommittally, casting a cursory glance over the great carved oak double doors that formed the entrance to the passage. Suddenly he stopped and peered at them more closely. Then he slapped his knee. 'Ma!' he exclaimed, sticking his snout-like nose against the wood and beckoning over his wife. 'You'll never guess what these goddam carvings actually say. HK! HK for Hilton Krankenhaus.'

Tally cleared her throat as politely as she could considering the outraged hammering of her heart. 'Actually, it's HK for Henry and Katherine,' she said, rather shrilly. 'Henry the Eighth and his first wife, Katherine of Aragon. The doors were carved for their state visit. In fact, the whole Long Gallery was built for it.'

'King Henry the Eighth of Britain came here?' exclaimed Mrs Krankenhaus, her expressionless marble eyes and immobile forehead belying the amazement in her voice.

'Well, no, as it happens,' Tally confessed. 'He was supposed to, but then the Third Earl, who lived here at the time, caught pneumonia and so the entire royal party went somewhere else. Rather bad luck, actually. But then the Third Earl was known as the Unlucky Earl.'

'I'll say,' said Hilton. 'What a bummer.' He returned to his scrutiny of the carvings. 'These here doors have given me an idea though,' he said to Mrs Krankenhaus. 'Imagine a scaled down, catflap-sized, miniature version of these. In oak. With my initials on them just like this. Classy, huh? They'll go down a storm in the Hamptons. The VIPs'll snap 'em up.'

'Hilton,' said his wife in an irritated voice. 'You know as well as I do that there are no VIPs in the Hamptons.'

'What ya say?' Hilton looked puzzled. It didn't make much sense to Jane either, and Tally had no idea what the Hamptons was.

'There are just Ps, remember?' finished Mrs Krankenhaus magisterially.

Hilton nodded. 'Sure, honey,' he said distractedly, his mind crammed with catflap possibilities. 'Or,' he added excitedly, walking forward into the Long Gallery, 'we could do a catflap that's like a picture, all scaled down in miniature, with a little gold frame round it and all. That miserable son of a bitch over there would do.' He pointed at the age-blackened portrait of a consumptive-looking man in a Regency striped waistcoat.

'That's Lord Vespasian Venery,' said Tally, stung on her ancestor's behalf.

'Yeah, so what's eating him?' asked Krankenhaus, temporarily diverted from the subject of feline exits and entrances.

'Well, he was always rather sickly, and died in a duel in the end,' said Tally, gazing sympathetically into her antecedent's sad eyes with their drooping lids.

'Doesn't look like a fightin' kinda guy to me,' said Krankenhaus dismissively.

'No, he wasn't,' said Tally. 'It wasn't his duel. He stumbled across someone else's by accident. He had very bad eyesight, you see.'

But Krankenhaus wasn't listening. His attention was now fixed on the linenfold oak panelling which ran the length of the Long Gallery. Tally hoped desperately he had noticed the woodworm. Surely he wouldn't buy the place if he had.

'Come to think of it, this old panelling along here would make a great showroom,' Hilton said, gazing speculatively along the length of the dusty, dark wood corridor with his bulging, boiled-egg eyes. 'You could just cut into the sides here and fix the flaps on. It's a sin to waste a great long room like this. Just imagine,' he added, as the idea took hold, 'fifty Krankenhaus Catflaps lined up all the way down this room, from one end to the other, and cats wandering in and out of 'em all, demonstrating 'em, all day long!'

Tally almost doubled over in horror. She looked at Jane in anguish.

'Ah disagree,' declared Mrs Krankenhaus. Tally and Jane looked at her gratefully. 'Ah think we should rip the lot out,' she pronounced, devastatingly, sweeping a bird-like, ring-encrusted hand through the dusty air. 'These filthy old cushions, for a start,' she said, stabbing with a gleaming red talon at a seat which had once supported Charles I.

Jane caught Tally's agonised glance. Desperate measures were needed. She took a deep breath. 'Quick, look,' she gasped, pointing into the gloomy far corner of the hall. 'Did you see it?'

'What? What?' said both the Krankenhauses.

'A mouse?' squealed Mrs Krankenhaus.

'The Queen,' said Jane in a low whisper.

'The Queen of *England*?' said Mrs Krankenhaus, as if she expected to see the familiar grey-haired, bespectacled figure of Elizabeth II trot briskly out of the shadows with her corgis at her heels.

'Queen Katherine of Aragon,' hissed Jane. 'She never got here in life, but . . .' Her voice fell away dramatically. She could not, in fact, think of anything else to say.

'She haunts Mullions,' Tally hastily joined in, knowing full well that the most the house held by way of apparitions was an occasional wailing from the cellar around Christmas which could have been anything from wind to the seasonal village help whom Mrs Ormondroyd didn't get on with.

The Krankenhauses looked doubtful. 'You mean Her Majesty – her ghost – walks here? In this corridor?' stammered Mrs Krankenhaus.

'Yes,' said Tally cheerily, now safely on the home straight.

'With her head tucked underneath her arm, naturally,' chimed in Jane helpfully, remembering too late that, of Henry VIII's wives, Katherine of Aragon was one of the divorced rather than beheaded or died persuasion. The Krankenhauses did not notice but Tally gave her an icy look.

'Well, isn't that kinda cool, though?' asked Hilton, clamping one huge, reassuring pink hand over his wife's tiny wrist. 'Ah mean, what's an old British home without a ghost? You gotta have one, it seems to me.'

Tally looked horrified. Was defeat to be snatched from the jaws of victory?

Jane's brain raced. 'Er, yes,' she ad-libbed heroically. 'But I think you need to think carefully about the *implications*.'

The Krankenhauses looked at her, puzzled.

'The cats,' Jane explained, as inspiration suddenly, brilliantly, struck. 'Animals react very oddly to supernatural phenomena, as I expect you know. Cats are especially terrified . . .'

Five minutes later, the Krankenhauses had gone amid much scrunching of gravel and grinding of gears. Relieved, Tally watched them depart, her long, lean frame slumped against the floor-length hall windows and her lanky shadow thrown back across the black and white tiles by the fading sun. Jane, also gazing out over the park, admired the way the light was so soft and low you could almost see every blade of grass.

'I love this time of the day,' Tally said. 'It's almost the only time when the light doesn't show what a wreck the poor old place is. And it's so quiet. Nothing and no one else around.'

There was silence for a few minutes. The sun sank further behind the conifers at the edge of the park, which stood as upright as a row of feathers. Red Indian feathers, thought Jane, wondering vaguely what Big Horn and Julia were doing. She gazed out into the gathering darkness so hard that her vision began to swim.

'Tally,' she said suddenly. 'You know what you were just saying about nothing or no one else around?'

'Mmm?'

'Well, it's just that . . . I can see someone coming.'

Tally's drooping eyes snapped open. It was true. A figure, just visible in the misty, milky distance at the bottom of the park, was coming slowly towards them up the drive. Fear gripped Jane's heart. Had Katherine of Aragon finally decided to drop in for a fino before dinner? Most terrifying of all, had Hilton P. Krankenhaus III changed his mind?

The apparition did not pause. It kept moving directly towards them. Neither Tally nor Jane dared stir. Their attention was fixed on the approaching figure, as if merely by staring at it they could somehow deflect it. But it was not to be deflected. Across the bridge and over the ha-ha it came. Round the bend and past the rose garden. Up the steps to the terrace. Hearts thundering, Tally and Jane dashed outside to meet it.

As they approached, they saw that the visitor was neither a coachman nor a headless queen. It was a man in modern dress. Very possibly Gucci.

'Good evening,' he said in a light, well-bred voice that nonetheless held a hint of steel in it. He held out a well-manicured hand to Tally. 'Saul Dewsbury. We met last night.'

Tally flushed. 'Yes, of course.'

'Lovely to see you again,' said Saul, nodding to Jane. His stark impeccability contrasted profoundly with the rioting decadence around him. Absolutely every hair was in place. Even his eyebrows looked groomed. 'It completely slipped my mind last night that I would be in this area on business today,' he said. 'It seemed rude not to drop in. From what you said I thought Mullions would be very beautiful, but it's even lovelier than I expected.' He looked fixedly at Tally as he spoke. To Jane's mixed horror and disgust, Tally actually blushed.

'How is Champagne?' Jane asked pointedly.

'Champagne is very well, thank you,' Saul replied. Jane looked fiercely at Tally to make sure she was taking this in. 'At least, she was the last time I saw her. You see our relationship, unfortunately, is over. As of this morning, in fact.'

Jane stared. Over? So suddenly? She gazed at Saul, who looked back at her boldly, one eyebrow inquiringly raised as if daring her to ask why. Champagne had seemed *terribly* keen on him. Was it possible he had finished with *her*? Could it be that for the first time in her life, Champagne was the dumpee, rather than the dumper?

'Look, I realise it's getting late,' Saul said, giving Tally another of his melting looks, 'but I wonder whether it might be at all possible to see round Mullions. I'd love to see inside what is obviously an exceptional sixteenth-century manor house.'

And could it possibly be, thought Jane, her head buzzing with more wild surmise than Cortes's men in Darien, that Saul had dumped Champagne because of Tally? Throwing over the famous and beautiful Champagne D'Vyne for the plain, flat-chested, decidedly eccentric-looking Tally seemed rather unlikely, admittedly, but what else was he doing here? She didn't believe for a minute his claim to be here on business. Whatever was going on? She had no idea but she knew she didn't like it.

'Oh, yes, of course, I'd love to show you round,' said Tally, beaming at Saul. 'I'd be delighted to. And you must stay and have some supper. Jane's just about to go back to London for work tomorrow, you see, so I'd be glad of the company.'

'No, no, I'm in no hurry,' said Jane, stretching her eyes warningly at Tally. 'I can stay for a while.' Until Saul Dewsbury is safely out of the place, she added to herself.

'You'll need to set off now to miss the Sunday night traffic,' urged Saul. Jane flashed him a furious look. 'Don't worry,' he added, giving her his most charming smile. 'I'll look after Natalia.'

Jane seethed. 'Well, if you're sure?' She made a final, direct appeal to Tally, who nodded and smiled reassuringly.

'I'll be fine,' she said eagerly.

She can't wait to get rid of me too, thought Jane miserably. Barely twenty-four hours after meeting Saul, she's completely under his spell.

Jane felt uneasy all the way back to London and not merely because the 2CV's petrol gauge had rocketed into the red zone. The image of Saul standing proprietorially with Tally on the terrace alternated with last night's ghastly scenes at Mark Stackable's flat. Damn Amanda. If she hadn't insisted on annexing Mark all the way through dinner, Jane would have established that he was single some considerable time before she was two gins and tonics, a bottle and a half of wine and three ports the worse for wear. At that randy, fuzzy-headed stage even Sholto was beginning to look promising, so Mark's whispered revelation during the coffee that he was still looking for the girl of his dreams had naturally had an electric effect.

Jane had accepted his offer of a lift home with alacrity and, after ten minutes' exposure to the low, thrilling purr of his Porsche Carrera, had jumped at the chance to come up and admire the mosaics in his bathroom. His flat had been extremely glamorous, Jane remembered dimly. It had been more of a loft, with a very fast lift that opened straight into the sitting room. Or perhaps that was just how it had felt.

Jane groaned. The whole ghastly, embarrassing experience could not have been more different than her night with Tom. She sighed, as she always did, at the thought of her by now completely imaginary-seeming lover, so utterly without a trace had he vanished. Recently, she'd even tried tracking him down through his work – if she found his publisher, she thought, then surely she could get his address. She had combed the shelves of every bookshop she came across for writers called Tom, and scoured their book jackets in the hope there might be a photograph of him. There wasn't.

Tom knew where *she* was, of course. But he thought she was living with her long-term boyfriend. Jane's heart sank as she pulled up outside the dingy Clapham flat.

Sliding her key into the lock, Jane felt more of a sense of doom than usual. For starters, some thrash metal band seemed to be playing loud and live directly above her sitting room. Damn Jarvis, she thought, coughing so loudly it hurt her throat, in the hope he would hear her and turn it down. He didn't.

In the corner, the answering machine was winking like a lecher with a twitch. Someone had been leaving a lot of messages. Jane's heart sank as the first one crackled on. It was Champagne.

'Help me. Oh God, help me.' Jane froze to the spot. The familiar, patrician tones sounded weak and desperate. Racking sobs boomed out of the machine's microphone, followed by several loud sniffs and choking coughs. 'Help me. For fuck's sake,' gasped Champagne, 'get over here, quick.' The suspicion that it might be another nail crisis crossed Jane's mind. Failing that, too deep a fake tan? A botched bikini line? On the other hand, did Champagne's desperate state have anything to do with the fact that the relationship with Saul Dewsbury was apparently over and he seemed to be quite happy about it?

The agonised sobs started again. The situation did not sound promising. Jane checked the time the last message was taken – fifteen minutes before. She picked up the phone, called 999 to give them Champagne's address and rushed back out to her car.

Chapter 12

It was not, Jane thought, exactly unusual to see Champagne in the arms of a muscular man. The difference this time was that the man was a paramedic. Draped helplessly across his broad, green boiler-suited chest, Champagne's tiny frame looked infinitely fragile and vulnerable.

'Na, 's all right. She don't weigh *nothing*,' said the paramedic, refusing offers of help from his colleagues. As he lowered Champagne on to the stretcher in the columned entrance hall, Jane felt tears prick the back of her eyes. Her throat ached from suppressed weeping. Champagne, admittedly, had had her irritating side, but not even her worst enemy would have wished her to die like this.

Champagne's head lolled back as the burly paramedic settled her body carefully on the stretcher. He pressed a freckled hand over Champagne's breast and began pumping her chest. Then he gave her mouth-to-mouth resuscitation. Watching his capable, businesslike actions, Jane reflected sadly how having one hand clamped on Champagne's bosom while their lips were locked on hers had once been the stuff of most men's fantasies. It didn't look like a dream come true from where she was standing.

'Well, you called us just in time, love,' said the paramedic, finally seizing the end of the stretcher and preparing to shift Champagne into the ambulance outside. 'Another ten minutes and I reckon she'd have been a goner.'

'You mean she isn't?' asked Jane, who had been convinced she was looking her last on her one-time tormentor. As relief swept over her, she realised how numb she had been feeling before.

'Well, she's taken a massive overdose, but if we get her stomach pumped in time, there may be a chance.' The paramedic looked up at Jane without smiling. 'Well, better get 'er down to A and E. Coming? You 'er next of kin?'

'Er, no,' said Jane, flattered despite the circumstances that anyone could think she and Champagne were related. But then again, looking at Champagne's exhausted, bruised and make-up-less face, perhaps it wasn't such a compliment. 'I'll follow in the car,' she said.

As the ambulance wailed off through the square, Jane did an automatic tour of the flat to make sure doors and windows were shut against burglars. Stooping to check that the curling tongs on the floor beneath the hall mirror were turned off, it struck Jane that any activity in the interests of Champagne's safety should be filed, at least for the moment, under Stable Door, Late Closing Of.

In the stuffy, airless bedroom, the entire contents of Champagne's wardrobe lay scattered about, although whether this was evidence of recent turbulence or Champagne's usual idea of orderliness, Jane could not be sure. Jimmy Choo shoes lay caught in Agent Provocateur underwear; Chanel suits were heaped upon piles of screwed-up pashminas. Selina Blow had fallen, Blow on Blow, and a rainbow tide of shoes ebbed and flowed around the edges of the pile. *Anyone who says money can't buy happiness doesn't know where to shop*, read an embroidered cushion lying amid the unmade bed. It sounded a hollow assertion now. As if in confirmation, a Coutts chequebook lay open on the floor, empty apart from the unfilled-in stubs.

A high-pitched squeaking noise was coming from the unhooked telephone which lay across the bed. Jane softly replaced it. As she did so, her eye was caught by the empty bottle of Krug which had rolled into the corner, its last drops soaking into the carpet. Beside it, a battered childhood teddy bear stood drunkenly on its head. An image of the laughing, blonde, pampered child Champagne had once been flashed before Jane's eyes. How sad that all that had come to all this. And how much sadder, Jane thought, that Champagne apparently had had no one to ask for help apart from herself. If, when in extremis, the only person the It Girl could turn to was the Shit Girl, things had come to a pretty pass. And not a celebrity backstage one at that.

Sitting in the hospital waiting room, Jane tried not to stare at the array of oddly-twisted limbs, bleeding heads and hanging-off fingernails hoping to be treated this side of Christmas. She buried herself instead in a creased and greasy issue of the local freesheet whose main source of stories seemed to be the local police station. Accordingly, the editorial consisted almost entirely of reports of attacks on pensioners, murders, robberies and fights, and did not make for particularly cheerful reading. Looking again at her companions in the waiting room, some of whom seemed to have clashed with something big and angry, Jane realised that she was probably getting a preview of what would be in next week's edition.

When she was finally ushered in to see Champagne, hidden behind bilious green screens in a narrow hospital bed, Jane stifled a gasp. Champagne looked dreadful. Seen in the harsh light of a hospital ward, the emerald eyes looked sunk and defeated and the famous six-seater lips were no more than a camp stool. The even more celebrated breasts looked saggy and deflated, apparently incapable of filling a trainer bra.

'Hello,' Jane whispered as the doctor pushed the screens back together behind her. There didn't seem much point asking Champagne how she was. Jane had often seen Champagne with a drip on her arm, but had never before seen her with one in it.

Champagne opened her eyes and looked straight into Jane's. There was, Jane was relieved to see, a hint of the old boldness there, but something else besides, almost anger, as if Champagne had finally come to realise what a sham her life was and how short-changed she had been by glamour and fame. Their relationship was going to be interesting from now on. Jane tried to imagine life with a chastened Champagne being grateful to her for saving, as she almost certainly had done, her life.

'What the *fuck* took you so long?' rasped out Champagne suddenly. The voice may have been weaker, but its imperiousness was not diminished one jot. Jane almost jumped a foot in the air with shock. It's the drugs talking, she told herself. Whatever were they pumping into her?

'Well, they kept me in the waiting room,' faltered Jane, surprised. 'It took a long time to get whatever it was out of you, the doctor told me. You could have died, you know.'

'Almost bloody did, thanks to you,' Champagne barked. 'Rang you hours ago, but you didn't bother to turn up until I'd practically snuffed it.'

'I don't understand,' Jane stammered. 'You tried to kill yourself. I saved your life. It's not me you should be blaming, it's that bastard Saul Dewsbury. He's the one who dumped you. He's the one who brought you to this.' She was, she knew, jumping to conclusions. But what other explanation was there?

It was Champagne's turn to look amazed. 'Kill myself?' she echoed. '*Him* dump *me*? You must be joking. I dumped *him*. Yesterday morning, in fact.'

'Dumped *him*?' stammered Jane, struggling to comprehend. Her head was already spinning with lack of sleep and the pitiless strip lighting. So Dewsbury had been lying.

'Too right I dumped him,' rasped Champagne, rolling her eyes. 'He's been boring the arse off me with his ghastly yawnsville businesses for weeks now. I'm sick of the sight of him. Anyway, I found out he hasn't any money. In debt up to his eyeballs. Especially now he's been running *me* for a month.' Her cackling laugh dissolved into a hacking cough.

'So why did you take an overdose? I don't understand.' Jane stared at her.

'For Christ's sake, you don't think I took those pills because of *Saul*, do you?' Champagne looked incredulous. 'They were *sleeping pills*,' she snarled. 'It's an exhausting business, being me, you know. I'm worked into the ground and I need my eight hours' beauty sleep. How the hell was I supposed to know how many pills you should take?'

'How many *did* you take?'

'No idea. Loads, I suppose. Just kept stuffing them in until I felt sleepy. But then I started to feel a bit weird so I rang you.'

Jane stared at the chipped vinyl floor. To think she had actually imagined, even for a second, that Champagne had any capacity for despair, any self-knowledge whatsoever. She should have known. The only deep thing about Champagne was her cleavage.

'But now you mention it,' said Jane, 'why did you ring *me*? There must be lots of other people you, er,' she groped for a phrase, 'um, know better.'

'Oh, yah, quite,' said Champagne airily. 'Stacks. Loads, in fact.' She looked calmly back at Jane.

'So why didn't you tell *them*?'

'I can't *believe* you're asking me this,' Champagne spluttered. 'Surely you don't think I'm stupid enough to risk anyone I know *socially* seeing me zonked out of my head? I didn't even have any *make-up* on. I'd never get asked anywhere again.' She shot Jane a withering look. 'I couldn't have called them anyway,' she added. 'Everyone I know goes out in the evenings. Apart from you.'

'I see,' said Jane, getting to her feet before the urge to pull the drip out of Champagne's arm overwhelmed her. 'I'm afraid I have to leave now,' she muttered.

'Oh, well, thanks for dropping by,' said Champagne sarcastically. 'Eventually,' she added.

'Yes, well, I'll try and be earlier next time,' said Jane with suppressed fury, trying not to think of the wasted six, no, seven hours she had just spent in the hospital and for which she would pay dearly at work tomorrow. Later today, in fact.

'I'll talk to you later this week,' Champagne said airily, by way of farewell. Insulting Jane seemed to have done her the world of good. 'Lots to report. New man, for a start. Met him last night. Footballer, Welsh international who plays for Chelsea. Thighs so huge he can't cross his legs.'

Champagne looked pointedly at Jane's far from perfect thighs.

Outside, Jane leaned briefly against the wall and took a deep, shuddering breath before attempting to find her way back down the maze of corridors to the exit. Blundering amid the blinding brightness of the shining vinyl floors, she became dimly aware of a voice calling, 'Excuse me.'

She turned. It was the weary-looking, clipboard-laden houseman who had taken her to Champagne's bed.

'Don't worry, she's going to be fine,' he assured her. 'She'll be out in a few days. She's recovering very well, and should be back to normal in no time.'

'Wonderful,' said Jane dully.

Saul, thought Tally, was a revelation. A miracle, no less. Holed up in her remote, crumbling manor house, she had, after the succession of disastrous would-be buyers, almost given up on ever being rescued. She had started to feel like Tennyson's Mariana of the Moated Grange. Marry Anyone of the Moated Grange, come to that.

What was most gratifying was how much Saul seemed to appreciate the house. 'This place is just *wonderful*,' he said as Tally started her tour. He clasped his hands and gazed around, shaking his head slowly in apparent amazement. 'It has such history. Such atmosphere.'

Such bloody *potential*, he thought to himself, keeping his eyes downcast to disguise their avaricious shine. He'd had a feeling about this place as soon as Tally had started to talk about it at the dinner party. And what a bonus that had been. He'd gone to Amanda's to warn that uppity bitch Jane to stop cutting him out of Champagne's columns, and come away with an entree into the best deal of his life. Which was just as well considering Champagne had dumped him the next morning. But, if he was honest, that had been something of a relief.

What a lucky dog I am, he reflected gleefully. To lose one golden goose might be seen as careless, but to find another within twenty-four hours was damn near miraculous. And what a golden egg Mullions was. Once you knocked the whole pile down and built a commuter estate in its place, of course. There were *bazillions* to be made here. But he had to be careful. Tally was obviously obsessed with the old heap. Softly softly catchee bulldozer, Saul warned himself, his head bubbling with plans.

'It has such atmosphere,' he repeated, pacing slowly round the drawing room, unable to think of what else to say. If he meant to be convincing, he'd have to work on his architectural vocabulary. Tally would probably prefer he admired her corbels to her cheekbones. He stolc a quick glance at her. Not that she had very good ones. Her face was thin and concave, rather like the reflection in a spoon.

'You mean it's freezing and it smells of mildew,' Tally grinned, self-deprecatingly. But she thrilled inside. Saul's interest was a pleasant and profound contrast to the Krankenhauses, the sandwich king, and most of all Champagne D'Vyne. Not to mention the fact he seemed, well, almost *interested* in her. She shrank from the full beam of his gaze.

Saul smiled at her with something approaching lust in his eyes. Tally really was a gorgeous sight. An estate worth several million standing before him in a baggy sweatshirt and the worst haircut he had ever seen. And, even better, showing signs of being mightily taken with *him*.

'Natalia . . .' he said.

'Call me Tally.' Her eyes shone and a blush rose from

her neck to her forehead. It did not suit her, Saul thought.

'May I look in here?' he asked, approaching the doorway of the Green Drawing Room and almost cringing with veneration for Tally's benefit. He stared, with every appearance of utter fascination, at the portrait of the Second Lord Venery as a be-ruffed, brocaded child. 'Such a noble face,' he said in fascinated tones. 'Even at that age. Such breeding.'

'I think it was more a case of such bleeding,' Tally replied, ecstatic at the intensity of his interest. 'He was a very unhappy child. Got the strap a lot from his father.'

'Oh, a belted earl,' said Saul, grinning at her in the semi-darkness. Tally started, then giggled nervously, and proceeded to lead him from treasure to treasure. 'Miraculous,' declared Saul, apparently almost asphyxiated with admiration on being shown the decorative ostrich egg Queen Victoria had given to the Fifth Earl. What really struck him as miraculous, however, was the fact that Tally was still alive after having breathed in the dank and dusty atmosphere of the house for twenty-odd years. It was incredible she hadn't died of consumption. On the other hand, she wore a lot of clothes. All of them at once, by the look of it. Pretty odd-looking, as well, with that funny snub nose. Still, ugly girls were always easy. They were so grateful.

And Tally *was* grateful. She was thrilled to have someone in the house so interested in simply *everything*. Saul had even been fascinated by the large pieces of lava on the downstairs corridor floor brought back by the Fourth Earl from Pompeii. 'Hot stuff,' he had said wittily, trying to disguise his disappointment that the rocks on the carpet were not, as he had thought, bits of the house that had already fallen down.

'Splendid,' he had said, feeling a piece of brocaded curtain dissolve in his hands at the precise moment Tally invited his admiration of the Eighth Earl's stuffed bustards. It was more than splendid. The place was even closer to collapse than it looked. Some of the wooden floors were so soggy and worm-eaten they were practically sponges. He probably wouldn't even need to bring in the bulldozers. Just leaning vigorously against one of the doorframes should bring the whole place crashing down.

His stomach surged with excitement. If he could pull this off, it would be the biggest success of his life. He looked speculatively at Tally's layers of sweaters. He needed to pull *those* off, too. If he could make Tally fall in love with him, and even better, marry him, things could really start moving. Big metal things, with cranes and drills attached.

'Oh dear,' Saul suddenly announced as they mounted the staircase under the baleful eye of the Ancestors. 'I've been so fascinated by everything you've shown me that it's *far* too late to drive back to London.' He was speaking nothing less than the truth. He had been *enchanted* by the disastrous state of the house. And Tally had been even more of a pushover than he had hoped. He still needed to push her over *properly*, however. 'I would just *adore*,' said Saul, his eyes fixed meltingly on her, 'to see the Elizabethan Bedroom.'

'Oh, yes, of course,' said Tally, wondering vaguely where Saul might sleep. Beds as most people understood them hadn't been much in favour at Mullions lately. Her own tiny single bed which she had had since childhood was about the only serviceable one left. Tally doubted Saul would want to curl up in Julia's smelly old bearskins, still less spend the small hours standing in the garden as Big

Horn had sometimes done. His idea of a good evening out, Tally supposed. But not everyone's.

She stopped short halfway down the Long Gallery. 'Here's one of our finest tapestries,' she said proudly, gesturing at a murky piece of cloth upon which Saul could discern practically nothing. 'Made to celebrate the wedding of the Fourth Earl and Countess. It depicts the legend of Jonah and the Whale.'

'Jonah and the Whale, eh?' smiled Saul. A mischievous glint stole into his eye. 'Not very flattering for the poor old Countess,' he remarked. 'Large lady, was she?'

Tally turned a horrified glance on him. Briefly, Saul felt his fate hang in the balance. He had dared to make light of the Mullions heirlooms. Then Tally's face split into a smile. 'You *are* dreadful,' she said and led the way onwards.

They reached the Elizabethan Bedroom door. Tally pushed but the door resisted.

'Here, let me,' said Saul, applying himself to the unrelenting oak, which immediately relented to such an extent that the door flew open and they both shot across the polished floor, narrowly avoiding a skirmish with a Georgian washstand.

'Wonderful,' said Saul, picking himself up and gazing upon the house's greatest treasure. The extent of the moth damage on the counterpane's embroidery made his heart sing. The heavy, carved bedposts were obviously as humming with woodworm as they were cavorting with semi-naked gods and goddesses, and his cup ran over when the electricity suddenly cut out. Tally fumblingly lit a candle whose flame sent Saul's profile, his nose curved and lengthened, jerking devilishly across the cracked, white-washed walls of the room. He turned to look at her, his eyes gleaming. 'You're gorgeous,' he said, addressing not

Tally but what he had by now estimated as the ten thousand acres of prime building land she represented.

Tally glanced demurely at the polished floorboards and shivered. Less from the cold than the excitement of being completely alone in the proximity of a bed with the handsomest man she had ever seen in her life. And who had just told her she was gorgeous into the bargain. Her heart thumped and her throat felt dry in profound contrast to the distinctly moist feeling in her gusset.

'I want you,' said Saul, urgently, to the rolling, curving acres of the Mullions estate standing before him in human form. A slow smile spread across his face and his eyes glowed as he looked deeply and (quite literally) speculatively into Tally's. Surrender, he saw, was written there in capital letters. 'I'm desperate for you,' he told her passionately.

Chapter 13

'Out of hospital and flat on her back again, I see,' said Josh fondly, holding up the centre spread of the *Sun*. Under the headline 'SEE NIPPLES AND DAI' was a huge picture of a scantily-dressed Champagne with her new football star boyfriend. ' "Dancing the night away in a skimpy gold bikini top and matching hot pants",' he quoted.

'Ooh, lovely,' said Valentine. 'And what was Champagne wearing?'

Jane pointedly said nothing. She was sick of Josh, sick of Valentine, sick of the job. Most of all, she was sick of Champagne. Once out of hospital, Champagne had lost no time telling every tabloid editor who would listen about the exhausting, stressful pressures of fame that had led to her near-fatal encounter with sleeping pills. Sympathetic spreads about burn-out syndrome had resulted, along with fact boxes covering everything you needed to know about insomnia.

Insomnia, Jane snorted to herself. It was the first time she had heard staying up all night at Tramp and the Met Bar count as inability to sleep.

Since their encounter in the hospital ward, Jane had been unable even to look at a photograph of

Champagne without foaming at the mouth. To be told that the person whose life you had saved was not only ungrateful but had actually hand-picked you to do it on the grounds that you were their social inferior was more than infuriating. It was devastating. Jane's self-esteem was currently lower than absolute zero.

Her telephone rang. 'Be quick with that,' Josh rapped out. 'We need to have a features meeting. Everything you've suggested to go in next month is rubbish.'

Jane thrust her middle finger up half-heartedly in the direction of her boss's temporarily turned back and picked up the receiver. 'Is this Jane Bentley?' asked a peremptory cut-glass voice, but one which didn't, mercifully, belong to Champagne.

'Victoria Cavendish here. I'm the editor of *Fabulous*, as you probably know.' Jane did know. Everyone knew. Victoria Cavendish had been around long enough to qualify for fully paid-up legend status. She had edited *Fabulous*, *Gorgeous*'s direct rival, for years, and was supposed to be every bit as shrewd and ambitious as Josh. She was also supposed to be the sort of editor who wouldn't even share a lift with you if you were wearing the wrong length of hemline that season. Rumours about her abounded. Whiplash thin, she reportedly existed on one rocket leaf a day, bathed in Badoit and sent her daughter's school clothes to be unpicked and recut by the Chanel atelier. She had, it was said, once resigned from a job because her office, while vast, was half a centimetre smaller than that of another of the company's editors. Size was also an issue when it came to Victoria's staff, some of whom, it was whispered, had been sacked for the ultimate crime of Putting On Weight. If true, Jane thought, it was certainly the most literal interpretation of gross misconduct she had ever come across.

'I'll come straight to the point,' said Victoria briskly. 'I'm looking for a deputy editor. I've heard great things about you and I wondered if you might be interested.'

Jane's eyes bulged. Interested? She was *fascinated*. 'Well, it certainly sounds like a strong possibility,' she said neutrally, conscious that Josh, who had a sixth sense where phone calls were concerned, was listening through his open office door with his ears out on stalks.

'Well, we'd better meet up then,' said Victoria briskly. 'Tonight? The Ritz? Seven?'

'Fine,' said Jane, echoing Victoria's monosyllabic style. She put the phone down with as much nonchalance as she could muster.

'So good of you to make it,' said Josh as Jane came into his office and sat down next to Valentine. 'Now, to work. We've got to get more celebrities in the magazine. Any ideas?' He looked round hawkishly.

Jane and Valentine shuffled uncomfortably, caught out again by Josh's favourite trick of calling meetings without notice when only he had had time to prepare for them.

'Well, fortunately, I've had one,' sighed Josh martyrishly. 'It's called Namesakes. We ask George Bush what his favourite bush is, Michael Fish what his favourite fish is, Mike Flowers what his favourite flowers are . . . geddit? Any other ideas?'

Jane blinked. 'You are joking?' she said. 'I thought we were supposed to be a sophisticated magazine.'

Josh raised an eyebrow. 'I happen to think it's a rather good idea,' he said, in a tone that brooked no argument.

'OK, how about asking Jean-Marie Le Pen what his favourite pen is?' said Valentine, the faintest trace of weariness in his voice. 'Sir Peter Hall his favourite hall? John Major and his favourite major?'

'Damon Hill and his favourite hill?' said Jane, reluctantly getting her brain into gear. 'Jon Finch and his favourite finch? Oliver Stone and his favourite stone? Joan Rivers and her favourite rivers?'

'Excellent,' said Josh. 'Now off you go and ring them all up.'

Jane looked hard at the clock, as if she could force it by sheer effort of will to move round to seven and her meeting with Victoria. It seemed too good to be true. Was she really being offered an opportunity not only to escape from Josh but also from Champagne?

'Right, fire away,' barked Champagne when Jane picked up her ringing telephone several seconds later.

'Sorry?' asked Jane.

'Ask me questions, so you, um, I can write the column,' shouted Champagne. 'I'm back with a bang and raring to go.'

'You've made a lightning recovery,' Jane told her.

'Yes, well, I've had my inner labia pierced,' yelled Champagne. 'That sorted me out, I can tell you.'

'Ugh, how awful,' grimaced Jane. 'Did you sit on something sharp?'

'Course I bloody didn't,' boomed Champagne. 'Cost me a bloody fortune. My acupuncturist did it.'

'Acupuncture!' exclaimed Jane. 'That's not acupuncture. That's S and M. Why on earth did you do it?'

'Labias are the bit where all your stresses gather,' Champagne informed her with exaggerated patience. 'Apparently it's the ultimate place to be pricked. As it were. Ha ha ha.' The receiver exploded with her window-shattering laugh.

Jane stared dully into space. George Bush and his favourite bush paled into insignificance as she realised that she was spending hours of her life transcribing, nay, *inventing*, the thoughts of a woman who paid large amounts of money to be stabbed in the front bottom.

Meeting the editor of a glossy magazine in The Ritz was definitely Jane's idea of journalism. Even if the editor had not yet arrived. Pastel satin sofas and low-slung chairs lurked invitingly in gilded corners. A pianist tinkled soothingly in the background, while penguin-suited waiters glided smoothly about bearing trays of champagne and bowls of fat nuts.

Refusing all offers of refreshment – she didn't want to commit herself to a mineral water and have Victoria roll up and order a champagne cocktail – Jane fished in her bag for the virgin copy of *Hello!* that lurked in its depths. She waded greedily through the glossy pages, wallowing in the usual smorgasbord of washed-up rock stars in stonewashed jeans, lovely homes with a firm emphasis on leopardskin, face-lifted film stars flogging autobiographies and, Jane's personal favourite, Euro-royal gatherings featuring dresses apparently designed by people who had heard about clothes but never actually seen them. Grinning to herself, Jane turned the page. Her good mood evaporated instantly as her eyes fell on a large photograph of Champagne and her latest lover gurning at the camera from the frilled and flower-printed depths of a large four-poster bed. 'Britain's Most Famous Party Girl Talks Frankly About Fame After Her Recent Illness And Introduces Us To The New Man In Her Life' ran the big red and white headline. Jane hesitated. She knew reading on could seriously damage her mental health. But she couldn't help herself.

Champagne, you're a model, TV personality and, most famously, a writer. How do you fit so many things into your life?
I'm fantastically well-organised, basically. And very self-disciplined. The early bird catches the modelling contracts, after all.
You're obviously ambitious. What drives you?
A chauffeur, mostly. Ha ha ha. No, but seriously, I love working. I have a very strong work ethic.
Champagne, what is the secret of succeeding in so many different areas?
Sheer perfectionism, I think. I also make it an absolute rule to be pleasant, patient and punctual at all times.

Jane gasped and stretched her eyes.

Your life seems very glamorous. Endless parties and celebrity premieres. Is it as glittering as it looks?
Not at all. Making small talk with famous people is completely exhausting, and I'd like to see the average builder manage five hours a night in my Gucci stilettos.
Did all this have anything to do with your recent illness?
Yes. I was burnt out, basically. People just don't realise the hard, hard work that goes into being a star. They think they'd like my money and fame but they wouldn't last two minutes with my timetable. Most of the time, it's unbelievable.

Unbelievable was the word. And two minutes, thought

Jane, was about the longest Champagne spent on any item on her timetable.

Champagne, you have achieved so many things. Is there any ambition you would still like to fulfil?
I would love to be appreciated for my writing. Not for who I am. And I would love to develop my film and TV career. This morning, for example, I visited a beekeeper for a guest slot on a nature programme. It was amazing. So many bees. I told him I couldn't imagine how he remembered all their names. I would also love to do some charity work. I'm looking into doing something for the Centreparks charity for the homeless, taking over where the Princess of Wales, God rest her, left off.
Finally, Champagne, could we ask you about your relationship with Dai Rhys?
Dai is the first man in my life I would seriously consider settling down with. He's so supportive and, being so well-known himself, he completely understands the enormous pressures of fame and the endless demands.

Tell me about the endless demands, thought Jane sourly.

Are you a football fan?
I wasn't, but I am now. Dai's explained so much about it. I even understand the offshore rule – very important when you earn as much as Dai does.
Do you prefer rich men?
I really don't care about money. Love is the most important thing to me. If Dai hadn't a penny in the world I'd still adore him.

Jane snorted so loudly that a couple of elderly duchesses on the next sofa almost dropped their glasses of sherry. They glared over their bifocals at her in fury.

Are wedding bells in the air?
Marriage is certainly on the cards.

You bet, thought Jane. Dai's credit cards.

Would you have a traditional wedding?
Yes. With my darling little pet poodle Gucci as Best Dog, of course.

Jane could read no more. As there was still no sign of Victoria, she decided to head for the loos. That would also get her out of the way of the hovering waiters. They probably think I'm a prostitute, she told herself, before realising that the prostitutes on this particular patch were probably better dressed than she was.

In the powder room, Jane stared at herself in the mirror, looking miserably at her shiny nose and forehead. Her crimson jersey brought out the red of her eyes beautifully.

When Jane returned to the lounge, a woman with a helmet of black hair, a slash of red lipstick and spike heels was occupying a minuscule area of one of the sofas. Jane had seen enough pictures of the *Fabulous* editor to know who it was. The woman was talking urgently into a mobile phone. Or was she? As Jane approached, she realised there was a mirror glued to the inside of the mouthpiece flap. Victoria Cavendish was evidently checking her lipstick the executive way.

'Hi,' said Victoria, holding out a cool hand clanking with rings. 'Two champagne cocktails, please,' she added, waving imperiously at a passing waiter. Jane felt relieved. At first glance, Victoria had looked dangerously like the skinny, self-denying sort whose idea of a racy drink was Badoit and Evian in the same glass.

Although probably in her mid-forties, Victoria had the figure and, perhaps less advisably, the clothes of someone half her age. That someone, however, was not Jane. Victoria's sharp suede jacket and matching miniskirt were far snappier and more costly than anything she had in her own wardrobe. Round Victoria's neck was a soft brown shawl, which Jane recognised as one of the wildly expensive kind which were, as far as she could remember, made from the beard hairs of rare Tibetan goats. Victoria's, of course, was probably made from the facial hair of the Dalai Lama himself.

Jane crouched on the edge of the seat, crossing her legs to minimise the spread of her flanks and wishing she had remembered to clean her shoes. Come to that, she wished she had had her hair cut, lost a stone and spent a day in Bond Street in the company of a personal shopper and an Amex card.

'Well, as you know, I need a deputy,' said Victoria, lighting a menthol cigarette with a lipstick-shaped lighter. She crossed her bird-like black legs, the razor sharp heels just missing her bony ankles. Jane shivered. There was more than a touch of the Rosa Klebb about all this.

'You're very highly recommended,' said Victoria. 'Apparently you handle contributors very well and I particularly need someone I can trust with a very high-profile new writer we have coming on board.' A thrill ran through Jane. A famous writer. How wonderful.

'Who is it?' she asked.

'Can't tell you, I'm afraid, until you're all signed up,'

said Victoria, taking another swig from her champagne glass. 'But someone who will hopefully send our circulation into the stratosphere.'

Martin Amis? wondered Jane. Iris Murdoch? She thrilled at the thought of day-to-day contact with a proper author. 'Sounds wonderful,' she said, reaching for her own glass, then realising it was empty. As was the dish of nuts. Jane realised she had shovelled in the lot in her excitement.

'So I take it you're interested,' said Victoria, clicking her metallic blue-tipped fingers for the bill.

Jane nodded. 'Yes please.'

'Good. I'll bang you a contract over tomorrow.' Victoria levered herself upright. 'Must run now,' she said, which struck Jane as no less than fighting talk, given her footwear. 'I'll be in touch tomorrow.' She shimmered away across the carpet in a cloud of the sort of delicious perfume Jane instinctively knew one didn't buy in Boots.

Jane wandered slowly out of the hotel and along the darkening street back towards the Tube station. The 2CV, which had not worked for several days now, lay languishing by the Clapham roadside waiting to be put out of its misery. It probably would not live to see another MOT. The potholes of Mullions had seen to that.

It was flattering though odd, Jane thought, as she wandered absently down the stairs into Green Park Tube, to be suddenly so much in demand. Odd, too, that Victoria Cavendish should be eager to sign her up without so much as asking for her opinion of *Fabulous*, let alone without a CV, references and especially without the reams of sparkling features ideas invariably demanded on these occasions and never referred to thereafter. Especially as Victoria, if rumour was to be believed, had her own special methods of selection.

Candidates for employment were, so it was said, generally invited to lunch with her so she could observe their table manners and satisfy herself that they didn't cut their salad with a knife or belong to what she designated the HKLP (Holds Knife Like Pen) brigade. Victoria, reportedly also used these occasions to ensure that any of her would-be co-workers were not prone to the verbal social *faux pas* that would condemn them without trial into what she called the PLT (Pardon, Lounge, Toilet) category. Jane could believe it all. Victoria, as was well known, was completely unrepentant about both her magazine and the social aspirations it enshrined. 'Snobbery,' she was often quoted as saying, 'is merely an acute awareness of the niceties of social distinction.'

Even candidates who scraped through Victoria's restaurant tests were far from home and dry. They still risked one of the editor's celebrated spot checks in which she had a member of staff call the would-be employee's parents' home (the number, with address, was demanded on the *Fabulous* application form) to make sure that the person answering had a suitably patrician tone of voice. By these combined methods any social chameleons of humble origin were prevented from getting their plebeian feet under *Fabulous* desks. Some, it was said, were filtered out right at the beginning of the process simply by Victoria's casting an eye over the parental address. If it was a number rather than a name, the letters were filed straight in the bin, a process which had always struck Jane as somewhat unreliable, ruling out as it did any members of the Prime Minister's family, for starters.

Yes, it was certainly strange that none of the usual hurdles had been placed before her, thought Jane now, crossing the dirty platform to her Northern Line connection at Stockwell. Especially as she was not at all sure she could have jumped over any of them. The word 'toilet' had certainly passed her lips from time to time, and she had yet to see anyone, herself included, eat a Caesar salad without resorting to a blade of some sort. And, although thinner than she used to be, she was certainly not racehorse skinny.

There was, however, one highly plausible explanation for Victoria's keenness to get her on board, one quite detached from all the flattery about her superior editing skills. Josh. All being fair in love and circulation wars, it was entirely within the rules of the game for Victoria and her rival to poach as many members of each other's staff as possible. Bagging as key a person as the *Gorgeous* features editor was certainly a feather in the *Fabulous* editor's cap, and would be even if Jane's parents had lived at 13 Railway Cuttings and she ate her salad in the lounge with a saw held like a Biro.

The contract duly arrived next day. As Jane had expected, Josh affected utter insouciance when she handed in her notice. His casual acceptance, however, lost some of its conviction after Valentine spotted him half an hour later smoking furiously in one of the stairwells.

Yet Jane's bombshell was short-lived in its effects. Midway through the afternoon it was superseded by a bigger bang altogether – Valentine's news that Champagne was leaving Dai Rhys the footballer. He had overheard it being discussed at a neighbouring table at San Lorenzo that lunchtime.

'Surely not,' said Jane. 'She's just been all over *Hello!*. All over him.'

Valentine raised an eyebrow. 'Well, she's given him the

red card now. Brought on a substitute.'

'But who?' asked Jane, faintly surprised at Valentine's apparently sound grasp of the argot of the terraces. 'Who could possibly be left?'

'Remember when she did the National Lottery draw a few weeks ago?' asked Valentine.

Jane shuddered. The memory of Champagne in a pink sequinned dress struggling before an audience of millions over a task as simple as selecting a set of numbered ping pong balls was still fresh. 'Mmm?' she said, wondering where this was leading.

'That young unemployed scaffolder from Sheffield won it. Wayne Mucklethwaite, wasn't he called? Biggest Lottery winner ever?'

'Ah, yes,' said Jane, light dawning. 'I think I see what you're getting at.'

At least, she thought, she would no longer be around to chronicle the inevitable demise of that relationship as well. Which reminded her. Champagne had not yet been told she was leaving. No point putting off the blissful moment, Jane decided, picking up the receiver.

She almost sang her news when Champagne answered. In reply there was a sharp gasp at the other end, followed by another, and another. 'Uh, uh, uh,' went Champagne. Jane's stomach contracted with concern. Was Champagne having a seizure with the shock of it? Or had she caught her *in flagrante* again? Jane listened carefully. Limited though her experience was, it didn't sound orgasmic to her.

'Champagne? Are you all right?' she asked, feeling vaguely guilty. Was Champagne, after all, capable of human feeling? Was she finally realising how much she depended on Jane?

'Uh, uh, uh,' went the dreadful, rasping gasps. 'Yah, I'm, uh, uh, fine. On the, uh, uh, Stairmaster, actually. I'm in the, uh, uh, gym. Leaving, are you? Oh well, good luck.'

And that, it seemed, was that. No 'Thank you for all you've done'. It would, Jane thought, have been unbelievable, had it not been so eminently believable.

'Um, well, good luck to you too. I, um, hope it works out with Wayne,' Jane said.

'Oh, yah. Absolute sweetie,' said Champagne smugly. '*So* generous. Just bought me a necklace with the most *humungous* diamond in it. I suppose I do rather deserve it though. After all, I *did* pick his balls on *National Lottery Live*.'

Chapter 14

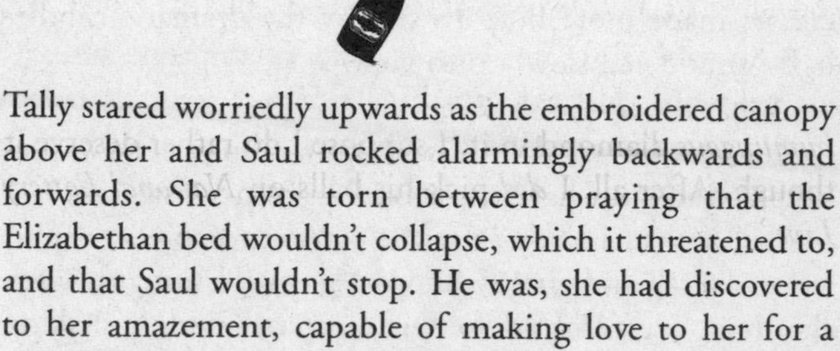

Tally stared worriedly upwards as the embroidered canopy above her and Saul rocked alarmingly backwards and forwards. She was torn between praying that the Elizabethan bed wouldn't collapse, which it threatened to, and that Saul wouldn't stop. He was, she had discovered to her amazement, capable of making love to her for a whole hour, which was exactly fifty-seven minutes longer than anyone else had ever managed.

And that, Saul realised, about to collapse himself from exhaustion, had clearly been quite some time ago. Even Champagne hadn't required so much servicing. He should have known. The quiet ones were always the worst.

His spine felt twisted beyond repair from the lumpy old mattress of the Elizabethan bed. 'But Elizabeth the First slept in it,' Tally had told him indignantly when he had suggested it was less than comfortable. No wonder she was called the Virgin Queen, then, it was on the tip of Saul's tongue to say.

'You're amazing,' he panted to Tally. 'I want to marry you. Now.' He was speaking no less than the truth

A loud, sudden knock on the heavy oak bedroom door pre-empted Tally's reply. Saul's face dropped in shock. There had been no one in the house except Tally since he first came here, well over a week ago now.

Drained of all colour, every hair on his body erect, Saul clung to Tally in terror. As he watched, rigid with fright, the door creaked open and light from a guttering flame shone into the room, sending the shaking shadow of a bent and fearsome-looking creature wobbling terrifyingly across the walls. Saul gibbered hysterically as a huge and brutish face, its brilliant eyes shining and its lines and creases made more hideous still by the dramatic candle-light, shuddered slowly into view.

'What's *that*?' he shrieked.

'It's Mrs Ormondroyd,' said Tally calmly. 'The house-keeper. She must have come back from her sister's.'

Saul looked in horror at the fearsome expression plus nylon overall and ghastly lumpy legs now issuing through the door. He fumbled for his cigarettes with a shaking hand.

'Dinner's in an hour, Miss Natalia. Oh.' Mrs Ormondroyd's gimlet eye alighted on Tally, sitting up in bed with the sheets pulled over her breasts, and Saul, who wasn't making much effort to conceal anything. 'Didn't realise you had comp'ny. Very sorry, I'm sure.' She couldn't, Saul thought, have sounded more disgusted if she had discovered Tally in bed with her father, her brother and a couple of Alsatians.

Dinner was, for Saul at least, a revelation. He poked uncertainly at the rapidly-cooling surface of what looked like a chop. He tried to cut it, only to find that it was so well done you practically wanted to give it a round of applause. Saul frowned. He hated overcooked meat. He much preferred it bleeding. Badly injured, at the very least.

'What's the matter?' asked Tally, discerning his disgrunt-led face through the gloaming of the freezing dining room.

'It's cold,' Saul said. He had to shout it twice before she heard him at the other end of the refectory table. Saul realised in a flash why so much of the aristocracy had loud voices. Conversation in places like this would otherwise have been impossible.

Tally sighed. It was too much effort to explain that food always arrived cold in the dining room. The distance between it and the kitchen, not to mention the icy blasts encountered in the various corridors en route, meant that only the hardiest of dishes arrived at the table in a vaguely eatable condition. Over the centuries, the Venery cooks had refined their menus by a process of trial and error (which was certainly how those eating them saw them) down to the few items that could cope best with the adverse conditions. Those dishes were but two: the Brown Windsor that had already featured on tonight's menu, and which Saul had instantly christened Primordial Soup. The other was the cutlets he was staring at now.

Saul gazed down at the meat, an island surrounded by a sea of thick, greasy slop. The plate hardly set the ensemble off to best effect, being made of what looked like tarnished tin. Saul pushed it away, noticing as he did so some marks and scratches on its rim. He screwed up his eyes to examine them in the gloom. 'Tally,' he asked, 'are these plates solid silver?'

'Yes,' Tally called back. 'Mrs Ormondroyd's smashed all the Sèvres now, and this is all we have left. Even she can't manage to destroy metal, although I daresay she's made a few dents.'

Saul raised his eyebrows and took a sip of wine. It really was remarkably good. He groped towards the bottle and read the label. 'But this is Margaux nineteen forty-five!' he shouted in amazement.

'Oh dear, I am sorry,' yelled Tally. 'It's just that I can't afford to send Mrs Ormondroyd to the Threshers in Lower Bulge any more. I told her we should economise and see if there was anything left in the cellar. There are quite a few bottles down there, she says, so I suppose she can use it to cook with if it's too horrible to drink. It might help her cutlets.'

The only thing that would put Mrs Ormondroyd's cutlets out of their misery, thought Saul, was a controlled explosion. 'No, no, no need to do that,' he said hurriedly, thinking of the excitement an influx of fifty-year-old Bordeaux would make on the London wine markets. And the profit he could make out of it. 'I'll get rid of it for you,' he assured Tally. 'No problem.' She beamed at him gratefully.

Later, shivering by a sickly fire in the Blue Drawing Room over the mugs of thin, tepid Nescafe grudgingly produced by Mrs Ormondroyd, Saul returned once again to the attack. 'We could do such wonderful things here together once we were married,' he urged, trying not to stammer with the cold and clasping both her chill hands in his. Tally hesitated. It wasn't that she had any particular objections to rushing headlong into matrimony with someone she had hardly met. Her ancestors, after all, had done it for generations; the Fourth Earl, for example, had married a Somerset heiress to whom he had been introduced only once before, in the cradle. But there *was* something she wanted to know first.

'What happened with you and Champagne D'Vyne?' Tally asked, screwing her courage to the sticking place. 'Weren't you quite keen on her?' Tally was desperate to be reassured that Saul was not still in love with the bird-brained philistine who had been so rude about Mullions, still less the glamorous, blonde, and beautiful party-girl-about-town whom, if Jane was to be believed, every man in the universe lusted after.

Saul took another deep drag on his cigarette. It was true that on paper his liaison with Champagne had been an ambitious entrepreneur's dream come true. Yet he had soon discovered that the cost of running her far outstripped any business benefits she might bring. Incidents such as being made to book an entire suite at the Savoy because she wanted a room service club sandwich hadn't helped. Nor had the time she demanded a Jacuzzi full of champagne because of all the extra bubbles.

Saul shuddered as the memories crowded in. Not to put too fine a point on it, going out with Champagne D'Vyne was one of the worst experiences of his life. She had been the most unstimulating woman he had ever met, which was odd when you considered she wanted seeing to at least three times a night. Then there had been her dreadful, loud, spoilt, braying voice. The people in the flat above had banged on the ceiling merely when he played back her answerphone messages.

'Um, it just wasn't to be,' he muttered eventually to Tally, not sure he wanted to relive the trauma by putting the details into words. 'We weren't quite, um, suited,' he added. 'She was a bloody nightmare,' he said finally.

'Was she *really* that bad?' sighed Tally, blissfully, thinking that Jane, who had frequently uttered those very same words, had more in common with Saul than she realised. 'I don't know her at all, you see.'

'Obviously you never read her column,' said Saul bitterly, 'otherwise you'd know everything about her including the colour of her knickers. When she bothered to wear them, that is.'

'No, I never read any of them,' confessed Tally,

wondering what it would be like to wear no knickers. Nothing short of dangerous in the winter at Mullions, she imagined. Mrs Ormondroyd, she knew, always wore at least four pairs in January. 'I don't buy magazines,' she added. She didn't admit that the real reason Mullions no longer subscribed to any publications was the cost. And the fact that she had hated to see the Lower Bulge newsagent's tiny, spindly son struggle the mile up the winding Mullions drive, his fragile old bicycle visibly sagging beneath the weight of all the papers and magazines Julia had once taken. 'So I'm afraid I haven't the faintest idea of what's going on anywhere.'

'In that case,' said Saul, dropping a kiss on her head, 'I think you and I are going to get on just fine.'

Suddenly, the telephone shrilled outside in the gloom of the passage.

'I think it might be for me,' Saul said, leaping up to answer it. 'I've got a couple of deals on the boil at the moment.'

'Who was it?' asked Tally, when he returned a few minutes later. 'One of your deals?'

Saul shook his head. 'Wrong number.'

In Clapham, Jane put the phone down in astonishment. Saul Dewsbury was *still* there. And what did he mean Tally couldn't come to the phone because she was having a shower? The only showers at Mullions were those that appeared unexpectedly through the ceilings during thunderstorms. Still, if Tally was having a fling with Dewsbury, on her own head be it. She had made her four-poster and now she could lie on it, Jane decided. She had more than enough to think about. Such as how to lose a stone overnight before she began her new job at *Fabulous* tomorrow.

Chapter 15

Beautiful, lissom girls with long blonde hair crowded the foyer of the *Fabulous* offices. Uncomfortably stuffed into her first-day-smart clothes, Jane's heart sank as she realised that everyone else was at least two sizes smaller than she was. And they all looked exactly the same, which was to say, different from her. Not only did they have identical clothes – tiny white T-shirts revealing brown navels, skinny black trousers and high-heeled boots – they had symmetrical features too. Waiting for the lifts, Jane decided, was like standing in the middle of an exceptionally glamorous multiple birth, twenty-two years on.

Everyone had a tan, a delicious little nose, cheekbones higher than the Andes, glossy hair and pert little breasts. They all wore minimal make-up and that type of dark nail polish that made their fingers look as if they had been trapped in the door. Talk about a clone zone, Jane thought. The people who thought Dolly the sheep was such a breakthrough should have come here first, where it had all obviously been going on for years.

There must be, Jane supposed as she entered the lift, an appearance-improving machine somewhere in the building, probably up by the managing director's office. She imagined it to be called the Glamourtron, a tall silver cylinder with sliding doors. It was here that Personnel summoned one on arrival, and into here one stepped, grey-thighed, mottled of face, split of end, stained of teeth, bloodshot of eye and bulging of waistline. One would stay inside the cylinder for ten minutes (possibly longer in extreme cases; Personnel to decide). There would be a mild humming and then the doors would spring back. Out one would step, tanned, blonde and glossy-haired, with a delicious nose, pert chest, and cheekbones as high as the Andes. Dressed in tiny white T-shirt, skinny black trousers and trapped-in-door nails. Jane felt excitement rise within her. Would Personnel call her today?

The lift finally arrived at the *Fabulous* floor and out Jane stepped, her nostrils filled with the same delicious perfume absolutely everyone seemed to be wearing, and entered the *Fabulous* offices. As at *Gorgeous*, about a third of the space was devoted to the large glass box denoting editor territory. Victoria's photographs, Jane could see through the windows, were blown up even bigger than Josh's. Victoria with Princess Diana, with Cherie Blair, with Karl Lagerfeld, with John Galliano, with Donatella Versace.

Jane wondered when Victoria herself would put in an appearance. Or, for that matter, when anybody would. The office was empty. Jane busied herself in the familiar task of flicking through the papers, in which, as usual, Champagne and her lottery winner received radioactive publicity.

Today's shots showed Champagne and Wayne Mucklethwaite, the richest 24-year-old man in Britain, almost invisible under designer carriers in Bond Street. Talk about label dame *sans merci*, thought Jane, making out bags from Chanel and La Perla that could hardly have been intended for Wayne. Relief that her days of dealing with Champagne were at an end flooded through her. The thought of never hearing those arrogant, barking tones again was nothing less than utter bliss.

'Hello,' said someone. A gangly girl with big eyes, a short, lacy skirt and long blonde hair had appeared in the office. 'I'm Tish. Victoria's secretary. You must be Jane.' Jane nodded, feeling suddenly self-conscious as the rest of the staff finally started to trickle in. 'I'll introduce you to everyone, shall I?' offered Tish helpfully.

Just then, an extremely thin man with an extremely flat bottom came mincing into the office in a pair of extremely clean white trousers. His frail build looked incapable of supporting his vast black sunglasses, let alone the two huge and clinking bags of duty-free swaying from each beringed and wrinkled hand.

'Should keep me going until lunchtime,' he remarked, crashing the bags theatrically into the middle of his desk.

'That's Larry, the travel editor,' said Tish. 'He's just got back from holiday,' she added, rather unnecessarily.

'And who's this?' Jane asked as a glamorous older woman with violent purple lipstick, white cropped hair and a pair of extremely tight cream leather trousers made her entrance.

'Oonagh, the picture editor,' supplied Tish. 'She and Larry are a brilliant double act. Just watch them.'

'How are you, dear one?' cried Larry to Oonagh. 'Well, I hope.'

'Ghastly, actually,' replied Oonagh, checking her reflection in a black Chanel compact. 'My husband actually wanted to have sex with me last night. Can you imagine?'

Larry shuddered. 'Not with *your* husband, darling.'

'Precisely,' said Oonagh. '*Such* a drag.' She snapped

shut the compact. 'Still, no *visible* damage. Anyway, how were the Bahamas, darling? Just beyond blissful?'

'Oh, beyond, beyond,' trilled Larry. 'Except that I nearly had a *very* nasty accident. I was putting on my bathers and there was a scorpion lurking in my crotch. Can you imagine?'

'Well, frankly, darling, I'd think yourself lucky,' sighed Oonagh. 'Nothing's lurked in my crotch for years. Apart from my wretched husband, that is. Right, now I need to talk to Jeffrey Archer, darling, *urgimento*. Any ideas how I can get hold of him?'

'Oh, just lean out of the window and shout, I should think,' replied Larry.

Jane's attention was distracted from this fascinating exchange by the arrival of four girls who immediately went into a huddle over the newspaper horoscopes.

'No *way*!' the tall, chestnut-haired one in the centre exclaimed dramatically. 'I just can't *believe* what he's said about my star sign. It's just, like, *uncanny*. He says I'm struggling with an impossible dilemma. So true. I've been invited to a fancy dress party on Friday and I can't decide whether to go as Sharon Stone or Grace Kelly.' She closed her eyes and shook her head in amazement at the perspicacity of the astrologer. '*Unbelievable*. I simply can't work out whether I'm more *Basic Instinct* than *Rear Window*, do you know what I mean?'

Jane gazed at her discreetly. Rear End was nearer the truth. There seemed little outward resemblance between the ice-blonde, stick-thin Princess of Monaco and this frankly rather buxom brunette, but Jane was not going to jump to conclusions. *Fabulous*, even more than *Gorgeous*, was famous for its wealth of well-connected employees. The brunette was probably a duchess at least. The only comfort was that she plainly hadn't been to the Glamourtron either.

'That's Tash,' whispered Tish. 'She's the drinks party editor.'

'What about me?' exclaimed a thin blonde. 'I've been asked to go to Woggle Wykeham's tonight to play Boggle, as well as being invited for drinks at Minkie Rochester's.'

'That's Tosh,' whispered Tish. 'She's the weddings editor.'

'So you can't decide between Boggle at Woggle's or drinkies at Minkie's?' asked Tash.

'Yah, 'xactly,' said Tosh.

Jane cast eagerly about for any handsome men. There were none. Nor were there, as far as she could see, any men at all, apart from Larry, who hardly counted. Her heart sank. The office had the atmosphere of a girls' boarding school dormitory. She never thought that she would miss Valentine and Josh, but . . .

A few minutes later, a throwing open of doors and rustle of bags announced Victoria's arrival. She marched in frowning, distracted and impeccable, swinging a tiny handbag violently back and forth. Behind her staggered Tish under a heap of boxes, bags, newspapers and dry-cleaning. Victoria didn't need a secretary, Jane decided. She needed a Sherpa. Nodding frostily in Jane's direction, Victoria stalked into her office and slammed the double doors.

It was hardly an effusive welcome. Inside the huge glass box, Victoria was gesturing dramatically, the phone glued to her ear.

'Who is Victoria talking to?' Jane whispered to Tish. The important new writer, perhaps. Or Archie Fitzherbert, the magazine company's dynamic-sounding managing director who, so rumour had it, was reasonably young, reasonably charming and reasonably presentable. He sounded, thought Jane, distinctly promising. 'It seems to be someone terribly important.'

'It is,' said Tish, pushing her bottom lip out as she tried to choose from among the myriad bottles of nail varnish on her desk. They were, Jane noticed, the only bottles there. Tippex, or anything else one might expect secretaries to need in the normal run of events, was noticeably absent from Tish's desk. There were no staplers, no letter-headed paper, no pens. There was a Sellotape dispenser, but it was innocent of Sellotape. With its lipstick, mirrors and nail varnish, Tish's desk bore more resemblance to a dressing table than anything appertaining to a professional amanuensis. 'Victoria's calling the agency for a new nanny for her children,' said Tish breezily. 'She often does on a Monday. They tend to leave over the weekend, for some reason.'

The novelty value of hearing people saying '*Fabulous*' instead of 'Hello, *Gorgeous*' when they answered the telephone was already starting to grate. Jane was dreading the moment when her phone rang and she had to say it herself. It wasn't long in coming.

'Hi there,' honked horribly familiar tones.

'Champagne, hello,' said Jane, vaguely touched that her old adversary was bothering to call her in her new place of work. 'How are you?'

'Pretty bloody chuffed with myself,' yelled Champagne. 'Just signed the Superbra contract. Half a million notes for lying around on a beach in my underwear. They're going to shoot the ads in the South of France. Talk about Monte Carlo or bust. Haw haw haw. God, I'm funny. But it's bloody annoying to think I've been doing it for free all these years at Cap Ferrat.'

'Well, that's wonderful,' said Jane briskly. 'I'm really very glad for you, Champagne.' After all, she told herself, she could afford to be generous now.

'Yah, bloody marvellous, isn't it? I'll be on massive billboards all over the country,' honked Champagne. 'And all over the back of buses. I'll look like the back end of a bus. Har har har!'

'Marvellous,' said Jane. 'I *am* glad you're doing so well,' she added through gritted teeth. 'It's lovely to hear from you but I've got to go now.' Victoria had finally detached the telephone from her ear and was gesturing at her to come in. 'I have a meeting with the editor.'

'Haven't finished yet,' Champagne shouted imperiously. 'Wayne and I have just got back from the new villa in Marbella, the one I helped him buy.'

'Is it nice?' asked Jane, making coming-soon movements to Victoria.

'Fabulous. Three swimming pools and ten bedrooms, one with a two-way mirror so you can spy on the guests. Hilarious. My idea. Love to know what other people are doing in bed. Staff are morons though. No one speaks a word of bloody English.'

'Really? Oh dear.'

'Yah. Bloody nightmare, basically. *And* I've gone and lost the yellow sapphire ring Wayne gave me. He'll go ballistic if he finds out.'

'Oh dear,' said Jane, with exaggerated patience. 'What a shame.' *Get off the phone*, she thought, furiously.

'But I've thought of a brilliant way round it,' Champagne continued mercilessly. 'I'm going to claim it on my car insurance. All I have to do is blow up my Lamborghini and pretend it was in there.'

'But didn't he give you that as well?' asked Jane, incredulous.

'Oh. Yah. Think you're right there,' bawled Champagne. 'I'd forgotten that, actually. Oh well. You are writing all this down, aren't you?' she added suspiciously.

'Writing it down? But why should I? I've moved magazines, you know,' Jane said as gently as she could. 'I'm working for *Fabulous* now.' Champagne was obviously in denial. How sad. And yet, in a way, how touching as well.

'Yah, I know you are,' Champagne yelled. 'So am I.'

'Oh, I *thought* you'd be thrilled,' beamed Victoria as Jane rushed, panic-stricken, into her office. 'Seemed such an obvious thing for *Fabulous* to do. Champagne's exactly the same age and background as our ideal reader, as well as being *slightly* more famous and glamorous. She should send our circulation rocketing. Not to mention,' she added, almost as an incidental, gazing complacently at her perfect nails, 'being a death blow to *Gorgeous*.'

'But why didn't you tell me?' stammered Jane.

'No point until everything was signed and sealed,' said Victoria, silkily. She grinned. 'I was going to just now, but Champagne beat me to it. But I *knew* you'd be thrilled. Champagne never stops telling me how *brilliantly* you get on together. But we couldn't let you in on our little secret because Champagne, bless her, was *terrified* that wily boss of yours would suspect we were after you and try to stop it.'

'Champagne was?' asked Jane, stunned. 'But why? You mean she *knew* you had approached me?'

'Knew? My dear, she was the only reason I *did*,' said Victoria, smiling incredulously. 'She made it a *condition* of her coming here that *you* would edit her copy. You know how temperamental these famous writers are. Most of them hardly need *anything* doing to their work at all, but they think they can't do anything without their dear old editor.' Victoria smiled pityingly.

The photograph-crammed walls of Victoria's office began to spin round Jane. A cold sweat broke out on her forehead. So Victoria hadn't approached her for her legendary editing skills at all. She had recruited her solely at the whim of Champagne who had been cunning enough to see that her lucrative new contract would be of very short duration once Victoria realised how poor her raw copy was. Not only that, Champagne had persuaded Victoria to keep her own move to *Fabulous* a secret from Jane.

The extent to which she had been outmanoeuvred sank in. Champagne had succeeded in making her her pawn, dependent on her for her job. The roles had been reversed. Jane saw with awful clarity that she was far worse off than she had ever been at *Gorgeous*. She was now utterly in Champagne's power.

'It's marvellous,' Victoria said, dimpling and beaming at Jane as she sipped a cup of black coffee. 'Champagne's first job for us will be to cover the New York fashion shows next week. Should be quite a read!'

Jane felt the soles of her feet fizz with envy. Champagne, doing the fashion shows. Crammed between the stars and the fashionably starving in a little gold front-row chair, watching as Naomi and Kate sashayed languidly by in a variety of unfeasible outfits. Rushing from one show to anothe rin a whirl of limos; drinking in gossip and cocktails at the post-show parties. Jane longed with all her soul to go.

'I see,' she said dully to Victoria, forcing the corners of her mouth up into a semblance of a smile and trying to sound enthusiastic. 'Well, it should be quite a read, as you say.' If only she could go as well, Jane wailed inside because there were no prizes for guessing who would write the reports in the end. And the expense of sending Champagne to New York would be phenomenal. Even Josh, who had given her a Bentley and a chauffeur without a second thought, would never have gone this far. Jane wondered what personal transport arrangements *Fabulous* had offered Champagne. A Learjet, probably.

'Features meeting!' Victoria suddenly shouted through the open doors of her glass box. 'May as well see what rubbish this lot have come up with for the next issue,' she added *sotto voce* and with a conspiratorial wink to Jane as Tish, Tosh, Tash and co. filed in. 'Thank goodness we have Champagne's column, at least.'

Thank goodness, thought Jane, sourly, noticing, as she took her seat, that another man besides Larry had appeared. He had, Jane noted with interest, undeniably film-star looks. With his thin, pale hair, long nose, little round rimless glasses and quivering chin, he reminded Jane irresistibly of Charles Hawtrey. He was, it appeared, one of *Fabulous*'s freelance contributors.

'Right, let's get started,' rapped out Victoria, revolving in her executive swivel chair with a pen between her teeth. 'We need more *Fabulous* people, *Fabulous* homes and *Fabulous* lifestyles for the next issue. In particular, we need someone *Fabulous* for the cover. A real star. Any suggestions?'

'What about Lily Eyre?' ventured Jane. 'Up and coming actress. Going to be huge. Apparently Hollywood wanted her for *Full: Throttle* with Schwarzenegger, but she turned it down because she wants to do small, quality British films. I thought she sounded quite interesting.'

It was evident from the silence around her that nobody else did. Victoria looked as if she hadn't heard.

'Ugh, not her,' said Oonagh at length from the back of the room. 'Dreadful common ankles.'

Jane looked blank. What on earth was Oonagh talking about?

'Oh yes,' continued Oonagh. 'It's an absolute fact. Upper-class women have thin, elegant, bony ankles while lower-class women have big, thick, shapeless ones. You can always tell.'

'Any other ideas?' asked Victoria.

Lily Eyre, Jane realised, had been consigned to the dustbin. She felt uneasy, unable to understand why there wasn't a chorus of approval. Josh had been after Lily Eyre for months. She was not only an interview-shy rising star, in itself enough to make her intensely sought-after, but one with that delicate English pink-and-blonde prettiness beloved of upmarket glossy magazine editors. She was, in short, textbook-perfect cover material.

Charles Hawtrey suddenly roused himself. 'Well, what I'd certainly like to know,' he piped up in a high-pitched, reedy voice, his fists clenched in his lap, 'is where one can get a jolly good spanking these days.' A sudden, violent convulsion shook his weedy frame. He had, Jane realised, quite a bad twitch.

Victoria raised her eyebrows. Jane stifled a giggle.

'Apparently,' Hawtrey squeaked, by now purple-faced with exertion and indignation, 'there's hardly a single school in the country where they still have cold baths and corporal punishment. Now it's all warm beds and TLC. I've been to several dinner parties recently where people have been complaining about it. The fathers, in particular, are all furious. They don't see why their sons should have an easier time at school than they did. And speaking personally,' Hawtrey stammered, as a series of twitches threatened practically to throw him off his seat, 'it didn't do me any harm.'

'Well, there *has* been a certain amount of anti-bullying legislation passed,' ventured Jane.

Hawtrey shot her a withering look. 'I'm aware of that,' he spluttered, as another twitch convulsed him. 'What I'm saying is that it takes a magazine like ours to stand up and say that there shouldn't have been. We built an Empire on being flogged senseless by the Upper Sixth. We must campaign,' he said, now jerking up and down like a bucking Bronco, 'to bring back Matrons with warts and being chased around the quad by the randy Latin master.'

'No, surely not,' said Victoria, much to Jane's relief. 'Latin's a dead language. Being chased by the randy French master, perhaps. That's much better. It's a seriously brilliant idea, Tarquin. Make a great think piece. Look into it, will you?' She gazed sternly round the room again. 'Well, that sorts out our *Fabulous* Dinner Party Debate for this month. But we still need our *Fabulous* Lifestyle. Someone very rich and glamorous, preferably.'

'But weren't we doing that piece about that very beautiful actress, Sonia Svank, going back and discovering her family castle in Lithuania?' asked Larry. 'I thought that sounded marvellous.'

'It would have been, had the castle not subsequently been turned into a rustic hospital,' retorted Victoria. 'When the photographer turned up, there was a Lithuanian farmer having boils removed from his willy. *And* it was tiny.'

'Well, size isn't everything, you know,' smirked Larry.

'I'm talking about Sonia's *castle*,' snapped Victoria. 'In other words, I don't think she had one.'

'But that's impossible,' said Tash wonderingly. '*Everyone* has a castle somewhere.'

'Look,' said Victoria, looking determinedly at her watch, 'I was due at the Caprice ten minutes ago. Everyone keep thinking about the cover interview. And keep an eye out for possibles at the Movers and Shakers party on Friday.'

Friday was four days away. 'Movers and Shakers party?' Jane asked Tish after Victoria had flounced out of the office.

'Mmm. *Fabulous* does it every year,' said Tish nonchalantly. 'It's a publicity thing really. We invite all the most happening people in London to a party and drown them in poo.'

'Poo?' stammered Jane, wondering why she had never heard of this extraordinary event before.

'Shampoo,' said Tish, looking at her in astonishment. '*Champagne*, in other words.'

Jane blushed deeply. She clearly needed a crash course in upmarket rhyming slang. Despite her embarrassment, a spasm of excitement gripped her intestines. A party full of happening people, some of whom had to be single and some of whom might even be men. So there was at least one advantage to this new job. 'It sounds wonderful,' Jane breathed, thinking excitedly that she could smuggle Tally in too. Then she remembered Saul Dewsbury and scowled.

'Yah, last year Bonkers Brixham was snogging Bruiser Baddeley-Byng for hours,' supplied Tash, overhearing their conversation. This intelligence left Jane none the wiser as to who was the female half. If either.

* * *

'Darling, must you wear that skirt *again*?'

Tally, buttoning her faithful old Black Watch tartan over two pairs of long johns and her grandfather's First World War army fatigues, turned in surprise to see Saul watching her from the bed.

'You have superb legs,' he said. 'Such a shame to keep your tights under a bushel.' It was true, he thought. Tally did have nice legs. But that was about the size of it. After the Himalayas of Champagne's exuberant physique, the foothills of Tally had been a comedown in every sense of the word. But there were compensations. Saul was not a religious man, but he still sent out a prayer of thanks for his deliverance every morning he woke gibbering to find his recurring nightmare was just a nightmare. He was not, after all, trapped with Champagne and a stream of deafening anecdotes in a taxi from London to Paris where she leapt out and left him with the fare. After Champagne's extravagance, it was refreshing to find that Tally's idea of luxury was a new bar of soap, a fire that managed a flicker and lights that did not fuse once all evening.

Saul, however, found it rather more convenient if they did. Under cover of darkness, he could turn on all sorts of useful little taps to do some nifty bits of damaging flooding here and there to speed up the decaying process, although rather irritatingly someone – he suspected Mrs Ormondroyd – usually managed to turn them off before too much damage was done. He was sure she was spying on him. He had come across her unexpectedly twice yesterday, once when he was gazing with admiration on the work of a particularly vicious and destructive colony of deathwatch beetles and again when he was staring speculatively at a fine Tudor fireplace in one of the upstairs bedrooms. She had looked at him long and suspiciously.

She had had good reason. Saul had recently bought a share in an architectural salvage company and Mrs Ormondroyd caught him in the act of calculating how much his target customer, an Islington film producer, would pay to install the Red Bedroom fireplace in his weekend home near Southwold. The less worm-eaten sections of the panelling in the Long Gallery would certainly be received gladly into one of Fulham's larger bathrooms and Saul had instantly earmarked the Jacobean staircase as a centrepiece for a second gym he was planning to open. Mullions' huge cast-iron baths, meanwhile, which probably hadn't been full or hot during the reign of the present Queen, were sought after for Georgian townhouses from Hackney to Harlesden. As for the pestles, mortars, toffee hammers, bone-handled knives and chopping boards scattered about the kitchen, there wasn't a theme pub in the country that wouldn't rush to stick them up on its wall for period atmosphere. The house's eponymous mullioned window frames, equally, would fit seamlessly and extremely profitably into the footballers' mansions currently being flung up the length and breadth of Cheshire.

Tally's breath, Saul noticed now, was clearly visible in the freezing air. It was little wonder they spent so much time in bed. Buried several feet beneath blankets and sheets was the only warm place in the house, and even then Saul half expected to wake up and find some of his frostbitten toes lying on the floor. It was like *Dr Zhivago*, he decided. Only Tally looked slightly less like Julie Christie than he himself looked like Omar Sharif.

Much as he dreaded flinging back the sheets and exposing his warm flesh to the cold, Saul knew he had to scowl and bare it. He had things to do, after all. Today he planned to walk the estate and make a rough calculation of the maximum number of houses that could be crammed on the site. And there were other decisions to make too. Herringbone or straight brickwork driveways? Cul de sacs or ovals? Video entryphones or traditional enamel bells? Fitted kitchens or freestanding units? The penthouses, he had already decided, would have their own private roof terraces, but there was still the parking to think about. Would he really be able to drain the oxbow lake and build an underground multi-storey as he planned? There were a few more calls to make about the financial backing as well. And, of course, he still had work to do on Tally. He was within an ace of getting her up the aisle, he knew. But victory was not yet his. Tally hadn't quite given in.

He leapt off the bed and felt the usual twinge in his spinal column as he went striding, naked, over the splinter-ridden floorboards to kiss Tally. As the morning sun, struggling through the dusty diamond-paned windows, gilded his tautly-muscled body and haloed his tousled black hair, her heart did a forward roll.

'Don't you think it's too cold in the house to wear short skirts?' she asked.

'Well, that's one very good reason why we have to start thinking about ways to get the place warm again,' said Saul briskly, pulling his damp and chilly shirt over his head and belting his trousers round his trim waist.

He was aware that the log supply was running low, but he was damned if he was going to chop any himself. He'd sooner put the furniture on the fire; in fact he would, without a second thought, had not the oak refectory table had Hampstead basement kitchen written all over it. He'd get a fortune for that. Saul was confident a similar dazzling future awaited the pair of fine Jacobean chairs that had somehow escaped the attentions of the woodworm. Perhaps they were saving them for dessert.

Mrs Ormondroyd could get the logs, he decided. She looked as if she could fell entire forests before breakfast. Oh, for a few creature comforts, he thought, bracing himself for a Mrs Ormondroyd breakfast, normally prunes and burnt toast. Prunes were hardly the thing to get one firing on all cylinders. On the other hand, perhaps they were.

'Tally, I've been thinking,' said Saul, now glued to the looking glass where he was, ostensibly at least, tweezering out an ingrowing hair. 'I know exactly how you can get this place back on its feet. Imagine it. New roof, new wiring, new window frames and a brand spanking new heating system.' Tally gazed at him raptly. 'New paint-work,' continued Saul. 'Repointing the brickwork. New grass on the lawn.'

'Oh,' sighed Tally ecstatically, an orgasmic light in her eyes. He was reminded of when Champagne demanded he talk dirty.

'Meet me in the Blue Drawing Room after breakfast,' said Saul. 'Tell Mrs O I'm giving it a miss today. I have more important things to do.'

Mrs Ormondroyd's broad back radiated disapproval as Tally entered the kitchen. She crashed the kettle on to the Aga, banged a few pots about and in case Tally still hadn't got the message, the scraped, blackened and torn toast she was finally presented with spelt it out in Hovis of fire.

'What's the matter, Mrs Ormondroyd?' Tally asked innocently.

'Back's playing up,' muttered the housekeeper. She clamped a large, sausagey hand to the bottom of her spine.

To the small of her back, if her vast back could be said to have a small.

Tally sighed. 'Mrs Ormondroyd, I think we both know what's really the matter,' she said. 'I just don't understand why you hate Saul so much. He truly loves Mullions and really wants to find a way to get the place going again. He has tons of ideas,' she ad-libbed in anticipation of the revelations awaiting her in the Blue Drawing Room, 'and we may as well see if any of them work. After all, the alternative is to sell the place to the type of ghastly person we've had looking round recently, and while Mummy's away we should explore every option before she comes back and turfs us all out.' She bit into her toast and grimaced. It was like buttered coal from the grate. She wondered vaguely whether a loaf of carbonised bread would burn in the Blue Drawing Room fireplace. 'Give him a chance, at least.'

Mrs Ormondroyd's back remained silent and impassive.

Outside in the hall, the telephone bell shrilled. Almost immediately, it was picked up. The low voice of Saul floated into the kitchen, although his words were impossible to make out. There was a ting as he replaced the receiver. Half-turning so Tally could see her massive profile, Mrs Ormondroyd heaved her Brezhnevian eyebrows upwards. Tally finished her toast in as much silence as was possible given the crashing of her jaws against the carbon. Then she left the kitchen.

Billows of smoke greeted Tally on her entrance into the Blue Drawing Room. Saul was crouched in the vast hearth, eyes streaming, trying in vain to persuade a smouldering, resentful pile of still-damp wood into warm, blazing life. 'Whoever said there was no smoke without fire was talking utter shit,' he snapped as Tally came up behind him. 'No wonder this is called the Blue Drawing Room. Look at the colour of my hands.' The patches that were not black with soot were, Tally saw, almost indigo with chill.

'Here, let me,' she soothed, taking the tattered bellows from him and trying not to mind that he had been thrusting their Elizabethan carved oak end straight into the burning embers. 'I'm used to it.' A few well-directed wheezes later, she had persuaded a respectable blaze into being.

Saul gazed at her pinched face in astonishment. How did she manage to be so thin and yet apparently immune to the worst the cold could throw at her? She really did have the constitution of an ox. Mrs Ormondroyd, on the other hand, just *looked* like an ox.

'Why do you never get colds?' he asked.

'We were never allowed to wear socks after March,' Tally answered. 'And we took cold baths every day. It was very good training for learning to live in an English country house.'

'We?' asked Saul.

'My brother Piers and I,' said Tally.

'Your *brother*?' gasped Saul, alarmed. He had not bargained for this. Visions of a patrician, urbane head of the family in a fifteen-piece tweed suit suddenly appearing brandishing a riding crop and grilling him in merciless detail about what he was up to loomed large and hideous before him. His heart thundered like the last furlong of the Grand National as all his carefully-laid plans swayed and shuddered in the balance. Penthouse balconies, herringbone brick drives and video entryphones swooped mockingly before his racing vision, then faded dramatically away. The figures on his imaginary bank balance morphed from the hoped-for brilliantine black to an angry, frustrated red. Tally had a brother. What a nightmare. Was the brother here? Spying on him? Concealed somewhere in this vast, rotting warren of a house?

'Where is he?' asked Saul. He had intended the query to sound insouciant, but it flew out in a high-pitched yelp.

'Oh, I'm not sure,' said Tally, sighing into the flames. 'He could be anywhere.'

Saul, having heard what he most feared, was somehow able to stifle the cry of panic that threatened to loose itself from the moorings of his throat. But he was able to do nothing about the shocked, colourless white of his blood-drained face.

'The last we heard he was underneath a runway at Gatwick,' Tally added.

Saul's head spun. 'Wh-what?'

'Under a runway at Gatwick,' repeated Tally. 'He's an environmental protester, you see. He went AWOL from school and the only time I see him now is in the papers if he's been throwing mud at a minister or something. He hasn't,' she ended sadly, 'been near Mullions or his family for months.'

Saul let out a sigh of relief so vast he feared it might extinguish the hard-won fire. His feet tingled with the joy of the reprieved. 'How fabulous . . . I mean, how dreadful,' he stammered. But Tally was too lost in her thoughts to notice. It made her sad to think of her brother. They had been close as children, had clung together in the face of their mother's more eccentric excesses and affectations. Tally had written regularly to him at school, bowled up frequently with picnics and chatter and advice about girlfriends and in between times had sent him money she could ill afford to spare. Piers's current lack of communication was a disappointment she felt keenly.

'Who was on the telephone, by the way?' she asked, changing the subject. It hadn't occurred to her to wonder before, but the faint hope that it might be Piers struck her as she edged into a mice-dropping-free corner of the sofa.

'Wrong number again,' said Saul smoothly, after an infinitesimal silence. It was, too, he justified to himself. His business contacts had strict instructions from now on to call him on his mobile.

Feeling more in control again, Saul lit a cigarette and stood in as upright a manner as he could muster given that he was several spine-twisting nights on Mullions' mattresses the worse for wear. He felt gingerly at his left cheek. Shaving in wobbly Elizabethan mirrors had done nothing for the symmetry of his sideburns. No wonder the Tudors had always gone in for beards. Much safer. He cleared his throat; his ticklish cough was getting worse. Tally looked at him expectantly.

'You ought to be in pictures,' announced Saul.

Tally flushed. It was true that someone had once compared her to Celia Johnson. It was very sweet of Saul to try and flatter her, but really, one had to be realistic.

'I'm much too tall to be a film star,' she faltered.

Saul looked nonplussed. 'No, not *you*,' he said, in rather more astonished tones than Tally might have wished for. 'The house. Here.' He thrust a brochure into her hand.

Tally gazed at it. 'The ultimate location' read a line of mock Elizabethan script rolling across the front of a familiar looking combination of golden stone and oriel windows, viewed from across a pearly lake. It looks astonishingly like Mullions, thought Tally, fascinated to see that some turrets of the gatehouse had fallen off to leave just the same gap-toothed effect as on the one at the end of their own estate road. She looked closer. It *was* Mullions. 'Where on earth did you get this from?' asked Tally, gazing up at Saul, bemused.

'From myself,' said Saul, turning up his hands for dramatic emphasis. 'I put it together, using a few of my contacts from the advertising world.'

'But what is it? What does it mean?'

Saul gritted his teeth. Some people really were slow. 'It's a brochure,' he said, with exaggerated patience. 'A brochure advertising Mullions to film companies.'

Tally looked at him blankly.

'It's a brilliant idea, don't you see?' Saul urged, a chilly touch of impatience creeping into his voice. 'The film world is crying out for locations like Mullions. Period dramas needing backgrounds. You know, *Sense and Sensibility, Pride and Prejudice*, that sort of thing. There are a few films that I happen to know are going into production at the moment. We can target them. They'd pay a fortune.'

'But wouldn't they need, oh, I don't know, electricity, loos, food and all that?' gibbered Tally, shrinking against the sofa back as she tried to think quickly. 'Wouldn't they wreck the house?'

'Oh, no, no, no,' said Saul, fingers firmly crossed behind his back. 'You'd never know that they'd been there afterwards. Film units bring their own jennies. That's filmspeak for generators,' he added, rather pompously. 'But you don't have to worry your pretty little head about any of it. All you need to do is pop out and say hi when Tom and Nicole roll up in their trailers.'

Tally gasped, feeling dazzled. Saul had obviously thought it through. 'I know so little about it,' she murmured. 'You're the expert. But it sounds harmless enough.'

Saul looked at her huffily. 'Well, don't overwhelm me with your enthusiasm.'

Feeling guilty as well as scared, Tally gave him a contrite and dazzling smile. 'It sounds a wonderful idea,' she said. 'Thank you so much, darling. We must,' she added, straining to please, 'get these brochures off as soon as possible.'

Saul grinned, a hint of triumph in his eyes. 'Actually, I sent them out yesterday.' In a lightning move, he grabbed both her hands and pulled her close, gazing into her face with heart-melting sincerity. 'I won't ask you again,' he croaked, reflecting as he did so that the combination of the bed, his cough and the freezing cold would probably see he didn't survive to, 'but now you have proof that I'm desperate to help you and Mullions, will you marry me?'

Chapter 16

Deciding what to wear for the Movers and Shakers party was a nightmare. Desperate, Jane had even considered asking Champagne if she could borrow one of her dresses, but thought better of it after realising they probably wouldn't fit over her head. Just as she was juggling the idea of her all-purpose black trousers teamed with an all-purpose black jacket, or all-purpose black jacket teamed with all-purpose black trousers, or perhaps a daring combination of both, the telephone on her desk shrilled.

Ten minutes later she put it down. Her ears were singing as she went into Victoria's office. 'I've just had Champagne's hotel in New York on the line,' she reported.

Victoria looked up from the card, personalised in neat serif capitals, on which she was writing in the thick, black-inked oversized hand developed at prep school to make sure it got to the other side of the paper.

'They say Champagne has checked out.'

'Why?' said Victoria, absently. 'I thought it was the best one in town. We even got her the Presidential suite.'

'It is and we did,' said Jane through gritted teeth. 'But it's not good enough for Champagne. She's just checked out in a fury because the lifts to the penthouse are too slow for her.'

Victoria nodded. 'Quite right too,' she said with the air of one who'd seen more penthouses than Bob Guccione. 'Slow lifts can be *very* frustrating.'

'There's something else,' Jane said, keeping the urge to scream and throw things just about under control. 'The photographer called me earlier and said he and Champagne were among those invited to the exclusive dinner Ralph Lauren held after his show. Apparently it was unbelievably lavish. Champagne, caviar, lobster, you name it.

Victoria nodded, looking bored. So far, so run-of-the-fashion-mill, said her face. 'Yes? And?'

'Well Champagne apparently decided in the middle of it all that she wanted lasagne,' said Jane. 'She stormed out of the dinner when she was told there wasn't any and went back to the hotel and demanded they found some for her.'

'Well, I jolly well hope they did,' said Victoria hotly. 'Those hotels are supposed to be able to get you anything. A white elephant steak at four in the morning if you want it.'

'Oh, they got it all right,' said Jane. 'It's just that Champagne's exclusive at-home interview with Ralph Lauren, which we fought off all the competition to get, may now be in some doubt.'

Victoria breathed in deeply and exhaled, flaring her nostrils dramatically as she did so. She fixed Jane with a look of pitying patience. 'Sooner or later,' she said, in exaggeratedly patronising tones, 'even the most sophisticated and privileged among us gets the urge for something simpler. Many's the time I've come back from some A-list premiere or party, thrown off my heels and asked for nothing more than the maid to rustle me up a simple eggs Benedict.'

Jane sighed. OK, if Victoria wanted to play hardball, she'd got herself a game. She hadn't wanted to tell Victoria this, but . . .

'That's not all. I've had a call from the British Consulate as well. There's been some trouble with Customs. Champagne was held at Heathrow on the way over.'

Result, this time. The colour drained from Victoria's face. Jane saw her mind flicking swiftly through the Rolodex of possibilities, of which there seemed really only one. A drugs charge would mean the column would certainly have to go.

'Why?' Victoria croaked, the fingers of her right hand clenched into a white-knuckled knot round her Mont Blanc.

'She refused to hand over her passport on the grounds that the photograph in it wasn't flattering enough,' said Jane. 'They had to practically prise it out of her hand, apparently. She held up Concorde for half an hour. Joan Collins is talking about suing for the delay.'

To disguise the relief she felt, Victoria put on her most indulgent expression. 'Well, say what you like about Champagne, she's never boring.' Equanimity restored, her pen hovered over the card again. 'And, more to the point, she's certainly had an effect on the circulation.'

I'd like to have an effect on her circulation, thought Jane as she left Victoria's presence. Like cut it off completely.

She returned to her desk, just in time to answer the telephone which had been ringing for ages, ignored, as usual, by Tish who was otherwise occupied flicking through the latest *Vogue*. Jane's heart sank as the familiar honk blasted through the receiver. After the exchange she had just had with Victoria, Champagne choosing now to call – collect, naturally – from New York was like a blow upon a bruise.

'Four bangs,' squawked Champagne. 'I've managed four bangs so far!'

'What?' It sounded positively modest by Champagne's usual standards. So why was she boasting about it?

'Four crashes because people were staring at my underwear ads when they were driving!' Champagne boomed. 'One fatal.'

'Oh, I see,' said Jane. 'How awful.'

'No, it's brilliant. Proves the ads are really working. Superbra are thrilled!'

'I'm delighted for you,' said Jane. 'Is that everything?'

'Yah, think so,' said Champagne. Then, 'Oh, no, hang on, there *is* something else. I've packed in Wayne.'

Why aren't I surprised? thought Jane.

'Just too much of an oik, really,' declared Champagne, even though Jane hadn't asked. 'Hasn't a clue. His idea of a seven-course meal is a six-pack and a hamburger. Thinks Pacific Rim is something sailors get. The last straw was when we were in a restaurant and he pronounced claret claray. *So* embarrassing.'

'Quite,' said Jane, not sure how else to respond.

'But I've met some scrummy men in New York,' Champagne continued. 'The *sweetest* English politician at the Donna Karan show last night. *Bloody* nice guy.'

Jane had seen the coverage of Champagne at this particular fashion bash in the tabloids that morning. Coverage, however, had hardly been the word. Champagne's clinging silver dress had made her cleavage look like the San Andreas Fault.

'Yah, he was really interesting,' Champagne gushed. 'We talked for hours about politics.'

'Really?' said Jane faintly. Surely, as far as Champagne was concerned, Lenin was the guy who wrote songs with Paul McCartney. Her idea of a social model was probably Stella Tennant and dialectical materialism meant wearing a velvet Voyage cardigan with a leather Versace miniskirt. Champagne's concept of social security, Jane felt sure, was ten million a year, a country house in Wiltshire, flats in Paris and New York and a Gulfstream V.

'What's the politician called?' asked Jane, realising she hadn't thought about Westminster for what seemed like a lifetime. 'And what on earth was he doing at a fashion show?'

'James Morrison,' barked Champagne. 'Used to be the transport minister, apparently, and he's just been made Secretary of State for Pop. I told him I thought it was amazing that the prefects at Eton had their own minister, but I supposed it wasn't that surprising if you think that most of them end up in the Cabinet anyway. But he meant pop *music*. And popular culture in general, which includes fashion, apparently.'

'I see,' said Jane, vaguely wondering if that meant Nick, too, was now on cheekbone-crashing terms with supermodels. She had no idea whether Nick still worked for Morrison, and didn't care. She hadn't, she realised, thought about *him* for ages either.

'Well, must dash. My masseuse is waiting,' Champagne said by way of finale. 'Oh,' she added nonchalantly, 'tell Victoria I probably won't be back for the Movers and Shakers party. I know she wanted me there, but some producer wants to talk to me about a film part.' She stifled a yawn. 'He must be *desperate* for me. He's paid for a new Concorde return ticket so I can stay on an extra day.'

Jane felt weak with envy. Film parts were falling into

Champagne's lap now as well. If only a *real* film part would. Like the lighting rig. 'How wonderful,' she said sincerely. 'I'd *love* to go on Concorde,' she added longingly.

'Terrifically boring the tenth time, I can assure you,' yawned Champagne.

'Oh, Tish,' wailed Jane after a lunchtime spent trailing despondently round Bond Street looking at dresses she could neither fit into nor afford. 'What *am* I going to wear to this party?' Everyone else in the office seemed to be pulling glittering garments out of plastic bags and exclaiming over them. 'Look at what the others have been buying,' she moaned.

'Buying?' said Tish. 'You must be joking. No one's bought a stitch. Everyone's had the fashion department call things in for them. Apart from *you*, that is.'

'Oh,' said Jane, feeling foolish. It had never even occurred to her to borrow.

'Follow me,' said Tish.

The fashion department was a riot of racks stuffed with brilliantly-coloured clothes. Emaciated long-legged girls bobbed between them like exotic birds, clutching armfuls of shimmering dresses. Shoes lay scattered all over the floor, spilling from boxes lined with brightly coloured tissue paper. Jane was reminded of Champagne's bedroom.

'This is what *I'm* wearing,' Tish announced, producing a tiny dress made of ivory silk embroidered all over with tiny pink roses. 'Isn't it pretty? It's amazing anything's left,' she added. 'Tash has already been up here and was trying to wear practically everything at once to make sure no one else got a look-in. Oh, Tiara, Jane needs a dress for tomorrow,' Tish called as the fashion editor, a willowy redhead with huge green eyes and a vague air, wafted in. 'Got anything?'

Jane flushed beetroot as she submitted to Tiara's scrutiny. She doubted anyone as huge as herself had ever been seen in the fashion department before.

'Mmm,' said Tiara, putting her hands on her non-existent hips. 'Mmmm,' she repeated, putting her head on one side and tossing her curtain of hair in a shimmering arc as she did so. Jane felt nervous. Why had she allowed Tish to put her through this? There probably *had* been something in M&S if she'd looked hard enough . . .

'Mmm. You're in luck. I've got just the thing. Bias-cut.'

Tiara thrust a scrap of cream-coloured fabric into Jane's arms and shoved her into the fashion cupboard. Wispy bits of sequins and feathers tickled Jane's nose as she struggled into the dress while bent double underneath racks of clothes. She felt like a contortionist. Bias-cut, Tiara had said. Hopefully not biased against her.

'Wow,' said Tish as Jane emerged a few minutes later. 'That's *incredible*.' Which, thought Jane, walking resignedly to the mirror, could mean practically anything. At first glance, through half-closed eyes, it looked fine. Up close it would probably look dismal. Good from afar, but far from good.

'It really suits you,' said Tiara encouragingly. And, looking at herself critically in the long mirror, Jane had to agree. The extreme plainness of the long cream satin dress emphasised every curve and, by means of clever boning, wiring and general wizardry, contrived to give her a bust to rival Champagne's. A long slit up one side revealed a long, miraculously slender-looking and for once completely unbruised length of leg. Delight and excitement fizzed in

Jane's stomach. She certainly looked the party part now. My cups, she thought, looking at her *embonpoint*, runneth over.

But Tish hadn't finished yet. Next, Jane was frog-marched to Sash the beauty editor for a make-up lesson. It was astonishing how a few well-placed strokes of charcoal eyeshadow could transform her eyes from small and piggy to huge and mysterious. Sash also showed her how to fill out her lips, normally the only dependably thin parts of her body, to look plump and luscious.

'Remember to lick before you drink anything, so the lipstick won't come off on the glass,' Sash warned. 'And *don't* eat. Don't even nibble. Remember, little pickers wear bigger knickers.'

Jane grinned. She was planning to take a leaf out of Champagne's book and not wear any knickers at all. She was determined to avoid visible party line.

'Archie Fitzherbert's office called you,' Tash said casually when Jane got back to her desk. 'Wanted a word, I think,' she added vaguely.

'What, Archie Fitzherbert the managing director?' Jane's stomach was suddenly thundering with panic. 'A word with *me*?'

Tash nodded. 'You're to call his secretary.'

Jane fumbled for the phone. Visions of instant dismissal, unpaid mortgages and repossessed flats floated through her panicked mind. Had Champagne been complaining about her? 'Which secretary?' she asked. Archie Fitzherbert, she knew, had two. A dragon called Mavis and an angel called Georgie. Tash shrugged.

Jane dialled, tremblingly. She got Mavis.

'One mayment,' said Mavis sternly. 'I think Georgina is dealing with this.'

Jane caught her breath. *Dealing* with this? What on earth was happening?

'Sorry,' said Georgie, bouncing on to the line like a friendly dog. 'I know this is awfully short notice . . .'

'What is?' croaked Jane, her worst fears assuming hideous, three-dimensional reality.

'Oh, didn't Tash tell you? Tomorrow morning. Archie would like you to attend one of his staff breakfasts.'

Jane sank in her chair with relief only to sit bolt upright again with terror. Archie Fitzherbert's 'meet the people' staff breakfasts were famous throughout the industry. Or notorious. Ostensibly, they were informal meetings to discuss staff-related issues, but most people suspected their real purpose was for Fitzherbert to spot check how switched-on his employees were. Jane saw her planned evening of collapsing in front of the telly metamorphosing into a night of frantically ripping through every issue of every competing magazine in order to be able to discuss its strengths and weaknesses confidently should her opinion be sought.

As she left the *Fabulous* building that drizzling evening, Jane noticed with a pang that the road outside, as usual, looked like the most fantastic outdoor car showroom. It was filled, nose-to-tail, with the shining, glamorous vehicles belonging to the boyfriends of the magazine company members of staff. They revved impatiently as their lissom girlfriends came rushing out of the revolving doors, tossing their shining hair and throwing their expensive handbags in the back seat before sliding into the front and roaring off. Jane strode on, trying not to care that there was no one to whisk her away to cocktails and candlelit dinners. Trying not to care, too, that the rain was now smashing against the pavements like gobbets of wet, cold lead.

She dashed into a newsagent and bought every magazine she could lay her hands on. Clutching her slippery armful, she hurried through the downpour to the Tube station. A speeding bus spattered the contents of a deep and dirty puddle all over her from the thighs downwards. Looking with loathing at the offending vehicle, which screeched dramatically to a halt at a bus stop a few feet away, Jane saw that it bore on its side one of the posters of Champagne in her Superbra underwear. Her bra was the same level as the top deck, while the lower one lined up with her skimpy G-string. Jane watched as the men in the queue, office drones with overpadded shoulders dragged down by the straps of their laptops, gawped at the advert before clambering aboard the bus and sitting on the bottom deck. It was, Jane realised, the nearest any of them would come to getting inside Champagne's knickers. Certainly for the price of a bus fare.

Chapter 17

It was over twelve hours later that Jane entered the fetid mouth of the Tube again, but it might as well have been twelve minutes. Her eyes felt as hard, dry and heavy as golf balls. She had spent half the night hunched over her pile of magazines, and had fallen asleep over them in the end. She had woken up at five in the morning to find her nose pressed against a pageful of advice on dealing with irritable bowel syndrome.

Still, no one could accuse her of not preparing, she thought. And once the ordeal of the Fitzherbert breakfast was over, there was this evening's Movers and Shakers party to look forward to. Jane thought happily about the creamy liquid perfection of the party dress hanging in the cool darkness of her wardrobe. She focused her mind firmly on it as more and more people surged into her carriage at the next station.

The stop after that brought an even bigger influx. As her head became wedged under the armpit of a plump, perspiring businessman, who was evidently very fond of garlic, Jane tried to divert herself by thinking about her party shoes as well.

She had laughed when Tiara first suggested she try on the tiny, gossamer-light silver sandals, doubting she could get one, ragged-nailed, unpainted, bunioned toe in them, and had been amazed to find that they not only fitted, but gave her feet a grace she had never thought possible. They had even encouraged her to paint her toenails for the first time in years. She was, Jane realised, entering dangerous, perhaps fatal waters. She was beginning to see the point of spending a fortune on looking good.

'Ow!' Jane growled into the businessman's armpit as someone stood heavily on her toe. She moved her head the fraction that was possible to glare at the offender, and instantly wished she hadn't. An extremely spotty youth, his yellow-tipped, angry red bumps shining hideous and near in the harsh overhead light, gazed fishily back at her. Clamped to his ears were a pair of cheap headphones from which a grinding, sneering sound, interspersed with a fizzing rattle, emanated.

Jane sighed, loudly, knowing she was far from being the only unhappy traveller. The sense of mass irritation was almost as palpable as the overwhelming heat. She tried to prepare a selection of choice observations about the magazines she had read for the Fitzherbert breakfast, but was distracted by the sensation of her carefully moussed-up hair melting in the moist, sulphurous fug. She wrinkled her nose. The carriage, frankly, stank. It was one thing to travel like a can of sardines. To smell like them as well was just too bad. Desperately seeking distraction, she gazed through the window in the door at the back of the carriage, into the next one.

There he was. About eight feet away from her, his blond head clearly visible above the mass that pressed about him. Was she hallucinating? Had she finally gone mad?

No, she hadn't. It *was* him. No doubt about it. Tom.

Suddenly, incontrovertibly, unbelievably here. Not in New York. Not anywhere else in the world, but here, alive, in the flesh, in London, in the very Underground carriage next to hers. He looked well, tanned, the ends of his hair bleached by the sun. He also looked even handsomer than she remembered.

Jane stared urgently at him. Surely he must see her. But Tom was gazing vacantly out of the carriage windows, seemingly oblivious to his surroundings. Jane tried to move, to make a gesture. He would, he must, sense her presence. She struggled again, but she was packed too tightly between the armpit and the acne to move. She was trapped. Until the next station, that was. Please, God, let it come soon.

Between Leicester Square and Tottenham Court Road, the train ground to a halt in the tunnel. Jane twisted herself desperately about, but could have been no more securely pinioned if she'd been bound hand and foot. And gagged into the bargain. For there was no point shouting. Tom would never hear her through two panes of glass and a mass of people. Feeling dizzy with panic, Jane locked her gaze on to him, burning into his leather jacket like a laser, willing him with every fibre of her being to turn and look at her. He must. He had to.

He didn't. The eyes that had melted her heart looked blankly out of the window at the black tunnel walls. The hand that had played her body like a harp, plucking deep, throbbing notes that still resonated, hung limply from a ceiling strap. Jane wanted to scream. Her eyeballs ached with the intense staring. She felt her gaze to be a lasso, thrown round him, connecting him, an invisible thread that would break if she so much as blinked. As long as she was looking at him, she thought, he could not get away.

Eventually the train gave a juddering, shuddering lurch and moved on. Seconds later, it had drawn into Tottenham Court Road station and flung open its doors. Jane was forced to look away now. She had to get out. Desperately, she scratched, pushed and clawed her way out on to the platform and elbowed against the tide of people pouring out of the train. She struggled towards the next carriage. It was half empty when she gained it. And Tom had gone.

'Tom!' screamed Jane, turning desperately round in the midst of the raft of commuters and glancing wildly about her for the blond head and the leather jacket. The wide, unwieldy crowd moved with a pitiless shuffle up the stairs, making it impossible for her to move at more than a snail's pace. In the escalator hall, Jane scoured the length of the commuter-crammed moving staircases with her eyes, but Tom was nowhere to be seen. She pushed her way up, muttering apologies, attracting angry glances, crashing her shins painfully into the sharp, heavy edges of briefcases. Tom *couldn't* have disappeared into nothing. Not when she'd been so close to him.

Through the ticket gates the crowds moved, as thick, slow and dense as treacle. Finally, Jane rushed out into Oxford Street, panting, her head bursting and dizzy with hot, pounding blood. For the next fifteen minutes she dashed up alleyways, down dead-end streets, across busy roads and around squares, but with no success. Tom had completely vanished. Eventually she slumped on a bench in Soho Square and burst into tears. No one passing batted an eyelid. You got all sorts of nutters wandering around Soho, after all.

When Jane entered the Archie Fitzherbert breakfast, she was half an hour late and felt a hundred years older. The breakfast was practically over but she didn't care. Nor did she care that her hair was all over her face and her mascara, despite automatic-pilot efforts in the loo, hopelessly smudged. She had walked the half mile from Soho Square to the *Fabulous* offices in a fragile daze, trying not to let the dreadful truth hit her that she had been mere feet away from the man she had been thinking of almost nonstop since he had left her, and she had let him get away. *Again.*

'Jane! Good morning,' called the managing director, half bouncing up from his chair as she came in. '*So* pleased you could make it.' He appeared to speak without irony. Jane bulldozed a smile across her face as he motioned her to sit down, waving a tanned, square-fingered hand across the array of croissants and toast wrapped in linen napkins. 'Have some breakfast,' Fitzherbert smiled. Jane nodded and drew in the chair beneath her, noticing that no one else had taken up the offer so far. The food was untouched.

Jane was too distracted to notice much else. All she took in about Archie Fitzherbert was his rather theatrical lilac suit, fashionably jarring orange tie and air of focused enthusiasm. Motivation shone from his every pore. He radiated energy and success. He was, in short, a deeply depressing sight, and the last person on earth Jane wanted to see at that moment.

He introduced the others at the table to her, an assortment of deputy editors, managing editors and advertisement and promotions people from other titles in the group, whose names Fitzherbert was evidently proud to be able to recall from memory. In her frazzled state, however, Jane forgot them as soon as he said them.

'We were just talking about *Lipstick*,' Archie Fitzherbert said, training a polite but penetrating gaze on her. As she picked up her coffee cup, Jane heard the unmistakable sound of a gauntlet hitting the floor. She was expected to make a contribution. Well, she could. Launched by a rival publishing company, *Lipstick* was the latest women's magazine to hit the already gorged market. It had been judged a great success, but Jane had thought from the start that it was boring. She said as much now.

'*Really?*' said Archie Fitzherbert, leaning forward and looking utterly fascinated. He clutched at the tablecloth with his fingers. 'How *very interesting*. Why *is* that?'

'There's nothing original about it,' Jane said, conscious, for once, of not giving a damn what anyone else thought. 'It's derivative, it takes the successful bits of practically every other magazine and mixes them together, but it's got no soul of its own. It's less than the sum of its parts.'

There was a shuffling silence. Jane suspected that before she came in, *Lipstick* had been the subject of considerable praise. But she didn't care. She felt oddly clear-headed and detached, as if the shock of seeing Tom and the misery of losing him again had left her no energy for worrying about trivia. She took a sip from her coffee cup, aware that Archie Fitzherbert was still staring at her. As was everyone else in the room.

Fitzherbert suddenly looked at his Rolex. 'Well, thank you for coming, everyone,' he said, and stood up, smiling politely as his guests drained coffee dregs and stumbled to their feet. There were a few crashes as the more maladroit dropped cutlery. Everyone mumbled their thanks, grabbed coats and bags and hurried out of the room. As Jane prepared to leave, she suddenly became aware that Fitzherbert had glided to her side. 'I'd like a quick word,' he said, sitting back down and motioning her to do the same. A few of the last to leave gazed curiously over their shoulders as the doors swung shut behind them.

'May I ask, since you seem to have such strong views, what you think of your own magazine?' Fitzherbert inquired in carefully neutral tones, locking his eyes on to hers. He was, Jane noticed, really quite handsome. But she also noticed the wedding ring. Taken, then.

She hesitated. It was, she knew, her cue to say something flattering about Victoria, to laud her to the skies, to say what a great and inspirational editor she was.

'Fairly dull really,' someone said. Jane heard the voice ringing round the silent room and realised it was her own. 'I think,' the voice continued, 'that it needs to move with the times more. It's quite witty, which is important, and has a certain amount of glamour. But there's a lot that could be done with it nonetheless.'

'Such as what?' asked Fitzherbert, his light, pleasant tones still betraying nothing of what he thought.

Jane took a deep breath. She'd clearly talked herself out of a job anyway, so she may as well speak the truth. What had she to lose? Somewhere out there in the mockingly bright sunshine, Tom was wandering about London and she had no way of finding him. She had been given a second chance and had wasted it. What did anything matter now?

'Well, I think it could be better informed,' she heard herself saying. '*Fabulous* staff don't seem to think they need to read the newspapers, apart from the horoscopes, which is a pity. Which means that everyone else spots the big stories first and gets their interview requests in. And big interviews and stories, as you know, are what sell magazines.'

Fitzherbert nodded. He seemed to be encouraging her to say even more. Probably because after this she would have to offer her resignation and it would be cheaper than sacking her. Oh well. Since he'd asked . . . 'It's also not very sexy,' Jane continued recklessly. 'Or perhaps as hip as its rivals.' That much *was* true – Josh had placed a far greater emphasis on predicting trends and spotting rising stars than Victoria did.

She stopped and took a sip from her coffee, feeling scared but strangely unburdened. Fitzherbert kept up a sphinx-like silence for a few seconds. Eventually, he cleared his throat.

'Well, I'm *very* interested in what you say,' he remarked. 'Very interested indeed.' The interview, such as it was, was evidently over. Jane scrambled to her feet, certain she would find her P45 on her desk that very afternoon. Once Victoria got wind of this, she would be out faster than a Porsche Boxster.

As she passed through the mirrored entrance into the Movers and Shakers party, Jane smiled. A beautiful stranger smiled back, dazzling in a clinging satin dress, perfect make-up and a Grace Kelly ripple of blonde hair curling down over her shoulders. She felt pure Hollywood. Or, looking down at the vast glass of champagne in her hand, perhaps pure Bollywood.

Jane planned to drown all thoughts about Tom in gallon after gallon of champagne. And all thoughts about her no-doubt-wrecked professional future. She had, so far, been spared the expected post-Fitzherbert tongue-lashing from Victoria, who had been out of the office all day having her legs dyed and her eyelashes waxed for the party. Or was it the other way round? There had also been something about a seaweed wrap, eyebrow reconstruction, mud treatment and cellulite-blasting. Victoria was, for all Jane knew, probably having a damp-proof course put in as well.

'Jane, darling, you look delicious,' cried Oonagh, bustling up atop a pair of high black boots.

'Wonderful boots,' said Jane.

'Thank you, my darling,' said Oonagh. 'They're my fuckits,' she added, unexpectedly.

'Fuckits?' said Jane. Did she mean fuck-me shoes? Or was it the new Patrick Cox label?

'That's right,' grinned Oonagh. 'Expensive things I treat myself to even though I can't really afford them. I just think, oh fuck it, and buy them.' Oonagh smoothed her heavily beringed hands down her body. Her clinging black dress showed off her tiny waist to perfection. For a fifty-something, she really had the most wonderful figure.

'How do you keep in such good shape?' Jane asked her, smiling gratefully at the waiter glugging champagne into her glass.

'Sleep in my bra, darling,' Oonagh said briskly. 'Always have done. Never take it off, except for gala occasions. Not that there are many of *those* these days.'

'Who's here?' Jane looked around at the sea of braying, grinning faces and wondered who they all were.

Oonagh on the other hand knew everyone. Being the *Fabulous* picture editor, Jane supposed that she probably had to. Nonetheless, she seemed to know more about the guests than might be deemed strictly necessary.

'Busty Binge-Fetlock's over there,' Oonagh whispered, gesturing in the direction of a stout, shock-headed man in tartan trousers who seemed to be deep in conversation with a coat stand. 'Terribly well-connected. On first-name terms with most of Europe's royal families. Rather near-sighted, though, as you can see. Probably thinks that fur's Queen Silvia.'

'And who's that?' Jane asked, looking in the direction of

an impossibly lithe brunette whose legs went up to shoulder blades which protruded like Cadillac fins. On her head was something that looked like a meringue with a feather in it.

'Oh, that's Fluffy Fronte-Bottom,' twittered Oonagh. 'Great girl. One of the Basingstoke Fronte-Bottoms. They say she eats nothing but chips and pizzas, but you can't believe *that*, can you?'

Depends if they ever reach her stomach, I suppose, thought Jane. The girl was so thin that in profile she was almost invisible.

'And who's that over there?' she asked. A stunningly arrogant-looking man with a riot of thick dark curls was looking over with an appreciative expression. A thrill ran through her.

'Careful,' whispered Oonagh. 'That's Sebastian Tripp. Apparently has the most *enormous* you-know-what. Women have been hospitalised, I'm not joking. Don't touch him with a bargepole. He's a serial shagger.'

'A case of wham, bam and see you in Casualty, ma'am,' said Jane.

'Exactly,' said Oonagh. 'Oh, and that's the Hon. Barnaby Fender over there, talking to Princess Loulou Fischtitz.' She nudged Jane in the direction of a tall, gangly man stooping to talk to a very short, plain, plump girl. 'He's a very sought-after banker. Bonuses are quite beyond belief, apparently.' Oonagh gave Jane a dirty wink. 'But bats on the other team, they say. Friend of Dorothy. Shame, as Loulou's his perfect woman. Just the right height to give him a blow job. Standing up. Anyway, I'm off, dear. Must circulate. I'll leave you to your own vices.'

As Oonagh disappeared into the throng, Jane looked warily around for Victoria, whom she was determined to avoid at all costs. Thankfully, she was nowhere to be seen in the vast crowd. Time, Jane decided, to put her best front forward. The champagne was beginning to have an emboldening effect. Knocking back a third glass, Jane launched herself into what she hoped was a sea of possibilities.

Her progress was made hazardous by both her high heels and the waiters who, elaborately dressed in Nehru collars and turbans, also bore ceremonial swords which threatened to shred the material of any passing dress. They reminded Jane strongly of Kenneth Williams in *Carry On Up the Khyber*. Anyone planning to squeeze by them also had to take into consideration their huge and unwieldy platters piled high with curries and Indian nibbles. Bearing in mind Tish's warning, Jane declined all offers of food. There seemed little point in dressing up to the nines and then spoiling your chance with the handsomest man in London by having a samosa between your teeth at the crucial moment.

There really were some *extraordinarily* handsome men in the room, obviously all scions of families who for centuries had had the pick of the gene pool. And the deep end at that. Everywhere Jane looked there were cheekbones, golden tans and more floppy blond fringes than you could shake a silver-backed hairbrush at. None of the women seemed larger than size eight, or sounded older than age eight. 'Oh, Bunter, you shouldn't!' Jane overheard them squealing at their escorts in high, babyish tones as she pushed by.

She slinked towards the back of the room, feeling like sex incarnate. Feeling like sex with anybody, in fact. Never had her blood pounded so hard and fast in her ears. She looked down with awe at the unaccustomed sight of her wobbling Mansfieldesque cleavage. A little over the top? she wondered. Actually, there was rather a lot over the top. Oh well, she told herself. Men like breasts. No boobies, no rubies, as Zsa Zsa Gabor once said. And tonight was the best chance she was going to get of picking up some family heirlooms.

'Allow me,' murmured a voice at her elbow just as Jane found herself gravlaxed between two braying members of the minor aristocracy. They were locking overbites like stags locked antlers. Jane gratefully allowed a cool hand to lead her into a relatively uncrammed spot at the back of the room.

'Thank you,' she gasped, looking for the first time at her saviour. 'Mark!' she exclaimed. 'Mark Stackable!' Deep, crimson shame filled her. The last time she had seen Mark Stackable was in the company of a large pool of artichoke vomit she had deposited all over him, his floor and his waffle-cotton bedcovers. 'W-what are you doing here?' she stammered.

'First things first,' said Mark. He lifted two brimming glasses of champagne from a passing tray and handed one to Jane with a dazzling smile. 'Nice to see you again. Your very good health.' Jane blushed as she sipped. He had more reason than most people to say that.

'Are you a Mover and Shaker?' she asked. It sounded graceless, she realised, as soon as the words were out. Because *of course* Mark must be. His bonuses could probably even give the Hon. Barnaby Fender's a run for their money. And she'd forgotten quite how handsome he was.

He, on the other hand, seemed to have forgiven her. His thick-lashed dark eyes, which may or may not have been midnight blue, were looking warmly, if not directly at her, then certainly at the area of her cleavage. He switched on a large and brilliant white smile and pushed back his thick dark hair. Jane's knees felt weak as the surging crowd suddenly pressed her closer to him. His skin was close-shaven and tanned. He smelt rich.

'Apparently, although I'm not sure which,' grinned Mark. 'It's good to see you.'

'I'm so sorry . . .' she began, not wanting to bring up, as it were, the subject of the artichokes but feeling it had to be broached.

'Don't mention it,' Mark said, making it sound more of an instruction than an act of politeness. 'Let's pretend it never happened?' He flashed another glimpse of his stunningly white tombstones. It was obvious that he bore no grudge. He seemed to have simply wiped it from his memory.

'You're looking very well,' Jane said. She felt surprised and relieved and grateful. Not to mention extremely randy. Her mind fumbled for some useful neutral territory that she might steer towards his asking her out for dinner.

'And you look wonderful.' He gazed appreciatively at her cleavage again. Jane, unsure whether he was addressing her breasts or herself, grinned. The evening looked more or less in the bag. She was about to start a conversation about restaurants but noticed, just as she opened her mouth, that his eyes had slid over the top of her head and had fastened themselves on someone behind her.

'Mark, *darling*,' honked a familiar voice. 'Here you are, you *naughty* poppet. I've been looking for you *everywhere*.'

Jane froze. Champagne, she thought in horror. But how? She was supposed to be thousands of miles away in New York. How could she possibly be here? Jane could hardly bear to face her. Only the thought of Champagne getting a close-up view of her well-covered shoulder blades and random moles persuaded her. She turned round.

Champagne had never looked more beautiful. Her white-blonde hair streamed over her fragile shoulders. Her knuckleduster cheekbones glowed with the merest hint of blusher and, through the clinging folds of her thin Voyage dress, her nipples protruded like screwed-out lipsticks. Her brilliant green eyes raked Jane up and down like searchlights as she stretched out a chilly hand heavy with rings. Her wrist was so thin it was exactly the width of her Cartier watch face. You could not see the straps at all.

'I don't believe we've met,' Champagne said frostily.

'We have, actually,' Jane said boldly. 'I'm Jane from *Fabulous* magazine.'

Champagne's six-seater lips parted in astonishment.

'Well, you scrub up well, I must say,' she blurted. She looked pointedly at Jane's dress.

'I tried that one on,' she added sweetly. 'But it looked cheap and nasty on me.'

She paused.

'Suits you, though.'

Around the base of her champagne glass, Jane's fingers itched. She longed to empty it in that arrogant face. Instead she said, 'Aren't you supposed to be in New York? With your film director?'

'We flew back together in the end,' barked Champagne. 'Talked about the film idea on the way.' She reached towards a passing platter. 'Whoops! Oh dear. Clumsy me. *So* sorry.'

Jane felt a hot, slithering sensation down her front as a vast pile of chicken tikka masala streamed off the serving dish and slid down her front. Thick, greasy sauce of a bright orange hue spread slowly across the pristine cream satin of the dress. Gasping as the hot, smelly slime seeped between her breasts, Jane briefly contemplated bludgeoning Champagne to death with one of the passing bottles of Bollinger. She did not have the faintest doubt that the food had been tipped over her on purpose. Clutching her arms to her breasts, impervious to the shouts of Mark behind her, Jane shoved her way through the crowd to the door and a taxi, her only thought to get home and change. She had been planning to take her dress off, admittedly, but not in these circumstances. Her hot, spicy evening had suddenly turned very cold.

Chapter 18

The staff of *Fabulous* were rarely at their best first thing on a Monday morning. In common with the rest of the nation, they shuffled slowly and unwillingly into the office. It had taken Jane a few weeks to realise that their reasons for doing so were rather different than most people's.

The clue was in the fact that they all carried large, expensive-looking weekend bags into the office on Mondays, and they all had bruises on their foreheads. Their dazed appearance, Jane gradually gathered, was the result of practically the entire *Fabulous* workforce spending its weekends in Grade One listed buildings. She knew from Mullions that banging one's forehead repeatedly against low doorways was the occupational hazard of the country-house guest. So perhaps it was hardly surprising the staff weren't the quickest of thinkers. All that cranium-crashing was bound to take its toll on the brain.

This ingenious theory, Jane realised, also explained why everyone smoked like a kipper factory during those first few hours in the office. The fear that you'd only stayed at Chatsworth while the person next to you had been to Windsor informed all discussions. The exaggerated, laid-back drawls with which information about weekends was exchanged obviously disguised panic of the highest order.

The Monday after the Friday of the Movers and Shakers party, however, Jane entered to find the joint positively jumping. 'Wasn't Grotty *unbelievable*?' Tash was shouting as Jane came in. 'Taking off those knickers and putting them on her head. Shame they were Totty Fotheringay's knickers, though. She looked furious . . . And didn't Loulou look *completely out of it*? Apparently at least four Rolls-Royces' worth have gone up her nose since January . . . Wasn't Bumzo hilarious? Trying to stick his tongue down Victoria's throat. She looked as if she was quite enjoying it, actually . . . And isn't Mark Stackable a *dream*? Hunktastic or *what*? Champagne certainly seemed to think so. Did you see them go off together?'

Jane's heart sank. Another one bites the dust, she thought miserably. Mark must think her utterly mad anyway. As well as disgusting. Throwing up everywhere on the first date, getting covered in food the second. She was beginning to wonder if there was a curse on her.

'And did you see *Jane*?' Tash sniggered conspiratorially. 'Rushing out with CTM all down her front! Talk about an *Indian takeaway*.' Various coughs and agonised stretching of eyes alerted Tash to the fact that Jane was sitting at the desk behind her. Jane derived some comfort from watching the tide of mortified puce that now rose swiftly up the back of Tash's neck.

'Uuurrggghh.' Everyone was suddenly distracted by a profound groan coming from Oonagh's direction. Head bent over the lightbox, she was examining a set of wedding photographs for the social pages. 'All that inherited wealth and not one of them seems to own a full-length mirror,' wailed Oonagh, holding one of the offending images between her finger and thumb as if it was something very nasty indeed. 'This poor woman's hat looks as if a poodle's died on top of her head. And look at all that jewellery. And that *food. Pork chops* for goodness' sake. Talk about swine before pearls.'

'Whose wedding was it?' asked Tish.

'Pandora Smellie-Lewes,' sighed Oonagh. 'She's married someone called Conte Juan Paz de Barcelona de Cojones de Soto.'

'Who everyone knows doesn't have a bean,' said Tash, 'but poor Dora was *so* desperate to marry a title. Talk about a wannabe.'

'You mean a Juannabe,' snorted Tosh.

Jane was relieved that Victoria, so far, had not made an appearance.

'I'm not sure we'll be seeing Victoria today,' said Tish as if reading her mind. 'Hermione's had a relapse.'

'Hermione?' asked Jane. 'That's not one of her children, is it?' Visions of a distraught Victoria bending over the bed of a sick child flashed before her. Her soft heart dissolved with pity, with a powerful slug of guilt. How *could* she have said all those things about poor Victoria to Archie Fitzherbert?

'No, Hermione's her daughter's kitten,' said Tish breezily. 'Had to be rushed to hospital with a suspected ingrowing toenail or something. But she's fine now. Has a private room with her own nurse. I've sent some flowers from all of us. A card is going round the office for everyone to sign.'

'I see,' Jane blinked. 'Well, anyway, Tish, perhaps you could give me a hand with this interview request. I need to get it out today. Could you type it for me?' She handed a scribbled sheet of paper to the secretary, whose attention was now focused on painting each nail a different colour. She looked up from the paper to Jane in astonishment.

'I don't do much typing, actually,' she drawled in what, for her, passed for surprise.

'She's not the type,' said Tash, standing at the fax.

Jane raised an eyebrow and opened a file on her computer to type the letter herself. It was a request to Lily Eyre's agent for an interview. Common ankles or not, Jane was determined that *Fabulous* should do something about the pretty actress before everybody else did. As she typed the opening sentence, her telephone rang.

'Hello,' said an American voice. Jane froze as she recognised the businesslike tones of Mark Stackable.

'Hi,' muttered Jane in astonishment. What on earth did he want? Surely having seen her covered in undigested food for the second time was enough to put him off seeking her company for ever.

Apparently not. 'I wondered whether you might be free for dinner tonight?' he said. 'It strikes me that we haven't managed to have a proper conversation yet.'

'Er, yes, I mean no, we haven't,' Jane said, amazed. 'I mean yes, I'd love to.'

'I've booked a table at Ninja,' said Mark. Ninja was a wildly expensive new Japanese restaurant where only the eye-wideningly rich or universally famous had a hope of being admitted. Nonetheless, Jane was surprised at his choice. After the CTM fiasco, one might have imagined Mark would want to give exotic food a rest for the moment.

'Look, I've got to dash,' he said briskly. 'Bit of a salmon day. Meet you in the Ninja bar at eight thirty, OK?' The line went dead.

It was nice, Jane thought, to be in the hands of someone decisive for a change. But that, she determined, was as far as Mark's hands were going to get. At least, until the question of how well he knew Champagne had been satisfactorily explained.

Ninja was one of those irritating restaurants which didn't bother having a sign outside, presumably on the grounds that the people who mattered knew where it was anyway, and those who didn't simply didn't matter. Jane realised she must be in the latter category, after spending ten heart-stopping minutes rushing up and down the street before finally realising the stark, anonymous, utterly signless black glass doors that looked exactly like an office were in fact the portals of Ninja.

There was no sign of Mark in the bar, which was of the minimalist, understated persuasion that looked far better without people. Anyone, however smart, who dared sit on one of its perfectly-aligned beige-covered stools ran the risk of making the place look hopelessly untidy. Intimidated, Jane decided to powder her nose instead.

Signs, it seemed, were not Ninja's strong point. Squinting at the tiny sexless figure on the black marble lavatory door, Jane assumed it was the ladies until she suddenly found herself in the men's. Ricocheting into the women's room, Jane looked at her appearance in despair. The faithful old black jacket and trousers were showing distinct signs of wear and tear; she had realised too late that her only other suit, along with the remains of Tiara's ballgown, was at the cleaners. 'I don't even have any clothes of my own,' she grumbled to herself. 'I just rent them from Sketchley's.'

She had done her best with her floppy, insubordinate locks, but it was still less of a hair-do than a hair-don't. It collapsed in a vague bob about her shoulders, perfumed with the smell of the sandwich bar in which she had queued at lunchtime. Why was it, Jane wondered, that her scent faded into nothing only a few minutes after application, while the odour of fried bacon and chips clung on more determinedly than the Ancient Mariner's albatross?

It took her a good few minutes to find her way out of the loos. The doors were innocent of anything as cumbersome or unaesthetic as a handle, and Jane scrabbled at panel after relentless panel of shining black marble before finding the one that opened. When, red-faced and flustered, she arrived back in the bar, Mark was sitting in the corner, talking urgently into the smallest mobile phone she had ever seen.

'Look, I'll have to get back to you tomorrow,' she heard him say as she approached. 'I'm late for a meeting now, so I have to go. *Ciao*. Hi there,' he grinned, snapping his mobile away. 'Krug?'

'Yes, please,' Jane nodded, shifting her bottom on to one of the tiny beige stool cushions.

'Shame you had to leave the party,' Mark said.

'Yes, wasn't it?' said Jane, thinking that it was more of a shame Champagne had seen fit to throw a trayful of chicken tikka masala all over her.

'How do you know Champagne?' she asked. There seemed no point in beating about the bush.

'Known her for years,' Mark said breezily. 'Her family's been with Goldman's practically since it started. Nice girl. Knows an awful lot about money.'

A waiter of inscrutable Orientalness came to escort them to their table. Jane decided not to pursue her inquiries further. Why spoil the evening by discussing Champagne? Better stick to drinking it. And what did it matter anyway? What was Mark Stackable to her? There was only one man she really cared about, and she could never find him now.

At some unseen signal from Mark, the waiter shimmied over with two more chilled glasses of champagne. Jane tried hard not to knock them over as she struggled to push aside with her knees the several layers of thick, white starched linen under the table. It was the type of restaurant where sitting down was like getting into bed.

Mark, buried in the menu, suddenly began to make a succession of noises of mixed agony and surprise which the waiter began to note down. He was, Jane realised, ordering in fluent Japanese.

'I'll have the same,' she smiled at the waiter, who looked back at her impassively.

'I've already ordered for you,' Mark said, snapping the menu shut. 'I used to work in Japan,' he added airily, 'so I like to get it out and dust it down every now and then.'

'Do you now?' grinned Jane.

Mark, however, did not smile. It dawned on Jane that perhaps his sense of humour was not his strongest point after all. Then again, he was so good-looking, it was probably greedy asking him to be funny as well.

A wooden board of sushi arrived and was placed on the table between them. Jane stared at the neatly arranged diagonals of cold fish and rolled rice and felt her appetite desert her. What she wouldn't give for a vast, steaming plate of spaghetti.

'It's very difficult to find food in London that doesn't destroy your body, don't you find?' Mark observed, plucking his sushi elegantly between tiny chopsticks and dipping it expertly into a bowl of soy sauce. Determinedly Jane nodded, shoved a piece of sushi in her mouth and swallowed it as quickly as possible.

'How was your salmon day?' she asked.

Mark raised his eyebrows and made 'I'm eating sushi'

gestures. 'Oh, fine,' he said when his mouth was empty. 'Not too many CLMs in the end.' Mark glanced at her uncomprehending face a trifle impatiently. 'Career limiting manoeuvres?'

Jane noticed that everything he said ended with a strange, upward, interrogative note that made each sentence sound like a question, even when, as almost always, it wasn't.

'Best overcome and remedied by efficient blamestorming and arsemosis?' said Mark. 'Blamestorming,' he explained, rather tersely, 'is like brainstorming, but the idea is to find some other guy to blame for when everything goes wrong?'

Jane giggled nervously, hoping he wasn't going to do the corporate talk all night. She knew nothing about the financial world. Her idea of a bear market was the cuddly toy section at Hamley's.

Mark gestured to the waiter to fill up her glass again. 'I can see I'm going to have to teach you a thing or two about the City?' he remarked, reading her thoughts alarmingly easily. 'Do you, for example,' he asked, shoving in a mouthful of rice and seaweed, 'know about leverage?'

Mark's mobile phone shrilled just as she was about to confess that she didn't. Flashing her a terse look which Jane interpreted as 'This is important so you'll have to excuse me?' Mark got up quickly and walked to the bar, his heels clicking on the marble like Fred Astaire.

After what seemed an eternity, Mark clicked back again. 'Sorry, but I'm afraid I'm involved in a pretty mega project at the moment?' he said. Jane was beginning to find his note of permanent inquiry maddening. 'Big bucks, if it comes off?'

Mark's eyes, Jane noticed, positively blazed at the mention of money. Perhaps the City was exciting after all.

Being rich *must* be interesting. It struck her as strange that, although he ended each of his statements with a question mark, Mark had yet to ask her a single question about herself. She hadn't noticed before, being too drunk the first time she had met him, and not having had time the second, but his mind, she was beginning to realise, had a strangely incurious cast. The only thing he seemed to be interested in was interest.

She laid down her chopsticks and drank the rest of her champagne. The room was starting to spin faster than Alastair Campbell.

'I'm not too hungry either?' Mark said, noticing Jane had stopped eating. 'Too much at lunchtime?' he added, patting his perfectly flat stomach. 'Tell you what, why don't you come back to my flat for, um, a peppermint tea? It's just around the corner?'

A corner half an hour away by taxi in the depths of Clerkenwell, as it turned out. Jane could have lived in the entrance hall of Mark's apartment block alone, she thought as she was ushered through the gleaming, concept-lit brick-lined space which seemed very different to the chandeliers-and-gilt-lobby she remembered going back to after Amanda's dinner party.

It was. 'Like it?' said Mark as they zoomed upwards. 'My new loft apartment. It's awesome. So cool. I've only been here a week or so.'

'When did you move?' asked Jane. She felt embarrassed. She had been meaning to move for months and hadn't done as much as look in an estate agent's window.

'Last week?' said Mark. 'I saw this place after a meeting and just had to have it. I had to get out of Cheyne Walk. There's no buzz there any more?'

Almost as soon as they had closed, the lift doors sprung

open again, straight into a vast, light room which Jane realised must be the sitting room. 'Yeah, the lift opens straight into the flat?' said Mark. 'Cool, huh?'

It was completely empty apart from two colossal white sofas which faced each other, as if squaring up for a sumo wrestling match, over a huge expanse of polished, honey-coloured wood. Behind them, a spiral staircase of the same wood wound up and away into the ceiling, and, further back still, two huge windows covered with thin-slatted Venetian blinds stretched film-noir-like to the floor. On a glass coffee table between the two sofas, a single white lily rose from a huge glass flowerpot. It was the barest room Jane had ever seen.

'Space,' Mark said, spreading his arms and grinning at her eagerly. 'The ultimate luxury, don't you think?'

Jane managed a smile. The discovery that Mark's idea of a good thing was basically thin air was not encouraging.

'And this is the cuisine,' said Mark, leading her into a vast white kitchen illuminated by a sloping glass roof. Its expanses of stainless steel and smooth white surfaces were more suggestive of an operating theatre than anything to do with eating. The vast fridge, which Mark proudly opened to show how it was shaped like a huge mobile phone, was bristling with ice-makers and water dispensers. Definitely a fridge too far, thought Jane. The front of the stove had so many buttons and lights it looked like the flight deck of Concorde. 'Not that I use it?' Mark confessed, mock-embarrassed. 'Haven't eaten in for, gee, must be five years?' he added proudly.

Jane could believe it. Nothing looked as if it had ever been touched. It was all so clean she felt as if she ought to be fumigated, or at least slip on protective clothing.

'Drink?' asked Mark, trotting across the brilliant white

space and returning with a bottle of red wine and two gleaming glasses. 'Nothing under fifty pounds a bottle is ever worth drinking, don't you agree?'

Jane nodded dumbly.

Mark took a tiny, restrained sip of the wine, then gave her a wolfish grin, evidently flossed to within an inch of its life. 'Want to see upstairs?'

As he led her out of the kitchen, Jane caught a glimpse of a bathroom beyond containing the biggest pair of weighing scales she had ever seen. Mark, Jane realised, was beginning to make Narcissus look self-deprecating.

'You've gotta see my bedroom?' said Mark.

Up the spiral stairs he went, into a room the size of a small airport terminal. Like downstairs, it contained the absolute minimum of furniture – a vast bed covered in a spotless white duvet and a huge mirror bolted to the wall opposite. It would almost have been kinky, Jane thought, were it not for the fact that the mirror was so far away from the bed you'd need binoculars to see yourself.

'Like my chandeliers?' asked Mark, pointing upwards to a ceiling as white and radiant as eternity. 'Cost a fortune. Specially designed for the loft. Great, aren't they?'

Jane looked up at the bright, twisted mass of cracked teacup, wine glass and coathanger, interspersed with the occasional bulb, which hung from the centre of the bedroom ceiling. It was, she supposed, witty. But she'd heard better jokes.

Mark picked up a small, slim remote control from the floor at the side of the bed and pointed it upwards. The chandelier immediately dimmed. 'Come and look at my million-pound view?' he smiled, clicking over to the floor-length windows. Jane walked over and stood beside him, gazing out as directed to the prospect of the City. The box-like buildings, centre of the world money trade, only reinforced Jane's feeling of unease. Mark's flat was so sterile. There seemed to be no books anywhere. Nor pictures. The only thing framed was mirrors.

Mark stretched out an arm and drew her to him. He started to kiss her neck, his mouth moving slowly up to her face. As he held her to him, Jane felt something big and hard pressing against her.

'Oh, excuse me?' Mark said, suddenly rummaging in his trousers and extracting his bulging wallet.

He began to kiss her again. The taste of the wine as he explored her mouth was now sour and metallic. Jane felt unable to respond. The truth was, she realised, that she could never really feel anything for Mark Stackable. There was nothing warm or witty about him. Nothing human. He was rich, but that really was about the size of it. Or was it? Something that was definitely not his wallet was rubbing urgently against her pudenda.

But it couldn't have been more different from Tom's tender caresses, and his thrilling subtlety. Jane stood as rigid as a statue as Mark grasped her breasts as eagerly as if they were fistfuls of banknotes, tears sliding down her face as he unbuttoned her jacket and roughly pushed it off. He stopped and looked at her in amazement as sobs began to shudder through her body. She shook her head, buttoned her clothes and squeezed his hand as she detached herself and went downstairs into the sitting room in search of her bag. After all, it wasn't Mark's fault that he wasn't Tom. Nor was it necessarily a bad thing he was obviously so obsessed with money. Some women, including, no doubt, most of the *Fabulous* staff, would kill for a man like him. It was just that, as far as Jane was concerned, Mark Stackable had feet of K.

Chapter 19

'Bollocks,' said Tosh to Oonagh.

'No, darling. Bollocks Beaufort-Baring wasn't *at* this wedding,' said the picture editor, bending over the lightbox and squinting at the pile of photographs she was examining with Tosh in her capacity as wedding editor. 'You're probably confusing him with Bruiser Aarss, who was there with the Hon. Bulymya yl Bowe.'

'Are you sure?' asked Tosh, picking up a photograph and scrutinising it closely. 'This looks like Bollocks to me. Don't you think so, Jane?' She held it up to the light.

Jane squinted at the image of a short, stocky young man with a novelty waistcoat and an alarmed expression. 'Complete Bollocks,' said Jane, who actually knew nothing about him save the fact that he had clearly emerged from the shallow end of the gene pool and was, as far as she could see, still dripping wet.

Oonagh sighed. 'I probably need a break,' she said. 'I've been wading through those pictures for so long I can't tell my Aarss from my yl Bowe any more.'

Jane's telephone rang. She gazed at it in terror. What if it was Mark? Three days had passed since she had left him with his expectations quite literally raised, and there had been much agonising in between. Had she done the right thing? Had rejecting the advances of the richest man she was ever likely to meet been a good idea?

Jane took the receiver with a shaking hand. For once, she was almost relieved to hear Champagne at the other end of the receiver. 'I've got some *brilliant* news,' came the triumphant honk. 'I'm going to be a film star. Marvellous, isn't it? I saw Brad again last night.' Naturally, she made no mention of, still less an apology for, the CTM incident.

'Brad who?' asked Jane. 'Pitt?'

'No,' came the outraged squawk. 'Brad Postlethwaite. The hot new British director I told you about. The one I met in New York. Anyway, we had dinner at Soho House last night and afterwards he offered me the most *amazing* part.'

I bet he did, thought Jane. 'A part in what?' she asked.

'He's making a really cool new film,' bawled Champagne. 'Sort of like *Four Weddings and a Funeral*, but it's called *Three Christenings and a Hen Party*. It sort of sends up English society christenings. He wants me to play myself. So obviously I've signed up for the best acting lessons money can buy. I'll be sending you the invoices, of course.'

'Playing *yourself*?' said Jane slowly. 'It's tongue in cheek, then?'

There was a silence. 'I'm not putting my tongue in anybody's cheeks,' blustered Champagne at the other end. 'It's a seriously challenging artistic opportunity. Brad says it's a cameo role,' Champagne gushed, 'but I do hope he lets me wear my diamonds.'

'When do you start?' asked Jane.

'Monday,' boomed Champagne. 'That's why I'm calling you. About the stretch limo. To take me to the set. Brad says the film hasn't got the budget to pay for one, so you'll have to sort it out for me. Want it big, black and shiny. Oh, and with a TV, telephone, fax, blacked-out windows, white suede seats and a cocktail cabinet.'

'You must be joking,' said Jane. 'We can't afford that.'

'Well, you'd better bloody *try*,' shrieked Champagne, slamming the phone down.

'Champagne's got a part in a film,' Jane told Victoria who was busy filling out her expenses slips in her office. 'She seems to expect us to provide a stretch limo to drive her to the set. As well as paying for her acting lessons.'

Victoria stopped stabbing her calculator and stared at her. Jane felt uncomfortable. She didn't know quite where she was with Victoria these days. The expected blow had not yet come. Victoria had not said a word about the conversation with Archie Fitzherbert. There must be a reason for this, as it was impossible that he had not told her. She was obviously biding her time. Waiting to strike. It made Jane nervous.

'Champagne,' Victoria explained patiently, a dangerous gleam in her eye, 'is our biggest asset. Whatever she wants, she can have. If she's in a film, great. Get her to write about it. Go on set with her. Do a big number. Come to think of it, let's put her on the cover.' Victoria's eyes blazed feverishly. 'Yes,' she breathed, like one witnessing an ecstatic vision. 'Let's put her in a director's chair, with her legs either side of it like Christine Keeler. What a great idea.'

Jane reeled out of the editor's office.

'By the way,' Victoria's voice floated out behind her, 'I've been meaning to have a word with you about this interview with Lady Dido Dingle, the interior designer.'

Jane blanched. The Lady Dido Dingle piece had been an editing nightmare. Like many of the *Fabulous* pieces which crossed Jane's desk it needed a rewrite so heavy she could have brought in a JCB.

'What about it?' Jane asked through gritted teeth. She had, she thought, done a reasonably good job on it.

'Well, it mentions her fifth home in St Tropez and her downstairs toilet,' said Victoria, putting her head on one side and looking questioningly at Jane.

'Yes that's right,' said Jane, nodding. 'With a solid gold seat and a diamond flush button.'

'*Fabulous* readers,' said Victoria, closing her eyes in exasperation, 'do not go to toilets.'

Which explained, thought Jane, the expressions on the faces of some of the people on the party pages.

'They use *lavatories*,' said Victoria. 'Or *loos*.'

When Jane rang Champagne back to say she could have a car, and was next month's cover story into the bargain, she was as magnanimous in victory as ever. 'Yah, I should bloody well think so,' she honked indignantly.

'So where is this set?' Jane asked. 'Although I suppose we could travel up together in the limo.'

'We bloody well could not,' Champagne shouted furiously. 'I'm the star. I'm not sharing my limo with anyone. You make your own sodding way there.'

Jane called the film production company, where a squeaky-voiced girl called Jade said she'd have to get back to her about the location. She was more forthcoming about the cast. It turned out that *Three Christenings and a Hen Party* was to star none other than the up-and-coming British actress Lily Eyre. After an excited discussion, Jane shot back into Victoria's office. There could be no excuse now for not putting Lily on the cover.

'She'll be the next Andie MacDowell,' Jane pleaded.

After all, she reasoned, Lily Eyre was the star of the film. Champagne was just a walk-on. 'And we could do her first. Have her exclusively, the film company says so. She's beautiful. She'd make the most brilliant cover.'

'Look, I'm sorry,' said Victoria sternly, sounding anything but apologetic. She did not like being argued with the first time, let alone the second. 'Champagne's our cover, and that's all there is to it.'

'But . . .'

Victoria's eyes flashed fire. She stood up, her leather miniskirt creaking indignantly. 'I'm not discussing it any further. Have you the faintest idea how busy I am? How many things I have to do today?'

'What *is* she doing today?' Jane whispered to Tish after Victoria stalked out of the office clutching a make-up bag, obviously en route for the loos.

'Erm, lunch at the Caprice,' murmured Tish, flicking through Victoria's diary. 'Then she's having her highlights done. Then she's going to her aromatherapist. Then she's seeing her dressmaker. Then she's off to Bali for a week on holiday. She didn't tell you? Oh. Do you want me to get that?'

Jane's phone had by now been ringing for some time. 'No, it's OK,' said Jane diving for it, thinking she'd rather have it answered this side of the millennium. It was the *Three Weddings and a Hen Party* film company.

'Sorry about the confusion earlier,' said Jade. 'It's just that we've been juggling locations slightly until we got the price we wanted. It's now definite that Champagne D'Vyne will be filming her scenes in the West Country.'

'How lovely,' said Jane. Visions of rustic, verdant bliss unfolded before her. 'Where, exactly?'

'Well, don't get your hopes up too much,' said Jade.

'The place is falling apart from what I hear. Rotting old pile called Mullions. The nearest village,' she paused and sniggered, 'is called Lower Bulge.'

The next day could not have been more beautiful. As the 2CV, given an unexpected stay of execution by a new garage down the road, backfired its way through the hedge-lined lanes leading to Mullions, Jane caught occasional glimpses of ploughed fields through which running pheasants lurched drunkenly from side to side. Placid ponies stood nibbling on green hillsides. A more soothing scene could not be imagined.

Jane was consumed with curiosity about what Tally had been up to. Guiltily, she realised it had been weeks since she had spoken to her. And what tumultuous weeks they had been. She had started a new job and she had found and lost once more both Tom and Mark Stackable, with varying degrees of regret. She had thought she had finally rid herself of the dead weight of Champagne, only to be proved hideously wrong. Tally, meanwhile, had hardly been idle. She had apparently converted Mullions into Ealing Studios.

Jane had thought at first that Jade was mistaken, but the directions she was given confirmed that Mullions was indeed where *Three Christenings and a Hen Party* was being immortalised on celluloid. It must be part of Tally's push to generate new business. An admirable and uncharacteristically enterprising effort, thought Jane, but it was a shame, nonetheless, that the production had Champagne in it. After her previous experience showing Champagne round Mullions, Tally had sworn on the heads of all the Venerys never to have her within a million miles of the place again. It was odd that she had changed her mind.

As the weather was so crisp and fine, Jane decided to leave the 2CV by the gatehouse and walk through the parkland to Mullions. She would be late for the arranged on-set meeting with Champagne, but not significantly. And certainly not later than Champagne herself. Champagne could be late for Britain.

After a pleasant ten minutes wandering along the estate road with the afternoon sun on her face and the sleepy church bells of Lower Bulge floating drowsily across the fields, Jane rounded a corner and stopped dead in her tracks. A scene seemed to be in full swing. Not wishing to disturb the filming, Jane slipped behind one of the bushes bordering the path, blessing Mr Peters and his slatternly pruning for such a convenient and copious screen. She peered out and watched.

The actors looked a decidedly scruffy bunch, all with straggling beards, metal-framed glasses and cagoules in every hideous fluorescent shade from violent pink to acid yellow. All wore hiking boots, were hung around with rucksacks and compasses like Christmas trees and were looking angrily in the direction of someone Jane could not quite see. She wondered where this scene fitted into the plot.

'What do you mean we can't walk across this land?' one of the cagoule-wearers was shouting, shaking his skinny fist. 'This is a right of way, this is. Marked on all the Ordnance Survey maps. Just look.' He waved a handful of much-creased cartography in the invisible someone's direction. 'You've no right to stop us, you haven't.'

'I have every right,' shouted a threatening, familiar voice. *Saul Dewsbury*, thought Jane in horror, shrinking further back into the bush. *Still around.* She imagined he had got bored of Tally and gone back to Chelsea ages ago. But no, he was here, larger and louder than life. This was obviously nothing to do with the film. This was another plot altogether.

'Don't want my land messed up by a load of wandering outward-bloody-bounders like you lot,' Saul was yelling, still out of sight.

His land? thought Jane in panic. Surely to God Tally hadn't *married* him. That would be a disaster. Not to mention insulting. They had always sworn to be each other's bridesmaids.

'Stomping around with bloody knapsacks,' continued Saul's echoing, contemptuous tones. 'Just piss off, will you? If you don't make yourselves scarce this minute, I'll horsewhip you off. I'll give you blisters where your boots have never been.' There was a cracking sound. Jane knew without having to see that Saul was slapping a riding crop over his thigh.

The ramblers' glasses flashed with impotent fury, but they decided not to call his bluff. Instead, they walked as slowly and defiantly as they could back along the path to the gate, muttering into their beards as they went. 'Won't get away with this,' the leader vowed as they passed Jane hidden behind the bushes. 'Breaking the law. We'll get him for this. Arrogant tosser.'

'Yeah. Who the hell does he think he is?' demanded another plaintively. 'Ruined our walk, he has. I'd just got into my stride and all. And what about all these egg sandwiches? I spent all last night making 'em.'

'Never mind the sandwiches,' said the leader, looking resolute. 'They'll come in useful, don't you worry. An army marches on its stomach. An' this is war. There've been some odd rumours about what that bloke's up to 'ere as it is. Time to get in touch with a few of our mates, I reckon.'

The little group stomped out of the gateway and disappeared behind the hedge along the road. Jane wondered who their mates were. And even more about the rumours.

She waited a few minutes until she was sure Saul had gone, then stepped out on to the path, almost colliding with Saul as she did so. He was passing the bush, presumably en route to the gate to make sure the ramblers had disappeared.

'Ow,' he shouted, as Jane's knee collided with that part of his thigh which still smarted from overzealous application of the riding crop. 'You!' he exclaimed, glaring at Jane. 'What the hell are you doing here? You're trespassing. I've a good mind to call the police.'

'I'm here for the filming, actually,' Jane said, trying to disguise how rattled she felt by his assumption of control. *Surely* Tally couldn't have . . . 'I'm here,' she continued lightly, 'to bring the sights, the sounds and if I'm very lucky the scenes of Champagne D'Vyne's cinematic debut to the printed page for the benefit of the glossy magazine-reading public.'

Saul stared at her, the colour draining out of his face. 'Champagne?' he gasped, his lordly tones dropping several decibels. 'Is *Champagne* in this bloody film?' He gasped at Jane in horror before recovering himself rapidly. 'I haven't seen the final cast list yet,' he muttered.

'She's got a starring role,' said Jane, amused at his consternation. 'I'm surprised you haven't popped down to say hi. Although,' she added slyly, 'I don't suppose Tally would particularly appreciate that. Is Tally around, by the way? I was rather hoping to be able to stay at the house.'

'Tally's not here at the moment,' said Saul firmly. 'I'm looking after the place for her. She's gone to London.'

'London?' exclaimed Jane, not believing him for a minute. Tally's loathing of London was legendary. Had he, she suddenly thought wildly, got *rid* of Tally? Hidden her under the floorboards and taken control of the estate? Saul, Jane was quite sure, was capable of anything to get his own ends. And there was no one around to stop him.

'Yes,' said Saul, smoothly. 'She's gone shopping. Buying a wedding dress, as it happens. We're getting married next weekend.'

Jane gasped. Next weekend. Relief that it had not yet happened mixed with horror that it was going to. 'Where's Mrs Ormondroyd?' she demanded. If she could get any sense out of anyone about what had been going on she'd get it out of the housekeeper.

'Mrs Ormondroyd, alas,' said Saul, admiring the signet ring on his little finger and playing with one of his elegant cuff-links, 'is sadly no longer with us. We had to let her go.'

Jane stared. The ring on his finger bore the Venery crest. Tally's ring. 'What, you mean you've sacked her?' she gasped. 'But Mrs Ormondroyd's been here for years. Centuries.'

'Exactly,' said Saul, lighting a leisurely cigarette. 'Mrs Ormondroyd didn't fit in with the, well, *enterprising* spirit that Tally and I are trying to introduce at Mullions. Nor, for that matter, did Mr Peters, who has also sadly left us. And now,' he said smoothly, 'I'll have to leave myself. Regrettably I won't be able to put you up at Mullions tonight. None of the bedrooms is fit to receive guests, unfortunately.'

When, thought Jane, watching Saul's dapper form retreating, had they ever been?

Jane walked rapidly down the slope into the park. There

was little more she could find out until Tally returned from London. If she had ever gone there, that was. Jane glanced up at the rambling old house and calculated that her chances of finding Tally inside that maze of rotting rooms if Saul wished to keep her hidden were nil. Mullions was the kind of place where people got up in the night to find the nearest lavatory, lost their way and were discovered forty years later as a skeleton in the Clock Tower broom cupboard.

Jane headed towards the film set. Even to her jaded and preoccupied eye it had something of the excitement and romance of a fairground. Caravans and lorries were parked haphazardly on the grassland, and ponytailed, T-shirted people bustled importantly about clutching clapperboards. On the grass immediately below the house, a gaggle of people with clipboards, cameras and loudhailers were concentrating on the scene about to be filmed.

As she approached, Jane saw that it was a scene between Lily Eyre and her co-star, a gangly young man with a tousled fringe and a disorganised air who was evidently meant to provide the Hugh Grant factor.

Lily was even more beautiful in the flesh than in her pictures. She had a vivid heart-shaped face in which two huge blue eyes shone like naughty sapphires, and a large, infectious grin. Her long, gold hair was as yellow and crinkly as spiral pasta and, as far as Jane could make out under the jeans, her ankles were slender and irreproachably upper class. As she waited for her cue, giggling with her co-star, she seemed to radiate charm and good humour.

'Take twenty-four,' shouted a red-haired girl with a clapperboard as Jane sidled in next to her at the edge of the set.

'A-aaa-aand ACTION!' shouted a shambolic-looking

man in a baggy sweater and geeky glasses, evidently the director, Brad Postlethwaite. He looked too cerebral to be tempted by Champagne, Jane thought. Whatever state he had been in when he offered her whatever part he had offered, he was clearly regretting it now.

'CHRIST!' he yelled as a figure suddenly appeared and ran across the back of the scene being filmed. 'Champagne, you've arsed up the eyelines again. For FUCK'S SAKE!' He spoke, Jane thought, amused, with the acid vehemence of the truly bitter.

'What do you mean?' bawled back Champagne indignantly. 'There's nothing wrong with my eyeliner. I know a damn sight more about make-up than you do.'

'Not eyeliner,' yelled the director furiously. '*Eyelines.*' His voice dropped, suddenly weary. 'You're distracting the actors on set so they keep looking at you and not at each other.'

You could hardly blame them, Jane thought. Champagne was wearing a fluorescent pink minidress so tiny one wondered why she had bothered putting it on at all. Her tanned thighs were exposed in their entirety while her breasts soared outwards and upwards like a couple of moon-bound Apollos.

'That dress should win an Oscar,' whispered the redhead with the clapperboard. 'Best supporting role.'

'A couple of Golden Globes at least,' giggled her blonde companion, whose bag, bulging with brushes, pots and tubes, proclaimed her to be a make-up girl. 'Unbelievable, isn't she? Talk about star attitude. Have you heard, she's even been demanding her own trailer?'

'Yes. And Brad told her she could have the honey-wagon if she wanted,' grinned the redhead. 'She was thrilled until she found out it was the toilets.'

'She's not very good at the jargon, is she?' smiled the blonde. 'When she first came to have her make-up done she had a very odd idea of what touching up was.'

'She thought a dolly grip was some sort of sex position, apparently,' snorted the redhead. 'Ooh, I'm on,' she added, suddenly realising the filming had ground to a halt and the director was staring at her furiously. 'Take twenty-five,' she called, slamming down her clapperboard so hard it made Jane wince.

'Get out of shot, for God's sake,' bawled the furious director at Champagne. 'For the millionth time, and almost the millionth take, THIS ISN'T YOUR SCENE!' Brad pushed his glasses on top of his unkempt hair and rubbed his eyes. He looked utterly defeated. 'OK, OK,' he said. 'Let's do your bit, Champagne. Your big scene. You walk across the set, grin at the camera and walk off again. That's all there is to it.'

'That's all there is to it *now*,' grinned the clapperboard girl. 'She had a line to say at the beginning but Brad got so fed up with her fluffing it he made it a non-speaking part. Lily's been very good about all this, I must say,' she added. 'Most stars would have a major fit if they had Champagne to put up with.'

Indeed, far from being annoyed, Lily, now smoking a cigarette beside the cameraman, actually seemed to be enjoying it. Her eyebrow was raised and her face shone with suppressed laughter. It was, Jane realised with a pang, the most perfect, provocative expression for the cover of *Fabulous*. Really, she was beginning to be obsessed with the magazine.

'AACTION!' shouted Brad.

Champagne stood up, took a deep breath and tottered across the set on her high heels. 'Break a leg,' murmured the redhead as Champagne closed her eyes and started to flex her tyre-like lips in what was evidently some sort of pre-performance ritual.

'Well, she'd certainly rather break a leg than a nail,' observed the make-up girl. 'I should know, I spent about three hours painting them this morning in exactly the right shade of nude she wanted. If nothing else, there's no end to her talons.'

'Shush, it's her Moment,' cautioned the clapperboard girl. 'We don't want to miss a piece of acting history.'

Pausing for a good few minutes in front of the camera, Champagne stuck her chest out and flashed a prolonged and utterly plastic grin before sashaying slowly off set.

'Cut!' said Brad. 'Perfect, Champagne. Got it in one. Take a break, everyone. Lunch.' He passed a weary hand across his forehead, looking as if food was the last thing on his mind and strong drink the first.

The two girls exploded. 'That bit wasn't even filmed,' hiccuped the redhead. 'There's no one sitting on the camera.'

Jane smiled broadly. It was true. The seat behind the lens was empty.

'Is it a shawl?' honked Champagne, wobbling across the grass towards Brad.

'She means a wrap,' tittered the make-up girl.

Jane, giggling, suddenly felt the smile freeze on her lips. Champagne, looking furiously in the direction of the sniggering, had spotted her.

'Where the hell have *you* been?' Champagne honked, stumbling over, her green eyes flashing furiously. 'What about this story you're supposed to be writing about me?'

The clapperboard and make-up girls melted away,

leaving Jane feeling alone and unprotected. 'I got delayed,' she said hurriedly.

'Well, you'd better catch up quickly then,' Champagne barked. 'I'll have to show you round, I suppose. I bet you don't know the first thing about a film set, do you?'

'Er, not much,' Jane admitted.

Champagne rolled her eyes and tossed back her white-blonde hair. 'Well, you'd better come with me,' she huffed. 'But first, you can take me to lunch.'

'Fine,' said Jane, looking at the queues of actors starting to form at the trestle tables some distance away. It would be fun to eat with the cast. And useful. She'd pick up lots of good anecdotes for the piece and it would be a chance to meet Lily.

'You surely don't think we're eating *on set*?' Champagne declared, looking at Jane in amazement. 'I'm sorry, but I think a star of my calibre has the right to expect something a bit more upmarket than the filthy crap they serve here. Can you see Demi Moore queuing up with that lot?'

'No,' said Jane, truthfully. Demi Moore was, indeed, nowhere to be seen. Lily Eyre was though, chatting happily to a bunch of cameramen as her plate was loaded with what looked like the most delicious noodles. Jane's stomach rumbled. She adored noodles. And the smell was heavenly.

Suddenly, from somewhere close by, something started playing an irritating and familiar-sounding tune in high-pitched, tinny notes. Looking around without success to identify where it came from, Jane realised it was 'There's No Business Like Showbusiness'. To her surprise, Champagne suddenly put her hand down her cleavage and extracted a tiny gold mobile phone. She snapped it open. The tinny music stopped.

'Yah?' Champagne listened for a few seconds. 'Yah,' she

said finally, closing the phone and shoving it back down her dress. She sniffed and tossed her hair. 'That was my New York acting studio,' she said loftily. 'Calling to tell me to make sure I'm projecting enough. Do you think I'm projecting enough?'

Jane's eyes dwelt briefly on Champagne's bulging bust, straining against the thin material of her dress like a dam about to burst. 'Oh yes,' she said with complete truth. 'You're projecting more than enough.'

'The food on that set is simply uneatable,' Champagne complained ten minutes later, her temper not improved by having to hobble all the way to the gatehouse where Jane had parked the car. 'Can you believe it,' she huffed from the front seat, 'Brad won't even let me have my own chef. I mean, it's the bare minimum a star expects on set. Julia Roberts would freak out. Tom and Nicole would go ballistic.'

'Brad should think himself lucky,' said Jane, starting the engine, 'that you didn't insist on a chef for Gucci as well.'

Champagne looked at her in contemptuous astonishment. 'Well of course I did,' she honked. 'I told him that Gucci needs a very special Russian diet. Can't eat anything but caviar at the moment, poor lamb. But of course Brad took *absolutely* no notice. Callous *bastard*. Can't think what I ever saw in him. Wouldn't even let me have a bodyguard, let alone a personal trainer. Stingy *bastard*.' She paused for breath. 'Still, he *had* to give me a trailer in the end. He actually thought he could make me stay at the local pub with everybody else. Can you *imagine*?'

Jane didn't bother to reply. By now they had reached Lower Bulge.

Lunch, in the event, was nothing more substantial than

a bag of cheese and onion crisps each and a half of Old Knickersplitter in the Gloom. 'Can't believe no one in this town knows how to fix a lobster club sandwich,' huffed Champagne as, a mere half an hour later, Jane drove the 2CV back to Mullions as hard as she dared, hoping the piles of noodles would still be on offer when they returned. But when they arrived back on the set, not so much as a beansprout remained.

Champagne climbed out of the car in such a manner as to expose as much tanned bottom as possible. 'I'm back now,' she announced to no one in particular. 'You can carry on filming.' She staggered over the grass towards the girl with the clapperboard. 'Where's my call sheet?' she demanded.

Not batting an eyelid, the girl detached a piece of paper from a folder in her bag. 'Here you are,' she said, handing it to Champagne, who scanned it eagerly before looking up in fury.

'But I'm not in any scenes at all this afternoon according to this,' she shouted. 'What the fuck's going on? Where's Brad?'

'Filming the big love scene,' said the production assistant. 'The set is closed, I'm afraid.' How much full frontal nudity could there possibly be in a film called *Three Christenings and a Hen Party*? thought Jane. Could Brad be barricading himself inside the set for other reasons altogether?

'I *demand* to see him,' raged Champagne. 'What do you mean, big love scene? I'm the one who makes the big scenes around here.'

There was an acquiescent silence.

'Brad was so happy with what you shot this morning that he thought you probably needed the afternoon off to rest,' said the redhead quickly. Whatever was she doing in films, Jane wondered, when she obviously had a brilliant future in diplomacy?

Champagne tossed her head, faintly mollified. 'Yes, I was rather good, wasn't I? Oh well.' She turned and looked at Jane. 'Suppose I'd better fill you in on some of the jargon,' she declared. 'For the piece you're writing about me. Got your notebook ready?' She pointed at the lighting rig behind her. 'Lights,' she boomed, as if Jane had never seen one before. 'Big ones are called redheads and the little ones are called blondes.'

'Er, other way round actually,' murmured the redheaded clapperboard girl.

Champagne ignored her. 'And that big machine they are slung up on is called the cherry popper,' she announced.

'Cherry *picker*, actually,' said the girl before beating a retreat under Champagne's furious glare.

Champagne wandered over to a group of men surrounded by wires, microphones and speakers. 'This is Nigel, one of the sound men,' she revealed, pouting at a handsome, bronzed six-footer with blond hair tied back in a ponytail. 'Nigel has a very large and hairy thing he waves around everywhere.' Champagne gave Nigel the most blatantly suggestive smile Jane had ever seen.

'I think Champagne means the boom microphone,' said Nigel, grinning back.

'And this is Chris, the chief cameraman,' Champagne continued, dragging Jane into the personal space of a tanned and muscular hunk in a New York baseball cap. 'Otherwise known as the gofer.'

'You mean the gaffer,' said Chris in a broad Australian accent. 'Rather a different thing in the pecking order,' he grinned. 'But that's not me, anyway. The gaffer's the chief electrician. And his deputy, that's Ian rummaging in that box over there, is known as the best boy.'

Champagne lowered her lashes and smouldered at Ian, who started to scrabble even harder in what looked like a case of electrical leads. 'The best boy, eh?' she repeated loudly. 'Best at what, I wonder?'

As a flush crept up Patrick's pale and somewhat pimply neck. Champagne returned to pouting at Chris.

'Chris and I have discovered we've got lots in common,' she honked. 'We've both got some Scottish in us, apparently. His name is McCrae, and my grandmother was from Edinburgh.'

'What an astonishing coincidence,' said Jane, ironically.

Champagne glanced suddenly at the Rolex weighing down her wrist. 'Look, can't stand here all day. Come and find me later,' she ordered Jane. 'Must dash. I've got the runs.' She staggered off over the field.

'She means the rushes,' said Chris. 'It's when what's been filmed during the day is shown. Hardly worth her turning up, really. I don't think she's going to appear on much of it, to be honest.'

'Never mind,' said Jane, turning round to see Champagne flirting wildly with Nigel some distance away. 'I'm not so sure she intends to go and watch it. She seems to be more interested in the sound.'

Chris grinned as he watched them. 'Well, she's wasting her time with Nigel,' he said. 'He may look macho but he's as gay as New Year's Eve. Fancy a drink later?' he added. 'Are you staying in the pub?'

Jane hesitated. She had not considered the question of her overnight accommodation since unsuccessfully raising it with Saul Dewsbury. 'Yes,' she said. 'I think I probably am.'

Chapter 20

Tally shrieked as the bright red bloodstain began to spread over the virgin white satin of the wedding dress. 'Shit,' she yelped. 'Bugger.' The needle had driven right into her finger. It had been a charming thought of Saul's that she should embroider her wedding dress with the Venery family mottos of deer and hares, but they had not come out as successfully as she had hoped. Her hares looked like hamsters, and the deers' antlers like TV aerials. Not to put too fine a petit point on it, her sewing was a shambles. And, boringly, it had kept her practically imprisoned in her bedroom throughout the first few days of the filming.

The bloodstain, fortunately, was less of a disaster than it first seemed. It was on the inside of a sleeve and if she kept her left arm to her side throughout the wedding, no one would be any the wiser. Not that anyone would be anyway. Saul's insistence on a speedy, private register office wedding meant the two of them would be practically the only people present.

As she plunged the needle once more into the satin, Tally determinedly tried to bury all thoughts of the traditional ceremony in the family chapel which she had always imagined she would have. With flowers by Mr Peters and serried ranks of Mrs Ormondroyd's quiches alongside knockout glasses of the Fourth Earl's punch. And her mother's veil, but not, alas, the family tiara. That had been sold long ago to cover one of someone's less fortunate evenings at Monte Carlo.

The family chapel, in any case, had been ruled out of the proceedings the week before, when the crested and pilastered Venery family gallery high up at the back of it had finally come crashing down. It was a tragedy, Tally had thought as she surveyed the damage with brimming eyes, that she and Saul could not marry on the same spot where so many of her ancestors had celebrated their union.

'Such a shame,' she said to Saul. 'The Fourth Earl married no less than three wives here.'

'What did he do with the first two?' Saul stammered as best he could between his chattering teeth. Like the rest of the house, the chapel, as always, even in the scorching height of summer, was freezing.

'They died in childbirth, I think,' said Tally vaguely. 'Then there was the Fifth Earl,' she added, brightening. 'He got married here. Quite a wild chap, by all accounts. Took his mistress on honeymoon with him and his wife.'

'What did his wife make of that?' asked Saul, clutching his herringbone tightly round him.

'Went mad and died of diphtheria, I believe.'

'Well,' said Saul, still shuddering, 'looks like we're doing the right thing then. A wedding here sounds about the worst start to married life imaginable. Just as well the place has collapsed.'

If only it was just the chapel that had collapsed, Tally thought. The rest of the house seemed poised to come crashing down at any moment as well. Tally fretted about the fretwork every night as she went to sleep, and she felt guilty about the fading and black-flecked gilt everywhere, so desperately in need of renewal. The cracked console tables were no consolation whatsoever and the bas-reliefs were a source of deep anxiety. There was also nothing remotely amusing about the ha-ha. The only comfort for Tally was that she no longer had to face the increasingly baleful-looking Ancestors. A furious and shaken Saul had removed them from the walls of the staircase some weeks earlier after another leap for freedom by the Third Earl had narrowly avoided crushing him to death. 'Bunch of miserable old bastards anyway,' Saul had said, watching the then-still-employed Mr Peters heave the Ancestors' reproachful and indignant countenances into a storeroom.

Tally sighed. Where was Saul? she wondered, letting her sewing fall into her lap. He had dashed off a good half hour ago saying that he thought he had heard something suspicious downstairs. Something suspiciously like Champagne D'Vyne, she imagined jealously. She may have spent the last few days in thimble-wielding purdah, but Tally knew perfectly well Saul's old girlfriend was on the set. No one within a four-mile radius of that unmistakable voice could possibly be innocent of the fact.

Saul was definitely up to something, Tally was sure. He was practically nowhere to be seen these days. Once or twice she had rounded corners to find him muttering into his mobile phone and, despite his protestations that he was talking business, she had not quite believed him. Business with Champagne, maybe, she thought crossly.

It's just pre-wedding nerves, Tally told herself briskly, dismissing her demons. She knew from the ancient and dog-eared copy of *Brides and Setting Up Home* she had bought from the newsagents in Lower Bulge that engaged couples were often beset with doubts and fears about each other before getting married. The best cure for cold feet, she decided, was a brisk trot along the chilly corridors to the kitchen, where a ready-meal lasagne had been heating in the Aga for what seemed like hours.

The kitchen seemed impossibly huge, dark and empty without Mrs Ormondroyd. Her sheer bulk had somehow made it look smaller. The lasagne, meanwhile, was dried out and dead. Tally was prising it sadly from its foil coffin when Saul walked in.

'What's *that*?' he said, throwing a disgusted glance at the lasagne. 'Something Mrs Ormondroyd's left behind in the bottom of the oven?

'You're not in the Fulham Road now, you know,' said Tally furiously. 'You're not with Sha-Sha-Champagne D'Vyne now either,' she added, her scant bosom heaving. 'Though you ob-ob-ob-viously wish you were.' She dissolved into tears

The look of absolute horror on Saul's face was some comfort, at least. 'I can assure you I don't,' he said, with feeling. Understanding dawned in his face. 'Is *that* what's making you so baity?' he breathed, sending up a silent prayer of thanks that Tally wasn't, as he had feared, pregnant. 'Let me tell you,' he said, taking his fiancée's heaving form in his arms, 'that woman was the worst mistake of my life. She practically bankrupted me. I've been avoiding the film set like the plague rather than risk running into her. Oh, Tally,' he said, kissing the top of her head and trying not to mind she had not brushed her hair for what looked like a week at least. 'You mustn't. It'll all be fine, you'll see. You have to admit the film idea was a huge success.'

Tally sniffed and nodded, not quite daring to remind Saul that a condition of the film crew's coming had been that no shooting was to take place inside the house. To date at least one love scene had been filmed on the Elizabethan bed and a riotous party scene in the Blue Drawing Room had caused the room's great treasure, the precious Eagle chandelier with its delicate arms fantastically wrought with birds of prey, to rock wildly. A network of terrifying-looking cracks had since spread across the ceiling surrounding it.

Tally was about to tell Saul a few stately home truths when, somewhere beyond the hall, the shattering sound of glass crashing on the floor stopped her. She sighed. The Eagle, it seemed, had landed.

Rather surprisingly considering the number of people on the film set, the Gloom and Sobbing turned out to have plenty of room to spare. Jane was as relieved to get a bed for the night as she was disappointed to find the promising-looking cameraman called Chris was nowhere to be seen. It dawned on her, as she sat in the deserted bar with a book and a half-pint of Old Knickersplitter, that he was perhaps staying in another pub altogether. On reflection, it seemed more than likely that everyone else on the film had chosen the more cheerful if more distant Barley Mow in Upper Bulge to the lugubrious Gloom.

The Gloom's lumpy bed and scratchy sheets not being conducive to a lie-in, still less a good night's sleep, Jane was up and about on the film set by ten. Breakfast was being served and she headed gratefully for a plate of creamy yellow scrambled eggs and a mug of steaming tea.

'Looking for Champagne?' called the redheaded clapperboard girl who, despite her tiny size, was tucking into an enormous plateful of fried bread, tomatoes, sausages and bacon. Jane, who had in fact been hoping for a morning encounter with Chris, nodded anyway. 'Try her trailer,' said the redhead.

Jane looked around for a Demi Moore-style gleaming silver pantechnicon. 'Where *is* her trailer?' she asked.

'Over there,' said the girl, pointing in the direction of a tiny, battered, domestic caravan. 'We borrowed it for her from the continuity girl's parents. They live near here, thank goodness. They're invited to the world premiere of the film to make up for not being able to go to Skegness all summer.' She finished her sausages and gathered up her clapperboard. 'Tell Champagne she's on soon,' she called. 'There's a crowd scene coming up where she has to smile at the camera. If she gets on set now we might get it right by midnight.'

Jane knocked on the caravan door. A flurry of hysterical barks announced Gucci was within, but the expected accompanying growls from his mistress did not materialise. 'Champagne?' Jane called, rapping again. The top half of the door creaked reluctantly open to reveal the head of a tousled-looking Champagne who, maddeningly, looked more glamorous than ever with wild hair and sleepy eyes.

'You!' she said disgustedly. 'Why the hell did you have to come now? I'm busy, um, perfecting my technique.'

'Well, apparently they want you on set in a minute,' Jane said, 'I'm here to collect you.'

'Well, I can't come just like that, you know,' snapped Champagne. Was she hearing things, thought Jane, or was there a stifled guffaw from within? Her suspicions were confirmed when Gucci, scenting escape, threw himself against the lower door which swung open to reveal Chris the dark-haired gaffer lying on the floor, naked and in a state of supreme excitement. Completely unabashed, he grinned winningly at the astonished Jane.

'What's the matter?' he asked. 'Never heard of making love to the camera?'

'I'll, um, see you on set,' muttered Jane, backing away in embarrassment tinged with disappointment. So this was what Champagne had meant by having some Scottish in her. No wonder she hadn't seen Chris in the Gloom and Sobbing.

Jane walked away, trying to concentrate on the scenery rather than what she had just seen. It really was a beautiful morning. A powerful sun was burning the last mist off the lake to reveal a dazzling silver mirror beneath. Brilliant green grass swayed ecstatically in the rosemary-scented wind like a music and movement class, each blade shining as if Nature had not only washed it, but given it a squirt of hi-gloss conditioner as well. The leaves on the thick-trunked trees dotted here and there across the undulating parkland tossed and shimmered like a row of chorus girls' feathers.

Et in Arcadia ego, thought Jane as her feet swished through the grass. Well, she could vouch for the ego bit, certainly. She looked up to find herself approaching the tiny ornamental rotunda that stood on a gentle slope on the other side of the lake. She had walked further than she thought.

As she approached the little building, Jane realised she was not the only one pacing about the park that morning. Propped up against one of the encircling pillars was an ashen-looking Brad, smoking furiously. He was evidently a man with a lot on his mind. Probably recharging his spiritual batteries for the day's filming, Jane thought, skirting gingerly past him so as not to disturb the creative process. She gasped as a cold and bony hand shot out and grabbed her by the wrist.

'I've just seen the rushes,' Brad blurted out. 'Couldn't face seeing them last night. And in every shot from yesterday morning that stupid tart's wandering around in the background flashing her tits and her knickers. The christening scenes look like they've been filmed at Raymond's Revue Bar.'

Jane looked at him, not knowing what to say. Much as she agreed with Brad, she had her professional responsibilities to consider. After all, if Brad threw Champagne off the set, *Fabulous* would be left without a cover and the deadline was looming. Once again, Champagne had her by the short and curlies. 'Her acting method is very, er, avant garde, isn't it?' she murmured.

Brad turned glittering and feverish eyes upon her. 'I think it's more avant a clue,' he hissed.

Deciding he was better left to himself, Jane continued on her way and walked up the slope behind the lake to the estate road and the old gateway. As the estate entrance came into view, Jane noticed a flash of silver turn off the main road beyond and come flying through the ancient archway like a Cruise missile. As it bounced over the potholes Jane stumbled out of the way on to the verge, expecting the car to plunge past her towards the house. It didn't. There was a mighty screech of brakes as the wheels locked and what looked like a hundred thousand pounds' worth of prime babe magnet shuddered to a halt a foot or so in front of her. Jane looked up at the windscreen. Sitting behind it, to her astonishment, was Mark Stackable.

The tinted driver's window glided electronically down to reveal Mark's stern, unsmiling profile. Jane stared at him, embarrassed, wondering what on earth he was doing here. Had he come to try and persuade her to give him another chance? If so, he looked very surprised to see her.

'You really didn't need to come all the way up here,' she stammered. 'We could have met in town.'

Mark stared at her in astonishment. 'Met *you*?' he repeated in tones that implied he would have crossed continents to avoid her. 'I'm afraid I'm up here on business. Nothing to do with you, I'm afraid. At all,' he added emphatically. It was the first time Jane had ever heard him not end a speech with a question.

Of course, thought Jane. Business must mean the film. The success of *Four Weddings and a Funeral* meant that no City investor worth his salt could afford to ignore the potential of a follow-up made in the same style. *Three Christenings and a Hen Party* was worth a punt of anyone's money.

'You know what I think,' she said to Mark eagerly, and wanting to make amends for her behaviour at his flat. 'You should have some male strippers from Sheffield as well.'

'Excuse me?' asked Mark, astonished. His fingers stopped their impatient tapping on the steering wheel. 'What the hell are you talking about?'

'Yes,' enthused Jane, swept away by the brilliance of her idea. 'You can't afford to ignore the success of *The Full Monty*. If you have a gang of unemployed Yorkshiremen getting their kit off at the posh hen party, you'll have both the top British hits of recent years in one. And,' she added, inspired, 'you shouldn't call it *Three Christenings and a Hen Party* either. You should call it *The Full Fonty*!'

'I haven't the faintest idea what you mean?' Mark said wearily, his fingers now drumming a tattoo.

'The film, of course,' said Jane. 'The film that's being made over there.' She gestured in the direction of the now-buzzing set from where the occasional loud bray could be heard. Champagne was obviously now up and about and ready for her close-up.

'I've got no interest in *that* whatsoever,' said Mark, casting a contemptuous glance at the straggling conglomerate of caravans and lighting rigs. 'That's small fry. I'm here to have a meeting about the house.'

'Oh, so you've come to see *Mullions*?' Now that made even more sense. What else, thought Jane, would a rich young banker about town be doing on a Saturday apart from buying himself a mansion in the country? It was odd, admittedly, that Mark's choice should have fallen on Mullions, but the house, as Champagne and the film set demonstrated, was proving to be the sort of place that attracted unlikely coincidences.

She wasn't sure, however, that Mark buying Mullions was altogether ideal. Jane shuddered at the thought of him making the ramshackle old house the same sterile temple to contemporary interior design as his Clerkenwell flat. Visions of Mark using the suits of armour as novelty linen baskets in his surgically precise bathroom and replacing the Elizabethan four-poster with a circular waterbed flashed before her. The only remotely appropriate thing she could imagine him doing was returning the ancient dungeons below the house to their original use as torture chambers and making them into a gym.

'Are you sure you're interested in Mullions?' Jane asked, alarmed. 'The place is collapsing, you know. Rotting on its feet. Practically rubble.'

'Yes, I know,' said Mark. 'That's precisely why I *am* interested. It's got *megazoid* potential?'

Jane blinked. He thought Mullions had potential? This was not what she had expected to hear. Perhaps she had got him wrong. 'Why don't you leave the car here and walk over to the house with me?' she suggested enthusiastically. 'That way you get the best view of it. Over the lake.' Mark looked at her doubtfully, then nodded and opened the door which ran the entire length of his gleaming vehicle. His jeans, Jane couldn't help noticing as his legs swung out on to the path, had creases so sharp they looked dangerous. He was obviously not a man who was used to casual dressing. 'Nice car,' she remarked, privately considering it flasher than a warehouseful of kitchen cleaner. 'New?'

'All my cars are new,' said Mark crushingly, grabbing a large black folder out of the passenger seat and pointing the car alarm key at the lock. There was a swishing, clunking sound as his security system came on stream. 'I change them every six months, or sooner, if the ashtray gets full?' He gave her a wintry smile. Jane was not entirely sure he was joking. But she was relieved he had de-iced a bit. As with the vomit episode, he seemed to be erasing her rejection of his advances from his memory. Part of the reason, she was touched to see, seemed to be his enthusiasm for Mullions.

'The place has had a bad time lately,' Jane began as they set off across the greensward in the direction of the house. She grinned. 'You can practically smell the dry rot from here.'

'Yes,' said Mark, clutching his folder to his chest. 'Wonderful, isn't it?'

Jane gave him a quizzical look. What was so wonderful about it? Still, perhaps he meant that the opportunities for sympathetic refurbishment were endless. Jane hoped fervently that Tally was somewhere in the house to show him round. Mark had arrived in the nick of time. He was just what she was looking for.

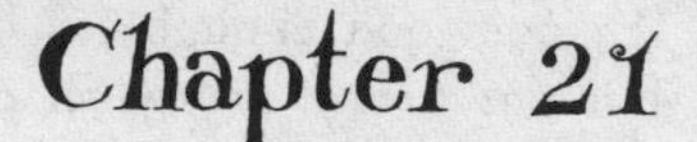

Tally gazed forlornly round the rose garden. What once had been a civilised area for after-dinner strolling was now, with its rampant thorns, something that the Prince in Sleeping Beauty might recognise. The roses were not so much rambling as rioting.

Trowel in hand, Tally peered through the bushes at the park beyond. She could just about see the film set and the people moving about on it. Relief flooded her when she recognised the strutting figure with white-blonde hair, who, from the sound as well as the look of her, was enjoying a full and frank exchange of views with a tall man with a megaphone. Champagne D'Vyne was safely on set. So, wherever Saul had disappeared to again, it wasn't to be with her.

Really, I'm getting paranoid, Tally thought to herself as she poked half-heartedly with her trowel at the long-untended earth. Saul was doubtless making some arrangement or other for the wedding. Or the honeymoon, which she imagined must be a surprise, as Saul hadn't uttered a word about it. But try as she might, she couldn't quite quash a feeling of misgiving. 'Something's rotten round here,' she thought, feeling like a prophet as a bush bitten to death by blackfly collapsed into her lap.

As usual when she was not quite certain about anything, Tally decided to blame herself. Perhaps I feel, subconsciously, that I'm not good enough for him, she told herself. That I'm not pretty or stylish enough. This morning's events alone were enough to support this theory – Saul had been unimpressed when she had appeared at breakfast in her father's old shooting suit.

'You'll be wearing the suits of armour next,' he had snapped.

'But I've nothing else left,' said Tally, thinking that the suits of armour idea was not such a bad one. Once you got them warmed up, they would be very hard-wearing and perfect for walking, although fiddly tasks like washing up or gardening might be tricky.

She was also slightly worried about Saul's attitude to Mullions these days. His former awed respect seemed to have been replaced by something bordering on the cavalier. And not the Charles I variety at that. When, for example, she had shown him Mullions' other single remaining treasure beside the Elizabethan bed, a tiny sketch of the infant Edward VI thought to be by Holbein, Saul had observed breezily that he thought Holbein was a stop on the Central Line.

Perhaps, Tally reasoned with herself, sitting back on her heels and letting the trowel slide from her lap, she felt uneasy because she was getting married without a single member of her family present; an unprecedented step for a Venery. Yet Julia and Big Horn were still away at their ashram with no definite date for their return. 'We'll come back when the time is right,' Julia had breathed enigmatically as she and Big Horn piled into the astounded minicab driver's back seat on their way to the airport. Piers, of course, had not been seen for months. Still saving the earth two hundred feet under some runway, Tally supposed wearily, wondering if she would ever see her only sibling again.

If only she could talk to Jane about it all. She had suggested to Saul that her best friend be witness at the wedding, but Saul had been so appalled at the idea she had dropped it without further ado. The very mention of Jane's name got him in a rage for some reason. It had seemed better, more loyal to him at any rate, not to get in touch with Jane at all for the time being. Passions were running too high. Plenty of time for everyone to make friends after the wedding. Nonetheless, Tally missed her. Jane was so straightforward. Her opinions came directly from her heart, and her advice was always sensible, except, of course, when it came to addressing her own love life. Tally wondered what Jane's romantic status was at the moment. Chaotic as usual, she imagined.

Or perhaps not. Tally, getting to her feet and stretching her back, stared in astonishment as she saw someone who looked rather like Jane walking rapidly down through the rose garden towards her, accompanied by someone, a man, whom Tally didn't recognise. She squinted at the couple. The man looked astonishingly handsome. With extraordinarily clean jeans.

'Tally!' called Jane, breaking into a run. She dashed up and caught Tally in a bear hug. 'Haven't seen you for ages,' she muttered into Tally's scratchy and rather smelly tweed shoulder. 'God, I've missed you!' She held her friend at arm's length and stared into Tally's hesitant grey eyes. She looks thinner, thought Jane. Strained, even.

'Natalia Venery, meet Mark Stackable,' she said with a flourish. 'He's come to look at Mullions. You must be expecting him.'

Tally frowned. Unreliable though her memory was, apart from when recalling the more recondite episodes of family history, she was sure the estate agents had stopped sending people to look round the house at least two weeks ago. After Saul had been to see them, in fact.

'They say the place is just too near to collapse to sell,' Saul had reported, the picture of regret. Tally had dolefully agreed, unaware that Saul's purpose in going to the estate agents was to take the place off the market himself. 'Don't worry, I'll think of something,' he had told her. She had given him a watery grin, unaware that he already had.

'Oh,' Tally now said to Mark, who was staring at her in the astonished way everyone who came to Mullions seemed to. 'I'm not sure I was expecting anyone actually. But you're very welcome. Would you like a cup of tea?' She prayed not. The Aga had been playing up so much lately it was quicker to go on foot to the cafe at Lower Bulge than wait for a kettle to boil.

'I had an arrangement to see your husband?' Mark said crisply. He felt impatient with this obviously batty woman. He'd wasted enough time already. 'Mr Dewsbury? He and I have been discussing the estate quite a lot recently?'

Jane stared at Mark, puzzled. He'd come to see Dewsbury?

It made slightly more sense to Tally. 'Oh, I *see*,' she said slowly. So Saul had decided to take the matter of finding a buyer into his *own* hands, had he? There was, Tally supposed, no reason why not, although he *might* have discussed it with her first. 'Well,' she said to Mark, 'I'm afraid my, er, Mr Dewsbury's not here, but I'm sure I can tell you anything you might want to know.'

'Good,' said Mark. 'I just wanted to check that the bulldozers are still on schedule?'

Tally gasped and took a step back. 'B-b-bulldozers?' Jane shot to her side.

'What do you mean, bulldozers?' she demanded. This sounded serious.

'Well, Dewsbury should have arranged it all?' said Mark. Never had his ludicrously interrogative tones irritated Jane so much. 'They're coming in a fortnight to flatten the place?'

'*What*?' said Jane, taking over the role of official spokesperson. Tally looked too shocked to speak. One hand was clapped to a face more drained and grey than the Mullions gutters. She looked as if she was about to be sick.

'Yeah, though Dewsbury says if we wait three weeks the house will probably fall down on its own. Sooner if somebody sneezes?' Mark grinned.

Tally removed her hand. Her mouth opened and closed like a goldfish.

'Then,' said Mark, snapping opening his folder and riffling through its pristine white pages, 'we slap up the houses.'

Tally's face had now changed from grey to ripe tomato. She started to sputter something. Jane put a quieting hand on her arm. Here, at last, was the evidence she had been waiting for. She had *known* there was something fishy about Saul from the start.

'Houses?' she asked, trying to sound as calm and matter-of-fact as possible.

'Yeah,' said Mark, flashing his tombstone teeth. 'Hundreds of them. Making astronomical profits for everyone involved?' He looked at Tally. 'I bet you're thrilled, aren'tcha?' He licked his lips.

Tally made a choking sound.

'Astronomical? Really?' croaked Jane, squeezing Tally's

arm warningly. Her head echoed to the thunderous sound of everything crashing into place. So *this* was what the marriage was all about. Saul had seen millions in Mullions the minute he clapped eyes on it, and seducing poor, batty, scatty Tally was the way to get his hands on it. He must have cooked up his plan almost immediately after Amanda's dinner party and had roped in Stackable to finance it.

'Astronomical,' Mark almost sang. 'So you haven't been filled in on the details, huh? Best left to the men, huh?' He paused and grinned at them.

Jane was by now almost breaking Tally's wrist, so desperate was she to keep her friend quiet. They needed Mark to tell them as much as possible.

'Well,' Mark drawled, gazing at his documents with love in his eyes, 'we thought three hundred and fifty K a time for the smallest two-bedroomed rabbit hutch? And, as you know, we're building four hundred of them? Only the best breeze block, and each house comes ready-equipped with satellite dish, herringbone brick drive, carriage lamps and automatic garage door?' He stopped and looked at Tally's and Jane's astonished faces. 'Dewsbury doesn't seem to have briefed you very well, I must say?'

'No need, now you've done such a great sales pitch,' said a smooth voice behind Tally. 'Couldn't have put it better myself.' Saul sauntered into view, his eyes glittering boldly. 'Sorry I wasn't here when you came,' he added easily to Mark, 'but I was in the loo and the door fell in on me. Took rather a while to lever it off.' He grinned widely all round.

Tally and Jane's mouths stayed as straight and flat as spirit levels.

'I think you owe me an explanation, Saul,' said Tally, in

low, fierce tones Jane had never heard her use before.

The law of the Dewsburys was if in doubt, brazen it out. Saul now proceeded to apply that law to its last letter. 'But my darling,' he said, smoothly, 'just think of the advantages. The astonishing profits. With the sort of money we're talking about we can dismantle Mullions brick by brick and re-erect it in Arizona. On the moon, if you like. Just think of the . . .' His pleading voice died away. His expression widened and deepened into abject terror. It seemed to be reacting to something behind Tally. 'Oh God, no,' he gasped, as if the Grim Reaper himself was coming across the park behind them. 'Please. Anything but that.' Saul took a few steps backwards, then suddenly spun on his hand-tooled leather heel and shot off round the back of the house.

'Hey, hey, not so fast,' bellowed Mark, seeing millions, if not Mullions, disappearing before his eyes. He skidded after Saul across the gravel, the papers flying out of his folder as he went.

Both woman craned round to stare at whatever had so terrified Saul. Picking her wobbling, skyscraper-heeled way determinedly over the muddy grass in a pair of unfeasibly tight leather trousers and shades so profoundly black they looked opaque came Champagne D'Vyne.

'Where the bloody hell have *you* been?' Champagne brayed, looking straight at Tally as her metal Gucci heels dragged excruciatingly over the soft old stone of the steps. 'I've been all over this dump looking for you.'

Tally drew in her breath in a short, indignant gasp.

'Don't worry,' whispered Jane. 'I don't think she can see a thing in those glasses. She thinks she's talking to me.'

'I gathered that,' hissed Tally. 'I just object to my home being described in that way. Although I suppose,' she added ruefully, 'judging from what I've just heard, I'm lucky to have a dump left. I just can't believe—'

'What's the matter?' Jane asked Champagne hurriedly. Now was not the time for Tally to embark on an orgy of agonised heart-searching. That could come later.

'That bastard Brad has only *sacked* me from the *film*, that's all,' honked Champagne. '*Outrageous*. How *dare* he? Who the *bloody hell* does he think he is?'

'What happened?' asked Jane. 'Artistic differences?'

'Well, for some reason,' Champagne boomed, still addressing Tally, 'he seemed to think I was being unreasonable, asking for a double to film some of the party scenes.'

'Body double? I thought they were only used for stunts,' said Jane.

'Yah, but in these party scenes, we're supposed to be drinking champagne, and of course I never drink anything less than Krug,' Champagne spluttered indignantly. 'And Brad was actually expecting me – *me* – to drink filthy *supermarket stuff*. So I *insisted* on a body double because otherwise I'd probably be throwing up all night. But he refused and threw me off the set.' Champagne fumbled furiously for a cigarette. Her efforts to light it were so severely hampered by the restrictions the sunglasses placed on her vision that Jane took pity on her and stepped forward to help. Without muttering a word of thanks, Champagne stuck the cigarette between her blood-red lips and took a deep, rasping draw.

'Well, anyway,' she demanded, staring at Tally again, 'you've got to get down there *now* and tell that bastard Brad he's got to put me back in that film *this minute*.' She stabbed a red-taloned finger in Tally's direction. 'Tell him,' she declared grandly, 'that if he comes on his bended knees and gives me Lily Eyre's part, I'll reconsider.'

'Look, I'm sorry to interrupt,' said Jane suddenly, 'but something slightly odd seems to be going on over there.'

Tally and Champagne followed the direction of her gaze to the park entrance. Wending its way over the rise behind the lake was a strange little procession of about thirty people. Capering figures in flowing clothes and brightly coloured pointed hats led others brandishing flags and playing bongos and flutes. People were clapping, waving their arms and letting out little cries.

Tally peered in their direction. She hadn't thought the day could possibly get more surreal. She had thought wrong. 'It's like the Pied Piper of Hamelin,' she breathed wonderingly. 'There's even someone on stilts.'

How could she see that far? wondered Jane in awe. To her, the approaching figures were just a blurred and slow-moving block. But then, Tally always had had superior eyesight. This honing of the optics came, Jane imagined, courtesy of the genetic inheritance of generations of Venerys scanning the horizons of their vast acreage. Being grand, however, had its downsides too. Like the girls at *Fabulous*, Tally had always suffered the most agonising of periods. Blue blood was evidently more painful.

'They look positively *medieval*,' Tally breathed, gazing at the approaching ragged band and thinking that it looked like a scene out of Brueghel. 'Apart from those people in ghastly fluorescent cagoules at the back, of course.'

This rang a Saul-shaped bell with Jane. Sure enough, bringing up the rear of the procession, were the grim-faced hikers she had encountered yesterday morning. So this was who their mates were. But what were they here for?

A sudden shriek from Tally made her jump.

'Piers!' Tally screamed, dashing helter-skelter down the

slope of the ha-ha. 'It's Piers! It's my brother! Piers!' she shrieked, rushing to the figure at the front of the crowd and launching herself upon him. 'Where on *earth* have you been?' She buried herself in his neck which, even from the distance of the terrace wall, Jane could see was far from clean. Blood, it seemed, was thicker than shower gel. She walked swiftly up to join them.

'Well, a hundred feet under it, actually,' Piers said good-humouredly to Tally. 'We've been living in a hole under the new runway site at Gatwick for the last two months.'

As she approached, Jane stared at Piers in astonishment. How on earth had Tally recognised him? His fair hair, once as smooth and shining as a gold ingot, hung in matted ropes about his shoulders. Gone was the pink and white schoolboy face Jane remembered, and gone, too, were the Eton coat tails, brushed to within an inch of their lives by Mrs Ormondroyd. Instead, Piers wore layer upon layer of mud-caked sacking that made him look like an Arthurian hermit. With studs through his eyebrow, nose and upper lip as well as through his earlobes, he was not so much Piers as Pierced.

'Oh Piers, how could you?' cried Tally. 'Why didn't you get in touch?' she wailed, half furious, half ecstatic. 'I've been *desperate* to see you. So much has happened. M-m-mummy's disappeared and M-m-m-mullions was nearly bulldozed, and it was all because of m-m-m-*me*. How could I have been so *m-m-m-mad*? Oh, *Piers*!' She buried her face in his neck again and shook with sobs.

'Shush,' said Piers, his braceleted wrist rattling as he patted her on the back. He grinned at Jane. His smile, she noticed, was as brilliantly white as ever, but then it probably took more than two months down a mudhole to undo a lifetime of expensive orthodontics. 'And by the way,' he added to Tally, 'I'm not called Piers any more. I'm Muddy Fox now. Muddy, for short.'

'Oh *Piers*,' gasped Tally, completely ignoring this and emerging from his dirt-crusted shoulder, her face swollen and red with tears, 'I nearly lost *everything*. Oh, *Piers*!'

As Tally flung herself on her brother once more, Jane looked nervously around at his companions. Next to Piers stood a tall, solidly-built figure with a long grey matted beard, a rough-woven cloak of mud brown fixed with a Celtic clasp, and greasy grey locks hanging almost to his elbow. He looked like something straight out of Malory, thought Jane, blanching as she noticed the long, dull-grey metal object in his hand. It looked terrifyingly like a weapon of war. Is that a broadsword in your hand or are you just pleased to see me? she thought nervously.

'Don't worry, it's only ceremonial,' said Piers, following the direction of her eyes. Jane wasn't sure how reassuring that was. After all, the Druids had held some pretty gory ceremonies. 'This is Merlin, my right hand man.' Piers waved a tattooed hand at the brown-cloaked figure.

Merlin bowed gravely. 'Good morrow, fair maiden,' he boomed.

Tally looked astonished.

'And this is Laughter,' said Piers, drawing to his side a hostile-looking girl clutching a baby. 'Merlin's wife. But the baby belongs to us all. Concepts of fatherhood are so limited and bourgeois. Not to mention,' Piers added, grinning, 'the fact no one really knows who the father is.'

Laughter looked thunderous.

'So what's been going on here?' Piers asked, waving towards the film set. 'I heard there was some strange dude around ordering everyone off the rights of way, which is why I thought I'd pop over. But I didn't realise it was Steven Spielberg.'

'It's not,' said Tally. 'Oh, don't ask.' She clutched her hair with her fingers and rolled her eyes. She took a deep breath. 'The film set is, or at least it was, an attempt to bring some money in to keep Mullions going. It seemed a better idea than Mummy's, which was to sell up.' Briefly, Tally filled Piers in on the events of the past few weeks.

Piers took the news, even the episodes concerning Saul and the bulldozers, with his impressive sang-froid. 'The Red Indian guy sounds pretty cool,' he remarked. 'Shame I missed him. And I wouldn't have minded meeting this Saul cat either. Merlin could have given him a good seeing to with Excalibur. Couldn't you, Merl?' Beside him, Merlin grinned, exposing blackened teeth in his beard. 'So what are you going to do now?' he asked his sister. 'Want to see what the crystals have to say about it?' He rattled a bag which hung at his belt. 'They're very wise.'

Tally tried not to shudder. 'Er, thanks, but no, I'll be fine,' she said nervously. 'I'll just get back to the drawing board. Think up some more business ideas. More films, perhaps.'

'What about a rock festival,' suggested Laughter, looking almost enthusiastic. 'Like Glastonbury. It'd be brilliant. You could have floating stages in the lake.'

Tally's eyes bulged. 'Well, I *was* perhaps wondering about a few classical music concerts,' she faltered.

Piers grinned round at his companions. 'Well, if we're not needed here, we'd better get back to the runway,' he remarked to the assembled troops. 'We could catch that earth-healing ceremony at Avebury on the way back.'

'What? You're going already?' stammered Tally. 'Wouldn't you, er, like some tea?'

'No thanks,' grinned Piers, clapping her on the back. 'So many green belts, so little time. I'm at Gatwick if you need me. When you next need someone to throw themselves in front of a bulldozer, don't hesitate to get in touch.'

As she watched Tally once again launch herself on her brother, Jane saw something move out of the corner of her eye. She looked round to see another, smaller and altogether different procession snaking across the parkland in white vans, bearing what looked like satellite dishes and aerials. A cameraman and soundman, whose equipment sported the livery of the local news station, were already moving in on Piers, while a gaggle of other lens-laden and boom-microphone-waving types were swiftly approaching. Piers, Jane realised, must be rather well known. Famous, even, by the looks of it. On the outskirts of the crowd, young men and women with notebooks, obviously from local papers, were earnestly scribbling down vox pops. One unfortunate, whose career as a journalist Jane suspected might be shortlived, had hit upon Merlin as an interviewee.

'What can you tell us about today's protest, Muddy?' a grey-anoraked news reporter asked Piers eagerly, thrusting a fat black-tipped microphone at him.

'It's cool,' Piers replied, not batting an eyebrow stud at all the attention. 'It's over, in fact. We're heading back to Gatwick now.'

'Back to the runway protest?' asked the man. 'How's that going, Muddy? You've been down there quite some time now, haven't you?'

'Two months,' said Piers. 'And we're not giving up. We'll be down there for as long as it takes.' He turned to his followers and thrust a triumphal fist to the sky. They cheered and threw their caps and bells in the air. The stilt-walker waved a stilt. Piers, Jane realised with surprise, had real charm. He was a figurehead. The shy little schoolboy she remembered had grown up to be a charismatic leader of men.

She wasn't, it seemed, the only one who thought so.

'Filthy's just *so* wonderful, isn't he?' breathed a low, husky voice at Piers's side. The interviewer blanched and extended his shaking microphone to the stunning, pouting blonde in tight leather trousers who had suddenly appeared in the crowd and was snaking her slender arm round Piers's shoulders.

'Filthy, my hero,' simpered Champagne, grinning at the cameras as she ran a perfectly-manicured fingernail over his much-pierced countenance. 'Such a *stud*, isn't he?' she pouted into the lens. Piers looked astonished but not horrified. Beneath the dirt on his face, Jane swore he was blushing. Laughter, meanwhile, looked livid.

'Champagne D'Vyne, isn't it?' said the reporter, jostling with about ten others who had suddenly zoomed in, in every sense of the word, on the unexpected drama that was unfolding. 'The famous It Girl?'

'That's right,' breathed Champagne in her best Sugar Kane tones. 'At least, it *was*. But not any more. I've always been *fascinated* by preservation and conservation. I'm very keen on recycling.' She paused. 'I *always* get the maid to take my champagne magnums to the bottle bank.' She shot the bearded reporter a glance so sizzling you could have fried sausages on it, then grinned and ran a hand through her gleaming hair. As the movement rucked up her blouse to reveal an expanse of brown tummy, Champagne was rewarded with her favourite sound, a fanfare of whirrs and flashes from the cameramen.

'Who *cares* about films, parties and premieres,' pouted

Champagne passionately, running a finger up and down Piers's mud-encrusted sleeve, 'when there are so much more *important* things like runway protests going on?' She tickled Piers under the chin with an alabaster finger. He looked both shy and delighted. 'From now on, I'm giving up the high life for life underground,' Champagne announced in ringing tones. 'I'm joining Filthy and his intrepid band. From this moment on, I'm no longer an It Girl. I'm a Grit Girl.'

There was a gasp from the reporters, the crowd and Jane most of all. 'Terrific,' shouted one of the newsmen. 'Britain's favourite party girl joins Britain's favourite environmental protester. Who would have thought it?'

Who indeed, thought Jane sardonically, watching Champagne, in her element once more as she held court to the TV cameras. Joining Piers and his band of high-profile crusties was, of course, a heaven-sent, if not heaven-scented, self-publicity opportunity. No self-respecting narcissist could pass it up. Particularly one like Champagne, whose latest venture, the film, had ended rather less gloriously than she had anticipated.

'Yah, I know Swampy really well,' Champagne boomed into a phalanx of microphones. '*Such* a sweet guy. I was on *Shooting Stars* with him once . . .' She had totally stolen Piers's thunder, Jane noticed. Not that he seemed to mind. He was gazing at Champagne with all the helpless fascination of a rabbit caught in the headlights. Which, Jane thought, probably wasn't all that far from the truth.

As soon as the interviews were over, the TV van raced away across the parkland in order to be first back in the studio with the great exclusive. Behind it, the young reporters, newsroom-bound, ran for their cars and careers.

Left alone at last, Piers's crowd began to pick up its

bags, shoulder its children and get back on its stilts, ready fòr departure. Piers gave a thumbs-up sign to Tally by way of farewell.

Champagne did not so much as look at Jane as she tottered away, clinging like a limpet to the latest person to save her career. As Jane accompanied Tally up the steps to the house, she had the rare feeling of being able to predict the future with absolute accuracy. Give or take an adjective, she knew exactly what was going to be on the front pages of the tabloids next day.

Chapter 22

'What exactly *is* an integral, double-aspect utility room?' asked Tally several hours later, looking up at Jane and frowning. Sunk in a leather armchair so battered it could have been served with chips, she was looking wearily through the papers that had fallen from Mark Stackable's folder as he ran after Saul. 'Integral. Double aspect. It sounds rather philosophical,' Tally added.

'I think it's a sort of lean-to scullery with two windows,' said Jane. All those weekends trailing around flats with Nick had left her better versed than Tally in the argot of estate agents.

Tally gave another deep sigh. 'I just can't believe I was so stupid as to have been taken in by Saul.'

'Well, he's very charming,' Jane said heroically, even though she had never found him anything of the sort.

Tally nodded, grateful for the excuse.

'And you can't choose who you fall in love with,' added Jane. 'As I know only too well.'

'Yes, but Nick was *ghastly*,' said Tally, displaying none of Jane's diplomacy.

I wasn't thinking of *him*, thought Jane. She fell silent and gazed into the fireplace.

'Now I'm back to square one,' said Tally. 'I have to find

a way to keep this place going.' Her despairing gaze took in the whole of the chilly, peeling, rotting, collapsing, ageing gloom of the Blue Drawing Room. She slapped the palms of her long hands down on the worn armrests of her chair.

'Well, we'll just have to think of a thriving business idea,' Jane said briskly, pouring herself another tot from the rapidly-diminishing bottle of Bowmore that Tally had discovered in one of the kitchen cupboards along with a litre of gin and a bottle of flat tonic. Mrs Ormondroyd, it turned out, had squirrelled away quite a stash. 'I know what I'd like to do. Not that it's much use to you.'

'What?' asked Tally, holding her glass out to Jane and rustling in a bag of stale peanuts which constituted the rest of the treasure trove from under the butler's sink.

'I want,' said Jane, raising her eyes to the mould-spotted and peeling ceiling, 'to set up a company that records the omnibus edition of *The Archers* for people who miss it on Sunday mornings. You know, people who are away, or on holiday, or forget that the clock's turned back or forward or whatever, or it's Armistice Day.'

'Yes. That's a brilliant idea,' said Tally, sitting up. 'Because if you miss the omnibus, you lose the plot for about the next six months. And then your life has no meaning.'

'Exactly,' said Jane. 'My company would provide a solution to that sad fate. And I know what I'd call it as well. *Ambridge Too Far*. Like *A Bridge Too Far*.'

Tally grinned. 'But it won't make a million,' she said. 'Not unless you branch out into recording *EastEnders* and *Coronation Street* for people as well.'

'No chance,' said Jane. 'I can't work a video.'

'I wonder what I could do,' mused Tally, pushing one

of Mark's brochures away from her with the tip of a wellington. 'Piers always used to talk about opening a shop that sold nothing but bacon sandwiches,' she said. 'But that would hardly make enough to keep this place going. Even if Piers wasn't vegan now, which I expect he is.' She sighed. Her face looked suddenly older, and infinitely tired. Give it up, Jane urged her friend silently. Just abandon the struggle. It's a losing battle, and even Mullions isn't worth sacrificing your youth and life to. But Tally would never give in, Jane knew. 'I can't be the one to let it all go,' Jane recalled Tally saying once. 'I can't be remembered for all time as the one who lost the house.' Yet she had come close.

Jane gazed into her glass wondering why she was worrying about Tally so much. Her own prospects were, after all, hardly glittering. Personally, they were a disaster, and professionally they were little better. The disappearance of Champagne a hundred feet under the runway at Gatwick, which she would normally have greeted with joy and relief, also meant *Fabulous* would have no cover. Jane groaned at the thought of Victoria's wrath now the film story could no longer be run.

Tally sat up suddenly. 'Did you hear something?' she hissed at Jane. 'Something banging somewhere?'

Jane's ears strained in the singing silence. Tally was right. A faint noise could be heard from the Marble Hall. They gazed at each other in terror.

'It might be,' gasped Jane, her throat dry with fear, 'the wind.'

Tally shook her head. 'You can always hear that.'

It was true. The building had so many holes you could use it to drain pasta.

'Something's coming in,' gasped Tally, drawing her

gangly legs into her chair and hugging them tightly. 'Look. The door.'

As they watched, terrified, the Blue Drawing Room door started to open slowly, revealing the hall beyond. A full moon was just visible through the top pane of one of the hall windows, a brilliant silvery pearl, positioned, as if by some celestial jeweller, on a bed of dark blue velvet. Tally gasped sharply. 'Not Saul come back?' she breathed, putting into words what Jane, too, most feared. 'Please don't let it be him,' panted Tally.

It wasn't. A figure in a white flowing robe slowly appeared through the door. Tall, dignified and slow-moving, it glided into the room as if in a trance. Even from across the distance and the gloom, the brilliance of its burning eyes could clearly be seen.

'Mummy!' exclaimed Tally, thrusting her legs back out and sprawling in relief across the chair. 'You *terrified* me!'

'*Darling*,' breathed Julia, moving swiftly over to her daughter, and gazing intensely into her eyes. 'I have only one question to ask you,' she said dramatically, grasping Tally's thin shoulders. '*Have you?*'

'Have I what?' asked Tally, alarmed at her mother's earnest expression. Seen the light? Strayed from the path of righteous wisdom? Got a bun in the oven? Turned lesbian? What would have been an open-ended question for most people was practically limitless with Julia.

'Sold Mullions, of course,' gasped Julia.

'No,' said Tally apologetically. 'I'm afraid I haven't.' She braced herself for her mother's wrath.

'Thank Goddess!' proclaimed Julia dramatically, sinking to her knees in a billow of cheesecloth. 'I'm *so* relieved,' she said, in low, dramatic tones. 'There are great opportunities ahead for us all. Big Horn has had the most *wonderful* idea for Mullions.'

'Oh really?' said Tally guardedly. She had had quite enough brilliant ideas for Mullions for one day. Did this one, she wondered, involve integral double-aspect utility rooms?

'Yes. Yes,' breathed Julia, ecstatic. 'He's so *creative*, that man, I can't *tell* you.' She clasped her hands and gave a semi-orgasmic shudder at the mere thought of it. Around the base of Jane's stomach, something twinged with envy.

'Come here, my darling,' Julia called over her shoulder. 'Tally's *dying* to see your wonderful plans.'

Something tall detached itself from the shadow of one of the windowledges. A pair of strong, tanned thighs glowed in the firelight as Big Horn, still sporting his chamois leather miniskirt, came slowly towards the group of women. In his braceleted, tattooed arms he carried a large black folder which he deposited ceremonially on the rug in front of Tally. She looked at it suspiciously. It was not, after all, the first one she had seen that day.

'Big Horn and I,' declared Julia, 'and, of course, the Mother Goddess,' she added, quickly glancing upward, 'have come up with a plan for Mullions which would cost us practically nothing and,' she added, dropping her ringing tones to a discreet, excited whisper, '*make us a fortune*.'

Big Horn, his face impassive, gave a slow, dignified nod of agreement.

'We want,' continued Julia, her face ablaze with excitement, 'to make Mullions into an ashram. A retreat.'

Jane and Tally looked at each other in mixed disappointment and incomprehension. 'A retreat?' asked Tally doubtfully. 'What exactly *is* a retreat? Isn't it something to do with monks?'

'Not necessarily.' Julia serenely ignored the bad vibes. 'It's somewhere to cleanse yourself spiritually and internally. *Not,*' she added sternly, 'to pamper yourself physically. A retreat is very basic, preferably with no heating, TVs, telephones or radios.'

'It doesn't sound much fun,' ventured Jane.

'It's not meant to be *fun,*' said Julia, almost pityingly. 'It's meant to be a place where you unlock your human potential. You spend hours meditating, fasting, chanting. Some people simply lock themselves away in isolation for days on end, visualising, learning to listen to their inner selves.'

So that was what Nick had been doing in the bathroom all that time, thought Jane. If only she'd realised.

'You take classes in yoga, go for long walks, tune into world harmony and learn humility by doing menial household tasks like cleaning the lavatories, fixing shelves and doing the washing-up. And, of course,' Julia cast her eyes modestly to the floor, 'paying really rather a lot of money for the privilege.' She beamed triumphantly and clapped her hands. 'Mullions,' she pronounced, 'could not be more suitable.'

Silence ensued.

'But surely,' said Tally, struggling to find a polite way to say what she thought. 'Surely,' she gabbled, failing, 'you don't really expect people to pay a fortune to eat practically nothing, lock themselves away for weeks in sheds, spend hours contorting themselves and clean the loos into the bargain? Only nutters would pay to do that.'

'Yes. Nutters like me and Big Horn, obviously,' said Julia, offended. 'We've just come back from doing it ourselves.'

There was an embarrassed silence. Then Jane, who had been thinking furiously for the past few seconds, barged in. 'It's a brilliant idea, Tally. Don't you see? You *can* make a fortune out of ashrams. They're terribly nineties. I've read about them. They're springing up everywhere, even in this country. In California, all the film stars go to them and pay the earth to stay there.'

Julia clapped her hands and Jane blushed as Big Horn gave her a stiff nod of approval and curved his magnificent lips upwards in what might even have been a smile.

'That's right,' Julia gushed. 'Just look at the figures.' She opened the folder. 'It'll cost next to nothing to set up. Why, Big Horn and I are practically an entire ashram in ourselves. I can take Breathing for the Millennium, Workshopping Your Pain, Locating Your Inner Child and World-Harmony Yoga classes and Big Horn can do Group Hugging and Lacto-vegetarian Meditation. We don't need telephones or TVs, and the food is really basic. Even Mrs Ormondroyd can manage to chop up a few carrots and boil a few lentils for dinner.'

There was another silence. 'Um, Mrs Ormondroyd's not around at the moment,' Tally hesitatingly confessed.

'But I'm sure we can find her,' added Jane quickly.

Julia smiled absently. 'And people don't even need to stay in the house,' she said. 'In California, lots of them sleep outside in the woods for that extra back-to-nature experience. We can get Mr Peters to knock up a few teepees.'

Tally nodded. Wherever Mr Peters had got to, she had better find him fast. Something told her that he had not been snapped up by another estate just yet.

'Some people pay up to fifteen hundred pounds a week to stay on ashrams,' said Julia, running her finger down a column of figures, and displaying a grasp of financial matters that would have impressed even Saul Dewsbury. 'We could undercut that by hundreds and clean up in this part of the country.'

'Gosh,' said Jane. 'It certainly puts the money in harmony, doesn't it?'

Chapter 23

Returning to London from Mullions, Jane found the capital an oasis of calm after the tumultuous events in the countryside. While life, admittedly, continued manless, it also continued Champagneless, and as the fashion season came round again it had the added bonus of being Victoria-less as well. After a week in Milan, Victoria was now in Paris. Left in charge of *Fabulous*, Jane for the first time was enjoying the freedom of selecting features and planning entire issues herself.

She had not, as yet, dared to move from her deputy's desk into the glass-windowed sanctum that was Victoria's office. This was less fear of hubris than the fact that Tish would be completely incapable of putting her calls through to another desk. But in any case, Jane did not want to tempt fate. Archie Fitzherbert had left her to her own devices so far. Her criticisms over breakfast about Victoria and *Fabulous* had, unbelievably, apparently been forgotten. Fitzherbert had, Jane decided, probably just dismissed her as mad. Which was probably fine by him. Mental instability, after all, seemed practically a requirement of the job for senior magazine staff.

It was wonderful to be left alone to get on with things. There was only one cloud on Jane's horizon: the question of who would replace Champagne on the magazine's cover. The printer's deadline was approaching and she would have to make a decision soon.

At least, Jane thought, she didn't have to worry about Tally any more. Any scars left by Saul had apparently healed quickly. Tally, indeed, seemed to have emerged practically unscathed. The extent of Saul's deceit and his true intentions towards her beloved home had evidently extinguished any feelings for him other than disgust. Not that there was time to dwell on anything anyway. Having finally accepted Big Horn's plan to convert Mullions into what amounted to a cosmic Center Parc, Tally, together with Julia, was now frantically preparing for an influx of stressed-out celebrities.

'It's amazing how many people have signed up,' Tally gasped excitedly down the telephone. 'Especially when you see the brochures Mummy's sending out.' She paused. 'Because they're not brochures at all, really. Just pebbles with the telephone number engraved on them. But they seem to be bringing in the business. Mummy says it's because the pebbles are lodestones and draw the person they are sent to towards Mullions. And you should see Mr Peters. Slapping up teepees quicker than you can say General Custer.'

'So you found Mr Peters, then?'

'Yes, he was wreaking havoc at the Lower Bulge bowling club,' Tally giggled. 'They'd had to cancel games for the first time since 1910 because Mr Peters had practically destroyed the green, and he'd cut the electrics off twice by running the lawnmower through the cables. They seemed rather glad to see the back of him.'

'What about Mrs Ormondroyd?' asked Jane. 'Did you track her down as well?'

'Yes,' Tally said. 'She was working in the local dentist's surgery. Apparently business was down by almost fifty per cent. People were frightened enough of going to the dentist, but the thought of having to see Mrs Ormondroyd as well just finished them off. She's having a wonderful time now, though. Giving huge simmering pots of chick-peas the occasional stir whilst gazing uninterruptedly at Big Horn.'

'How is Big Horn?' asked Jane, smiling.

'A revelation,' said Tally sincerely. 'He's running the place like clockwork. He's got more business acumen than the entire City put together.'

'He was probably a top fund manager in a former life,' said Jane sardonically.

'Well, funny you should say that, because it turns out that he was in this one. According to Mummy, Big Horn's originally a barrow boy from Bethnal Green who went to work for a merchant bank in New York. He used to get the biggest bonuses on Wall Street until it all got too much and he burned out and went to live on the reservation in Nevada where Mummy met him.'

'No!' said Jane. 'So Big Horn's a Cockney?'

'Yes, and he's a film star now as well,' Tally said. '*Three Christenings and a Hen Party* is finished but Brad decided at the last minute to reshoot some of the christening party scenes with Big Horn as a guest. Brad thought he would add a certain—'

'*Je ne sais Iroquoi*?' butted in Jane.

'Exactly,' giggled Tally. 'After all, as Brad said, look what a big, silent Red Indian did for *One Flew Over the Cuckoo's Nest*!'

Entering the *Fabulous* office the next Monday morning,

Jane found Tosh shrieking with laughter at something a white-faced Tash had just said.

'What's the matter?' asked Jane.

Tosh screwed up her face, evidently unable to speak for mirth.

Tash looked agonised.

'Good weekend?' pressed Jane.

'No,' burst out Tash. 'I've had the most *ghastly* weekend actually. I was staying with the Uppe-Timmselves when my hostess came into my bedroom without knocking to have a bedtime chat with me and caught me *peeing* in the sink. It was *beyond* embarrassing.' She crimsoned at the memory.

Tosh exploded once more.

'You should have told her it was part of your yoga routine,' said Jane.

'Yes, well, sadly one never thinks of these things at the time, does one?' said Tash. 'But as I said to her, if you don't provide en suite bathrooms for all your guests, what else can you expect? I mean, who wants to walk miles down a draughty corridor in the middle of the night in the pitch black looking for the lavatory?' She looked at Jane in anguish. Jane tried to appear sympathetic and not catch the eye of Tosh. The giggles bubbling up in her throat would certainly damage the fragile *esprit de corps du bureau* she had managed to establish in Victoria's absence.

'Speaking of outside lavatory arrangements,' drawled Tosh, rubbing a hand roughly over her streaming eyes, 'did you see Champagne D'Vyne at the runway protest on the news last night? She's *beyond*, isn't she? Said she was passionate about green belts, particularly the ones you get from Mulberry.'

'Yes,' Tash joined in, glad of the distraction. 'She's

certainly the first environmental protester I've ever seen who gets her entire wardrobe from Voyage. And apparently Michaeljohn have to send a stylist down to Gatwick every week to give her hair that fashionably tangled look. Hilarious, isn't she?'

'It's all very well for her to try and save the planet,' remarked Larry, 'but I'm not sure she's on the same one as the rest of us in the first place.'

Talk of Champagne and holes reminded Jane again of the one she had left on the *Fabulous* cover. Jane had considered many options over the past few days, but no one seemed quite right. Except Lily Eyre, and Victoria had already vetoed her. Still, thought Jane defiantly, if Victoria was going to go swanning off round the minibars of Europe and leave someone else to run her magazine, she would have to take the consequences. Deciding, for once, to act on instinct, and before she could change her mind, Jane picked up the telephone, dialled Lily Eyre's agent and offered her the cover and an interview.

'Lily Eyre's going to be our next cover,' Jane told the rest of the staff at a features meeting that afternoon. Lily Eyre's people had accepted with alacrity and Jane had briefed one of her best and wittiest freelance writers to interview the actress. Her stomach felt tight with mixed apprehension and triumph as she thought about it. It was a bold move, but there seemed no reason why it would not pay off.

'But what about her ankles?' asked Tash doubtfully. 'Aren't they supposed to be dreadful?'

Jane shook her head, trying not to stare at Tash's own distinctly solid lower calves. 'They're fine,' she said reassuringly. 'Right, ideas. Anyone got any?'

There was a silence.

'There's this artist I read about,' said Tash hesistantly. 'She's the daughter of the Earl of Staines and she makes papier-mâché lamp bases out of prostitutes' telephone box calling cards.'

Another silence.

'Well,' said Jane brightly, determined to be encouraging, 'we *do* need to beef up the arts side. You're certainly on the right track, Tash.' Albeit stuck in a siding on a branch line, she thought to herself.

But the message seemed to be getting through. The staff seemed to be trying a bit harder, and were even venturing into areas of the newspapers other than the horoscopes.

'Have you seen this?' said Tosh a day or so later, proffering a copy of a recently-launched literary magazine. '*The Scribbler*'s main interview this month is with a writer called Charlie Seton who they're raving about as the new James Joyce.'

Jane raised a sceptical eyebrow.

'He's sex on a stick, apparently,' sighed Tosh. 'I only know because a friend of mine works there. She says Charlie Seton's just *gorgeous*. Just *amazingly* good-looking. Oh, and really, really talented, of course,' she added quickly.

Amused, Jane looked closer at the piece. 'Eton, Oxford, bedsitter in Soho,' she read. It was, as Tosh said, great *Fabulous* material. Jane squinted at the picture of the author. It was very heavily art-directed, so much so that beneath the scribbles and pasted-on cutouts of lightbulbs and lips, it was impossible to see what Charlie Seton actually looked like.

'I thought I could go and interview him this morning,' suggested Tosh.

Jane looked at her sternly. Tosh knew perfectly well she had a mountain of beauty copy to rewrite. 'Sorry,' said Jane. Tosh's face went into freefall. 'You're much too busy. You've got that piece about the new blue lipsticks to tidy up.' Tosh pushed out her bottom lip.

Unmoved, Jane picked up the magazine and read the piece again. Was it, she wondered, worth giving Charlie Seton a call? He might make an interesting piece. And the bits of his face that you could see looked reasonably promising.

Hell, I deserve it, thought Jane. I'll go and see him myself. I don't get to pull rank very often. In fact, I don't get to pull *anything* very often.

'Busty Models' read the badly-written sign on the shabby Soho door. Walking slowly up the other side of the street, Jane looked at the very young, sunken-eyed girl in a black PVC waistcoat and miniskirt lounging against the door-frame. She was chewing languidly and obviously waiting for business. She didn't *look* very busty, Jane thought. But then, with her scraped-back, lifeless blonde ponytail and greyish skin, she didn't look much like a model either. She was, however, looking suspiciously at Jane.

Jane couldn't blame her. She had been wandering up and down this street for the last ten minutes at least and still hadn't been able to locate Charlie Seton's flat. Because he was a writer, she had assumed that he would be in the garret. But as she peered up to the crumbling second-floor windows with their cracked windowboxes containing long-dead plants, it occurred to her that writing by the light of a red bulb might be difficult. Jane cleared her throat and crossed the litter-strewn street towards the girl in PVC.

'Does a writer called Charlie live round here?' Jane asked.

The girl carried on chewing her gum. 'No,' she said. 'There's no one called Charlie round here.' She spoke, somewhat surprisingly, in the pleasant, enunciated tones of a vicar's wife.

Jane turned away, disappointed. She was in the wrong place, obviously. Odd, because this had definitely been the name of the street. That, evidently, was that then. She began to walk away.

'But there *is* a writer round here,' the girl called after her. Jane turned. The girl was chewing her gum, grinning. 'Down there in the basement.' She pointed beneath her feet. 'Say hello from me.'

Jane quickly retraced her steps. She bent slightly and peered down into the lighted basement window directly below, whose top four inches were exactly level with her ankle. The room inside was lit by a single bulb. Cigarette stubs overflowed from an ashtray all over the desk below the window, and a rumpled duvet covered a mattress on the floor. Papers, both newsprint and manuscript, were scattered everywhere. Yes, it looked like a writer's room. If she inclined her head slightly to the right it was just possible to see the back of a T-shirted figure sitting at the desk. Charlie Seton was obviously hard at work.

Absurdly aware of her smart little herringbone suit and brand-new high-heeled ankle boots, Jane went through the open front door of the scruffy building and descended the stairs at the back of the passageway. She tapped at the battered door at the bottom. The paint on its ancient surface was so blistered and cracked it was possible to see every colour it had ever been. Jane counted burgundy, mustard, bilious green and diarrhoea brown before the door creaked open to reveal Charlie Seton.

Only it wasn't Charlie Seton. It was Tom.

'Tom!' croaked Jane. 'Tom!' she squeaked, fumbling for the right words to convey the explosion of excitement, confusion and hope that had just detonated within her. She gazed desperately from one to the other of his eyes. She felt like a bad actress in a straight-to-video romantic turkey.

'What an amazing coincidence,' she gasped eventually in strangled tones. The film seemed to have switched to *Brief Encounter*. 'You see, I've come here to interview you. Isn't it hilarious? From the magazine.'

'Oh,' said Tom. 'Of course. Right.'

So far he had conspicuously failed to gather her up in his arms and murmur 'At last, my love, I've found you' into her neck. Jane wasn't sure what film he was in. Something inscrutable, perhaps one of those tortuous coming-of-age-in-eastern Europe sagas that win all the Best Foreign Language Film Oscars. Still gazing intently into his face, Jane felt dizzy with the almost overwhelming desire to shout 'Do You Still Love Me?' from the rooftops.

What she actually said was, 'What are you doing here?'

'I came back,' Tom said simply. 'New York didn't work out exactly as I expected. Look, why don't you come inside?'

'Why didn't it work out?' asked Jane, following him into the room which looked even scruffier from inside than it had from the pavement. There was no furniture apart from the mattress, the desk, a rickety chair and a sink at the back with a shelf over it.

'I suppose you could call it a misunderstanding,' said Tom, smiling faintly.

Jane's heart started thumping with terror. A woman.

She might have known the dead hand of the Manhattan blonde would be involved. 'Girl trouble?' she croaked bravely.

'No!' laughed Tom. 'Not at all. My agent here sent me over there to work on the script for the new *Godfather* film. I was thrilled. It sounded like a dream come true.'

'So what went wrong?'

'Well, when I got there,' Tom said, rubbing his hair ruefully, 'it turned out the agent had misheard and I was expected to write the script for a cartoon about a mafioso fish called the Codfather. Not *quite* Robert De Niro.' He lit a cigarette.

Jane giggled and felt sufficiently emboldened to probe further. 'But why have you changed your name since you came back? And why,' she was unable to stop herself blurting out, 'didn't you get in touch with me?'

'I haven't changed my name,' said Tom. 'Charlie Seton is the name I write under. Always has been. My *nom de plume*.' So that explained why she could never find him in the bookshops, thought Jane. 'And in answer to your other question,' he said lightly, 'I didn't really see the point in coming round to see you at the flat in which you live with your boyfriend. Cup of tea?'

'But . . . I don't. I mean, I do. But he doesn't. Any more. That is.' A slight frown furrowed Tom's forehead. Jane wondered if he had understood her. The second cue for him to gather her into his arms and whoop . . . passed. They were still, it seemed, in different films.

'Why did you move in here?' Jane asked awkwardly, feeling so *Brief Encounter* her throat ached. Of all the ecstatic reunion scenarios with Tom she had imagined, she had overlooked the possibility of this one.

'It's a good place to write.' Tom filled an old Russell

Hobbs kettle at the sink. 'A real slice of old Soho. It's very stimulating.'

Jane's thoughts automatically flickered to Busty Models upstairs. She wondered *how* stimulating, exactly.

'Although,' Tom added, reading her thoughts, 'you have to be careful when you live below Busty Models. Looking up at the window is distracting. Most of the girls who work that pavement don't wear any underwear, and I can see straight up their skirts from here.'

'Really?' said Jane sourly. 'One of them sends you her love, anyway. The blonde in black plastic.'

'Oh yes. Camilla.' Tom dropped two teabags into a couple of chipped mugs that he held in one hand and poured on a stream of boiling water with the other. 'Poor thing. It's a dreadful story. Upper-middle-class family, promising student at Oxford, got fed up, ran out of money, came down here and became a prostitute. Doing well now, though. Runs that place like clockwork.'

'She runs it?' gasped Jane, amazed. 'But she only looks about ten.'

'She's nineteen,' said Tom. 'Going on ninety. And very funny with it. Some of the stories she tells are hilarious. You wouldn't believe who goes up there. Several MPs, for a start.'

'Really?'

'Oh yes.' Tom extracted the teabags from the mugs. 'Camilla has to be very careful. Not all of them are in the best of health. If she comes on too strong with the whips and masks, she could cause a by-election. When the Tories were hanging on to a majority by their fingernails she could have brought down the government. And the things she tells me about what she does you wouldn't believe.'

'Like what?' asked Jane, genuinely curious.

'Well, one of Camilla's favourite tricks, apparently,' said Tom, not quite meeting Jane's eye while she, for her part, wondered how apparently 'apparently' was, 'is to take a mouthful of Coca-Cola before giving someone a blow job. Apparently you get the most amazing sensation.'

Silence followed this astonishing piece of intelligence. They were not, Jane realised, in *Brief Encounter* any more.

'Look, shall we start the interview?' she asked, hoping to get the conversation out of the rather embarrassing siding it seemed to have got stuck in and remembering why she was here. She may as well try to salvage something, if not her dignity or the relationship, then at least a few hundred words of page-filler for *Fabulous*. 'I haven't got much time, you see,' she added. 'I've got an advertiser's lunch.'

Stepping into Victoria's Manolo Blahniks, Jane had discovered, involved more than just sitting in the office hammering out feature ideas. She had also to turn up to the ghastly events known in the trade as 'lipstick lunches' – launches of new beauty products by the magazine's advertisers. Jane's heart sank at the thought of the one that lay ahead – for a perfume called Orgasmique. Ghastly name for a scent, she thought. Who in their right mind would want to go round smelling of sexual activity all day? Who indeed, she thought, forcing herself not to gaze too longingly at Tom's invitingly rumpled mattress. Had someone spent the night there with him?

'Shall I sit here?' she asked, deciding to take charge and lowering her bottom on to the rickety chair at the desk. She felt absurdly formal standing up in her high heels and neat suit.

'I . . .' said Tom as Jane's tailored rump made contact with the chair, 'wouldn't sit there,' he finished as the chair seat slid away beneath and left her sprawled on the floor, skirt around her waist, giving Tom a gala performance of her underwear.

'Sorry,' said Tom, lingering rather longer than perhaps he should have done on the contemplation of her La Perla. 'Everything in this place is falling apart, I'm afraid. The only really safe place to sit is the deck, and even that's a bit dodgy in places. Tread softly, for you tread on my floor, as Yeats didn't say.' He sat down on the mattress.

Jane rearranged her legs. 'Well, you told me a bit about your career before,' she said determinedly, switching to interviewer mode to cover her embarrassment. 'What are you working on now?' she pressed. 'Did you ever get round to writing that bonkbuster?'

Tom raised his eyebrows. He shook his head. 'No. I never did, sadly.' His sexy, sleepy eyes crinkled with amusement. 'Still, it's not too late to start.' He looked at her speculatively. There was silence again.

Jane sighed. She knew that, despite her best efforts, she was going nowhere with this interview. She was wasting both her time and his. 'I'm afraid I've got to go,' she said, struggling to her feet and shoving into her bag the notebook in which she had only just started to write. 'I'm late for this dreadful, boring lunch, and it's all my fault because I got here so late. I'm sorry.'

'Don't be so hard on yourself,' said Tom easily, drawing on a newly-lit cigarette. 'It really doesn't matter.'

That much was abundantly clear, thought Jane, stumbling in her high heels up the rotting stairs on the way out. Tom could obviously take her or leave her. Leave her, preferably. She felt desperate with disappointment. Tom had been ambiguous to the point of incomprehensibility. Only the thought of Camilla loitering outside stopped her from dissolving into tears as she picked her way down the scruffy passageway.

Chapter 24

Fortunately, the lunch provided Jane with the opportunity to drown her sorrows in a great deal of champagne. She had hung on to every word the Orgasmique Nose had to say about the top and bottom notes of his new perfume. He had seemed the only stable thing in a whirling, Bollinger-fuelled world. Flattered by her apparent rapt attention, the Nose had been charmed.

Damn Tom. Who needs a man when you've got a career? were the alternate trains of thought occupying Jane as she lurched drunkenly from side to side in the taxi on her way back to the office. When she eventually, after much reeling, gained her desk, she noticed the office was practically empty apart from Larry.

'Wheresh everyone?' Jane asked. It was, after all, ten to four. Even *Fabulous*-length lunches should be drawing to a close by now.

'Tish has gone shopping,' said Larry. 'And Tash and Tosh are seeing their psychics.'

'Their *pshychics*?' slurred Jane. 'What on *earth* for?'

'Well, psychics *are* the shrinks of the nineties,' said Larry. 'Anyone who's anyone goes to one, basically.'

'*Do* they?' said Jane.

'Absolutely,' said Larry blithely. 'I wouldn't be without

mine. So *entertaining*, for one thing, hearing all about your future. Psychics are so *relaxing* in that way. They do all the talking and thinking for you and you don't have to bang on tediously about your childhood to a psychologist like we all did in the eighties. *So* exhausting, trying to remember whether it was Uncle Jasper or Uncle Henry who groped you in the gun room.'

Tish appeared with an armful of shopping bags to rival Champagne in her heyday. 'Uncle Jasper, definitely,' she grinned.

'I see,' said Jane, still wondering vaguely why girls on *Fabulous* were at all curious about what lay in store. If anyone could predict the future to within five pounds of their future husbands' bank balance, surely it was Tash, Tosh and Tish. From girls' school to upmarket former polytechnic to photocopying at *Fabulous* to marrying a suitable ex-public schoolboy, their lives had been programmed since birth. Her own future, on the other hand, might benefit from a bit of forewarning and forearming.

'Laetitia in the art department started it all off,' said Tish. 'Her psychic predicted that she would marry a tall, dark, handsome stranger whose name began with D. And she was bang on, apart from the fact that Laetitia's husband's blond and his name's Caspar. *Strordinary*, don't you think?'

'*Amazhing*,' said Jane, knowing Tish would be oblivious to her sardonic tones. Tish was one of those people, to quote Julian Barnes, who thought irony was where the Ironians lived.

Jane stared down at her desk and began shifting papers from one pile to another, trying to stop her slowly-sobering thoughts straying back to Tom. There was no point dwelling on him any more. He had made it pretty obvious what he thought about her.

The telephone rang. Jane reached for it. 'Hello?' she said.

'Hello,' said a voice both familiar and unfamiliar at the same time. 'How did your lunch go?'

Jane caught her breath and tried to prevent her hands from shaking, her heart from giving out, her liver from failing and her feet from beating a tattoo on the floor.

'Tom! I mean Charlie,' she gasped.

'You mean Tom,' said the voice. 'So? How was it?'

'Oh, fairly ghastly,' stammered Jane, as her hangover now beginning to kick in. Her throat was dry and she felt slightly sick.

'We didn't seem to get very far with our interview,' said Tom breezily.

'No,' said Jane. 'We didn't.'

'Perhaps you'd like to finish it,' said Tom, utterly matter-of-fact.

'Ye-es.'

'Well, if you want to meet up again,' said Tom briskly, 'tomorrow evening would be best for me. I've got a short story to finish during the day.'

Jane's stomach shot to the floor, bounced up and hit the ceiling and continued yo-yo-ing between the two for almost half a minute. Was she imagining things, or was Tom asking her out to dinner?

'I'd *love* to,' she breathed passionately. 'Er, I'd like to very much,' she repeated stiffly, aware that she was in danger of scaring Tom off completely.

'Well, I hope you like pasta,' he said. 'If you do, I know a great little place called San Lorenzo.'

Jane's eyes bulged. San Lorenzo. The Belgravia headquarters of the ladies-who-lunch brigade, preferred pit stop of every passing international celebrity worth their hand-chipped sea salt. She had hardly thought Tom could stretch to that. Perhaps he was doing better than she thought.

She should have realised there was something odd when Tom suggested they meet outside Leicester Square Tube, rather than Knightsbridge. But the restaurant was indeed San Lorenzo, although not quite as Jane imagined it. This San Lorenzo was a tiny, old-fashioned Covent Garden Italian where the only ladies lunching – or dining – looked like ladies of the night. The menu was innocent of anything even approaching truffle oil and the waiting staff was made up of two elderly, boot-faced Italian waitresses who clacked around in sloppy mules with tea towels flung over their shoulders. The straw Chianti bottles on the walls were obviously there from the first time round and not as part of some post-ironic retro-kick. It was so traditional it practically got up and did a jig as they entered.

Having dressed for Belgravia, Jane felt slightly *de trop* in her new Joseph suit and cursed her extravagance at blowing a week's salary on a haircut at lunchtime. Tom, meanwhile, was wearing his usual uniform of battered leather jacket, tired jeans and another T-shirt from his collection of jumble-sale specials. This evening's one was emblazoned with the dates from a Whitesnake tour of 1981.

'Aaah, Meester Tom,' said the waitresses, their hatchet faces melting into expressions of starstruck charm as he led Jane into a tiled foyer of Barbara Cartland pink which, she noticed, clashed beautifully with Bob-Monkhouse-tan walls. 'Thees way,' fussed one, pulling out an oilcloth-covered table for Jane to get behind while the other arrived with a brimming carafe of black-red wine.

'Wonderful,' said Tom, grinning and rubbing his hands. The gnarled old waitresses had by now melted so much they were almost a puddle on the floor. They gazed at him adoringly as they handed over the menus.

'Wonderful fresh pasta tonight, Meester Tom,' said one. 'Bring back childhood memories. Like Mamma used to make.'

Tom smiled. 'You forget, Bianca, that I'm not Italian.'

'Ah, but Meester Tom you 'ave an Italian soul,' giggled the old woman. 'Romanteek. Artisteek.' She waved her arms expansively.

'And I don't want to bring back childhood memories either,' Tom grinned. 'Can't think of anything more ghastly. I'd much rather bring back naughty adolescent memories.' He darted a teasing look at Jane, who blushed deeply.

'In that case,' said Bianca delightedly, 'you must 'ave the 'ouse speciality. *Pollo alla principessa*. Chicken for a princess. *Ecco!*' She gestured at Jane and beamed.

'Two of those then,' said Tom. 'I hope you don't mind me ordering for you?' he said to Jane after Bianca had gone. 'But I promise you it'll be delicious.'

Jane couldn't have minded less. Having Tom order for her in this cosy, candelit, unpretentious place could not have felt more different from having Mark squeaking and grunting in his show-Japanese as he ordered ostentatiously from the menu at Ninja. Nor could the food, when it came, have been more different. Instead of fish so raw it was practically still breathing, the chicken arrived roasted to golden perfection.

'Beakerful of the warm South?' asked Tom, proffering the carafe and crinkling his eyes at her in the candlelight.

As they talked, Jane could well believe he was a story-teller. His accounts of life on his Soho street were positively Dayglo in their luridness. He was a skilled listener too, she realised as he began delicately to probe her recent disastrous romantic history. Slowly and reluctantly at first, then willingly and eventually torrentially, Jane talked a lot about Nick and a little about Mark. Tom listened intently, rolling his large, candlelit eyes sympathetically now and then. For his own part, he said little about his love life. And Jane could never quite find the right moment or phrases to start asking.

'Coffee?' Tom asked, as the lovestruck waitresses loomed after the homemade tiramisu.

'No, thank you,' said Jane. 'Actually, I'd better go,' she added reluctantly as Tom produced a fistful of grubby notes out of his pocket.

'My treat,' he insisted when Jane started to scrabble for her purse.

'It's been lovely to see you again,' she said. Please ask me back for a drink, her eyes begged him.

'Come back for a drink,' said Tom right on cue. 'It's only round the corner, and you can call a cab from there.'

'All right,' said Jane, her eyes turned determinedly aside from the endless fleet of empty, available cabs clearly visible through the restaurant windows. Her legs trembled as she got to her feet.

Soho seemed a city of light as they walked through it. It was raining, and the neon signs of the restaurants and bars were brilliantly reflected in the wet pavements. Figures hurried by in the hissing rain, intent on their own business, silent and hooded as monks. Taxis honked and hustled their way through the traffic-crowded streets. Tom, apparently almost unconsciously and so delicately she could scarcely feel it, took her hand in his as they turned off Old Compton Street. Delirious happiness flooded through Jane's veins. She wanted nothing else in the world.

Someone else, however, did. The thin, desperate face of a young girl gazed pleadingly up at them as they passed the dark and rotting recess of an abandoned restaurant doorway. 'Here you are,' Tom muttered, stopping. Jane heard the rattle of change as he unearthed a handful of silver and put it gently into the dirty, proffered palm which protruded from the end of a plaster cast. 'Can I sign your cast?' asked Tom, smiling at the beggar.

'You can sign me wherever you like, darlin'.'

Camilla was on duty as they arrived at the flat. Her black plastic outfit shone in the street lights and a cigarette hung from between her wet, red-slicked lips. As they approached, Jane felt under scrutiny.

'You look very glamorous,' Tom said to her cheerfully. 'How's business?' He spoke to Camilla, Jane noticed, with as much courtesy and respect as if she had been a doctor or a barrister.

'Booming,' said Camilla, in her ironic, well-spoken voice. 'The good wives of Woking seem to have been having a lot of bedtime headaches recently. Not to mention,' she added, leaning forward conspiratorially, raising her eyebrows and shooting a loaded look at the red-lit window above her, 'the good wives of Westminster.'

Inside Tom's flat, Jane looked around in surprise. 'Tom! You've tidied up.' The papers were still there, but they were heaped rather than scattered. The duvet, although unrepentantly unironed, was actually pulled over the mattress and the pillows had a suspiciously plumped-up look about them. Had he expected her to come back with him? Oh, what did it matter anyway? It was a bit late to play hard to get now.

Jane avoided the chair and lowered herself on to the edge of the mattress while Tom lit candles and poured two tots of whisky into glasses. A low, calm swell of music swirled gently into the air. 'What's this?' Jane asked, gazing at the flickering flame through her glass and admiring the way the amber fluid turned to liquid gold.

'Vaughan Williams' Fifth,' said Tom, lighting a cigarette and settling himself against the pillows. Jane felt the space between them quiver. 'Preludio.' The haunting, insistent, plaintive notes increased in intensity.

Jane closed her eyes. 'It's lovely,' she said, aware it was a horribly inadequate description. She had, after all, said the same thing barely two hours ago about the San Lorenzo chicken. 'I'm afraid I don't know anything about music,' she added apologetically.

'Well, all you really have to know is whether you like it or not,' said Tom simply. 'I like this because it's very calm and relaxing. It's one of those pieces that puts into notes all that longing you could never put into words.' He said it without a hint of theatricality, as if merely stating a fact. Who or what was he longing for? Jane wondered. Gazing silently into the middle distance, drawing on his cigarette, Tom did not enlighten her.

As much to relieve incipient cramp as to break the tension, Jane got to her feet. For once, her knees did not crack like pistol shots. She crossed to look at the mass of books piled against the wall at the back of the room. It was her turn to examine his library now.

Suddenly, a finger lifted her hair from the back and she felt a warm mouth exploring the nape of her neck. Her spine exploded into shivers. She closed her eyes and gave herself up to blissful oblivion as Tom gently nibbled her ear.

'I didn't know what to say to you yesterday,' murmured Tom. 'You see, I had spent all this time persuading myself that you were living with your boyfriend and there was no point in trying.'

Damn, thought Jane, her fists clenching. What sort of deluded fool had she been to want to move in with Nick in the first place? It had ruined everything ever since.

'But then you came round here and I thought you'd come to tell me it was over with him,' Tom mumbled, 'that somehow you'd found me, but you said you had come from the magazine to do an interview, which, naturally, rather threw me, and then you *did* tell me it was over with him, but I didn't know what to think by then. If you understand what I mean.' Tom paused. 'I'm not sure that I do, though.'

Jane smiled and did not answer as his lips started nibbling round her cheekbones. She stood stock still, terrified to move in case he stopped. Tom gently turned her round and pushed her trembling lips apart with his own. He smelt of soap and tasted of salt, thought Jane, melting into his mouth and arms as her legs gave way beneath her. Pressing her gently to him, Tom pushed a warm hand beneath her Joseph and fondled her stiffening nipple.

'I've wanted you ever since that night,' he breathed. 'I just couldn't stop thinking about you. I thought you must have forgotten me ages ago, that you must have thought of it as just a one-night stand. Which it was, of course. Only it wasn't.'

'No, it wasn't,' Jane murmured, clutching his rough-soft hair in her fingers.

'But will you respect me in the morning?' Tom muttered as he slid the exploring hand into her knickers.

'I certainly hope not,' murmured Jane.

Chapter 25

Jane had not slept all night. It had seemed a good idea at the time; in fact, it had seemed a crime to do anything else. But now she was paying the price. Concentrating on the recondite detail of the next issue's fashion pages was almost more than she could manage. Just what was Tiara talking about?

'What do you mean, boars' pelvises?' Jane felt a migraine coming on. This meeting had been going on for an hour already and there seemed no end in sight.

'Boar's pelvises. Alessandro uses boars' pelvises in his hats. He's, er, the sort of Damien Hirst of millinery,' said Tiara, proffering some dim Polaroids featuring a pale, rickety, bony structure wearing another on her head.

'Don't tell me. He's the next pig thing,' sighed Jane, hoping it wouldn't catch on. There were quite enough boneheads around in fashion as it was. Tiara tightened her lips. Her sense of humour, thought Jane, had gone the way of her puppy fat and original facial features. Wiped away without trace. Perhaps that was what the Glamourtron did to you.

'We're planning a spread on the couture, of course,' said Tiara.

Of course, thought Jane. To justify Victoria's

continuing absence at fashion shows, if nothing else. Yesterday Victoria had returned from Paris Fashion Week and declared it the most tedious experience of her life. Then she had promptly boarded Concorde for the New York shows.

Tiara produced more Polaroids and spread them on the big desk before Jane. 'These are the latest batch. Amazing, aren't they?'

In one, a topless, emaciated woman wearing what looked like a gas mask and the ripped bottom half of a ballgown was staggering up the runway with a Doc Marten on one leg and a moonboot on the other. In another, a woman was wearing what looked like a green hospital gown. Tiara was right. Amazing was the word.

'Couture really is astonishing, isn't it?' muttered Jane. 'I mean, all those customers at the shows paying upwards of fifty thousand pounds for something they'll only wear once.'

'What do you mean?' asked Tiara indignantly. 'Some of them wear it *twice*.'

After the fashion meeting, Jane wandered out into a features department more deserted than the *Marie Celeste* after a bomb scare. 'Where's Tash?' she asked.

'Gone to a wedding,' said Tish, as if this was the most natural thing to do on a Tuesday morning. But then, at *Fabulous*, Jane supposed it was. No one here went to anything as tacky as a Saturday marriage. She looked at the clock. Half past twelve. Seven long, miserable, endless hours before she met Tom for the concert at the Barbican he had promised her to start her musical education.

Unclamping herself from his warm body that morning had been like leaving part of herself behind. Too happy to sleep, she had lain there wide awake all night, gazing through the gaping curtains to the dark blue sky in which passing planes glowed like slow-moving stars. Light-headed with tiredness, Jane closed her eyes and escaped into the inner world where she could see him, smell him, feel him again. How on earth did people in love manage to get any work done at all? she wondered. How did they fit anything else in?

She reluctantly dragged herself back to the film magazines and the burning question of her next front cover. Most of the 'ones to watch' sections seemed very excited about an American actress called Jordan Madison who was variously described as famously moody, notoriously uninterviewable, utterly beautiful and star of a string of indie films of which the latest, *Fish Food*, had been a huge critical and cult success.

'Oh yah, Jordan Madison,' said Tosh, passing Jane's desk en route to the fax. She rolled an over-made-up eye at the full-page pictures of the frail-bodied actress with her colt's legs and long, flat, black hair. 'You'll never get her. She *never* does interviews.'

Jane immediately picked up the telephone and began placing calls with and sending faxes to Jordan's LA press agent, New York press agent and the New York press agent's LA press agent. She knew a challenge when she heard one.

As the last note hung in the air, the tears continued to flow uncontrollably down Jane's cheeks. Tom, silent beside her, gave her hand a sympathetic squeeze. Jane cast a quick, blurred glance around and saw that almost everybody else in the concert hall was sitting ramrod straight with eyes as dry as the desert. Had they no souls? she wondered. Or, more likely, had she had one too many resistance-weakening gin and tonics before the beginning of the concert? 'It was so beautiful,' she gulped afterwards as Tom handed her yet another large gin and tonic from the bar. 'It was the saddest thing I've ever heard. What was it called?'

'*Pavane pour une infante défunte*,' said Tom. 'Pavane for a dead princess. Ravel used to make his students play it, and yell at them that he'd written a pavane for a dead princess, not a dead pavane for a princess.' He grinned and kissed her on the tip of her nose. 'Cheer up. Let's go and have that romantic dinner you promised me.' The lyrical moment was shattered in an instant as Jane remembered the mess her flat was in.

Having sent Tom round to the off-licence to buy some wine, Jane let herself quickly into the hall. Without even pausing to take her coat off, she rushed frantically around tidying up heaps of clothes, shoving her tampons and Ladyshave into the bathroom cupboard and spraying perfume liberally over the pillows.

Moving on to the kitchen, she emptied the pre-washed salad she'd splashed out on in honour of the occasion into a bowl and threw the potatoes into a pan. Next she tackled the scarily exotic-looking red snapper in the fridge. She was relieved to note from the cooking instructions that it required no more attention than the cursory slick of butter she had been planning to give it. Just as she lowered the fish into their crematorium, Tom came through the door. Rushing to meet him, Jane noticed a pair of grey knickers on the bedroom floor and kicked them swiftly under the bed.

'Why haven't you taken your coat off?' he grinned, brandishing a bottle of Moët at her. Jane hurriedly divested herself.

'What's for dinner?' he asked, picking two champagne

glasses from the kitchen cupboard and giving her his crinkle-eyed smile.

'Fish,' said Jane.

'Sounds brill,' grinned Tom. He shrugged off his battered leather jacket and lit up a Marlboro.

'I suppose you think that's very finny,' said Jane, twining her arms round his neck. 'But you're certainly a dab hand,' she added, as his warm fingertips slipped inside her knickers again. He certainly wasn't one to flounder, she thought, gasping as he rubbed gently at the warm, willing wetness between her legs.

'Cod we go to bed?' breathed Tom, grinding his cigarette out with thrilling force in the base of the cheeseplant.

'Just give me time to mullet over,' said Jane, walking slowly backwards towards the bedroom and pulling Tom with her.

As he pressed her gently down into the perfume-scented pillows, Jane prepared to give herself up to pure pleasure as Tom began to kiss her slowly. Very slowly. In fact, he almost seemed to have stopped. Jane opened her eyes. Above her, in the semi-gloom, Tom had raised his head slightly.

'What's that funny smell?' he asked. Jane felt panic shoot through her. Perhaps she *had* been a bit heavy-handed with the Number 5.

'Scent,' she admitted, shamefacedly. Would he think she was irredeemably naff? Dabbing perfume on pillows like a twelve-year-old.

'No, not that,' said Tom, sniffing. 'A sort of burning smell.'

'Aaaargh!' Two nanoseconds later, a naked Jane had leapt out of bed with a speed that would not have disgraced an Olympic high jumper and raced into the kitchen where the red mullet was now distinctly black.

She pushed aside her tangle of hair and looked at Tom helplessly as, also naked, he loped up to the kitchen door. She was encouraged to see that the sickening smell of burnt fish, which she knew would linger around the flat for days, did not seem to have dampened his ardour one iota. A splendid erection rose triumphantly out of his abundant dark-blond pubic hair. He looked, she decided, rather like one of those fertility statues in the British Museum. 'Fancy a takeaway?' she asked with a weak grin.

'No, but I fancy you,' said Tom, giving Jane his slow-burn smile.

'Oh no,' wailed Oonagh.

Jane started reluctantly out of the most wonderful daydream at the crucial moment when she was just going up the aisle with Tom. As there was no further interruption, she lapsed back into it, to find herself fast-forwarded to their honeymoon in the sort of Caribbean luxury hideaway where you just stuck a flag in the sand when you wanted another cocktail. The daydream then changed scene to a sunny garden path down which she and Tom were walking with two merry, blonde, fish-finger-advert children.

'No. No. No,' cried Oonagh, burying her perfectly-coiffed head in her elegant arms. 'I don't believe it. It can't be true,' she moaned from the muffled depths of her cashmere. 'That has to be the most embarrassing thing that's ever happened to me in my entire life.'

'What?' asked Jane, looking up distractedly. 'What's happened?'

Oonagh raised a despairing head. 'The Duchess of Dorchester has just rung me,' she said in anguished tones.

'So what's the matter with that?' It sounded like a *Fabulous* dream come true to Jane.

'The matter is that she's an old friend of mine,' wailed Oonagh. 'Or *was*. I went to her daughter's wedding last week. Apparently there's a *video*.'

'Oh *no*,' chimed in Tash, looking outraged. 'I just *don't* believe it. I mean, how *naff* can you get? Only *common* people have wedding videos. You're *quite* right to be furious, Oonagh.'

'Not *that*,' spat Oonagh. Tash blinked. 'I'm more concerned,' Oonagh gasped, 'about the fact that quite a large part of the video features me making very loud and rude remarks about some of the other guests. Apparently my seat was practically *next door* to the video and sound recorder. Daisy Dorchester is *incandescent*.'

Jane looked quickly down at a pile of faxes on her desk before anyone could see her laughing.

Most of the faxes were refusals from Jordan Madison's seemingly limitless band of press agents. Refusing to take no for an answer, Jane had pursued them by telephone and had still ended up with no for an answer. 'She doesn't do innerviews,' everyone had snarled, leaving Jane wondering why Jordan Madison needed press agents at all in that case. On the other hand, what was the point of not giving interviews if no one knew you didn't give interviews?

Jane sighed. She had to get this piece in the bag somehow. Having one good cover simply wasn't enough. Two and she'd be home and dry. And she needed to do it soon, before Victoria swept back, as she must eventually, and took all the credit for her efforts. Jane's heart sank at this most depressing of depressing thoughts. She was getting used to running the place on her own; more than that, she was enjoying it. Good ideas were finally starting to come out of the features department.

The telephone rang, providing a welcome excuse to leave Oonagh to her somewhat unsolvable problem. It was Tally.

'You won't believe how well it's going,' she exclaimed. 'People are just pouring in to the retreat. We even had a wedding here the other day.'

She spoke, Jane noticed, entirely without longing for her own near-miss nuptials. Clearly Tally had had enough of men for the time being.

'It's going to be in *Hello!* next week,' Tally twittered. 'It was some heir to a vitreous enamel fortune marrying his psychic, apparently.'

'Not the Hon. Rollo Harbottle, surely,' said Jane.

'Yes, how on earth do you know him?' Tally sounded astonished.

'Don't ask. Marrying his psychic, was he? Very trendy. I'm glad to hear he's finally got himself a relationship with a future.'

'You should have been there,' said Tally. 'It was hilarious. Mummy arranged it and you know what that means. A mad New Age ceremony where the bride and groom were naked and coated with mud and sang to each other at the top of a hill as the dawn rose. They were standing,' Tally added, snorting, 'in the middle of a giant representation in leaves of the male and female genitalia and exchanged oak saplings instead of wedding rings.' She giggled.

'What else is happening?' said Jane, trying not to look too amused for Oonagh's sake. The picture editor was still staring into space, contemplating the smoking ruins of her social life.

'Well, the retreat is full already and Mummy wants to

build more tents,' said Tally. 'She says there's no more beautiful sight than the dawn rising over teepees.'

'Not my idea of a morning glory,' giggled Jane, thinking instantly of Tom. Really, she was becoming one of those people who thought about sex every six seconds.

'How's it going with you?' Tally asked.

'Fine,' said Jane, not wishing to start the Tom story now. She'd tell Tally when she saw her. 'Everything's fabulous, in fact. All I need now,' she muttered, almost to herself, 'is Jordan Madison and my world will be perfect.'

'Sorry?'

'Oh, nothing.' Poor dear Tally, stuck in what were quite literally the medieval backwoods of Mullions, was hardly likely to have heard of Hollywood's latest hip, hot and happening star.

'Oh, it's just that I thought I heard you say Jordan Madison,' said Tally.

'I did,' said Jane, surprised. 'Why, have you heard of her?'

'She's Hollywood's latest hip, hot and happening star, isn't she? I only happen to know because she's staying at the retreat at the moment.'

'WHAT?' yelled Jane.

Tash whipped round and stared.

'She's a great friend of Mummy's. Worships her, in fact. Mummy helped her to discover the goddess inside herself or some such guff while they were cleaning out the loos together at that ashram in California.'

'It's amazing what you find down a U-bend, isn't it?' Excitement rose in Jane like a geyser. 'Gosh, do you think you could get Julia to ask her . . .' Her voice dropped to a murmur as she explained the *Fabulous* cover situation. 'Having Jordan on the front would practically make my *life*,' she ended. 'Oh, and could you find out if we could bring a photographer?' Don't ask, don't get, she told herself, feeling cheeky.

'All right,' said Tally breezily. 'She's in a tree-hugging seminar at the moment, but I'll ask her the minute she's out. Call you back.'

Why did I bother going through the agents? wondered Jane. It seemed so obvious, in retrospect, that mad, hippy Julia would have an address book starrier than the Milky Way. Everyone knew that these days the real deals were done in AA meetings, drug clinics and holistic retreats, not the agents' offices. Why hadn't she thought of the New Age network before?

Despite this excitement, it didn't take long for her mind to drift back to Tom. What was he doing now? He wrote in the afternoons, she knew. She devoted a blissful few minutes to imagining Tom, sleepy of eye and furrowed of brow, scribbling furiously in longhand like a schoolboy taking Common Entrance.

Almost exactly an hour later, Tally called back. 'That's fine,' she said. 'No problem.'

'What? You mean Jordan will do it?'

'She'd love to,' said Tally. 'Anything for a friend of Julia's, she says. She's here for the next fortnight at least, so any time you want to come up is fine. And it's perfectly all right to bring a photographer.'

'Holy shit.' Jane crashed the receiver joyfully down, leapt up from her desk and danced wildly round the room. Never, never would she laugh at Julia and her New Age eccentricities again. 'We've got Jordan Madison for our cover,' she shouted. 'Thank Goddess,' she yelled, punching the air and running out of the office, feeling like a winning-goal-scoring footballer doing a lap of honour round the stadium. This would show Victoria, she thought. This would put a bomb under the opposition on the news-stands. This would confirm her position as a hot new editor who could make things happen. She was much too excited to stay in the office. She decided to dash out and tell Tom straightaway. How wonderful it was, she thought happily, running down the back stairs, to be in love and have someone to share good news with.

Scattering a giggle of camp-looking photographers and their assistants in her wake, Jane shot through the foyer, out of the doors and on to the street. Plunging straight through the crowds of improbably tall Scandinavian schoolchildren wandering impassively up and down Carnaby Street, she dashed across Soho, skipping down the narrow streets, dodging parking meters and people, running across roads in front of taxis, sidling through narrow spaces between cars. At Busty Models she bolted through the door without even tapping on Tom's window and narrowly avoided falling flat on her face on the stairs leading down to his flat.

'Tom, Tom,' she cried excitedly, bursting through the door. 'Tom?' she repeated, a nanosecond and a whole world of difference later. Because Tom was not writing. He was not even alone. Tom was standing in the middle of the room embracing a beautiful blonde. And not any old bog-standard, run-of-the-mill beautiful blonde either. The girl he held in his arms was Champagne D'Vyne.

Chapter 26

Huddling deep in the dark, warm, foetal fug of her duvet, Jane heard the answerphone repeatedly click on. Whoever was calling, she didn't care. She'd turned the sound right down, just as she'd switched off the entrance buzzer by the flat door. If only she could switch off her life. Her dehydrated brain throbbed from the entire bottle of gin she'd drunk the night before. But coping with a hangover was nothing compared to catching Tom in flagrante with Champagne.

Jane had no idea what time it was. She didn't care about that, either. She just knew that from now on, every second of every minute of every hour of the rest of her life was going to be utterly, painfully, blackly miserable. For a brief moment, the world had been her oyster. Now it was just a shell. She was back in the bad movie again. Or perhaps the bad oyster.

She stared at the ceiling and wondered how she could have got it so wrong yet again. Why hadn't she seen what was coming? Tom hadn't given her many clues, it was true, but she should have known it would end badly. It always did. With Nick, with Mark, and now with Tom. And all within a few weeks. True, married, trusting, hi-honey-I'm-home happiness was beyond her reach, now and for ever. If it wasn't for bad luck, Jane decided, she'd have no luck at all.

She was cursed, there was no doubt about that. But not just by a failure to pick the right man. Her life was blighted by a beautiful blonde, a glamorous albatross hanging round her neck with six-inch stilettos and a pressing appointment at Michaeljohn. Champagne was utterly inescapable. Try and move magazines and you found she'd come with you. Visit your friend in the middle of nowhere and you'll find her in the garden. Bury her two hundred feet under a runway and she pops back up with her arms round the man of your dreams. Jane screwed up her eyes in despair. It might be caprice on the part of Fate to bind her life up with Champagne's, but it wasn't her idea of a joke. Almost worse than Tom's betrayal was the contemplation of a future not only manless but clamped as firmly to Champagne's side as her Chanel handbag.

Jane could not blank out what she had seen in Tom's flat. The sight of him clasping Champagne seemed tattooed on the inside of her eyelids. For the millionth time, she ran and re-ran the fatal ten seconds of footage in the video machine of her brain, but still managed to make no sense of it. *Why* hadn't he told her he had a girlfriend? He had been so open about everything else. She had *trusted* him, for God's sake.

She got up and staggered, head throbbing, to the shower. But if washing Tom right out of her hair was simple, washing him out of the bathroom, or any other part of the flat, was impossible. Although he had only visited it twice, Tom's presence seemed now to permeate its very fabric. He had walked on *that* floor, sat in *that* chair, laughed at her cooking in *that* kitchen and, most of all, *slept in that bed.*

She could barely glance at a written word in case she thought of him. If she turned on the radio, the merest hint of classical music set off a waterfall of weeping. Even the soap powder in the kitchen cupboard reminded her of the blonde children that would never now run merrily down the pathway.

The day after the day after she had discovered Champagne and Tom together, Jane finally sought refuge in the *Fabulous* office.

It was a hideous mistake. Here, more than anywhere, reminders that she was the only single, betrayed woman in the world seemed brutally abundant.

'I'm having *just the worst* time with my boyfriend,' Tosh was drawling to Tash as she entered. Jane pricked her ears up. This sounded promising. 'He's being *such* a pig. He told me yesterday he was taking me to Bali.'

'Well, what's wrong with that?' asked Tash. 'Although,' she added, raising her eyebrows, 'I suppose Bali *is* a bit five-minutes-ago now that everyone who's anyone is going to Sardinia. Actually, I *do* see your point.'

'No, no,' said Tosh. 'The problem is it turns out he's taking me to the *Nutcracker*. To the boring old *ballet*! Can you imagine *anything* more *yawnsville*?'

Even in the loos, where Jane retreated frequently during the morning to indulge in some spontaneous weeping, there was no escape. The basins were, as always, positively blazing with the flowers that were sent to the *Fabulous* office. From hopeful PR companies, hopeful designers and, worst of all, hopeful lovers they came, a never-ending stream of fashionable bunches. Brilliant gerberas wrapped in brown paper; withered twigs in glass pots; vast, rope-bound sunflowers the height of a tree; massy bunches of heady lilies; they were all plunged unceremoniously into the basins waiting to be taken home by their recipients. Or, as often happened, forgotten and left in the loos to rot. Her own flower-receiving days having been cut off in their prime, Jane found the sight of these exuberant, neglected bunches almost too painful. She briefly considered patronising the men's loos instead.

Jane tried to take comfort in the Jordan Madison layouts stacked for approval on her desk. She signed them off almost without looking. The Madison coup now felt flatter than a week-old glass of Bollinger. What difference did it make to anything?

'Someone kept calling and calling for you yesterday,' Tish told Jane as the morning drew to a close. She had clearly only just remembered. 'A man. But he wouldn't leave his name. Um, and the advance copies have just come in. On the desk in Victoria's office.'

'Advance copies of what?' asked Jane dully. She did not comment on the mystery caller. She didn't care.

'*Fabulous*, of course,' grinned Tish. 'The Lily Eyre one. Remember?' she added, teasing.

'Vaguely,' said Jane. It seemed a lifetime ago. But she may as well look at them. Go through the motions.

Dragging herself into Victoria's glass box, she glanced cursorily at the new issues, gleaming beneath swathes of plastic packaging. She could barely bring herself to cut it open. The Jane who had edited that issue and sent it joyfully off to the printers was a different, younger and more hopeful creature altogether than the shattered wreck who stood looking at the finished product.

The cover was, indeed, a radical departure from *Fabulous*'s staple diet of demure debutantes. Dressed in brilliant red, her lips a slash of identical scarlet, Lily Eyre looked sexy and exciting. Inside, the interviewer had turned in a witty and incisive piece, with lots of hilarious quotes about the film business from Lily. When Jane had first read it, it had made her laugh. Now, looking at the cover, she wanted to cry.

She had no idea whether the issue was good or bad. Was it a bold departure from the norm or a disastrous experiment which might well backfire on the newsstands? What did she know? She couldn't even tell a good guy from a deceitful two-timing bastard.

Tish interrupted her reverie. 'I've just had a message from Archie Fitzherbert's secretary,' she said. 'He wants to see you in his office this afternoon.'

That was that then, thought Jane numbly. Fitzherbert had obviously taken one look at the issue and hated it. He'd probably *retched* at the horrid *obviousness* of it. He'd probably tell her to go and work on *Penthouse*. She'd lost her man, now she was going to lose her job.

The telephone on her desk shrilled. Miraculously, as if aware there was a crisis, Tish actually went to answer it. Jane stood cowering by the magazines in Victoria's office. She didn't want to talk to anyone.

'It's a woman,' hissed Tish, covering the receiver. 'Very grand-sounding. Shall I put her through to Victoria's phone?'

Tally, thought Jane gratefully. If there was one sensible, kind, concerned voice she needed to hear just now, it was Tally's.

'Yes please,' she instructed Tish, sitting down heavily in Victoria's huge leather revolving chair. Her relief was shortlived. It was not Tally on the line. It was Champagne. The woman she had last seen all over Tom like a rash. Jane felt weak with hatred. She prepared to slam the phone down, but Champagne's opening remark caught her off guard.

'Where the bloody hell were *you* haring off to the other day?' barked Champagne. 'You didn't even say hello. *Bloody* rude, I thought.'

Jane gritted her teeth. *She* had caught Champagne with her arms round someone she had imagined was *her* boyfriend. Was she expected to apologise for it? Should she have stayed and chatted? 'I suppose I was rather surprised to see you there,' she replied, dangerously evenly.

'Why?' demanded Champagne.

She obviously thinks I'm even more stupid than I think I am, Jane seethed to herself. 'Because I thought you were at the Gatwick runway protest, of course,' she snarled, biting each word as it came out. 'With *Piers*.'

'Oh. Yah, well, actually, that all turned out to be a bit of a misunderstanding,' honked Champagne. 'Got myself in a bit of a hole there, to be honest. In fact, as far as Piers is concerned I'm afraid my name's pretty much *mud* at the moment. Haw haw. Christ, I'm funny.'

'Oh,' said Jane, sarcastically. 'It's all over with him, then?' Poor Piers. Champagne had probably dumped him in her usual subtle fashion. She hoped Laughter wouldn't be too hard on him.

'Yah, actually,' boomed Champagne. 'Shame really. He's a bloody nice bloke. Bit grubby, could use a shower now and then. But *trifficaly* sweet guy. *Great* guy, actually. But we rather fell out over the whole runway business. The *hole* runway business. Haw haw haw.' Her ear-splitting laughter rolled like thunder through Jane's aching head.

'What happened?' asked Jane. She felt too weary to be angry.

'The problem was,' Champagne honked, 'that we were

there for different reasons. I thought they were protesting *for* a runway at Gatwick, not *against* one.'

Jane felt dizzy.

'Anyone normal would have thought the same,' declared Champagne remorselessly. 'I mean, the schedules to Nice are an utter *disgrace*. They need about four times as many flights as they're running at the moment. The times I've had to *slum* it in Club because First is already booked up. So when I heard that Piers and his gang were protesting about the runway, I thought, yah, *splendid* chaps. Those runways *need* protesting about. They need about four more of them, not to mention more planes.'

Jane opened and closed her mouth like a surprised flounder.

'But it turned out that Piers and co. were actually trying to stop the bloody runway being *built*!' exclaimed Champagne. 'Ridiculous. *Unbloodybelievable*. But then again,' she added, 'I suppose I can see their point of view.'

'*Can* you?' spluttered Jane, at last finding her voice.

'Yah,' said Champagne. 'I mean, none of them have ever been to Nice in Club Class, so they have no idea what a *complete and utter nightmare* it is. If they had, obviously they'd understand. It's just a question of education. Anyway, I'm not calling you to tell you all this rubbish,' Champagne barked imperiously. 'It's about something else. We need to meet. Now. Urgently. For lunch.'

'Why?' asked Jane. What could there be to say?

'Because I have some brilliant news for you,' honked Champagne impatiently. 'An amazing offer.'

Jane frowned. Was it to be a *ménage à trois*, then? Or Tom-sharing, with Champagne having custody and Tom being allowed out for weekend visits? Or was Champagne about to offer one of her cast-off chinless wonders as a compensation package?

Jane's instinct warned her to steer well clear, but hard fact, in particular her impending dismissal by Archie Fitzherbert, seemed to suggest that, if she wanted to keep body and soul together for the foreseeable future, she was hardly in a position to turn brilliant news and amazing offers down. And Champagne, as Jane now realised, was in any case her destiny. No point in resisting her.

Jane was delayed leaving the office for her lunch with Champagne, because the inside of her jacket collapsed. She'd heard of unstructured linens, she thought crossly, sticking the lining back together with Sellotape, but this was ridiculous. She hoped it wouldn't flap open and reveal her handiwork during the lunch. Champagne may not be most people's idea of observant, but there was no doubt at all that she would notice that.

Even more stressed out after ten minutes in a gridlocked taxi, Jane announced her arrival at the restaurant by attempting to push the revolving door the wrong way. She was late, but Champagne had not arrived either. A supercilious and speedy waiter led Jane to their empty table. His sinuous form slid through the tight-packed tables with ease, while Jane found that presenting her bottom in a sideways shuffle to pairs of elegant lunchers was the only way she could get through the gaps herself. She threw herself into her chair, stared fiercely and unseeingly at the menu and wished desperately that she hadn't come.

After a few minutes she looked up and started to examine the eaters around her. They were mainly, she saw, emaciated women, ladies who lunch, although most of them looked as if they hadn't seen lunch for years. They were so thin that probably the only thing holding them together was their plastic surgeons' stitches. Jane shuddered as a tall, oleaginous man who she assumed was the restaurant manager made the rounds of the tables, planting ostentatious kisses here and there. Those surgery-raddled faces, she felt, might well come away on his lips.

Time passed. Champagne was now over half an hour late and Jane was beginning to feel vaguely mortified. She had polished off an entire bottle of sparkling mineral water and was desperate for the loo but, having no idea where they were, was reluctant to perform the required bottom-shimmy through the tables again in what would doubtless be the wrong direction.

Suddenly, a wave of perfume so strong it could have wiped out Barbados came crashing into her nostrils. The waiters wiped the sneers off their faces and goggled. Champagne had arrived, clutching Gucci and an armful of vast carrier bags emblazoned with the best of Bond Street.

Jane stood up so Champagne could smash both her cheekbones into her face. 'Darling!' Champagne yelled. As intended, her look-at-me voice had the desired effect. There was a snapping of neck joints all round as everyone in the restaurant undid weeks of careful work by their masseurs and craned to stare. Once there were enough people looking at her, Champagne pushed her black lace microskirt up as far as possible and sat down.

Under her arm, Gucci stared out, his bead-like little eyes shining malevolently. 'Doesn't he look splendid?' gushed Champagne, lifting the poodle and dangling him towards Jane. 'Don't you just *adore* his collar?'

Jane stared at the row of diamonds glittering round the

dog's skinny neck. Economics was hardly her strong point, but the collar was, she realised, probably worth more than the GDP of a smallish East European country.

'It's Guccigoo's birthday,' Champagne explained, setting Gucci on the table where he lost no time sticking his nose in the bread and his tongue in the butter. 'That collar's got forty diamonds on it,' she boasted. She leant towards Jane conspiratorially, displaying a cleavage deep enough to bungee-jump down to two passing, plate-laden waiters. Four first courses wobbled perilously for a few seconds. Champagne cast a sideways glance at Gucci, who by now was scrabbling furiously at the tiny dishes of salt and pepper and scattering their contents all over the tablecloth.

'It's worth a hundred thousand pounds!' Champagne whispered loudly. Jane's mouth fell open. 'Of course, the whole thing was the most *enormous* secret,' Champagne continued, widening her eyes as if to convey the unimaginable subterfuge that had been involved. 'I didn't want Gucci to guess *anything*. It was the most *wonderful* surprise for him this morning.'

She leant back triumphantly in her chair and took a sip from the glass of chilled champagne from the complimentary bottle that had appeared as if by magic on the table. The oleaginous manager swept by, nodding and beaming. Jane wondered when Champagne would get to the brilliant news and amazing offers. She looked at her miserably. With her perfect, arrogant face unmarked by so much as a wrinkle, her white-blonde hair a shining mass on her shoulders and her tiny dress rucked up to show as much of her slender body as possible, it was not difficult to see why Tom had been tempted. Jane tried not to look at Champagne's perfect bare legs and tried to hide as much of her own stubby fetlocks under the table as possible.

Champagne was beaming at her. Her glossy lips parted to treat Jane to a smile so brilliant it could probably have been seen from Mir. Jane shifted uncomfortably in her seat. Being on the receiving end of Champagne's charm offensive somehow felt worse than when she was just being offensive.

'Darling! How *are* you,' Champagne gushed. 'It's *heaven* to see you. You're looking absolutely *wonderful.*' She raked Jane with her hard, green eyes. 'You're *so* lucky,' she declared. 'You *so* suit no make-up.'

Jane blushed deeply. Trust Champagne to zoom in on that. She knew she should have made time for a little mascara, at least. But lately she hadn't seen the point of putting it on. It scarcely improved the way you looked and it was a bore to have to clean it off at night. Besides, she thought miserably, it only streaked when you cried.

'You really do have the most *wonderful* cheekbones,' Champagne continued. Jane was aware that lack of sleep and general anguish had scooped great care-worn hollows from her cheeks. But she doubted they improved her appearance.

The waiter glided up. As she ordered, utterly at random, and barely glancing at the menu, Jane wondered if Champagne was ever going to get to the point.

'Christ, I'm absolutely *pooped,*' Champagne announced brightly, looking with deep satisfaction at the carrier bags crowding the floor. 'Signing all those credit card slips *really* takes it out of you. *Exhausting!*'

'What have you bought?' asked Jane. Everything, by the look of it, she thought.

'Oh, these aren't for *me,*' said Champagne, gesturing at

the bags. 'No, all *my* things are in the limo.' She waved a perfectly-manicured hand in the general direction of the restaurant window and the shining Rover visible outside. 'These,' she announced, waving at the bags which lapped around their table like a tide, 'are for my brother.'

'Your brother?' said Jane, dimly remembering the photograph on the top of the piano in Champagne's flat. It was the first time Champagne had ever mentioned him.

'Yes,' barked Champagne. 'You know. Or you should. You've been shagging him for the past week, at least.'

'What?' said Jane slowly. This was too incredible. Surely Champagne didn't mean . . . 'You don't mean . . . Tom?' she croaked.

'Of course I bloody mean Tom,' said Champagne, draining her glass. 'Unless you've been shagging someone else as well.'

Jane's bowels felt loose with shock and her tired head was spinning as she struggled to get a grip. Tom was Champagne's *brother*? He couldn't be. No two people could *possibly* be less alike. Tom was an obscure, impoverished writer who lived in a basement below a brothel in Soho, while Champagne was a Belgravia-dwelling professional socialite whose dog had a £100,000 diamond collar. Tom wrote seriously, and every word himself. The same certainly couldn't be said for Champagne.

Tom wore battered leather jackets and jumble-sale T-shirts. Champagne wore head-to-toe designer labels with little or no clothing attached. Tom had dirty blond hair that looked as if it was cut with a knife and fork. Champagne's shining mane was professionally blow-dried every day. And yet, Jane thought, gawping at Champagne as if seeing her for the first time, there *was* something about the cheekbones, the green eyes, the sultry, naughty smile . . .

'But you don't even have the same name,' stammered Jane. 'Tom's surname is Seton.'

Champagne drew on her cigarette and fired it out in two volleys from her nostrils. 'He *writes* under that name, sure,' she said. 'But his actual surname is D'Vyne. Tom's full name is, er,' she stopped and wrinkled her nose, as if preparing for a great feat of memory, 'Thomas Charles Gregorian Seton D'Vyne. Mine is,' she paused again, 'um, Champagne Olivia Wilnelia Seton D'Vyne,' she finished triumphantly.

Wow, thought Jane. Champagne's family had hardly held back over the font. Then again, there seemed to be an unwritten rule that the upper classes could have more names than everybody else. She remembered that from Cambridge. Along the corridor she had lived on, everyone but herself seemed to have three or more initials painted up above their door. Tally had had at least five.

'Tom dropped the D'Vyne because he said he thought it sounded too grand for a struggling writer,' said Champagne, a faint note of scorn in her voice. 'But I'm convinced the real reason is that he disapproves of my lifestyle. He hates socialites and the whole London party scene and didn't want anyone to connect him with my column inches. *Or* me. He's always been obsessed with money,' she finished, stabbing out her cigarette.

'*Has* he?' asked Jane, astounded. In the short time she had known him, Tom had seemed the most generous soul imaginable. He had practically emptied his pockets for the beggar they had met on the way back from San Lorenzo. He had not struck her as the mean type, still less the rich type.

'Obsessed with not having it, I mean,' honked Champagne. 'He refused his part of our trust fund because he wanted to make it on his own. And I was never allowed to mention him in the column, in case people stopped taking him *seriously* as a *writer.*' Champagne rolled her eyes mockingly. 'I mean, as if there was the faintest *possibility* that anyone could *not* take him seriously as a writer. He's hardly a laugh a minute on the subject, is he?'

Jane shook her head dumbly. If only she'd stopped a few more seconds and allowed Tom to explain. She'd blown it yet again.

She put her head in her hands and groaned. The horrible reality of the situation pressed in on her like a smothering pillow. And not just the dreadful misunderstanding, either. There was also the hideous fact that she had managed to fall in love with Champagne's *brother*. Of all the brothers in all the world, she had to fall in love with that one.

'Yah, he told me about this girl he's met,' Champagne said, eyeing Jane assessingly. 'Never thought for a *minute* it was *you.* Bit *odd*, though, I must say, the way you rushed off the other day. Tom was a bit cut up after you'd gone, actually. Dashed straight out after you, but you'd scarpered.'

'I, er, thought . . . I mean, I thought you . . . the . . .' She stopped and gazed miserably at Champagne.

'Oh, for Christ's sake,' Champagne boomed suddenly, so loud that the entire restaurant stopped to listen. 'You surely didn't think I was shagging my own *brother*?' She shrieked with mirth. The clatter of dropped jaws and forks all round was deafening.

'Oh God,' said Jane, panicking. 'What am I going to do now? I've ruined everything. Tom'll probably never speak to me again. He'll think I'm a hysterical freak.'

Champagne patted her hand. 'Oh, *all* his girlfriends are. I wouldn't worry. Ha ha ha.' She giggled at Jane's horrorstruck expression. 'Just teasing. Can't you take a joke? Pop round and see him tonight.'

'I'll go round now,' muttered Jane, getting to her feet. The room whirled around her. She swayed, feeling as if she was about to faint, and sat down again.

'He won't be there,' Champagne said, examining her nails with satisfaction. 'I tried to get him to come shopping but he told me he was spending every afternoon this week researching in some mouldy library somewhere. *Not* my idea of fun. Now look,' she boomed, 'there's something *really* bloody important I need to talk to you about now, OK?'

The earth-shattering revelations about Tom, then, were obviously just an aperitif, thought Jane. She dreaded to think what was coming next.

'Tom's not the only writer in the family,' Champagne honked, her green eyes blazing triumphantly. 'I've been offered a vast sum to write a novel myself. Brilliant, isn't it? Aren't you thrilled?'

'That's nice,' said Jane, wondering why on earth *she* should be pleased.

Champagne stared at her in amazement. 'What's the matter with you?' Several heads turned their way. 'You should be dancing on the *tables*. They're offering me half a million, OK? Serious dosh. Big potatoes.'

'I don't understand,' said Jane with as much dignity as she could muster, 'why *I* should be pleased that *my* work on *your* columns has got *you* a big fat novel deal. I'm *not* thrilled.' Her voice had risen to a faintly hysterical pitch. 'If anything I'm *furious*.'

There. She had said it. And if Champagne resigned from *Fabulous* as a result of it, she didn't care. She'd had enough. Of everything. The last forty-eight hours had left her drained, weak, bewildered and exhausted. And rather drunk. The bottle, she saw, was now empty. She had had a lot of champagne on an empty stomach. In more ways than one.

Champagne stared at her with amused astonishment. 'You *idiot*,' she honked. 'You don't understand, do you? I'm asking you to write this novel *for* me. We split the money. Two hundred and fifty grand each.' She smashed her empty glass against Jane's. 'Yah?' she boomed. 'Brilliant, eh?'

A sudden vision of freedom flashed before Jane's eyes. Two hundred and fifty thousand pounds. She could pack in her job. She was about to be sacked anyway, she thought, remembering her date with Archie Fitzherbert that afternoon. And what was the point of staying at *Fabulous* when Victoria was likely to sweep back into her editor's glass box any minute and make Jane's life an utter misery?

'We've got six months to do it in,' rasped Champagne, 'so you pack your shitty job in right now and we'll get cracking. All we have to do is rehash the columns and sort of link them together in some kind of storyline. Money for old rope.'

Jane looked away from Champagne's commanding gaze. Was she sure she wanted to get into this? The money was good, certainly, but would it be worth risking her sanity? Knocking out a monthly column with Champagne was torture enough. Six months' solid novel-writing would probably reduce her to care in the community status. She didn't feel all that far from it already.

'Can I think about it?' she asked.

'*Think* about it?' barked Champagne to whom this was obviously an alien concept. She glared at Jane with all the impotent rage of someone who has never been refused anything. For the first time ever in her dealings with Champagne, Jane experienced the amazing sensation of being in charge.

'I'll call you this afternoon,' she said, getting up.

'Well, I've got a colonic at three and my acupuncturist's at four,' honked Champagne. 'I don't want any sudden shocks during those or I'll have to spend the rest of my life on the loo. Call me at five. Oh, and could you get the bill? I'd love to treat you but I don't think my plastic will stand it.'

Why didn't she just accept Champagne's offer? Jane wondered as she climbed the stairs to the managing director's office. Flying in the face of Fate seemed foolish, particularly when she stood to gain a large sum of money and the sort of freedom she had hardly dared dream about before. As she knocked on Archie Fitzherbert's door, she made up her mind to say yes. After all, she was not likely to hear anything in the next few minutes that would make her want to change her mind.

'He's ready to see you,' said Georgie. 'Just go straight in.'

Jane knocked timidly on the oak door with the shining gold handle, wondering why she was bothering. She didn't need to go through this. She could turn and walk away, call Champagne and accept the book offer. But she was here now, and anyway she'd always wondered what Fitzherbert's office was like. Perhaps the Glamourtron was in here. She pictured the managing director sitting in a vast white leather swivel chair like Blofeld in the Bond films, stroking a white cat with a malevolent glare. The floor would be glass, with piranhas gliding menacingly beneath it, ready to slash to ribbons any editor whose circulation figures had slumped.

At a murmur from within, Jane pushed the door open. A pale room the approximate size of the entire *Fabulous* offices stretched away before her. Just as Fitzherbert in person resisted the stuffy, pinstriped manager stereotype, his office, too, was innocent of all mahogany or heavily framed oil paintings. Full of fat white sofas the size of stretch limos, book-piled glass-topped coffee tables, and concept bookcases of undulating wood, it resembled a film star's penthouse. The only clue to its inhabitant's profession were the framed magazine covers on the cream-painted walls. There was no desk. Fitzherbert, it was said, hated them, preferring to do all his work on sofas, or on the move. And rumour, for once, appeared to be true. The managing director, clad in a shirt of his trademark lilac set off with baby blue braces, was sprawled with his feet up on a white day bed, holding the *Daily Telegraph* inches from his nose. On top of the skyscraper of magazines beside him on the coffee table was the latest issue of *Fabulous*. Jane's heart sank.

Fitzherbert held his position for a few more seconds before sitting up, swinging his long, spare legs on to the polished wooden floor and grinning at her. He was, Jane decided, clearly trying to lull her into a false sense of security.

'Jane! Thank you so much for coming to see me. Sit down, do.' Fitzherbert pointed at the sofa opposite him with one dayglo pink-socked foot. Jane sank gingerly into the deep embrace of the cushions and wondered if she could ever get up again. Fitzherbert's office seemed deliberately designed to confuse and confound expectation. Which, of course, gave him more power over what went on in there.

'I asked you to come and see me because I have an idea to put to you,' Fitzherbert announced in a voice almost as bright as his socks. 'It concerns a slight change of, er, um, career.'

Jane nodded. This was what she had been expecting.

'I had a long conversation with Victoria yesterday,' said Fitzherbert, a slight frown rippling his tanned forehead.

Doubtless because one of the new issues had been biked round to her and she had hated it, thought Jane. 'She's back from New York, then?' she croaked.

Fitzherbert nodded.

'She's *back*, but she's not, ah, very *well* at the moment.' Fitzherbert agitatedly tapped the coffee table before him with the thick bottom of his Mont Blanc pen. 'In fact, she's apparently on the verge of a nervous breakdown. Stress. Overwork. Whatever,' he said, waving his hand in a half irritated, half dismissive gesture.

Jane stifled a gasp and cast her eyes down to disguise their outraged expression. *Victoria*, stressed? To her certain knowledge, the most anxious-making thing in Victoria's life was deciding between the Ivy and the Caprice for lunch.

'She needs a break,' Fitzherbert stated, raising his eyebrows slightly. 'Needs to get the city out of her system and all that stuff, find herself again et cetera,' he continued in a swift monotone, tapping his pen again. 'So the company's er, um, booked her into this place she wanted to go to. New ashram in the West Country. Called Millions or something, and from what they charge for a month there, that's about right.' He flashed Jane a wide but rather mirthless grin. She looked back at him blankly, failing to see what any of this had to do with her. Poor Tally, she thought vaguely. She must tell her to slam Victoria in a shed to get to grips with her inner child as soon as she arrived.

'The reason why I'm discussing Victoria's, er,' Fitzherbert raised his eyebrows, 'um . . . *indisposition* with you is that we've decided she should take a year off.'

Jane said nothing. What was all this leading to? Why didn't he just get to the point and put her out of her misery?

'So, I wanted to offer you the position. Acting editor, of course. For the time being, at least. Interested?'

Jane gulped. Was she hearing right? She had come here to be sacked, and now she was being offered what sounded suspiciously like Victoria's job. Acting editor of *Fabulous*. Jane's heart soared up into the back of her throat. She wanted to squeal with delight, jump up and down on the spot, turn cartwheels all round the spacious room. But she did none of these things. Instead she said quietly, 'Yes.'

'*Great*,' said Fitzherbert. 'Really great. I've just seen the new issue.' He stabbed at the shining cover on the coffee table before him. 'I thought it was really *excellent*. Very fresh, energetic, enthusiastic. One of the best issues for years, in fact.'

'Thank you,' stammered Jane, blushing a violent, confused and very un-editor-like red.

'*Great* cover, this girl, too.' He bashed Lily's nose with the end of his pen. 'Great pictures inside as well. And what *fantastic* legs she has. Terrific ankles.' Fitzherbert leapt to his feet. 'I understand you've got someone even better for the next. Well, that's *marvellous*.' Fitzherbert shook Jane's hand. 'Carry on the good, er, um, work. Personnel will be in touch about contracts and all that jazz.'

And the Glamourtron? Would Personnel be in touch about that as well? wondered Jane. Surely now, when she was poised to take over one of the house's glossiest titles, it must be her turn at last. It was on the tip of her tongue to ask Fitzherbert, as, wreathed in smiles, he ushered her out. But his door shut smartly behind her, and the chance was lost.

Outside, Jane hugged a puzzled Georgie and dashed downstairs to the foyer. She was captain of her own ship, finally. She had the job she had always wanted, and, at last, no doubt whatsoever that she could do it brilliantly. After all, did she not have Jordan Madison lined up for the next cover? Whatever mess her private life might be in, her professional one was shaping up just dandy.

Little did Victoria know, thought Jane, that she had no intention of relinquishing the editorship now she had her feet under the table. She had serious plans for *Fabulous*. They raced through her mind as she walked briskly along in the sunshine. More interviews. Better features. Funny pieces. Investigations. More sex. *Much* more sex.

Jane gazed joyfully up at the azure sky above the grimy buildings, a thank-you-everyone speech babbling through her head. Thank you, Josh, she thought, for being sufficiently horrid to drive me into the *Fabulous* job in the first place. Thank you, Champagne. If you had been one iota less nightmarish, I would have taken your book offer and never gone to see Fitzherbert today. And most of all, thank you, Victoria, for your blissful, hysterical self-indulgence. Thank you, everyone. I want to thank everyone I ever met, ever. Jane grinned ecstatically at a number of doleful passers-by. She buzzed with confidence. She felt brilliant with light. She radiated with energy. She felt like a human power station. Most of all, she was full of hope, which she needed, considering what she was about to do.

Rounding the corner, Jane spotted Camilla lounging, as usual, in the doorway. She raised an eyebrow as Jane crossed the street towards her. 'Hi,' beamed Jane, striding through the door and descending, sure and fleet of foot, down the stairs at the back. At the bottom, she paused just a second before throwing open Tom's scabby door.

He sprang up from his desk when he saw her, a half fearful, half hopeful expression in his exhausted, red-rimmed eyes. The bags beneath them were as big as suitcases. Caused by sorrow, or mere overwork? Thrown, Jane hesitated in the doorway, willing her confidence to come back. Tom had every right to be furious. She had judged and condemned him without a shred of evidence. Would he reject her? She scanned his strained face for clues, found none and decided to fling herself on his mercy.

Speechless with remorse, desperate for contact, Jane dashed across the room and flung herself into Tom's arms. 'Oh God, what a mess,' she whispered, burying her face in his neck. 'I'm so sorry. It was all a stupid misunderstanding.'

'I'd have tidied up if I'd known you were coming,' said Tom brokenly into her hair. 'And, by the way, just before you vanish yet again, will you marry me?'

An hour later, snuggled under the duvet with her head on Tom's chest, Jane thought ecstatically that she would rather be in this dingy Soho basement than in the finest suite at the Hotel de Paris. She quickly revised this. Being with Tom amid the splendours of Monaco's finest might just have the edge on where they were now. Well all that would come with her glossy new job. She smiled dreamily and pushed her hips closer still to Tom. I want to melt into him, she thought, so that we can never be parted again. But then, that wouldn't be quite so much fun. And it would certainly make sex difficult.

Jane felt she might die and go to heaven any minute. She had won the double. She had the man of her dreams and the job of her dreams and there seemed little more to wish for. Only one nagging, unsolved problem remained. Champagne was unlikely to be thrilled at the news that she wasn't going to be able to write her book.

Jane hugged Tom closer, pressing one ear into his warm flesh to muffle the honking, furious tones that seemed already audible. All the wrath of the Eumenides, she knew, would have nothing on the fury of a Champagne done out of half a million pounds. By her own sister-in-law, as well. Jane rolled her eyes at the thought of it. Josh had been right after all. Sisters under the skin.

She must have sighed, because Tom pressed her closer. He fumbled for another cigarette and lit up, drawing the smoke into his lungs with a happy sigh. Talk about the Duke of Marlboro, thought Jane worriedly. Tom smoked far too much. Not that she blamed him really. Even someone as certain of his own ability as Tom was must find it stressful to work so relentlessly on his writing without ever really knowing where his next rent cheque was coming from.

Jane had no doubt that Tom would eventually make it, but she worried about how he was going to support himself in the meantime. Or *themselves*, she corrected, half enchanted, half fearful. Her wages, even as an editor, would hardly be enough to set up a marital home from scratch. Oh, why had Tom turned down his trust fund?

It would have come in so useful just now.

She corrected herself sternly, knowing perfectly well that if Tom had kept his trust fund and spent it on cars, cocaine and Krug like everyone else, she would certainly never have met him. Jane pondered again on the amazing differences between Champagne and her brother, a train of thought that returned, with a circularity far from satisfying, to the worrying question of the book. *Could* she do it? *Should* she do it? It would be easy enough, after all, a mere matter of rehashing some of the columns, as Champagne had said. It might not take up *too* much time. She could do it and work as well, she told herself. Just about.

On the other hand there was another matter to be considered. Through Fitzherbert's offer, through achieving her own editorship, Jane had finally been granted an opportunity to break free, professionally at least, from Champagne. She had at last been given responsibility, a grown-up job that gave her a real place in the world, a profile of her own, a chance to run her own ship, in her own way, with her own ideas. Did she *really* want to go back to ghost-writing now?

Jane turned on to her back as she weighed up the options. She decided to consult Tom. After all, it might be selfish to turn down the money when they both needed it.

An idea struck her. Perhaps, if she found the right person, she could persuade Champagne to get someone else to do it instead. Using the existing columns as material, anyone who could string a sentence together and had the vaguest idea about plot construction and editing could write Champagne's novel for her. *Anyone* could do it really. Anyone . . .

'Tom?'

'Mmm?' said Tom, pulling her to him in the crook of one strong arm.

'You know you used to talk about writing a bonkbuster?'

The organ swelled as Jane approached the altar, light-headed with happiness and days of not eating. It had been worth it – the tiny waist of the wedding dress now fitted her with ease, and she was blissfully aware of her slender form moving gracefully beneath the thick satin. The air was heavy with the scent of freesia and white roses as, smiling shyly beneath her cathedral-length veil and perfect make-up, Jane drew up alongside Tom.

Looking at her with a gratifying mixture of awe and wonder, Tom gave her a tender smile. He looked exhausted, thought Jane, but then again, so would anyone who had spent the last six months writing his own book in the morning and knocking off a novel with Champagne in the afternoons. In the end, though, it had been relatively painless. The editor from the publishing house had been thrilled with it, so much so that the more literary arm of the house had made a substantial offer for Tom's own first novel. The advance for his sister's, meanwhile, had ensured they had one hell of a honeymoon ahead of them. And if half what was being said about German rights, US rights and film rights was true, they'd be holidaying on Mustique for the rest of their lives.

Jane glanced behind her, catching Tally's eye. Tally raised a gloved hand and grinned, looking as if she might burst with happiness. The Dewsbury business was obviously all over now; Tally had not even commented on the recent tabloid pictures of her erstwhile lover snapped with some unsuspecting anorexic heiress in a nightclub. Sitting in what passed for a beer garden at the Gloom, Jane had turned the page over quickly. Tally had merely smiled faintly and rolled her eyes, as if unable to believe any of it had ever happened.

Next to Tally, Julia blew Jane an exuberant, two-handed, bracelet-rattling kiss, almost knocking off Big Horn's headdress as she did so. Affecting not to notice, the majestic Indian remained as stock still as ever, his massive chest covered with even more feathers, bones and brilliantly coloured tribal beads than usual. It was obviously his gala outfit. As Jane's gaze passed to him, to her utter amazement he raised one magnificent dark eyebrow and tipped her the lewdest of winks.

Next to Big Horn, Archie Fitzherbert's attention was completely taken up by the person sitting on his other side. There, in a vast red hat under which her eyes burned smokily and her hair poured down as flat and black as tar, Jordan Madison, *Fabulous*'s most successful cover girl ever, sat in all her waifish glory. Her air of fragility was exaggerated by the fact that on her left sat the solid form of Mrs Ormondroyd, tissue clamped firmly to her nose. Jane shuddered at the memory of her most recent dealings with the huffy housekeeper. It had not been easy persuading her not to make the wedding buffet.

Jane turned her head back to the front, admiring how wonderful the restored Mullions altar looked now. Tally had insisted Jane's wedding should be the first to take place in the newly refurbished chapel. Even the eighteenth-century organ had been restored for the occasion and, as it struck up for the final hymn, the sound flowed out as confidently as when Handel, who was supposed to have inaugurated the instrument, first set finger to keyboard. It sounded, Jane thought, as smooth and strong as the well-aged brandy she had sipped to steady her nerves before the ceremony. As the quavering voices of the congregation struggled and failed to match the purity of the music, Jane felt Tom beside her fumble beneath her veil and squeeze her hand.

The service flashed by. Much to her relief Jane got Tom's many names right. She had spent a panicked night before whispering them into the dark surroundings of the Elizabethan bed, terrified that she'd get them all wrong like the Princess of Wales. She hadn't realised what a minefield this was. It would make a great problem for the *Fabulous* advice page. Only, on this day, her wedding day, she had vowed to try not to think of *Fabulous* once. She was, she knew, obsessed with the magazine, and thought of very little else except, of course, Tom. And *Fabulous* had repaid her devotion handsomely by soaring twenty per cent in circulation since she took over, leaving *Gorgeous* and Josh a very satisfactory distance behind.

Jane turned to walk back down the aisle with Tom. It was not difficult to spot Champagne's vast and violent magenta feather hat bobbing wildly as she waved at her brother. Beside her was her latest swain, an up-and-coming film actor in an electric-blue satin frock coat who had, it was said, ensnared Champagne with the promise of a cameo role in his next project. Jane wondered, noticing Brad at the back of the chapel with Lily Eyre, if the actor knew quite what he was letting himself in for. His subdued expression, contrasting profoundly with Champagne honking (and looking) like an excited Canada goose beside him, suggested that it had begun to dawn on him.

It was amazing, Jane thought, as she passed serenely by the exquisitely refurbished Jacobean oak pew where Champagne was sitting, to think they were now relations. She would never have imagined this possible. The strange fate which had intertwined their destinies from the start had by no means given up its influence. She had not only married Tom in the chapel at Mullions; she had also married Champagne. Jane plastered a vast, shaking but hopefully genuine-looking smile on as her new sister-in-law tottered up in the receiving line outside the chapel door.

'Ow!' Jane winced as, attempting an air-kiss, Champagne speared her in the eye with her huge and sprouting hat. A few guests down the line, Jane spotted Big Horn eyeing up the feathers with interest.

'Darling, you look *wonderful*,' Champagne gushed. 'It's so *interesting*, isn't it, how not everyone suits white? And so sweet of you to wear what is obviously your *own* jewellery,' she added, before passing on in a cloud of Jo Malone.

Jane gasped indignantly, as if a bucket of freezing cold water had been thrown over her. 'She's amazing, isn't she?' she stammered to Tom. 'I mean, it doesn't matter that I'm actually related to her now. She'll always see herself as the glamorous society girl and me as the slave. She'll always be the It Girl and I'll always be the Shit Girl.'

'Oh, ignore her,' said Tom, grinning. 'Let's go and have a drink.' He bore her off in the direction of the party, held in the newly refurbished and almost unrecognisably smart Blue Drawing Room.

A few circuits of the room later, her face plastered in lipstick from all the congratulatory kisses, Jane bumped into her new sister-in-law once more.

'Wonderful party,' Champagne gushed. 'Rahly marvellous.'

Jane grinned. Champagne had clearly not been stinting on her namesake beverage. 'Thank you for saying so,' she said, beaming delightedly. Champagne *could* be pleasant when she tried. Jane was almost beginning to feel fond of her. 'That's a real compliment,' Jane said, warmly, 'considering you've been to more parties than I've had hot dinners.'

Champagne pursed her lips, lifted an eyebrow and slowly scrutinised Jane's body from head to toe. 'Oh, I don't think so,' she smirked. 'Not quite *that* many.'